# INTO THE
# LOOKING GLASS

**Baen Books by JOHN RINGO:**

*A Hymn Before Battle*
*Gust Front*
*When the Devil Dances*
*Hell's Faire*
*The Hero* (with Michael Z. Williamson)
*Cally's War* (with Julie Cochrane)
*Watch on the Rhine* (with Tom Kratman, forthcoming)

*There Will Be Dragons*
*Emerald Sea*
*Against the Tide*

*Into the Looking Glass*

*The Road to Damascus* (with Linda Evans)

**The Prince Roger Saga
with David Weber:**
*March Upcountry*
*March to the Sea*
*March to the Stars*
*We Few*

# INTO THE
# LOOKING GLASS

# JOHN RINGO

INTO THE LOOKING GLASS

This is a work of fiction. All the characters and events portrayed in this book are fictional, and any resemblance to real people or incidents is purely coincidental.

Copyright © 2005 by John Ringo

A Baen Books Original

Baen Publishing Enterprises
P.O. Box 1403
Riverdale, NY 10471
www.baen.com

ISBN: 0-7434-9880-1

Cover art by Kurt Miller

First printing, May 2005

Library of Congress Cataloging-in-Publication Data

Ringo, John.
  Into the looking glass / John Ringo.
     p. cm.
  ISBN 0-7434-9880-1 (hc)
  1. Human-alien encounters--Fiction. 2. Explosions--Fiction. 3. Florida--Fiction.
I. Title.

  PS3618.I545I58 2005
  813'.6--dc22

                                                                        2005005210

Distributed by Simon & Schuster
1230 Avenue of the Americas
New York, NY 10020

Production by Windhaven Press, Auburn, NH (www.windhaven.com)
set in Elektra LT, design by Nancy C. Hanger

Printed in the United States of America

10   9   8   7   6   5   4   3   2   1

# DEDICATION

To Doc Travis, one hell of a physicist, without whom this book
would have made exactly no sense.

# AUTHOR'S COMMENT

There are a few deliberate mistakes made in the physics in this book (for reasons of security) and I'm sure there are some that are undeliberated. All mistakes, intentional or unintentional, should be laid upon my doorstep.

# 1

The explosion, later categorized as in the near equivalent of 60 kilotons of TNT and centered on the University of Central Florida, occurred at 9:28 A.M. on a Saturday in early March, a calm spring day in Orlando when the sky was clear and the air was cool and, for Florida, reasonably dry. It occurred entirely without warning and while it originated at the university the effects were felt far outside its grounds.

The golfers at Fairways Country Club had only a moment to experience the bright flash and heat when the fireball engulfed them. The two young men on University Boulevard selling "top name brand stereos" that they "couldn't return or their boss would kill them" didn't even have that long. The fireball spread in every direction, a white ball of expanding plasma, crisping the numerous suburban communities that had spread out around the university, homes, families, dogs, children. The plasma wavefront created a tremendous shockwave of air that blasted like a tornado outwards, destroying everything in its path. The shockwave spread to the south as far as U.S. 50, where early morning shoppers were blinded and covered with flaming debris. It enveloped the speeders on the Greenway, tossing cars up to a half a mile in the clear air. It spread to the north almost to the town of Oviedo, erased the venerable community of Goldenrod, spread as far as Semoran Boulevard to the west and out to Lake Pickett to the east. The rumble of the detonation was felt as far away as Tampa, Cocoa and Ocala and the ascending mushroom cloud, roiling with purple and green light in the early morning air, was visible as far away as Miami. Flaming debris dropped into Park Avenue in Winter Park, setting the ancient oaks along that pleasant drive briefly ablaze and crushed the vestibule of St. Paul's Church.

Troopers in the motor pool of Charlie Company, Second Battalion, 53rd Brigade, Florida Army National Guard, who were pulling post deployment maintenance on their Humvee and Hemet trucks, looked up at the flash and cringed. Those that remembered their training dropped to the ground and put their arms over their heads. Others ran into the antiquated armory, seeking shelter in the steel cages that secured their gear when they were at their civilian jobs or, as seemed much more common these days, deployed to the Balkans or Ashkanistan or Iraq.

Specialist Bob Crichton was compiling loss lists in his cubicle when he noticed the rumble. The unit had returned only a week before from a year-long deployment in Iraq and everyone seemed to have "combat lossed" their protective masks. Unit protective garments were at less than thirty percent of proper inventory. It was stupid. Everybody *knew* that sooner or later the riffs were going to hit them with a WMD attack, chemical, radiological or even nuclear now that Pakistan was giving the *Saudis*, of all people, nukes. But nobody liked protective garments or masks and they "lost" them as fast as they could. Convoy ambush? Damn, the riffs must have grabbed my mask. Firefight? Where'd that protective garment go?

He looked up to where his diploma from the U.S. Army Chemical Corps Advanced Training Course hung and saw the glass shatter even before it fell off the wall. He blinked his eyes twice and then dove under the metal desk and clamped his hands over his ears, opening his mouth to equalize the pressure, just before the air-pressure shockwave hit. Even over the sound of the explosion, which seemed to envelope the whole world, he heard the sound of the big windows in the armory crashing to the floor of the parade hall. There was a sound of tearing metal, probably one of the old girders that held up the roof of the parade hall, then relative silence except for a distant screaming. He waited a moment, catching creaking from the old building but figuring it was as safe as it was going to get, then climbed out from under his desk and headed for the company commander's office.

The first sergeant and the operations sergeant were just pulling themselves out from under their own desks when Crichton burst through the door without knocking, normally a cardinal offense but he figured this was as good a time as any to ignore the directive.

"Nobody goes outside for at least thirty minutes, Top," he said, bouncing from one foot to the other in the doorway. "And I need my survey teams, that's Ramage, Guptill, Casey, Garcia and Lambert. And as soon as it's clear I need a platoon to start filling sandbags for the Humvees—"

"Slow down," the first sergeant said, sitting down in his chair and then standing up to brush crumbs from the drop ceiling off of it. The first sergeant was tall and lanky. Up until the last year he'd been the chief investigator for the Lake County Sheriff's Department. When they got deployed, ignoring the Soldiers and Sailors' Act, he'd given the sheriff his okay to appoint his deputy to the job. So when they got back he took a cut in pay and went back to work as a sergeant. Give him a crime scene and he knew where he was at. He even was pretty good at recovering the company from a mortar attack or a convoy ambush. He was one of the best guys in the world at training his troops to sniff out hidden explosives, weapons and other prohibited materials—he thought of it as shaking down a dealer's house. But nuclear attacks were a new one for him and it was taking him a minute to get his bearings.

"I *can't* slow down," Crichton replied. "I need to set up a radiological station before anybody can go outside even *after* the first thirty minutes."

"What's with the thirty minutes?" Staff Sergeant Wolf asked.

The operations sergeant was medium height and well over what the Army considered acceptable weight for his height. And it wasn't muscle, like the CO's driver who was a fricking tank, it was fat. But he was pretty sharp. Not unflappable, he was clearly taking even more time to adjust than the first sergeant, but smart. When he wasn't in one third-world shit hole or another he was a manager of a Kinko's.

"Falling debris," Crichton asked. "We don't _know_ it's a nuke. It probably was but it could have been an asteroid hit. They throw chunks of burning rock into the stratosphere and they take a while to come down."

"Top?" Crichton heard from behind him. The chemical specialist turned around and saw that the mortar platoon sergeant had come up behind him while he was talking. The platoon sergeant, a staff sergeant who was a delivery manager for UPS when he was home, showed a physique developed from years of throwing often quite heavy boxes through the air. It was running to fat now that he worked behind a desk ten months out of the year, but he still was a big guy you wouldn't want to meet in a dark alley.

"Get Crichton his survey teams," the first sergeant said, looking at the suddenly irrelevant papers on his desk. "Send Sergeant Burell around to get everybody inside until the all clear sounds. Then get with the rest of the platoon sergeants in the Swamp. Wolf, head over to battalion, see what's up."

"Where's the CO?" Crichton asked, looking at the closed door at the back of the room.

"At breakfast with the platoon leaders and the battalion commander," the first sergeant answered, dryly. "We can handle this until they get back. Go."

FLASH is the highest priority communication in the military directory, superceding even Operational Immediate. Satellites in orbit noted the explosion and computers on the ground automatically categorized it as a nuclear explosion.

"Holy shit!" the Air Force sergeant monitoring the nuclear attack warning console muttered, his stomach dropping. In the old days he would have picked up a phone. Now he hit three buttons and

confirmed three separate pop-ups sending a FLASH priority message to the National Military Command Center in the bowels of
the Pentagon. *Then* he picked up the phone as sirens went off in
the normally quiet room in Sunnyvale, California.

The wonder of military communications and computers meant
that the President of the United States got word that a probable
nuclear attack had occurred on Central Florida a whole thirty
seconds before Fox broke the news.

"I know we can't say who did it, yet," the President said
calmly. He was at Camp David for the weekend but most of
his senior staff was on the phone already. "But I'll make three
guesses and only two of them count."

"Mr. President, let's not jump to conclusions," his national
security advisor said. She was a specialist in nuclear strategy
and had been doing makee-learnee on terrorism ever since the
attacks of September 11, 2001. And this didn't fit the profile
of a terrorist attack. "First of all, nobody thinks that they have
access to nuclear weapons of this sort. Radiological bombs, maybe.
But this appears to be a nuclear weapon. However, the target
makes no sense for a terrorist. It has been located precisely as
being on the grounds of the University of Central Florida. Why
waste a nuclear weapon on a university when they could use it
on New York or Washington or L.A. or Atlanta?"

"I gotta go with the NSA on this one, Mister President," the
secretary of defense said. "This doesn't feel like an attack. What's
the chance it could have been some sort of accident?"

"I don't know that much about UCF," the NSA admitted.
She had once been the dean of a major college but for the
last few years she'd been holding down the national security
advisor's desk in the middle of a war. Her stated ambition after
leaving government service was to become the commissioner of
the National Football League. "But I don't think they're doing
anything in the nuclear program, I'm pretty sure I'd remember
that. And you just don't *get* accidents with weapons. They're
hard enough to get to go off at all."

"So we're in a holding pattern?" the President asked.

"Yes, sir," the secretary of defense answered.

"We need to get a statement out, fast," the chief of staff said. "Especially if we're pretty sure it wasn't a terrorist attack."

"Have one made up," the President said. "I'm going to go take a nap. I figure this is gonna be a long one."

"Okay, Crichton, what do you have?"

The battalion headquarters of Second Battalion was collocated in the armory with Charlie Company. At the moment the Battalion, which should have had a staff sergeant and two specialists as a nuclear, biological and chemical weapons team, was without any of the three. Crichton had for the last year been the only trained NBC specialist in the entire battalion. He reflected, somewhat bitterly, that while he'd been holding down the work of a staff sergeant, a sergeant and six other privates it hadn't been reflected in a promotion.

"None of my instruments are reading any increase in background radiation here, sir," the specialist temporized. The meeting of the battalion staff and company commanders was taking place in the battalion meeting room, a small room with a large table and its walls lined with unit insignias, awards and trophies. The question hit him as he walked through the door. Crichton had been told only two minutes before to "shag your ass over to battalion and report to the sergeant major." At the time he'd been prepping his survey teams.

Radiological survey teams were taken from within standard companies and sent out to find where the radiation was from a nuclear attack. It was one of the many scenarios that the Army kept in its playbook but rarely paid much attention to. The privates and one sergeant for the company's team had been chosen months before and should have trained in the interim. But there were always more important things to do or train on, especially on a deployment. So he was having to brief them at the same time as he was trying to read all his instruments, prepare a NUCREP that was probably going to be read by the Joint Chiefs and make sense of the readings, none of which, in fact, *made* sense.

He knew all the officers in the room and, frankly, didn't like them very much. The battalion operations officer, a major, stayed on active duty as much as possible because his other job was as a school teacher, elementary level, and soccer coach. As a major he made three times as much as a civilian. He could run anybody in the battalion into the ground but the only reason he managed to keep his head above water in his present post was his S-3 sergeant, whose civilian job was operations manager for a large tool and die distributor. The battalion executive officer was a small town cop. Nice guy and, give him credit, in good shape despite the Twinkies but not the brightest brick in the load. How he made major was a huge question. The battalion commander was a good manager and a decent leader but if you asked him to "think outside the box" he'd get a box and stand outside of it while he thought. And there was nothing, so far, that fit in any box Crichton could imagine.

"The thing is, sir, this doesn't look like a nuke at all, Colonel," he admitted.

"Looked one hell of a lot like one where I was standing," the XO replied, his brow crinkling. "Big flash, mushroom cloud, hell of a bang. Nuke."

"No radiation and no EMP, sir," Crichton said, shaking his head.

"No EMP?" the battalion commander said. "Are you sure?"

"What . . ." the Charlie Company commander said, then shook his head. "I know I'm *supposed* to know this, damnit, but I don't. What in the hell is . . . what was it you said?"

"EMP, sir," Crichton replied. "Electromagnetic pulse. Basically, a nuke makes like a giant magnetic generator along with everything else." He reached in his pocket and pulled out a cell phone. "I called my mom to tell her I was okay and not to worry. Didn't think about it . . ."

"That's okay," the battalion commander said. "Everybody did the same thing."

"Yes, sir," Crichton replied. "But I meant I didn't *think* about it until I hung up. Nuke that size, sir, the EMP should have shut down every electronic device in East Orlando. I mean *everything* that wasn't shielded. Phones, computers, *cars*. But everything works. Ergo, it was *not* a nuke."

"Look, Crichton, I got a call, a personal call, from the Chief of Staff," the battalion commander said. "I mean the *Army* Chief of Staff. There's a NEST team on the way to check this out, but he wants data *now*. What do I tell him?"

Crichton cringed at that. The Chief of Staff was going to tell whatever he said to somebody even higher up. Probably the President. If he got it wrong . . .

"Right now this . . . event is not consonant with a nuclear attack, sir," the specialist said, firmly. "There is no evidence of EMP *or* radiation. Nor . . ." He paused and then squared his shoulders. "Nor does it appear to be an asteroid strike."

"A what?" the operations officer asked.

"Look," Crichton said, thinking fast. "Sir, you ever see a movie called *Armageddon*? Or *Asteroid*?"

"That's science fiction, right?" the major scoffed. "I don't watch that sort of stuff."

"An asteroid probably wiped out the dinosaurs, sir," Crichton explained, trying not to sound as if he was speaking to a child. "It's not science fiction, it could happen at any time."

"But we'd get warning, right?" the XO asked. "There's some sort of a group that watches for that sort of thing. They thought one was headed this way a couple of years ago . . ."

"No, sir, we wouldn't," Crichton said, shaking his head. "Not unless we were extremely lucky. Spacewatch can only scan about ten percent of the sky. An asteroid can come in from anywhere. But, again, there's no evidence that it's an asteroid strike. Asteroids will pick up debris, lots of it and big debris when you get a fireball like this, described as this one was which was that it seemed to be at ground level. Chondritic meteors can do an airburst, that's probably what happened in Tunguska . . ."

"They teach this in NBC school?" the operations officer asked.

"No, sir, but there have *been* recognized impacts in the last ten years; this is real information," the chemical specialist said. "Do you want it?"

"Go ahead, Specialist," the battalion commander said. "But your point is that this doesn't appear to be a meteor."

"No, sir," he confirmed. "I've caught what I can from the news while I've been running around. There's a big ball of dust over the explosion site and news helicopters have been staying away from it for safety reasons. But they've noted that the damage path is damned near circular. Very unusual for a meteor."

"Why?" the XO asked.

The Specialist sighed. "Angles, sir."

"Sit, Crichton," the battalion commander said. "Then explain. This is all new to me, too."

"Thanks, sir," he replied, grabbing a chair, then holding his hands up like a ball. "This is the Earth, right? For the damage to be circular it would have to have come in straight." He pointed towards where he'd had his hand cupped, then pointed from the sides. "But a meteor can come in from any direction. It's much more likely that it will come in at an angle. And if it hits," he clapped his hands together and then fanned them out, "it's like throwing a rock into a mud puddle. Most of the mud splashes away from the rock. Some splashes straight up. Some, a little, splashes back. They think the one that took out the dinosaurs hit down in the Yucatan. 'Splashes' from it hit in Europe and up in the tundra. The plasma wave crossed most of North America. Say one came in from the west for this. First of all, we should have seen, have reported, some sort of air-track. 'A shooting star in the day.' Then, we should have had flaming bits of rock raining all the way from here to Cocoa."

"Which we didn't," the battalion commander said, nodding his head. "The Orange County Sheriff's department wants to send a helicopter into the area to assess the damage and find out what's going on. They have their own chemical and biological response person, but they want a military presence who knows something about nukes. All we've got for that is you. Will you volunteer for the mission?"

"Yes, sir," Crichton said, his eyes lighting.

"It could be dangerous," the commander pointed out.

"So was driving Highway One, sir," the specialist replied. "But I'd give my left arm to be on the first survey team. For us it's like being the first one through the door is for infantry. This is the mother of all doors for an NBC specialist."

"Okay," the battalion commander said, smiling. "I'll give them a call and then call the Chief of Staff."

» » »

"Well, that was the Army Chief of Staff," the defense secretary said. It was forty minutes from Washington to Camp David by UH-60 Blackhawk helicopter. Three had been dispatched and picked up the national security advisor, the director of homeland security, the defense secretary and the Chief of Staff. The Vice-President was aboard Air Force Two circling over the Midwest but in contact by speaker phone. "He's been talking to the local National Guard commander. His survey teams so far report no evidence of radiation and there was no EMP. He also says that it does not appear to be a meteor strike. I'm not sure about how high a certainty to put on that, he's apparently depending upon the opinions of a private and evaluation of meteor strike is not part of his training."

"The private agrees with FEMA," the national security advisor said. "And Space Command. The evidence is not consistent with a meteor impact and I'm suspicious of meteors that hit research facilities."

"So what was it?" the President asked. He had taken a twenty minute catnap and now paced up and down the room occasionally looking at the TV. "What's the estimate of casualties?"

"We don't have one so far," the director of Homeland Security said. Technically he should have given the FEMA report, since it was under Homeland Security. But he liked and respected the NSA so he didn't make an issue of it. He also was phlegmatic by nature, a man who never hurried in a crisis but stayed calm and made rapid, rational decisions. Many thought that he had been tapped by the President because he was the former governor of an important swing state but it was his unflappable manner that had gained him the post. "FEMA didn't want to give even a wide estimate but the lowball I extracted from them was fifty thousand."

"My God," the President whispered.

"Yes, sir, it is very bad," the director admitted. "But it's contained and local emergency services are responding as well as can be expected."

The phone rang and was answered by the national security advisor, who held it out to the President. "Your brother, sir."

"Hey, Jeb," the President said, calmly. "A black day."

"Yes."

"Okay, right away. Good luck and God Bless."

He handed the phone back and nodded at the Homeland Security director.

"That was an official request from the governor to declare a state of emergency. I think this counts."

"I'll tell my people," the director said, standing up and walking out of the room.

News helicopters that had been loitering near the dust-ball zoomed in on a white and green helicopter that bore the logo of the Orange County Sheriff's department as it approached the scene of devastation. An area could now be seen that was stripped clean of all vegetation and homes although some foundations remained. The helicopter came in slowly and hovered low, stirring up dust from the ground to add to the pall that was drifting lightly to the west.

"There goes the first survey," the defense secretary said, quietly. The National Military Command Center had already sent in its estimate of casualties. NMCC had programs and protocols dating back to the Cold War for estimating casualties. The estimate they had given him, backed by high end modeling that had taken a series of servers nearly fifteen minutes to run, said that the FEMA estimate was low.

By nearly an order of magnitude.


"We just picked up some dust," Crichton yelled, cracking the door on the helicopter and holding out the wand on his Geiger counter. "Hold it there."

"You sure this is safe?" the Emergency Services guy shouted, his voice muffled by his chemical suit and almost impossible to hear over the sound from the rotors.

"No," Crichton responded. "But you want to die in bed?"

The Emergency Services guy, Crichton hadn't caught his name, was used to responding to spills on I-4 in Orlando. He knew all about how to contain a dumped tanker truck of carbon fluoride. He even knew about containment and cleanup of a dumped load of radioactive material. But responding to

a nuke was pretty much outside of his normal job descrip-
tion.

It was for Crichton, too. But he at least had manuals to go
by. And he'd boned up, fast, as soon as he got detailed to the
mission. He knew the sections on ground survey backwards
and forwards but all he knew about aerial survey was from the
books and they assumed that the helicopter had been fitted with
external systems. No external systems were available so, leafing
to the back of the manual, he'd found the section on "field
expedient aerial survey." Which was much less detailed than
the standard methods. Get close to the destroyed zone, staying
upwind from the site, kick up some dust and get a reading. If
it was hot, back the fuck up.

His counter was reading normal.

"This isn't a nuke," he muttered.

"What?" the pilot shouted. There were internal headsets but
they wouldn't fit over his gear.

"It's clear!" he yelled back. "Go in closer."

"How close?"

"As close as you can get," Crichton said. "Or set it down
and I'll walk!"

The chopper inched forward, slowly, as Crichton kept his
wand out against the prop-wash. Still nothing.

"Set her down!" Crichton yelled. "We're still clear! I need a
ground reading."

"You sure?"

"There is *no* radiation!"

"I've got the same," the Emergency Services guy said, looking
over at Crichton. "This doesn't make sense!"

"No, shit," the specialist muttered.

"Wait," the copilot called back. He had been looking out to
the front as the pilot searched for a reasonably flat place to land.
"You can see something at the base of the dust cloud."

The base of the cloud was dark, obscuring the light from the
sun that still hadn't reached zenith. But near the ground there
was a deeper darkness. There was a crater as well, one that
looked very much like an enormous bomb hole. The darkness,
though, wasn't at the bottom of the crater. Then an errant gust

of wind pushed some more of the dust aside and the darkness was revealed. It was a globe of inky blackness, darker than the spaces between stars on a cloudless night. It seemed to absorb the light around it. And it was hovering above the base of the crater, right about where ground level had previously been.

"It looks like a black hole," the copilot yelled. "Back away!"

"No!" Crichton yelled. "Look at the dust! If it was a black hole it would be pouring into it!" For that matter, he suspected that if there was a black hole *that* large the helicopter and most of Florida, if not the world, would be sucked into it faster than it could be seen. The dust wasn't being sucked in but he noticed that what dust went in didn't seem to be coming out.

"I'm calling the news service choppers and getting one in here for a visual," the pilot yelled. "You're *sure* there's no radiation."

Crichton glanced at the counter that had been forgotten in his hand and then shook his head. "Still quiet."

"Okay," the pilot yelled then switched frequencies and muttered on the radio. Crichton looked out the window and noticed one, and only one, helicopter inching closer; apparently the need to get a scoop did not outweigh common sense. He turned back to look at the ball, which didn't seem to be doing anything and shouted in surprise as something dropped out of the bottom and hit the base of the crater.

It was a giant insect.

No.

It was . . . It had black and red markings, mottled, not like a ladybug but some of the same color. It was . . . his sense of perspective zoomed in and out oddly. It couldn't be as large as it looked, but if it wasn't, then the pilot in the front seat was a child and his head the size of baseball. Crichton shook his head as the thing, using too many legs, wriggled and got to its feet. It was the shape of a roach, colored red and black and it had . . . more, way more, than six legs. It looked . . . wrong. Everything about it was wrong. It scared him more than any spider, however large and they got pretty damned large in Florida, he'd ever seen in his life.

It wasn't from this world. Not in this time. Or from any time in the past. And, hopefully, not any time in the future. It was from . . . somewhere else.

It was alien.

"Oh, Holy shit."

# 2

"Most of the faculty of the university was, presumably, off-campus when the event occurred." The briefer was from the FBI, which was one of a dozen agencies trying to make sense of the "event." No name had stuck to it, yet. It was not "Pearl Harbor Day" or "9/11" or "the Challenger." It was just "the event." The day still hadn't passed. By tomorrow, or the next day or the day after that some glib newsman would hang a moniker on it that would stick. But for right now, glued to their TVs, tying up the phone lines, people just referred to it as the White House spokesman had as "the event."

"Presumably because many of them lived near the campus," the briefer added. "The president, however, lived in Winter Park, outside the blast zone, and one of our agents contacted him. The center of the event, where the . . ."

"Globe," the national security advisor prompted. "Or hole, maybe."

"Where the globe now . . . floats . . . was where the high energy physics lab used to rest."

"Industrial accident," the President said, then laughed, humorously. He'd by now seen the Defense Department estimates and the "updated" estimates from FEMA, which were climbing higher as the day progressed. "The mother of all industrial accidents. Who?"

"The president was unwilling to directly point fingers but we believe that it was probably an out-of-control experiment by this man," he said, flashing a slightly Asian-looking face onto the screen. "Professor Ray Chen, Bachelors degree and Ph.D. in physics from University of California. Third-generation American despite his looks. Formerly a professor at MIT. Professor of advanced theoretical physics at University of Central Florida. He apparently moved there, despite a cut in pay and relative prestige of the facility, because of the weather in Boston."

"Why not California?" the President asked then waved his hand. "Never mind, irrelevant."

"Only slightly Mister President," the national security advisor said. "Thank God it was UCF and not MIT or JPL. We'd be looking at a million dead if it was either of those. And I know, vaguely, about Dr. Chen. But not enough."

"Bob," the President said, turning to the national science advisor. The science advisor was not normally part of the inner circle but he'd been called in for obvious reasons. His degrees, however, were in molecular biology and immunology; he'd been chosen for his background in biological warfare against the possibility of such attacks from terrorists. He knew he was out of his league.

"The security advisor probably is as good as I am at this. We need a physicist, a good one, that can think on his feet. Soon."

"Mr. President?" the defense secretary said. "When the high energy physics building was noted as the location I told my people to scrounge up a physicist. He's got background in advanced physics and engineering and holds a TS for work he does with my department. He's a consultant with one of the defense contractors."

"How soon," the President asked with a smile. "How soon can he be here, that is?"

"He's in the building, sir," the defense secretary said, quietly. "I'm not trying to step on toes. . . ."

"Bring him in," the President replied.

"Academic egghead," the Homeland Security director muttered, smiling, while they waited. "No offense," he added to the national science advisor.

"None taken," the scientist who hadn't published in seven years said. "What is his background Mr. Secretary?"

"NASA, then defense contractors," the secretary said, smiling faintly. "Ph.D.s in physics, aeronautical engineering, optics, electronic engineering and some other stuff. Smart guy. Very bright, very sharp, high watt."

"Fifty-ish, balding," the Homeland Security director added, chuckling. "Fifty pounds overweight, pocket protector, five colors of pens, HP calculator on his hip."

The defense secretary just smiled.

The man who entered, passed by the Secret Service, was just below normal height. He had brownish-blond hair that was slightly tousled and lightly receding on both sides. He walked like a gymnast or a martial artist and if there was an ounce of fat on his body it wasn't apparent; his arms, which had strangely smooth skin, were corded with muscles. He had light blue eyes and a face that was chiseled and movie star handsome. He was wearing a light green silk shirt and well-worn blue jeans over cowboy boots.

"Gentlemen and ladies, Dr. William Weaver," the defense secretary said, lightly with some humor in his voice. "Senior scientist of Columbia Defense."

"I'm sorry about how I'm dressed, Mr. President," the scientist said, sliding into a chair at a gesture from the President. "I didn't think I was going to need a suit this weekend; they're all at home." He had a slight, but noticeable, deep south accent. *"Ahm sorry 'bout how Ahm dressed, Mister Pres'dent."*

"Not a problem," the President said, waving his hand. Unlike his predecessor he insisted on suit and tie in the nation's work and never took his off when he was in the office. He had changed as soon as he got back from Camp David and all the senior staff were in suits or dresses. "Where's home? You don't live in Washington?"

"No, sir, I commute from Huntsville," Weaver said.

"We don't have much for you to go on," the President said. "But this event this morning appears to have originated at the high energy physics building at the University of Central Florida. We *think* that it might have been due to something that was being worked on by a physicist named . . . name?"

"Ray Chen," the national security advisor said, watching the newcomer.

Weaver closed his eyes and grimaced. "Ray Chen from MIT?" he asked, not opening his eyes.

"Yes," the NSA said.

"Well congratu-effing-lations, Ray," the scientist said to the ceiling. "You just made the science books." He looked back down at the President and then narrowed his eyes. "I can make some *guesses* Mr. President. That's all they are but they are informed guesses. Say about a seven on a scale of one to ten."

"That's good enough for now," the President said. "How bad is it?"

"Not nearly as bad as it might have been," Weaver answered, clearly trying to figure out how to phrase things. "One possibility is that we would all have just disappeared, as if we were never here. Unlikely, but possible. I'm going to have to explain and I'll try to tell you when I'm getting into completely raw speculation."

"Go ahead," the President said, leaning back.

"What Ray Chen was working on was the Higgs boson particle," the scientist said, shaking his head. "First thing to remember is that quantum mechanics can drive a normal man crazy so if it seems like I'm insane just keep in mind that it's the physics, not me. A Higgs boson is a theoretical particle that is named for the Scottish physicist Peter Higgs, who suggested it as a way to explain some phenomena in high energy and vacuum field physics. Some scientists and especially science fiction writers believe it *contains* a universe within itself. Me, I always thought it was just reinventing the zero point energy fluctuation energies, or vice versa."

"You mean a galaxy?" the defense secretary asked.

"No, Mr. Secretary, a *universe*. All the physics that make up a universe, which won't be the same as this one, all the math, *all* the galaxies if they form. Theoretically."

"That's . . ." the Homeland Security director stopped and chuckled. "It isn't insane, it's the physics, right?"

"Yes, sir," Weaver said, nodding. "The thing is they take really high levels of energy to form. CERN in Switzerland's been working on them for forever and couldn't get one. But the other thing is, there's another theory that when it formed it might just . . . supercede this universe."

"Supercede?" the President said. "As in replace?"

"More or less, Mr. President," the physicist said. "That's why I said: Not as bad as it might have been. We might not have even known anything happened, just all been gone. Moonshots to the Mona Lisa, gone as if we never existed. And anything or anyone *else* in the universe. Biggest argument against that happening is that it hasn't and *something*, somewhere in this big wide universe *must* have made a Higgs boson before."

"I see," the President said.

"Or even, and I think we might be onto something here, open a hole into *another* universe. You see, they don't last for long, even if you make one. Now, within the universe, it's *all* the time of the universe which might be, well, the whole thing. In the couple of nanoseconds they exist in this universe, in *that* universe they'd have the Big Bang, us making the universe so to speak, universal cooling, star formation, planet formation, the formation of life, contraction and then erasure. Billions and billions of years in *that* universe compressed to less time than it takes a computer to calculate two plus two in *this* universe. I know you're a God fearing man, Mr. President, but with Higgs boson theory, God might have been Ray Chen pushing a button as he said: 'Let's see what happens.'"

"So you *do* understand what happened?" the President asked. "If this was a possible result, why would anyone do such a thing?"

"Well, the recognized negative results were very low order probabilities, Mr. President," Weaver said. "They'd been studied over and over again and they were dismissed. I dismissed them and I still think I'm right. What would happen if you made a Higgs boson the normal way is a brief flash of light, some secondary particles and then it would be gone. Might not even be able to tell you'd done it. But that's the normal way, which involves great big linear accelerators."

"They had one in UCF," the FBI briefer said, glancing at his notes. "We'd first put the explosion down to an accident with that."

"Shows you don't know high school physics, much less this stuff," Weaver said in an equanimous tone. "Couldn't get anything like that out of even a big collider much less the four meter or so that they had at UCF. And you can't get a Higgs boson out of one normally at all. What we really needed was the superconducting supercollider they were building in Texas. That was one of the scheduled experiments. But Ray Chen wanted to make a Higgs boson."

"Why, in God's name?" the President asked. "If it was possible that it would erase all life on earth?"

"Why did you want your baseball team to win the World Series, Mr. President?" Weaver shot back. "Besides which, forming one and then watching it degrade would tell us a lot about how *our* universe really works. Understanding physics is the basis to everything, Mr. President. Everything from cellular telephones to the MOAB. And Ray was good at it. Very bright, very crazy in that way you have to be to understand quantum mechanics. And he thought, I've read the papers, that there was a way to shortcut to a Higgs boson. I won't get into what it is, but he thought that under certain conditions it was possible to change physics in a very limited area. And with the physics changed you could make a Higgs boson. And I think that it was his shortcut that went wrong."

"You think he changed the physics in a small area?" the national security advisor asked. "Would that have caused the explosion?"

"Possibly," Weaver said. "But probably not. What we have now is some sort of gate. Bear with me here, and I'll say that this is informed speculation, also known as a wild guess. But what we might have had was a universal inversion; we turned outside-in."

"What?" the President said.

"Think about a balloon, Mr. President," Weaver said, frowning as he tried to convert very complex theory into reasonable analogies. "You put a hole in the balloon and the air goes out. But you still have the balloon. Now, reach in and pull the balloon inside-out. We were actually the outside, now we're on the inside."

"That's . . ." the Homeland Security director said, then stopped.

"Crazy, right," Weaver replied. "The point is that if a Higgs boson was formed, it would be a universe. If the conditions were wrong, we'd be sucked into that universe and it would become the 'outer' universe. I could imagine some secondary effects would occur."

"Such as a nuclear explosion," the NSA said, dryly.

"Such as a very high-end kinetic energy release," Bill Weaver said with a nod. "Which would look an awful lot like a nuclear explosion. And at this point we get into pure speculation because there is no theory to support what we're looking at. That big black ball *could* be a boson, but it does *not* meet the theory of a Higgs boson particle or its effects. Yes, something came through, that might have been from a Higgs boson universe but, again, it doesn't fit the theory. Shouldn't be able to get in or out of the universe. Also, its physics should be different, so different that it would have either died right away or, more likely, exploded. Like, another nuke type explosion but larger as the full mass of the creature converted to energy. Didn't. What we're looking at is a gate or a wormhole. Obviously to another planet. Maybe, probably, to a planet in this universe. Might be to the future, probably not. The big question is: is it stable? Is it going to just go away? Is it going to release energy from that planet or universe into this planet? Is it expanding? Contracting? And, most interesting overall, what's on the other side? Another world? A world of gates maybe? Now I'm into skyballing which is the other side of speculation."

"Okay, so we have a gate and no theory as to why it formed?" the national security advisor said.

"No, ma'am, but I do have an idea *how* it might have been formed, based on some of Ray Chen's last papers, engineering rather than physics, and we might be able to figure out the physics before long. Once you know something's possible, especially if you can study it, that's nine tenths of the battle. Might, probably would, get the same explosion, though."

"The explosion we can handle," the defense secretary said, nodding. "Assuming it occurred somewhere like Los Alamos. On the ranges, not in the lab, obviously."

"I'm going to say something," the President intoned. "I do *not* want this followed up until we have a better handle on it. Not at MIT, not at California, not at Los Alamos. We have enough problems with terrorism. I do not want our cities popping like fireworks. I do not want another quarter of a million dead on our hands."

"I'm sorry, Mr. President," Weaver said, "if I was out of line."

"Not at all," the President said. "I just want that to be made clear."

"Dr. Weaver, may I ask a question?" the national science advisor said. "Dr. Chen's papers were open source, were they not?"

"No, sir, they weren't," Weaver said, shaking his head. "If they were, the President's order would, obviously, be impossible."

"Where did . . . ?" the science advisor said then stopped at a raised eyebrow from the defense secretary.

"Dr. Weaver, through his association with the Department of Defense, has access to restricted files . . ."

"Are you saying this was a DOD project?" the Homeland Security director asked, his fleshy face turning ruddy in anger. "That it actually *was* a bomb project?"

"No," the defense secretary said, definitely. "Let's try to leave the rumors to the press, okay? Dr. Chen had funding from the National Academy of Sciences," he said, gesturing at the science advisor, who blanched. "From at least three nongovernmental agencies and from the DOD. Most of it was private funding. But for the DOD grant, and we pass them out for quite a few things, he had to make his reports and projections classified. I'm not sure that there's *no* open source but everything in the last year or so is black. I don't even, frankly, know why or how he got funding from us. But we fund quite a few purely theoretical projects because, sometimes, they pay off."

"And it was these classified documents you saw?" the President asked.

"Yes, sir," Weaver replied. "I was interested in the physics. If you can change physics in a limited area you might be able to do a lot of things, Mr. President. I hadn't anticipated this sort of explosion or I would have rung the alarm bells. But there are other applications. Change gravity in a limited area and you've got a much better helicopter. Not to mention lightening the load on infantrymen. Change the physics another way and, yes, maybe you get a bang. I'd been thinking about some uses for the people who pay my salary, Mr. President. Besides being fascinated with the math. But I didn't anticipate this at all."

"Okay, so we have a gate and physics we don't understand but might eventually," the national security advisor said. "And since we don't understand the physics, we don't know what the eventual outcome might be."

"No, ma'am."

"But there's clearly a world on the other side," the President said. "Dr. Weaver, would you be willing to go to that world? Assuming it's survivable for a human?"

"Sir, it would take a platoon of marines to keep me away from that gate."

"Funny you should say that," the defense secretary said with a slight smile.

"I'm Spec . . . Sergeant Crichton, sir," Crichton said, saluting the Navy officer in desert camouflage. "I was the NBC guy that did the initial evaluation."

"Lieutenant Glasser," the SEAL said, returning the salute and then shaking his hand. "I saw the approach; good work."

"Thank you, sir," Crichton said. He knew he was getting a swelled head but didn't know what to do about it. The battalion commander had passed on good words from the Chief of Staff for God's Sake. His evaluation, that it wasn't a nuke, that it wasn't an asteroid and that it was a gate, had been ahead of FEMA's, the national science advisor and God Knows who else. And now he was being complimented by a SEAL.

Glasser just nodded his head and looked into the hole. The

team had been at McDill Air Force Base in Tampa, home of
the Special Operations Command, doing a dog and pony show,
read briefing, for the incoming commander. It was the sort of shit
that SEALs normally managed to avoid but the new SOCOM
commander was a Green Beanie, Army Special Forces, Green
Berets, who had limited experience in commanding or managing
SEALs or most of the other forces that fell under his command.
The team had been chosen because it was in country, not doing
anything important and it had a wide range of experience from
Command Master Chief Miller, who had been a SEAL since
Christ was a corporal and had been in every land and sea action
since Grenada, to Seaman First Class Sanson who still didn't
have the Coronado sand out of his boots.

And lo and behold they never even got around to shining those
same boots before they were loaded in vans and, preceded and
followed by a police escort doing about a hundred and eighty,
driven up to Orlando and dropped off in a howling wasteland
that looked suspiciously like Beirut. They'd caught just enough
on the tube to have some idea what was going on but there
wasn't much to see at the moment except a bunch of national
guardsmen standing around drinking coffee under klieg lights.

That and the globe.

"If there's a penetration of the globe, from our side that is,
we're tasked to do it," Glasser said. "There's no SOP for this;
we're into science fiction. Do you read science fiction?"

Crichton wasn't sure how to answer; most military officers
were death on SF. But Glasser didn't seem to mind.

"I used to," Lieutenant Glasser mused. "Used to read a lot.
I'm dead worried about biological or chemical contamination
from that side. What happened to that bug?"

"Well, sir, it's two bugs now," Crichton answered, gulping.
"Sergeant Grant and I got them both up out of the hole. We
wore our protective gear and decontaminated afterwards."

"Decon foam might not work on bugs from another world,"
Glasser pointed out. "As I said, no SOP."

"Yes, sir, but we also used bleach," Crichton said, stubbornly.
"Sir, if it can stand up to bleach, I don't think it can bond to
anything in *this* world."

"Where are the bugs?" the SEAL said, ignoring the comment.

"The sergeant and I trussed them up with duct tape and then dumped them in the back of a Humvee with all the windows rolled up and big signs on it not to open it. But they're both dead, sir. They just stopped twitching after a while."

"I guess something on this side is poisonous to them," Glasser said. "Which is the first good news I've had today. And bad, for that matter, it doesn't mean the other side *isn't* poisonous. Any idea what?"

"No, sir," Crichton responded. "They were moving fine and strong as bejeezus. Sergeant Grant helped me because he usually works in an alligator farm wrestling gators. And it took both of us on them to get the tape on them. They didn't attack us or anything but it was like riding an elephant if you know what I mean; they just didn't seem to feel the weight, even the smaller one. If I'd make a guess, sir, I'd say that it's a higher gravity world on the far side and that something in our air, carbon dioxide or oxygen, is probably what killed them. Too high or low of oxygen or too high carbon dioxide. Just a wild-ass guess, sir. I've gone up by the globe and taken readings but the instruments I've got don't show anything harmful coming out of it."

"You *do* read science fiction," the lieutenant said, smiling at him. "Crichton, right?"

"Yes, sir. I did. Still do for that matter when I've got the time."

"My boys can kill anything they can see," the SEAL said, reflectively. "They can move like lightning, go anywhere, do anything. But with the exception of the command master chief, who reads *Starship Troopers* once ritually before every overseas assignment, I don't think any of them have ever read an SF novel. Or thought about how an alien world could be different. Comments?"

"You'd better brief them carefully, sir."

"That is *we*, Sergeant. *We* had better brief them carefully. Believe it or not, SEALs *are* willing to listen to people who know what they are talking about. And, also contrary to popular opinion, they're smart. Which may matter one hell of a lot. Or not at all."

»          »          »

Orlando International Airport's call-sign was MCO, which stood for McCoy. It had previously been McCoy Air Force Base back when the security of the United States against the Soviet nuclear arsenal rested in Mutual Assured Destruction and intercontinental bombers were one leg of the triad that assured the Mutual.

As Orlando grew in size and importance from a small cow town with a few defense firms to an entertainment and research center, MCO had grown as well, adding flights, adding congestion and eventually adding runways. But the main runways were the same that had been laid down in the 1950s and they were more than adequate to handle an F-15. Which was how Dr. Weaver arrived after a flight from Andrews Air Force Base he would remember for some time.

FAA regulations prohibited military jets from breaking the sound barrier over inhabited areas. Jets which were supersonic, therefore, were limited to training over water or uninhabited desert areas.

Bill Weaver had flown in F-15s before, including aerobatics to try to make him sick. They hadn't. But this was radically different. The F-15, carrying conformal wing tanks, had climbed for altitude at what was called "maximum military thrust." Since an F-15 is one of the very few aircraft in the world that has more thrust than mass, that meant virtually straight up for a minute and a half. It was very much what he imagined being in the shuttle would be like, if you were able to look around in every direction. When it reached its optimum altitude, 65,000 feet, it had turned south and the pilot had pushed the afterburners to full. From that high it is normally hard to notice the change in motion relative to the ground at all. Just as high jets look as though they are moving slowly from the ground, from the air the ground itself tends to look stationary. Not at darned near Mach Three. It had taken thirty minutes from when the pilot turned south to when he flared out for a landing in Orlando. And the earth, which from their altitude had a very distinct roundness to it, looked as if it had shifted rotation from west-east to north-south. Even at their height Bill was pretty sure they'd left a string of broken windows behind them.

There had been very little conversation. Ground crewmen had helped him into a G suit, hooked him up, explained the two switches he was permitted to touch, pointed out the ejection system which he was not permitted to touch except in obvious circumstances and climbed out. The pilot had, if anything, less to say.

"Can I ask who you are?" the pilot, a lieutenant colonel, said when they reached cruising altitude and the bone crushing acceleration had eased off.

"I'm an academic egghead," Bill said, glorying in the view out the window. The sun was down in the west on the ground but they were still in sunlight at altitude. Despite that they were high enough that the sky was purple and he could see stars. It was as close as he'd ever been to space, the one place he'd wanted to go since he was a kid.

"Pull the other one," the pilot said.

"No, really, they're sending me down to look at this thing in Orlando. I'm a physicist."

"I figured that they weren't sending you to Disney World, but you don't look like any academic I've ever seen."

"You need to hang out at the Hooters in Huntsville more often."

Bill had heard it before. If you had a Southern accent and looked like a track and field coach everyone assumed you were a jock. But at the level of physics which was his specialty, you could get as much "work" done working out, or mountain biking, or SCUBA diving, or rock climbing, as you could sitting in a darkened office with the door locked and your clothes off contemplating your navel. Which was what one academic of his acquaintance swore by. It was all in the head until it came time to sit down and start drawing equations, which if you'd done the head work in advance practically drew themselves. And if you grew up with a body that only required two hours of sleep a night, a mind like an adding machine and the energy level of a ferret on a pixie stick, you had to find some way to burn off the energy, physical and mental. So he mountain biked, consulted with the DOD, went to national level Wah Lum Kung-Fu tournaments and, occasionally, stood in front of a white board for a few hours and then stayed up for three days writing a thirty-thousand-word paper which he sent off to the *National Journal of Physics and Science* serene in the knowledge that it would both pass peer review and be published.

Many of his friends, and most of his colleagues, referred to him jokingly as a rat bastard.

He'd recently considered going back to grad school to polish off another Ph.D. The only question was in what. Asshole physics, astrophysics to the uninitiated, was out. The whole field was filled with eggheads who couldn't tell reality from fantasy and most of them put their fantasies squarely on the liberal side of the political divide. Maybe atomic level engineering, but the only school that had a department, yet, was MIT. Bleck. Among other oddities in his field, Weaver was a staunch and outspoken political conservative of a seriously military bent. A year, about what it would take despite the "recommended" three years, in the People's Republic of Massachusetts was more than he could stand.

Maybe genetics or molecular biology, branch out a little.

But that had been yesterday, before "the event." If there wasn't a whole new *branch* of physics about to open up, he didn't have a nose like a hound dog. And he was in, practically, on the ground floor.

The math was probably going to kick his ass, though. At certain levels even the top-flight physicists sometimes had to resort to pure math guys. Ray Chen, for example, had been a go-to man for gauge boson and multidimensional field equations but even he bowed his head a few times and consulted with a pure mathematician in Britain. What was his name? Gonzales? Something like that.

Bill was coming up with a mental list of people he might need to consult with when he realized the plane was already flaring out to land. It had hardly banked at all and done a power-on approach. They must have cleared every other plane out of the way for the fighter. The pilot flared out, hit reverse thrusters and turned off the runway so hard it seemed as if they were going to fall over.

"In a hurry, Colonel?" Bill asked.

"Very," the pilot replied. "I got two in-flight requests for ETA. Somebody wants you pronto."

"Well, thanks for the ride, hope we can do it again some time."

There were soldiers waiting for the plane who obviously had no idea how to unhook all the umbilicals and straps that held him in the seat. The pilot unstrapped and got him unhooked, then he clambered out of the plane and onto the runway.

"Mr. Weaver?" one of the soldiers said. "I'm Sergeant Garcia. If you'll come this way?"

"Can I get out of the flight suit?" Bill asked, unzipping same. He reached up and managed to get open the small compartment he had seen his bag disappear into. He stuffed the G suit into the compartment and retrieved the backpack, then headed to the waiting Humvee.

"I understand you know what's going on here," the sergeant said as he climbed in as driver. The other soldier climbed in the back.

"No," Bill replied. "But I understand what might have happened, somewhat, and I've got some theories about what is happening and what might happen. And I know some of the questions to ask. Other than that, I'm in the dark."

The sergeant laughed and shook his head. "Can you explain it in small words?"

"Not unless you know what a Higgs boson particle is," Bill said, aware that he was going to have to explain it over and over again.

"A theoretical particle in quantum mechanics that can contain a universe," the sergeant replied. "But you can't form them unless you've got a really big supercollider. Right?"

"Right," Bill said, looking at the sergeant in surprise. "Did somebody call ahead?"

"No," the sergeant replied, making a turn onto the Greenway. For once it was nearly empty of traffic. He took the Sunpass lane despite not having a transponder. "I was working on my masters in physics and then things went awry. Optics, actually."

"I've got a Ph.D. in optics," Bill said. "And physics for that matter."

"Sorry, Doctor, I didn't know that," the sergeant said, wincing.

"I don't make everybody call me Doctor, Sergeant," Bill said, grinning. "I'm just an overeducated redneck, not some soi-disante academic. So how'd you end up in the National Guard?"

"Long story," the sergeant replied. After a long moment he shrugged. "I was working on my masters, working with blue-light lasers. One of my classes I had to have a peer reviewed paper published. You know the routine."

"Sure."

"Didn't have my experiments in lasers as far along as I wanted so I made the mistake of branching out. I got tired of everybody mouthing off about nuclear power so I did a comparative study of radioactive output from the Turkey Creek nuclear power plant vs. the big coal plant east of Orlando."

"Forgone conclusion," Weaver grunted. "Coal's nasty stuff."

"I knew that and you know that, but I'd done the research and there wasn't a single peer reviewed comparative."

"None?" Weaver said, surprised.

"Not one. So I did the tests, no detectable radiation outside of the plant itself for Turkey Creek and enough to cook a chicken in the tailings of the coal plant, which were, by the way, blowing into a nearby stream, and submitted it. To *Physics*. Got a response in a month. The paper was rejected for peer review and was not accepted for publication. My credentials were in optics, not nuclear physics."

"That's . . . odd," Bill said. "I smell a fish."

"So did I. Especially when I was summarily dropped from the master's program shortly afterwards. Nobody would talk to me except one of my professors, who made me swear not to say who it was or make a stink. Not that it would do me any good. Know the senior senator from West Virginia?"

"Oh, no," Weaver said, shutting his eyes. "King Coal."

"You got it. He apparently made a deal all the way back in the 1960s. Florida got NASA stuff but to power it they had to build a coal-fired power plant. And keep it running. He protects coal like it was his own personal child, which in a way I suppose it is. Anyway, a lowly master's candidate had attracted the personal ire of a senior senator. Said master's candidate needed to go away now. Please, don't bother submitting at other institutes of higher learning. You are the weakest link. Goodbye."

"I hate politics," Weaver said, then shrugged. "But that's why Huntsville has the Redstone Arsenal and Houston has the Space Center. Since I got my education because of the former, I suppose I shouldn't complain too much. But, yeah, that's a shitty story. On the other hand, it's good for me."

"Why?"

"Well, we're going to have to measure this thing and I've got my very own soldier who can handle laser equipment. That's going to help."

"Okay," the sergeant said, chuckling. "Do I get a pay increase?"

"Doubt it," Bill admitted. "But we'll see. Ever thought about going to other planets?"

"You'll get me through that thing kicking and screaming," the sergeant admitted. "I saw those bugs. I don't want to be on any planet that has them on it. Worse than arachnophobia. I just wanted to curl up and scream. I don't know how Crichton and Grant could stand to touch them."

"Touch them? What about contamination?"

"Wait until we get there, if you don't mind, Doctor, sir," the sergeant said. He had turned off onto the ramp to University Boulevard. They had been waved through a checkpoint and the ramp had been roughly cleared of rubble. But it was still a rough ride.

University Boulevard had been a four-lane highway connected to numerous side roads and residential communities. One lane had been partially cleared by an army of civilian bulldozers and military and a few emergency vehicles now picked their way down that single cleared lane. The suburbs on either side had been smashed, as if from a strong wind, and as they proceeded eastward it got worse until they entered an area that had been wiped clean of all vegetation except some burned stubby grasses and was devoid of anything but foundations. Bill shook his head as he mentally counted up the human life that had been erased in a bare moment. Families, children, dogs, cats, fish, birds in

the trees, the trees themselves, gone. It was shocking and hor-
rifying and, after a while, so overwhelming that his mind just
tuned it out.

"I'm glad our company got detailed to secure the site," Garcia
said, noticing his glances at the devastation.

"Why?"

"The other companies around have been pulled in for search
and rescue."

Crichton had finally gotten a chance to take off his protective
gear and grab some food. Battalion had gone to the Domino's
Pizza on Kirkman Road, one of the largest in the nation, and gotten pizza for Charlie Company at materials cost from the owner.
By the time Crichton got a slice all that was left was all the way
and it was cold. He preferred just pepperoni and hot, but it was
food and he realized as he bit into the slice that it was the first
food he'd had since a chicken biscuit for breakfast. He'd found a
bit of rubble, the foundation for one of the university buildings,
and was contemplating the activity around the hole when a small
voice said: "Excuse me."

He turned around and, right at the edge of the light from the
kliegs, a small child, a girl by her clothing and hair, was standing
watching him. In her arms was what looked like a stuffed animal,
probably some sort of "monster" animal. At least it looked stuffed
until it climbed up her clothes and perched on her shoulder.

"Hello," he said as calmly as he could. "Where did you come
from?"

"Home," the girl said. "I'm hungry."

"What's your name little girl?"

"Mimi Jones, 12138 Mendel Road, Orlando, Florida,
32826."

"Are you lost?" he asked. He wondered where Mendel Road
was and wondered who was going to hook this girl up with her
parents, assuming they were alive. She seemed uninjured, so
there was no way that she had been in the explosion. But there
wasn't anything standing for a kilometer around the explosion.
If she had come from outside the explosion area, then she'd
walked a long way.

"Yes," she said. "I couldn't find my house or my mommy. And Mommy said I shouldn't talk to strangers but she said that soldiers were okay one time when we were at the mall."

"Well, there's a policeman here," Crichton said, standing up. "He'll probably be able to find your mommy. And we'll get you something to eat. Come on."

He wanted to ask what that thing on her shoulder was but he thought it might be a good idea to wait until he got her into the light and got a better look at it. It might be one of those robotic toys that were turning up these days.

In the light the thing was no better. It was almost entirely fur except for some stubby and goofy-looking legs; there seemed to be about ten spaced equilaterally around its body. And it didn't seem to be threatening anything, just sitting on her shoulder.

A command truck had been parked at the edge of the light zone and he led the girl over to the group that was standing around at the back. Weaver was there and the SEAL commander along with a sergeant from Orange County Sheriff's that had been sent over as a liaison. There was also a woman he hadn't seen before, a tall brunette, just on the far side of chunky, with long brown hair. She was dressed in jeans and a flannel work shirt.

"Hi," he said when he got to the group. "This little girl just wandered up to me. I think she's from in the TD area. She says her name is Mimi."

"Hello, Mimi," the woman said, squatting down in front of the girl. "I'm Dr. McBain. I'm not a doctor like you probably know, I'm what's called a biologist. I study plants and animals. This is Dr. Weaver, he studies stars and stuff. What's your name? Do you know your address?"

"Mimi Jones, 12138 Mendel Road, Orlando, Florida, 32826," the girl recited again.

"And what's that on your shoulder?" McBain asked, eyeing it warily.

"That's my friend," Mimi said, patting the thing. "His name is Tuffy."

"Do you know where your mommy is?" the biologist said.

"No, I was watching *Powerpuff Girls* and then I woke up in

the dark. I was scared but Tuffy told me it would be okay and then I walked to the lights. I'm hungry."

"Tuffy told you?" Weaver said, squatting down by her also.

"Kinda," the girl said and giggled. "He doesn't talk, he doesn't have a mouth like us. But I know what he means. I was really scared but he made me be brave and told me to go to the lights and get some food. I'm hungry."

"We're out of pizza," Weaver said, waving at the SEAL officer. "Would you like some nice MREs?"

"I dunno," the girl admitted. "I don't like peas, though."

"No peas," Weaver said as the SEAL, shaking his head, went to get some MREs.

"Dr. Weaver," the cop said, coming over and squatting down with the others. "That's got to be impossible."

"What do you mean?"

"Were you at home, Mimi?" the deputy asked, softly. "When you fell asleep that is?"

"Yes," Mimi said.

"That's impossible," the cop repeated. "Mendel is about three blocks from here."

"Did you have a basement, Mimi?" Weaver asked. "Were you in the basement?"

"No," she answered. "We had an apartment. On the second floor. I used to throw water balloons at Manuel downstairs until Mommy found out what I was doing with them and made me stop."

"That's really impossible," the cop said. "Where were you, really, Mimi?"

Weaver didn't have children but he did know that they would make things up. However, there was no logic to Mimi lying and he felt she wasn't.

"I don't think she's lying, Sergeant," he said, quietly. "And do me a favor, don't bully her on it. I don't want her, or that thing, agitated."

"She can't have come from Mendel, Dr. Weaver," the deputy protested. "It's *gone*."

"*Quod erat demonstratum*," the physicist answered. "That which is demonstrated. Where *did* she come from, then? *Everything* for a half a mile in every direction is *gone*. She's six; there's only so far she could have walked. Ergo, she came from *somewhere* she could not have and Mendel is only one of many equally implausible possibilities."

"So how did she survive?" the cop asked, angrily.

"I don't know," Weaver said, honestly.

"Some sort of toroidal effect?" McBain asked.

"Nope," the physicist answered. "If there was a minimal effect toroid, and it doesn't look like there was, it still would have taken out an upstairs apartment. And she wouldn't be unscratched. Look, none of this is making sense according to standard theory so I'd have to go out on a limb and say that another gate opened and she fell in it as the blast front came across. Problem being even if it opened under her she wouldn't have had time to fall."

"Opened up on her?" the woman asked. "Then she fell out after the blast had passed?"

"Maybe," Weaver shrugged. "Or maybe Tuffy saved her."

"That's what happened," Mimi said, stoutly. "Tuffy told me he saved me."

"Well, then, that's the answer," Weaver said, smiling. "Problem solved."

"Not all of them," the deputy said. "We're supposed to isolate any ET stuff. And if that's not an ET I don't know what is. It could be carrying a plague for all we know. And she won't be able to take it to a shelter."

"And it doesn't explain *how* it saved her," McBain pointed out.

"The point is, we need to isolate that thing," the deputy said. "And her, come to think of it. Mimi, I'm sorry but you're going to have to give me Tuffy," the cop continued, pulling out a pair of rubber gloves.

"I won't," Mimi said, stubbornly. "Tuffy's my friend and he saved me. You're not going to take him away and put him to sleep."

"We won't put him to sleep, child," the woman said. "But he might be carrying germs. We have to make sure he's safe."

"He's not," Mimi said. "He told me he's safe."

"Well, you still have to give him to me, Mimi," the deputy said, reaching for the creature.

"No!" Mimi answered, backing up. "I won't give him to you. Leave me alone! You're a bad man!"

"Mimi . . ." Weaver said, just as the thing reared up. He caught a glimpse of what might have been a mouth and then two of the thing's legs extended enormously, forming or extending claws at the end. The claws caught the deputy in his upper arm, just below where it was protected by body armor. There was a sizzling sound and the deputy was flung back to shudder on the ground.

Weaver rolled up and back into a combat stance as the woman stood up and backed away as well. The deputy was shaking from head to foot and then stopped. He was still breathing, though.

"Medic!" Glasser called, dropping the MRE packet he had just carried over and grabbing the deputy. He dragged him to the rear of the command Humvee and then drew his sidearm.

"Mimi," Weaver said, as calmly as he could. "Tell Tuffy we're not going to try to take him away, okay?"

"Okay," Mimi said, turning her head and murmuring at the thing. "He says the man will be okay."

"Okay," the physicist replied.

"It looks like he's been tasered," Glasser said, walking over with the MRE packet. "Mimi, this is chicken ala king. It's got some peas in it, sorry, but it's one of the best ones we have. I heated it up for you." He pulled a folding knife out and slit the top of the MRE packet, then opened it up and carefully handed it to her along with a spork.

Mimi looked at the contents with the doubtful indecision millions of soldiers around the world understood, then poked at the contents. She spooned some of the mess up and tasted it, then picked at it greedily, pulling out the chicken bits.

As she did "Tuffy" climbed down her chest and, holding onto the front of her shirt, extended its legs to fish into the contents. It seemed to be rooting through for vegetables. Since the girl was only eating the meat it was a fair apportionment. Weaver watched in amazement as the thing fished up the bits in the sauce, hooked on small claws, transferring them to its underside where they were, presumably, consumed.

"Mimi," the biologist suddenly said with a tone of horror. "I just realized something. That might not be good for Tuffy."

"Tuffy says it's okay," the girl said around a mouthful of chicken. "He said that he can uh-just his fizz-ee-o-logical in-com-pat-ib-ility." She clearly didn't know what it meant or care.

"Holy shit," Weaver muttered.

# 3

"We're going to use the junior man rule, General," Lieutenant Glasser said, gesturing at a schematic on the whiteboard.

Brigadier General Hank Fullbright was the Assistant J-3 (Operations) of Special Operations Command. There was apparently a battle royale going on in Washington over who was to control the investigation of the gate but due to proximity SOCOM had control at the moment. Fullbright had been dispatched nearly as fast as the SEAL team and now sat in a rolling chair in the command Hummer nodding at the briefing. The "junior man rule" was well known to most of the military and certainly to the guys on the sharp end. In the event that you had no way to test for, say, poison gas, the junior man was the person you used for a guinea pig.

"Seaman First Class Sanson has been briefed for the initial entry," Glasser added, tapping the shoulder of the young SEAL standing at his side. He was wearing a blue environment suit and carried the full-face mask under his arm. "Just a reconnaissance. He will enter, ensure his own environmental and physical safety, do a brief video of the far side and then return."

"You up for this, sailor?" the general asked.

"SEALs in, sir!" the sailor blurted, nervously.

"Drop the hoowah, son," the general said, mildly. "I admit that the junior man rule makes sense, but I want to know if you have reservations about this."

"Am I worried, sir, yes, sir," the young SEAL said. "But I've been well briefed and somebody has to do it. I'm willing, trained and able, sir."

"Okay, you go," the general said, looking at his watch. "It's 2330. You planning on doing this tonight, Lieutenant?"

"Yes, sir," Glasser said. "The initial entry. It's been suggested that we do so as soon as possible due to potentiality of gate failure and to assess any threat on the far side."

"Other than bugs falling through," the general said, smiling faintly. Another had fallen out of the gate less than an hour before and was being examined by Dr. McBain.

"Yes, sir," Glasser answered.

"I don't know all this science fiction stuff," the general admitted. "You sure you've covered everything?"

"Everything that we can, General," Weaver answered. "We don't know anything about air conditions on the far side except that the bugs have book lungs, so there *is* air. And they can survive for a time on this side. Sanson will be wearing a full environment suit. He won't pop it open. We've come up with a very rough and ready air sampling probe. He could experience significant gravitational changes, significant light environment changes and the ground level may be different on the far side. Basically, he doesn't know what he'll find and we just hope he comes back at all. We sent in a roughed out rover set to roll in and roll back out. It didn't come back."

"That's not good," the general noted. "What about just sticking a video camera through on a stick?"

"We did, sir," Glasser noted. "The stick sheared off."

"Son, you still want to go?"

"Yes, sir," Sanson said.

"Well, good luck," the general said, standing up and shaking his hand.

The group moved out into the lights again. A platform had been rigged up under the globe. It was rickety as hell. At the base a man wearing a hard hat was looking up at it and shaking his head.

"Who are you?" Weaver asked when they reached the bottom of the stairs.

"Bill Earp, FEMA," the man said. "I'm the FEMA safety coordinator." He was tall and very heavyset, with a salt and pepper beard that had been cut back along the sides for a respirator; the blue jumpsuit that he was wearing made him look like a bearded blue Buddha.

"If you're going to tell me that platform is unsafe," Weaver said, "we'd sort of noticed. But we've got to make a penetration tonight."

"Oh, the whole thing is unsafe," the FEMA representative said, grinning. "I'm just here to do the required safety briefing. Who's doing the penetration?"

"Seaman Sanson," Weaver said, gesturing at the SEAL.

"Okay, Seaman Sanson, this is your safety briefing," the rep said, grinning again. "Be aware that the platform you are using for entry is poorly constructed and may collapse. Be aware that on the far side of the gate you may experience reduced air quality. Be aware that on the far side of the gate you may experience increased or decreased gravitational field. The far side of the gate may not be at ground level and you may experience vertical movement on exit. Upon returning you may find that you do not hit the platform in which case you will experience an approximately twenty-meter fall to ground level. The gate may not return to this same location at all in which case you may find yourself in any location in this universe or in any other universe. The environment suit that you are using is not warranted by the manufacturer for use in any nonterrestrial environment and, therefore, you are using it at your own risk. Do you understand this warning?"

"Yes, sir," the SEAL said.

"Has your mask been tested for fit?" the FEMA representative asked.

"I did a breath check," the SEAL said.

"Not good enough," the FEMA rep replied. "Come with me."

From the trunk of his rent-a-car the FEMA rep produced a mask-fit tester. He plugged the nozzle into the mask, hooked up the breath pak, then spent a few minutes ensuring that it was a perfect seal. Then he helped Sanson get the hood on. The hood was integral to the suit and flopped down in front when removed. The zipper was up the back of the suit. They got the hood on, sealed it, then zipped up the back. The FEMA rep ensured the seal of the zipper, put on the breath-pak harness and then tapped him on the shoulder.

"That's better," the rep noted. "You had a fifteen-percent leakage before; if there's anything harmful in the atmosphere on the far side you would have gone down in a heartbeat. Good luck."

"Thank you, sir," the SEAL said, his voice muffled. He kept his mask on as he went to the platform.

Glasser handed him an M-4 as he reached the platform and then buckled on a combat harness—which fortunately fit over the breath pak—and looped a video camera over his shoulder.

"Repeat your orders," he said.

"Start camera. Step through in tactical posture. Ensure my footing. One spin to check security. Drop weapon, pick up camera. One slow spin with the video camera. Return." Sanson dropped the magazine from the weapon, ensured it was clear, then locked and loaded and placed it on safe.

"If you don't return, we won't be going in after you for at least an hour," Glasser noted. "If it's due to being unable to reach the globe on the far side, assume a tactical posture and wait; we will send someone else through."

"Yes, sir," the SEAL answered, knowing he only had forty-five minutes of air. They'd been over that and as many other contingencies as they could imagine. "Can I go now?"

"Yep," Glasser said, gesturing up the rickety scaffolding stairs.

James Thomas Sanson had wanted to be a SEAL since he was seven years old and saw a show about them on the Discovery Channel. As he got older he studied everything he could find on the SEALs and what he needed to know before he joined. In high school he had played football and been on the track and field team. His high school didn't have a swim team but he went down to the river, winter and summer, and swam as much as he could. He would sometimes lie in the water in winter, training himself to ignore as much as possible the cold. He'd come near to dying one time from hypothermia but he considered that just "good training."

He'd also been a good student and an avid reader. He had graduated high school with a 3.5 GPA after having read every book of military history and fiction in the library.

He thought that he had prepared as well as he could for the SEAL course and with one exception Hell Week, while bad, had not been as horrific as it was for many of the other new meat. The exception had been fatigue. He had ignored the fact that SEAL students were kept awake for the entire period of Hell Week and that had almost finished him. But he made it. And he'd kept his head down in Phase One and Two and done pretty well, finished near the top of his class. When he got to the Teams he knew he'd face some harassment, nothing personal, just making sure he was adequate SEAL material. When they sent him out for flight-line he came back with a roll of climbing rope. When they sent him out for prop-wash he came back with a bucket of same, a civilian brand of aircraft cleaning solvent. He'd prepared and thought that he was ready to face anything that the SEALs could throw at him.

Until this.

He realized, as he reached the top of the platform, that instead of reading military fiction he should have been reading science fiction. For all his briefing he realized he had no clue what they were talking about. Different atmosphere? Different sun? Different *gravity*? And then there were those stinking, unworldly, bugs.

This could really, really suck.

He started the damned video camera then prepared to step through. At the last moment he stopped. If there might be a drop he wanted his feet together. He placed them side by side, held his weapon at high port in tactical position, and then jumped into the globe.

There was a moment of disorientation, like being on a roller coaster upside down in the dark and then rather than falling his toes caught on something and he tripped. He automatically rolled on something soft, hit something hard and came up in a crouch with his weapon trained outward.

Orange was his first impression; most of the environment was orange. There wasn't a lot of sunlight; it was cut off by overarching vegetation. The "trees" seemed to be giant vines that twisted together to reach upward for the light. It was something like triple canopy jungle. But instead of the vines and moss equivalent being green, they were orange. And they were everywhere. He'd hit a small patch of "soil" (orange) but it was a small patch. Most of the ground was covered by the roots of the vines.

He automatically stood up and did a slow turn, checking for anything hostile. There didn't even seem to be any large bugs around although he saw a small beetle-thing in the "tree" behind him. He also saw what the globe looked like from this side. Instead of being a globe it was a mirrored circle. It was almost hard to spot, except that it was actually *in* the tree itself, like some sort of looking glass embedded in the bark. Half in, half out, he decided. And not perfectly straight to local gravity, either, more at an angle, lying partially on its side and tilted a bit.

Gravity. Heavier than Earth's. It hadn't hit him at first; he just felt a little weak. But it was definitely the gravity. It felt like he was wearing a big pack but all over his body. He completed his first turn, then whipped up the video camera and did another. No hostiles, no signs of civilization, just these big honkin' trees.

It hit him, then, another wave of disorientation, not externally derived but internal. This wasn't Earth. This wasn't anything on or like Earth. This was an alien planet, completely and utterly different. For a moment he felt unbelievably frightened. This was like some hell; if the gate didn't work he might be stuck here and he really didn't want to stay here the rest of his life.

Training, again, saved him. He'd done his mission. One turn for security, one turn for video. And now . . .

"I am so fucking out of here," he muttered. He turned off the camera, checked his weapon was on safe and then turned to the gate.

"Shit, which way did I come in?" He wasn't right in front of the gate. If he went back at the wrong angle he might fall to his death. "Why couldn't they have put up a safety net?" he muttered. Finally, he looked at the marks from where he came through, spread his arms wide in case he missed and might be able to grab the safety poles on the platform, and jumped.

"We've put the full team through at this point and it appears to be a triple canopy jungle," Weaver said over the videophone. He was half amazed and half amused by the military's efficiency in setting up a headquarters around the hole. First there had been just the command Hummer and now there were tents, generators, a field kitchen, desks, computers, a video uplink to the White House, all in just the few hours since the general had arrived. "I've been through as well. Definitely an alien world; initial studies of the biology of the bugs that came through indicate that they don't even use DNA, at least Dr. McBain hasn't found any. They do have proteins, but they're like nothing we've ever seen: no terrestrial amino acids at all. Higher levels of carbon dioxide, much lower level of oxygen, other than that pretty much an oxy-nitrogen atmosphere. Gravity is one point three standard, pretty heavy but survivable. Frankly, strip out the biology around the entrance, wear some sort of breath mask and you could live on the other side quite successfully. It's all very interesting."

"That's great," the national security advisor said. "But I've really got to make sure; there is no sign of a threat from the far side? Either biological or military?"

"Not so far," Weaver temporized. "From the biology of the organisms I'd be surprised if they could even interact with our biology. Not impossible but very unlikely and Dr. McBain concurs. We're definitely going to have to get some good biologists down here including molecular. Or we need to send organisms to them."

"I'm working on that," the science advisor said. "We want samples for the CDC and the Emerging and Infectious Diseases Department at UGA. UGA's got an excellent molecular biology department."

"On the military threat, ma'am," the general interjected. "So far there's no sign of civilization on the far side."

"No sign as we define it," Weaver pointed out. "I'm not trying to disagree, General, but for all we know those lianas on the far side *are* their civilization. Not likely from the looks of things but don't get the mistake that you're looking at Earth."

"A point," the general admitted. "But if anything hostile comes through we've got a company of infantry and a SEAL team around the site. That should at least slow them down."

"Now, what about this little girl and the other ET?" the national security advisor asked.

"Well, ma'am, that's a puzzler and no mistake," Weaver said, grinning wryly. "She's definitely who she says she is; the local police contacted her school and pulled the files they have on her. Mimi Jones, from Mendel Road; there was even a picture. That's right in the totally destroyed area, practically ground zero. And the ET, initially, does not look as if it's from the same biological framework; we haven't seen anything with anything resembling fur on the far side so far. We sent some of the National Guard over to Mendel Road, using GPS; there's no way to tell where it was before the explosion. And they can't find anything resembling another gate. And let me point out that we're not sure we're looking at an alternate universe or another planet in this universe. There's no reason, frankly, that *any* gate should have opened on a habitable planet. It's much more likely to have opened into vacuum. Having two separate ET species turn up from one event is just mind-boggling."

"I see," the national security advisor said. "That's a very good point. Any theories, Doctor?"

"Not what you could call theories, ma'am," the physicist admitted. "We don't know a thing about the other side of the gate, really. There could be a reason it opened there. Some sort of alternate similarity that attracted the gate opening. Or it might be that there was once a civilization on the far side that opened a gate and the . . . resonance remains. Still doesn't explain Tuffy."

"Tuffy?" the national security advisor asked, smiling.

"That's what the girl, Mimi, calls the ET that turned up with her," the general interjected.

"Right now, ma'am, nothing's making a lot of sense," Weaver said. "We'll figure out what's going on, ma'am, in time. But right now all we can do is collect data and try to come up with some theories."

"Okay," she said, pinching the bridge of her nose and yawning. "What else do you need?"

"I've got a call out for some measurement devices, ma'am," the physicist said. "Long-term we're probably going to have to set up a lab right here. We need to clamp down on the biological protocols . . ."

"Definitely," the science advisor said.

"And we need to find out if this is a Higgs boson or not and if so if it's stable, increasing or degrading. And if it's degrading, what the secondary effects are." Weaver shook his head. "Lots of questions, not many good answers. Sorry."

"No, you're doing a good job," the security advisor said. "Keep at it. General, on my authority get a company or so of marines up there as well. But don't just kill anything that comes through; it might be their equivalent of a young SEAL just having a look around."

"Yes, ma'am," the general said dubiously.

"Put it this way, General," she said, smiling faintly. "We really don't want to start an interplanetary war on the basis of one itchy trigger finger. We've got enough problems in the Mideast."

"Yes, ma'am."

"And get some rest," she added, yawning again. "It's going to be a long day tomorrow."

Weaver nodded as the transmission ended but he didn't say he would. He'd be surprised if he could sleep for a couple of days; there was just too much to do, see and think about.

He nodded at the general and then walked over to the lab that he had set up in a tent. Garcia was there, nodding over the instruments, half asleep. They'd gotten laser measurement gear so far and set up a slightly more precise radiation counter but so far that was it. He hoped that by the end of the day tomorrow he'd have some way to *really* measure emissions. He'd be surprised if the particle wasn't giving off something, even if the radiation gear they had didn't detect it. The gear was standard military stuff, designed for detection of alpha particles and maybe beta. It wasn't set up to detect quark emissions.

"Any change?" he asked Garcia, punching up the program to the lasers.

"Nothing?" Garcia said, startling out of a half doze. "Not the last time I looked."

"Go get some sleep," Bill said, waving him out of the chair.

"Thanks," Garcia said. "See you in the morning."

Weaver didn't mention that it was already morning, about four A.M. He didn't really care. He just wished he had some halfway decent instruments. He wanted to understand this particle, if particle it was, completely. He needed more precise size measurements. He wanted to know if it had a mass. He wanted to know what it was putting out, if anything. He wanted it folded, spindled and mutilated.

But for now all he could do was watch it in impotent fury. It should be doing something. Not just sitting there, a big, black enigma. If this was proper science fiction it should be making a flashy light show. There should be electricity crackling over its surface. Not just this nothingness.

He snarled at his instruments and then stood up, walking out of the tent. He headed over to where light was coming from McBain's lab and knocked at the door.

"Mind if I come in?" he called.

"Come on," McBain answered, wearily. When he walked in she was bent over a table looking through a microscope.

"Got anything?" he asked.

"Strangest damned physiology I've ever seen," McBain answered. "Of course, you'd expect that. Some similarities to terrestrial. Book lungs, something that works for a heart, musculature, exoskeleton. But other than that, it's just weird. No visual sensors I've been able to find, no audio either. Something in the region of the head that I think are sensors, but of what I have no idea. Mandibles for eating. The book lungs look scarred; I'd say that this thing is extremely sensitive to additional oxygen and that's what killed it but it's just a guess. The next live bug they bring me I want to put it in a reduced oxygen environment if I can figure out how to rig one."

"Makes you wish Spock was here, don't it?" Weaver said, looking over her shoulder.

"Or Bones," she answered, looking up and grinning. "He was always my favorite. 'Damnit, Jim, I'm a doctor not a mason!' Well, I'm a *terrestrial* biologist, not a xenobiologist."

"You're one now," Weaver pointed out. "The only one, so far."

"There will be more," she said, darkly. "Get what you can while you can; you know this is going to be taken away from us."

"Oh?" Weaver said. "Why?"

"The military is all over it," she sighed. "SEALs doing the biological collecting, which could be done better by grad students. Soldiers on your instruments . . ."

"I asked for him," Weaver said. "He used to be a physics masters candidate."

"Yeah, but some Beltway Bandit corporation is going to take all this over and bury it deep; you know they will."

"Well, as long as it's Columbia I'm safe," Weaver said, smiling. "Where do you think they found me?"

"Really?" she asked. "You work for the Man?"

"Most of the time," the physicist replied. "And it's not like a social disease or something. Sure, some of your work gets classified, but most of the time you can publish. And the pay is a hell of a lot better than working for a university. Mostly I wear my engineering hat, anyway."

"Well, you're safe I guess," she muttered.

"So are you as long as you don't get all upset at what's going on," Weaver pointed out. "Some of this stuff is going to be classified. But I'm going to argue for declass of most of it. The classified community isn't large enough to handle the data we'll be getting and most of the world-class people we'll need to analyze it and make sense of it aren't prone to working with classified material. It makes sense to classify some of it, though. You don't want everyone and their brother making Higgs bosons if a nuclear bomb is the result."

"That's a point," she admitted.

"And they're already talking about bringing in the Tropical Disease people at UGA," he noted. "I don't think any of them are cleared for TS work. So don't worry about it for now. Have you been able to take a good look at Tuffy, yet?" he asked, changing the subject.

"A small one," she said. "Mimi was getting tired, no surprise, so am I. Just before she nodded off I got her to let me hold him for a moment. I was worried but he didn't do anything. He's decally symmetric, covered in fur and has a mouth on the underside. That's about all I could tell. I got a small piece of fur on my hand and I ran it through what I've got as an analyzer. It's got proteins and some dense long-chain carbon molecules in it. No DNA again. That's all I could get from it. And none of the molecules looked like what I was getting from this mess," she added, gesturing at the dissected bugs on the worktable.

"Where is she?" he asked.

"Bedded down in one of the officer tents," Susan said. "We're going to have to release her to her next of kin sooner or later."

"Only if they're in here," Weaver pointed out. "They don't want anything going out unless it's been decontaminated. I think it's a bit late; we had soldiers going in and out for a while. If there's going to be a purple plague, quarantine has already been breached."

"Let's hope not," McBain said, shivering. "But I'd be really surprised if this biology could interact with ours. I'm done in. I'm going to go get some rest."

"Go on," Weaver said. "I'm not tired."

He headed back to his tent and started making notes of everything they knew, not much, and everything he wanted to know. A lot. But Tuffy kept coming back to mind. If another gate had opened during the explosion, it wouldn't be a limited event. He suspected that they weren't anywhere near the end of the surprises.

"A closed world has opened," Collective 15379 emitted. "Intentional Boson formation from far side."

"Reconnaissance?" Collective 47 asked.

"Already ordered," 15379 answered. "Four gate parallels so far and expanding on available fractal line. Wormhole opened at one of the proximate parallels. Reconnaissance team entering now."

"Report back on viability for colonization."

"Nine-one-one emergency services," the operator said, noting the time of the call on a pad. "Police, fire or medical?"

"Police!" a female voice answered. The display read 1358 Jules Ct. Eustis. So far all normal, except for the boom of a shotgun in the background.

"Is that firing?" operator asked.

"Yes! There are demons attacking my house! My husband's got his shotgun!"

"Ma'am, just calm down," the operator said. She tapped her computer, dispatching a patrol car. Possible crazy person, guns fired. "You'll be okay."

"No I won't," the woman sobbed. "They're coming in the back door! Don't you hear them?"

It was then that the operator realized that she did hear something in the background, a strange ululation like an off-tone fire engine. It was . . . unworldly. She tapped the computer again and keyed for home invasion and multiple response.

"Ma'am, the police are on their way," she said as calmly as she could. "Is this 1358 Jules Court?"

"Yes, they're . . ." There was a scream in the background. "Please hurry! They're coming . . ." The call cut off.

Lieutenant Doug Jones was chief investigator for the Lake County Sheriff's department. He had gotten that position, and his promotion from sergeant, when the sheriff and his ex-boss agreed that it was unlikely the ex-boss, who had been called up in the National Guard, was going to be coming back for more than a year. Right now he regretted the promotion.

Generally he was in charge of investigations into burglaries, fairly frequent, rapes, not too frequent, murders, infrequent and, most of all, drug dealing and drug running. Lake County was at the crossroads of several major highways and drugs flowed up from the south, coming from Miami and Tampa, and often were distributed or transferred or dealt in Lake County.

What he wasn't used to was investigating home invasions by demons.

He looked at the patch of . . . what did the forensic tech call it? Oh, yeah, "ichor" on the ground and shook his head.

"This truly sucks," he said, looking over at the first-in officer. "And you didn't see anything?"

"No, Lieutenant," the deputy said. "When I got here there were neighbors out in the street. Based on my information I went to the back of the house. The rear door had been busted in; it was on the floor of the kitchen. There were shotgun shells on the stairs and upstairs landing and a twelve gauge pump shotgun. Blood patch on the landing, blood patch in the upstairs bedroom, wireless phone on the floor. And . . ." He pointed at the patch of drying green stuff. "That on the stairs, the landing and a trail going out the door. Also blood mixed with it in places."

"So, what we have here, is demons coming out of nowhere, invading a house, killing or injuring two retirees, dragging them out of the house and . . ." He looked at the hummock of oak and cypress behind the house. It was much the same as dozens he had walked through before but at the moment it was a dark and ominous presence. "And dragging them off into the darkness. I really don't like that."

"Neither do I," the cop admitted, gulping. "After I did an initial survey I called in and requested backup and investigators, secured the area and waited for response."

"Must have been fun," Jones said. He looked over at the head of the SWAT team and gestured with his chin. Like most small departments the SWAT team was a secondary duty for regular deputies. And, also like most small departments, it was made up of guys who were willing to shell out for their own equipment rather than being picked for being SWAT potential. But the Lake County squad was pretty good, all things considered. Most of the deputies were good old boys who had grown up with a rifle in their hand and knew how to shoot. That might help.

"Hey, Van," he said to the SWAT commander. Lieutenant

VanGelder was six feet six of muscle and bone and a crack shot. He'd gone to every training course the department would pay for and many that he paid for out of his own pocket. On the other hand, "fighting on the fringes of hell" wasn't one of the courses that was available. "I want to find out where the blood leads."

"Yep," VanGelder said. "I was just waiting for your okay; we're going to mess up any evidence going in."

"Well, I somehow don't think we're going to be standing any of the perpetrators up in court," the investigator said, wryly. "'Ma'am, do you recognize any of the demons that you saw on the night of the twenty-sixth in this lineup?'"

"Yeah," VanGelder said, waving at the rest of the team. "Okay, I'm going to take point. We'll follow the trail to wherever it goes."

VanGelder pulled down his balaclava, put on his helmet and hefted his shotgun. He'd considered using an MP-5 but the shotgun just had more authority. You hit something with a shotgun and it stayed hit.

He followed the trail, it was as clear as day, into the hummock. It curved around the cypress and oak with some side trails, moving in a generally northerly direction. Then, as he cleared a section of dense undergrowth, he saw it. A large, shiny, mirror sitting in the middle of the small forest. It extended from right at ground level up to about ten feet and was perfectly circular. And the trail went right up to it and disappeared.

"Son of a bitch," one of the team muttered. "Hellmouth."

"What?" VanGelder asked, turning around.

"Hellmouth," Knapp repeated. Knapp was, by nearly a foot, the shortest guy on the team. The rest tended to be over six feet but Knapp was five foot two inches tall. On the other hand, not only was he hands down the best martial artist, he was really useful for second-story entry; when the team competed five of them would just grab him and throw him through a window. Now he was pulling back his balaclava and shaking his head. "It's like Hellmouth, sir. They're saying there's a gate to another world at that ball in Orlando. I bet anything this is another one. Those weren't demons; they were aliens."

"Alien Abduction in Lake County," one of the squad muttered. "I can just see the headlines now. Just fucking great."

"Okay," VanGelder said, keying his mike. "Dispatch, this is SWAT One. We have what looks to be a teleportation gate in back of the incident site on Jules Court. Perpetrators appear to have escaped through the gate." He paused and was unsure what the hell to say after that. Fall back on the oldest call in police history. "Officer requests backup."

# 4

"Oh, this is so truly good," Glasser said.

"My thoughts exactly," Weaver agreed. McBain had already compared the ichor found at the site to the other two biologies and come up blank. All three appeared to come from different evolutionary backgrounds. "Any ideas? Other than digging in?"

A platoon of combat engineers was felling the hummock, violating numerous environmental regulations if anyone was interested at the moment, while a company of national guardsmen were attempting to dig in. As in much of Florida the water table in the area was high.

"Find out what's on the other side," Glasser said.

"If they're hostile, and I have to admit that appears to be the case, that might not be too healthy," Weaver pointed out.

"Toss a couple of satchel charges through first, sir?" the command master chief said. Command Master Chief Miller was about six feet tall and just about as broad with a bald head and a wad of chew bulging out the left cheek. He pushed the wad across and then spat on the ground, never letting his M-4 carbine track away from the glittering mirror. "Then go in tactical, get a look around and get back out?"

"What about blow-back through the gate?" Glasser asked.

"Well, the back side doesn't appear to be functional as a gate, sir," Miller answered. "I'd say we toss 'em, duck around back and hunker down, then go back around and through."

"Works for me," Glasser said. "Make it so. Oh, and Chief?"

"Yes, sir?"

"You are not the first guy through the gate."

"Yes, sir," Miller said, his face unreadable.

"Neither am I. But I am going to be on the team."

First the environment suits. The SEALs had been using them on the other side of the Orlando gate so much they were used to them now. Then the mask, then the hood, then the body armor. Then the air tank, then the ammo harness. Last of all the weapon and the helmet.

"Wish these face masks were ballistic protective," Glasser said as Weaver helped him get adjusted.

"Have fun," Weaver said.

"Don't I always?"

The five-man team had assembled by the gate, two of them swinging satchel charges in their hands. The satchel charge was a nylon bag filled with explosives. A timed fuse was connected to a detonator. Hit the timer, toss the bag and when the time's up big explosion.

"Just remember," Miller growled, over the radio. "Once you ignite the fuse, Mister Satchel Charge is not your friend.

Glasser, Miller and Sanson crouched behind the gate as the other two tossed the charges through and then ducked around with them. All five clamped their hands over their ears and then waited a moment. There was a tremendous crash that was at the same time oddly muted. Then the team went in.

Each SEAL had a number and a mission. The point, Howse, would enter, scan left and right and then concentrate on forward. Number two, Woodard, would scan as he entered, then concentrate on left. Three, Sanson, had right. Four, Command Master Chief Miller, had up and back. Five, Glasser, was in command.

They formed, fast, on the near side then, putting their left hand on left shoulder and holding their weapons out and down, went through the gate at a run.

This time there was no vertical discontinuity. The far side was at the same level as the world they had left. But it was an entirely different environment than either earth or the other, still unnamed, planet. They appeared to be in a large room, but the walls and floors seemed oddly organic. The light was low and either everything was green or the light was. It appeared to be vaguely oval but the most distant walls were beyond sight in the gloom.

Glasser switched on his gun-light and swept the beam around the room. It was large enough that the light didn't hit the far wall or the ceiling. The gate was in the middle of it, apparently. The floor, at least, *was* green and the diffuse light seemed to be coming up from it and the walls. The spot where the satchel charges had hit was dark as if whatever generated the light had been damaged. That was all the time he had to look, though, when Howse screamed.

Something like a giant mosquito was attached to his neck and more were flying through the air. Sanson shot at one and missed, then Glasser realized they were in an untenable situation. This was a place for Raid and shotguns, not M-4s.

"Back, back!" he shouted, backing into the gate and out.

The chief grabbed Howse and threw him over his back then bolted out the door as the rest of the team filled the room with lead. Howse, however, was the only one hit as the mosquitoes stopped well away from the gate.

Howse was on the ground with a local paramedic bent over him when Glasser, who may have been last in but was also last out, came through the gate. The thing that looked like a mosquito on the far side was, in the decent light of a normal sky, anything but. It had long wings shot through with veins and was colored light green. But the body was nothing but a blocky box and there was no apparent head, thorax or legs. It was attached to Howse's neck, though, and pulsed oddly in the light.

"What's it doing?" Sanson asked, stepping back.

There were tendrils extending out of its body and, as they watched, they burrowed into the environment suit and, presumably, into Howse. Howse's face was distended, his tongue sticking out, and he appeared to be dead.

"Okay, we have a real biological hazard, here," Weaver said. "Get him in a body bag. He needs to be in a level four bio-containment room, stat."

"He needs a hospital," Glasser objected.

"He looks pretty dead to me," Weaver said. "And I'd rather that we not contaminate the whole world with whatever that is. We need a way to stop them, for that matter, if they come through the gate."

"They stopped short," Miller said, walking over to the ambulance and coming back with a body bag. "Sanson, help me get him zipped."

"What the hell do we do?" Glasser said, shaking his head. "If those 'demons' come back, we can shoot them. But those things . . . they're too small. Too quick. Maybe with shotguns."

"Big cans of bug-spray," Woodard said as the chief and the seaman slid the late SEAL into a body bag and hastily zipped it over the flier. "One of those sprayer trucks."

"We don't know that bug spray will kill them," Weaver pointed out. "But we can catch them if they come through. We need to get some of those light-weight nets for catching birds over this gate. Those things don't, apparently, have any way to cut. What do they call them? Gossamer nets or something."

"Where?" Glasser asked.

"University of Florida will probably be closest," Weaver said, shrugging. "In the meantime . . ."

"Down!" Sanson yelled, triggering his M-4 into the first of the things through the gate.

Weaver understood why the, apparently late, Mrs. Edderbrook had called them demons. The thing stood about a meter and a half at the shoulder and was quadripedal. It had small eyes that were overshadowed by heavy bone ridges and more bone ridges graced its chest and back. The head, which was about the size of a dog's, ended in a beak like a bird of prey. The color was overall green with a mottling of an ugly purple. It had talons on front and rear legs. It had spikes sticking out of its shoulders and chest and a collar of them around its short neck. And it was fast.

The first of the things through the gate caught Woodard by the leg and threw him to the ground, worrying at the leg like a terrier, the beak crunching effortlessly through flesh with a brittle crack as it severed the bone. But there was more than one; they seemed to be pouring through the gate in a limitless stream.

Weaver took one look and decided that this was clearly not a place for a physicist. He turned tail and headed for the building line of entrenchments, hoping like hell that none of whatever those things were caught him and that he wouldn't get killed in the crossfire. Already the national guardsmen had opened fire and he heard bullets fly by as he sprinted for the lines. He also heard screams behind him and hoped like hell that the SEALs had had the sense to beat feet.

"Sanson, Miller," Glasser shouted, dropping to one knee and opening fire on the beast that had Woodard by the leg. "On me!"

The three of them formed a triangle, firing at the beasts as they piled through the gate. They would have been overrun in a second if it hadn't been for the National Guard, though. The guardsmen had kept all of their machine guns, both the platoon level MG-240s and Squad Automatic Weapons (SAWs) pointed at the gate and manned. So when the first of the beasts came through all they had to do was flick them off safe and open fire.

The result was a madhouse as six MG-240s and fifteen SAWs filled the gateway with lead. The beasts were heavily armored but enough rounds pouring into them killed them and they started to mound up in the gate, green ichor splashing in a wide circle, as the SEAL team backed away. As soon as they were clear of the immediate threat, and it was apparent that the infantry was piling up the enemy, the three turned their back on the gate and ran for the entrenchments.

Weaver was waving from a hole behind the main defenses and they made a beeline for him, passing between a shallow hasty fighting position where one of the national guardsman lay, firing careful bursts from an M-16A2 and crying, and a slightly deeper position where a SAW gunner was laying down three- and five-round bursts between what sounded like half-mad cackles.

Glasser, Miller and Sanson dove into the largish hole head-first, then the three SEALs turned around and began adding their own fire to the din.

Sanson drew a bead on one of the things and fired carefully, watching the placement of his shot. When they had first been retreating it had been a matter of laying down fire as fast as possible and he wasn't sure but he thought most of it was bouncing of the damned things. Sure enough, when he shot one in the head it didn't even seem to notice it. The things had overlapping scaly plates as well as the bone underneath. More shots in its side seemed to be effective, though, punching through the scales in a flash of green ichor. He wasn't sure whether it would have been a killing shot because even as he fired one of the MG-240s hit it and it went down. The ambulance that had supplied the body bag for Howse was in the way of fire from one side of the semicircle of national guardsmen and the things were trying to use it for cover. But the other side of the positions covered the dead ground and they were filling up the space with bodies of the things.

However, they were clearly spreading out from the gate, despite the fire.

"We need more firepower," Glasser shouted through his mask.

Even as he said it mortar rounds started dropping in the clearing around the gate. The mortars, however, didn't kill the things unless they dropped right on them and the shrapnel from the mortars didn't seem to affect them at all.

Weaver heard a truck engine revving behind them and turned around to see one of the support trucks, a big five ton, pull up behind the entrenchments. There was a big machine gun in a circular mount on the top and it started hammering away, adding its fire to that of the company.

"Ma Deuce," Glasser said, sighting carefully and firing a short burst. "Fifty caliber. And it's doing a job, too."

The big machine gun's bullets weren't stopped by the armor of the monsters. Head, chest, side, legs, the massive rounds punched right through. The gunner knew what he was doing, too, working his way from the outside in, pushing back the tidal wave of monsters until they were hemmed in around the gate again. But then he stopped firing.

"Has to change barrels," Glasser said when he saw Weaver flinch. "You want a weapon?"

"I wouldn't know how to use one," Weaver admitted. "But I'll be glad to learn if we get out of this."

"I need to go find the company commander," Glasser said. "Miller, Sanson, stay on the doctor. If it goes to shit, get him out." With that he stood up and sprinted off behind the line.

"What did it look like on the other side?" Weaver asked.

"Like being in a big, green, stomach," Miller responded. He had pulled off his mask and now had a chew in again. "I think it was the inside of some big organism. Big. The room we were in was at least a hundred meters long."

"Shit," Sanson said, dropping out his magazine and slapping in a new one.

The reason for his exclamation was clear. A new type of creature was pouring through the gate. These were bipedal and large but otherwise similar in general appearance to the earlier attackers. The big difference was in their armament. The tops of their beaks appeared to be hollow and as Weaver watched they stitched the line of defenders with projectiles. Two of them concentrated on the big machine gun, which had been gotten back into action, and the two man crew was riddled with the projectiles, their blood splashing all over the truck, which was still painted in desert camouflage.

The beasts were, also, heavily armored and seemed to shrug off most of the rounds coming their way. Only the heavy rounds of the MG-240s seemed able to penetrate their armor and the things were now concentrating on taking out the machine guns one by one.

"Joy," Weaver said, turning over and pulling out his cell phone. He noticed that a news crew had set up behind the line of firing. Alien invasion, live. Joy.

He pulled out his PDA and found the number he had been given then dialed it.

"White House, National Security Advisor's office."

"This is Doctor William Weaver," he said. "I'd like to speak to the NSA if she's available."

"I'm sorry, Doctor, she's in a meeting at the moment," the operator said. "Is that firing I hear?"

"Yes," he replied. "You might want to get a message to her that we're being invaded by aliens and the National Guard company trying to hold them off is about to be overrun. It should be on CNN by now. That was really all I called to say, anyway. Thanks. Bye." With that he cut the connection.

Lieutenant VanGelder's SWAT team had been more than happy to let the National Guard secure the site. But, on the other hand, this was Lake County and the gate was a clear and present danger. So he'd had them stick around and had taken over one of the upstairs rooms of the Edderbrook residence as his headquarters. When the firing broke out most of the team had been in the room and they had immediately stepped to the window to watch the growing firefight.

Most of the team was armed with MP-5s, which was not going to do much good in this battle. But in the team vehicle were heavier weapons. Some of them so heavy that the SWAT team got a good bit of ribbing for having them.

"Jenson, Knapp," he snapped as the smaller beasts started pouring out of the gate and the SEAL team retreated. "Go get the Barretts."

Weaver had stuck his head back up over the side of the hole just in time to see one of the big monsters go pitching back with a hole in its breast. From the rear there was a loud BOOM that was audible even over the sound of the firing around him.

"Barrett," Command Master Chief Miller said, spitting out a line of tobacco juice. "Probably them SWAT boys. Doctor, I think it's time for us to get out of here."

"Agreed," Weaver said, just as one of the things turned and sent a stream of projectiles their way. He ducked down and looked behind them where some of them had embedded in a tree. They looked like thorns about two inches long, glittering black against the grayish-brown trunk. "How?"

"Low," the chief said. "Crawl out the back. Keep your butt down and your head down. There's enough of a parapet in the front that if you stay low and go you'll be covered by it. We'll be right behind you."

VanGelder tracked right until the rifle was lined on another, then squinted through the scope. At this range it would have been better to use iron sights but there hadn't been time to take the scopes off much less rezero the sights. So he used what he had. He lined up the next beast through the crosshairs, stroked the trigger and then worked the bolt.

"Got him," Knapp said. He was standing by with another magazine and spotting for the lieutenant. "Left, monster in the open."

VanGelder tried not to laugh in near hysteria as he tracked left and shot another of the things. Unfortunately, it was like spitting in the ocean. The right flank of the National Guard company had been rolled up and most of their medium machine guns had been taken out. And more of the little monsters were pouring through now.

He shot another, changed magazines and then looked at the overall situation. Most of the national guardsmen were trying to scurry out of their holes and run. He didn't think anything against them for it; the situation was clearly out of control.

On the other hand, be damned if they were going to invade through Lake County if he had anything to say about it.

"Get on the horn. Call dispatch. Tell them to send everything we've got. If we can hold them by the gate we can hold them. Hell, send out a general call, anybody with big guns. Even a hunting rifle. Get your ass down here. We've got to hold them, here."

"I'm on it," Jenson said. "There's a news crew down there, I'll tell them, too."

VanGelder nodded and looked back through the scope. Monster in the open.

»      »      »

Sanson squatted by a window, firing single shots in rapid fire. Miller had scooped up one of the abandoned MG-240s, its two-man crew dead, and was laying down fire from another window.

Dr. Weaver had settled on the couch in the front room and was contemplating gate activity. So far there had been one gate caused by man and one that appeared, apparently as the result of a hostile alien force. The first one sort of made sense. The Higgs boson had caused some sort of wormhole effect, either to another planet in this universe or to another universe. The second one did not. And then there was the hypothetical gate through which Tuffy had appeared. Would there be more? And why were they occurring?

He dialed his phone again.

"Garcia."

"Have the detectors arrived?"

"About an hour ago, and you were right. There's a fairly continuous stream of subatomic particles coming out of it. I think it's degrading."

"Okay, good," Weaver said.

"Is that firing I hear?" Garcia asked.

"Yeah, we're being invaded," Weaver replied and yawned. "Monsters from the eighth dimension or something. I think we're about to get overrun."

"Jesus! Get out of there!"

"Well, we're sort of cut off," Weaver admitted. "Look, what sort of particles?"

"Muons and something else," Garcia said. "Do you really want to talk about this now?"

"Yes."

"Okay, there's some muons, like I said, but we're getting readings on others. They're not anything I recognize, not mesons, not quarks, very high mass. I'd guess they might be bosons."

"That doesn't make sense," Weaver said, squinting his brow as the machine gun set up an almost continuous clatter. "Not the big particles, the muons. I'd have expected neutrinos."

"I don't happen to have a neutrino detector on me at the

moment," Garcia said, sarcastically. Neutrino detection required very large tanks of chemicals, usually in the tens of thousands of gallons. When the neutrinos hit the chemicals they were accelerated to faster than light speed, creating Cherenkov radiation detectable as purplish-blue flashes of light.

"The Japanese have one down to, oh, the size of a container car or so," Weaver said, yawning again. "Maybe we can borrow it. But the rest makes sense. If it's degrading into the universe it's probably going to increase the charge of each of the released particles. That means you get small gates at first and larger ones as it continues to degrade. Or maybe they'll go further and further away. And the first gates that would open would be nearby. Finally things are starting to make sense."

Sanson walked over and slapped a pistol into the scientist's empty hand.

"You know how to use one of those?" Sanson asked.

"Point and click?" Weaver said, looking puzzled.

"Yeah, more or less." The SEAL laughed. "Round up the spout, cocked, not on safe. Touch the trigger and it fires. Just remember to point it at the bad guys."

"Look, one of the SEALs just handed me a pistol," Weaver said, keeping his finger away from the trigger. "I think that's a bad sign. We'll talk about this later, okay?"

"Okay," Garcia said. "Decaying, releasing particles, particles open gates."

"Something like that. And increasing charge, larger gates or further away as time goes by." Tuffy was small. Small gate? But large enough to take Mimi? The front door burst open and one of the smaller monsters came into the room, howling its terrible cry. Sanson turned and fired a burst that bounced off the armor but as it turned towards the SEAL Weaver lined up the pistol on it and shot. The first round was high, kicking dust out of the wall, but he lowered the pistol slightly and was rewarded with a green blotch on the second round. Two more bullets into it, and one in the floor, and it was kicking and twitching on the ground, spilling green ichor into the blue rug.

"Well, gotta go," Weaver said.

"Doc . . ."

"See you later, Garcia."

Another of the beasts sprang into the room and Weaver shot at it, missing, then two more times and hit. The second round hit it in the hindquarters and its back legs dropped, limp. But it continued to crawl forward on its front legs and his next two rounds missed, poking holes in the far wall and shattering a picture of a sailboat against the backdrop of a tropical island. That was his last round and the slide of the H&K locked back on the empty magazine.

"I think I'm out of bullets," he yelled, standing up and stepping back over the couch.

"Here!" Sanson yelled, tossing a magazine through the air.

Weaver caught it but had no idea what to do with it. However, he was an engineer; it should be easy enough to figure out. The thing had crawled up to him and he backed away, into the room, hoping to draw it away from the two SEALs as he attempted to determine how to reload. Let's see, two levers on the handle of the gun, one blocked by the slide. Lever near the trigger. He fiddled with the lever and was rewarded by having the empty magazine drop out onto the floor. Point bullets forward, insert magazine. Eureka! But the slide didn't go forward and pulling the trigger didn't work. He grabbed the slide and pulled back and was again rewarded by having it slide forward. By this time the thing had nearly crawled up to him again and he jumped backwards then pointed the gun at it and shot several times.

"Watch it!" Miller snarled as one of the rounds hammered into his body armor. "Save your rounds!"

"Hey, I got it, didn't I?" Weaver asked as his phone rang.

"William Weaver," he said, holding the smoking barrel of the pistol upwards where he wouldn't tend to shoot one of the SEALs.

"This is the NSA, we're watching the news, where are you?"

"In the Edderbrook house," he replied. "I think we're sort of cut off."

"Jesus! Get out of there!"

"I don't think that's possible," he noted as *another* of the damned things just strolled in the door. He aimed carefully this time and managed to hit it on the first shot. But the round only ticked it off and it turned and charged him.

"Hold please," he said, jumping to the back of the couch and over and then coming up with the pistol and shooting it in the back as it tried to make the turn. One of the bullets must have hit its spine because its back legs went out just like the other one. He aimed carefully and fired rounds into its neck until it stopped moving. He realized he'd gotten out of control when the slide locked back again. "I'm out of bullets again!" he yelled. "I'm sorry, I'm a little busy at the moment. Could we talk later?"

"Sure," the NSA said, bemusedly.

"I told Garcia what I think is going on, based on the evidence," he said, catching another magazine from Sanson and missing the toss from Miller. He reloaded and picked up the magazine he'd missed as he talked. Multi-tasking, that's the key.

"We'll talk later," the NSA said.

"Yeah, later," he replied as two more came through the door and one crashed through a window. "Guys! I don't think I can hold them this time!"

Sanson turned and shot the one under the window as Miller fired and killed one of the ones by the door. But that had emptied his belt and it was left for Weaver to finish off the last.

"Up the stairs," Miller said, pushing the scientist ahead of him.

At the top of the stairs, though, was a large barricade constructed from a bed.

"Hey!" Miller yelled. "Let us through!"

"Catch," a voice said from the other side of the barricade and a knotted rope came flying through the air.

The command master chief started to hand it to the physicist and then stopped, taking the pistol and manipulating a lever. "Safety."

"Right," Weaver said. "Thanks for the tip." He dropped his cell phone in one pocket and tucked the pistol in the other then climbed up the rope, with a push from the chief, and tumbled to the floor on the top landing.

The two SEALs followed him up the barricade and then spread out through the top floors.

"VanGelder," a voice said behind him. "Lake County SWAT. Who are you?"

Weaver tilted his head backwards and looked up at a blond mountain of a man.

"Dr. William Weaver," he answered. "I'm a physicist studying the gates."

"Come to any conclusions?" VanGelder asked.

"Yes, I wish Ray Chen had never been born," Weaver said.

VanGelder chuckled and pointed at the pistol. "You know how to use that?"

"I killed four or five of them downstairs," Weaver answered. "But the honest answer is no. And I'm pretty much out of bullets."

"Knapp carries an H&K," VanGelder said. "I'll get you some magazines. You want a shotgun?"

"I'd love a shotgun," Weaver admitted.

"Okay, you stay by the barricade and make sure none of them come up," VanGelder said, walking away. "And I'll get you a shotgun."

Weaver peered out through a gap in the barricade but none of the things seemed to be coming up the stairs. There was a crashing from downstairs and their weird ululation but they didn't seem to be interested in the upper stories. There was firing from all around the house, now and he heard the sound of some of the thorn projectiles hitting the sides along with a curse from someone in one of the rooms.

VanGelder stopped by and dropped four magazines on the floor, then handed him a shotgun.

"Four rounds in the tube and one up the spout," VanGelder said. "You know how to use it?"

"You pull the handle back," Weaver said, guessing. Sure enough when he did a shotgun round flew out the side. "I've watched television."

"You reload here," VanGelder said, dryly, pointing to the slot on the underside and handing him the ejected round. "I'll let you figure out the sights." He dropped a box of ammunition on the floor and then walked back into one of the rooms.

Weaver slid the round back into the shotgun and poked the barrel through the hole just in time to see one of the doglike creatures creeping up the stairs. It seemed to have trouble with the concept, raising its feet too high and missing the steps. He gave it a blast from the shotgun which knocked it off its feet. As it tumbled to the ground, howling, he shot it in the side. The load of double-ought buck put a hole in its side he could put two fists through. It twitched and then was still but by that time another was ascending the stairs. He shot it and this time it didn't fall but just kept climbing, belly down on the stairs. He shot twice more and the last round apparently found something vital because it stopped and rolled into a ball, biting at its belly. He shot it again and then the shotgun clicked on an empty chamber.

He loaded more rounds feverishly but no more were on the stairs when he looked. He leaned his head on the barricade and, just for a second, contemplated that this was a really stupid place for a physicist to die. When he opened his eyes again there were three of the things on the stairs, nosing at the dead monsters.

He shot one that was broadside, dropping it, then the other two clumsily charged upwards. He got one, somehow, but the third was scrabbling at the barricade and he was out of rounds. He dropped the shotgun and picked up the pistol, emptying it at point blank range into the belly of the monster. That stopped it, but its claws pulled the barricade partially down. More were on the steps now and he dropped out the magazine and started firing at them as fast as he could.

He was pretty sure he was done for when there came a burst of firing from outside the house. Shotguns, rifles, a heavy "BLAM-BLAM-BLAM" that sounded sort of like the big machine gun that had been on the truck and another louder boom that he couldn't place. The monsters were clawing at the barricade, though, so he kept reloading and firing. Then, suddenly, Sanson was at his side. He had a different rifle and he picked his shots, dropping the monsters one by one.

"What's happening outside?" Weaver shouted. All the firing had made him half deaf he realized.

"I think the cavalry got here," Sanson said.

Jim Holley had never had what most people called "a real job" in his life. After getting out of the Army he'd moved back to his hometown of Eustis and drifted from one job to another. He'd sold magazines, headed up a couple of charities, played at politics and spent a good bit of time working in retail. But what he mostly did was play with guns.

All of his limited free money went to his gun collection and it had, over the years, become quite extensive. He was well known to all the gun stores in the Eustis area and could be found every weekend that there wasn't a local gun show on one range or another firing a wide variety of weapons.

He'd been hanging out in Big Bob's Bait, Tackle and Armaments, wrangling amiably about the difference in quality between the British .303 and the .30-06, when they both heard the call from the SWAT team for any available unit to respond. If the National Guard couldn't handle it and the SWAT team couldn't handle it it had to be bad.

Big Bob had rolled his cigar from one side of his mouth to another and shook his head.

"I think it's time to break out the big guns, Jimbo, what say you?"

Jim had just nodded and they both walked into the back room of the store.

Now, Jim had quite a collection but Bob Taylor was in the business of supplying whatever a customer might desire. And his idea of what customers might desire was pretty eclectic. The back room of his store, which was only open to the right sort of individual, was the gun collector's dream. He had two Barretts, M-82A1 and M-95, semi-automatic and bolt respectively. There were Armalites, MP-5s, Garands, Thompsons, Sten, Steyn AUGs and hanging in pride of place a .577 T. Rex. On the floor was a huge gun with a stock and a bipod that was a Finnish Lahti m/39 20mm "man portable" engine of destruction.

By the time they had the back door open and were loading

ammunition the shop had started to fill up. Some of them were "help me" customers who, hearing what was happening had decided that this was the day to come in and purchase a weapon. But the vast majority were the usual crowd of hangers on. The latter filed into the back room and set to work unloading the room and loading the weapons.

In no more than fifteen minutes they had two pickups filled with enough weapons and ammo to arm a very eclectic company of infantry, and a convoy of half a dozen battered pickups, cars and SUVs was headed down the road to Jules Court.

They ran into the first monster nearly a block away. It was savaging a little girl's bike, said little girl being up a tree, screaming.

Jim was in the back of Bob's pickup truck and he let the monster have it in the side with a burst of 185-grain rounds from the vintage BAR he had laid across the roof. Even driving along at fifteen miles an hour he managed to put three rounds in the side of the thing, which dropped in its tracks.

"Time to unass," Bob yelled.

"No," Jim yelled back. "Drive closer. Less distance to hump this shit!"

But by the time Jules Court was in view, they could see that they were going to have to go tactical. Monsters were spilling onto the street. Some of them were like the first, the size of large dogs and covered in spikes. Others were bipedal and seemed to be firing something out of their snouts. Jim shot one of them with the BAR and then held on as Bob slammed to a stop.

"I've got just the thing for those bastards," Jim said, clambering over the tailgate and picking up the 20mm. He managed to get it set up on the roof and then slid in a magazine. "Eat Finnish hot-lead you alien freaks!"

The rounds from the 20mm were not, in fact, lead bullets but exploding shells. As each of them punched into one of the larger beasts it exploded sending bits of the monsters in every direction and covering the area in green gore.

The rest of the ad hoc militiamen had unloaded from the trucks and were laying down a base of fire, engaging the smaller beasts and letting the heavy weapons handle the larger ones.

One of the requirements to be a "regular" at Big Bob's Bait, Tackle and Armaments was that you had to "know what you were doing." That meant you couldn't just argue the relative merits of a Sharps Buffalo gun, you had to know what it was used for. Bob preferred people like Jim, somebody with real military experience. Cops were okay, but only if they knew how to shoot for shit and most cops, in Bob's experience, didn't measure up to his criterion.

Most of the regulars, therefore, had a more than adequate idea of what to do in a situation where demons were invading the earth through a gate into hell. That is: lay down as much lead as necessary to push them back.

Jim emptied the BAR magazine and reached back only to have another shoved into his hand. He slipped that one in and engaged another of the bipedal beasts, ripping a three-round burst into its torso that nearly severed it. There seemed to be about one of them for every ten or twenty of the smaller beasts. And the guys on either side with rifles and shotguns were clearing up the smaller ones.

It was only when the last of the bipedal beasts in view were down that he noticed there was firing from the second story of one of the houses. And at the far end of the road there was a group of soldiers in desert camouflage who had been holding a fall-back line.

"Bob, we got to move it in," he said. "Push them back to that gate, wherever it is."

"Yeah," the gunshop owner said, reflectively. He waved at an arm that had been thrust out of the second story window. There was firing from inside the house, too. "Everybody head for the house!" he yelled. "Get in and drive, I'm going to stay on the 20mm."

Jim got in and put the truck in gear, slowly rolling it forward as the infantry on either side kept pace. Twice he stopped as more waves of the monsters came out, one time ducking down as a line of something like thorns stitched the truck. They were tough and hard, though, he noticed, prodding at one that was shoved through the driver's side door. Sharp, too. He pricked a finger and hoped like hell they weren't poisoned.

Finally they made it up to the house and Bob called a halt. They'd left two bodies behind, both of them from getting hit by the thorn-throwers. As they pulled to a halt in the driveway the Lake County SWAT team came barrel assing out of the house and guardsmen started filtering out from other houses in the area.

"Glad you could make it," VanGelder said.

"Where's this gate?" Bob answered, sliding off the side of the pickup, then taking the 20mm that was handed down to him. The weapon was nearly two meters long and weighed right at fifty pounds, so it wasn't like you could fire it off-hand. But he slung it over one shoulder and grabbed a box of ammunition for it.

"Behind the house," the SWAT lieutenant replied. "The backyard is crawling with these things."

"I'll get up in the house and cover the advance," the gunshop owner said.

"Right," VanGelder nodded. "Get the thorn-throwers, we'll handle the dogs."

"Our cavalry is a group of rednecks in pickup trucks," Sanson said, dryly.

"Don't knock it," the command master chief said, spitting on the floor. "That's more firepower than I've seen outside Ashkanistan."

More of the locals had moved into the downstairs and a big man carrying an absolutely huge gun shouldered past Weaver into a back bedroom. Another of the locals wearing a Lynyrd Skynyrd T-shirt was following him carrying three large boxes of ammunition. More flooded up carrying a motley assortment of only *very* large guns. The last was carrying the largest "normal" rifle Weaver had ever seen. It had a bolt action and looked like what his friends back home used for deer hunting, but it was about twice as large.

"What's that?" he asked Miller.

"Is that what I think it is?" the chief said to the local at the same time.

"If you think it's a T. Rex, it is," the local said, smiling.

"Damn," the SEAL muttered. "I've got to move to Central Florida. They're death on those things in Virginia."

Firing had started up again from the back of the house and rose to a crescendo that was unbelievably loud. There was an occasional scream but the progress of the attack seemed to be steady. He could hear the firing from downstairs moving forward and thought about the gate. They couldn't stop the things by just shooting at them; they had to close the gate somehow.

"We gotta close the gate," Miller said, looking at him as if reading his mind.

"I don't know how to turn it off," Weaver said. "But what if we took one of the bulldozers and parked it in front of it? At the very least it would give us some warning that they're coming through."

"Well, I don't know how to drive a bulldozer," the command master chief admitted, sounding ashamed. "Do you?"

"No," Weaver said. "But I bet one of these locals will."

Sanson came back a moment later with the guy carrying the big "T. Rex" rifle.

"We want to block the gate with a bulldozer," Weaver said.

"So he told me," the local replied. "Makes sense. Where's the dozer?"

"There was one over to the left," the physicist noted. "But it's more or less behind the gate. I don't know if the monsters have spread that way or not."

"They seem to be heading for the houses," Miller pointed out. "They don't seem to be going *behind* the gate at all, yet."

"We could drive around back," the local said. "Try to drive right up to it."

"That might attract their attention," the chief pointed out. "So far we have a one-axis threat. That would make it multi-axis. And that would really suck."

"Hey, you're a SEAL, right?" the local replied, chuckling through his beard. "You wanna live forever?"

"Preferably," Miller answered. "But let's go see if you know what you're doing."

By the time they got to the pickup truck the locals and what was left of the National Guard company had retaken the fighting positions and, with the support of heavy weapons in the houses overlooking the gate, were holding the monsters in a small perimeter right at the gate itself. The monsters were still attempting to pour through but the additional firepower of the locals had them pinned at the entrance. As they crowded into the front seat of the pickup Weaver noticed some things that looked like the alien "mosquitoes" hovering near the gate now. He dreaded those more than the thorn-throwers or the "dogs" but it turned out that these were not the semiparasitic mosquitoes. What they were became apparent as a television helicopter drifted too close to the battle.

One of the things flapped its wings harder and began to ascend. When it got to about ten meters above the ground the wings dropped off and a jet of fire shot out of its rear. It accelerated fast on what appeared to be a rocket engine and then slammed into the helicopter. The helicopter exploded in midair sending flaming pieces far and wide.

"Jesus," the local said, putting the pickup in gear and backing out of the driveway.

"Great," the chief said. "They've got antiair capability. What next? Antitank? Organic tanks?"

"That room you were in," Weaver said. "It looked like a giant organism, right? So it's conceivable that they could grow something as large as a tank."

"That won't be good," Miller noted.

"No," Weaver said with a chuckle.

"Where are they, then?" Sanson asked.

"Probably the same place ours are," Weaver replied in a distracted tone. "Not near the gate. Okay, they form a gate. And maybe they're getting ready for an invasion. But that room was more or less empty, right?"

"Right," Miller replied.

"So . . . the mosquito thing that got your SEAL was something like a sentry, maybe an antibody. It was designed just to defend the hole and maybe send out an alarm. Although I'd guess getting a couple of satchel charges in the gut probably sent enough of an alarm through that thing anyway."

"Ouch," Miller said. "You're saying we caused this?"

"No," Weaver replied. "But you might have sped up their time-table. So they're throwing everything they have nearby into the gate. And, presumably, their real heavies aren't right there. Or, maybe, they haven't even produced them yet but will soon. Or are producing them now and they'll be here momentarily."

"We'd better block the gate pretty quick, then," the local noted, putting the truck in gear.

"Oh, yeah," Weaver said as his phone rang. He fished it out of his pocket and turned it on distractedly. "William Weaver."

"Doctor Weaver, this is the NSA. SOCOM reports they've lost contact with their SEAL team, the National Guard is out of contact with their company and the last news chopper to get into the area was shot down by something. I presume you've moved out of the area? I wasn't sure if you'd be there to answer, frankly."

"No, I'm still in the area," Weaver replied as the pickup took a corner on two wheels. "We're going to try to block the gate with a bulldozer. And I don't know what happened to Lieutenant Glasser but the last two members of the team are with me in the pickup truck."

"Pickup truck?"

"Some of the locals have rendered assistance," Weaver said. "I'd make a redneck joke but I are one. Anyway, they've got the monsters pushed back to the gate and we're going to try to close it, or at least block it, with one of the bulldozers that was clearing the area. But we've been discussing it and we think there are probably heavier monsters that haven't arrived yet. I think you need to get some really heavy forces down here."

"We will," the NSA answered. "There's a battalion on the way from Benning at the moment but they can't be there until tomorrow at the earliest."

"Well, in that case I suggest that you get whatever you *can* get here as fast as possible," Weaver said. "These guys seem to mean business. And so far I think we've only seen their equivalent of infantry. I don't want to think about what might be on the way. I'd say, ma'am, that it's a race to see who can ..." he paused. He'd heard the term before. Oh, yeah. "Who can get here the fustest with the mostest."

There was a pause and he could almost see the NSA nod. "I see. I'll point that out, with underlining, to the Pentagon."

"Yes, ma'am," Weaver said as the pickup braked to a stop by the bulldozer. "I've got to go now. Talk to you later. Bye."

"You know," Weaver said to the air. "This is almost as exciting as defending a scientific paper."

"You're joking," the chief replied, climbing out of the truck and scanning for monsters. There was one of the dogs on the bulldozer and he shot it off but that seemed to be the only one in the area.

"Sort of," Weaver said. "But you'd be surprised how brutal it can get." He hefted the shotgun and felt in his pocket for the remaining rounds. The pistol, on safe as he'd been shown, was shoved in the front of his pants, his last magazine shoved in his back pocket. "And they don't let you shoot people who are attacking you for no reason."

The four of them clambered on the bulldozer and the local got it started. It lurched into motion and headed right for the gate.

"I'm gonna pull it up to the side and pivot it," the local said. "That's gonna be the bad time; nobody will be able to fire because we'll be in the way."

"Well, I'll do what I can," Miller said. He had grabbed the T. Rex and had his M-4 slung over his back. "Sanson, take the dogs, I'll handle the thorns, Doc, you handle anything that gets on the dozer."

The local picked up the dozer blade as one of the thorn-throwers that had just exited the gate fired at them. Most of the thorns were caught by the blade but a few pinged onto the canopy over the driver's seat.

Miller leaned against the support of the canopy and fired the T. Rex, the recoil almost knocking him off his feet.

"Yowza!" he yelled, working the bolt and then rotating his shoulder.

"Got a kick, don't it?" the local said.

Sanson was picking off dogs on either side and Doc realized he should be watching for threats, not watching the chief. He looked around and, sure enough, one of the dogs had managed to jump up on the back of the dozer. He gave it a mouthful of buckshot which, if it didn't kill it, certainly knocked it off the dozer. Another was trying to get past the spinning treads on his side and he shot it in the back. It lost the use of its back legs but still tried to crawl forward.

Just then the local pivoted the dozer, incidentally crushing the wounded dog monster, and lowered the blade slightly, lining it up with the hole. There was a mound of injured and dead monsters by the gate and the dozer pushed them back into the hole along with a thorn-thrower that had just come through. The mound shrank as it was pushed back and then the dozer blades, which were wider than the opening, reached the gate. And stopped.

All four of them were thrown forward as the bulldozer lurched to a halt. The local geared down, but the treads just spun in place.

"Damn," Miller said. "That's weird."

"Very," Weaver admitted. He hadn't been certain what would happen since the blade was wider than the opening but if he had been willing to make a guess is was that the dozer would have gone forward as if the gate didn't exist, leaving the gate in the middle of the dozer. However, it appeared that the gate had a very real physical presence. It was, however, at least partially blocked. As he watched, though, a dog monster crawled out from under the blade, only to be shot by Sanson.

"Lower the blade a little," the chief said.

The local lowered it to the ground, leaving the top half of the gate open. A thorn-thrower clambered over the obstacle but was hit by fire from three separate machine guns and fell back into the gate.

"Let's dig a berm," Sanson said. "Push dirt up to cover it completely."

"They'd just dig through it," Miller said. "No, leave it this way. We'll realign the machine guns to cover it. I'm sure they'll figure out a way through but it will do for now."

The four of them clambered off the dozer and headed for the lines at a weary trot. They were halfway there when an explosion behind them threw them off their feet.

Weaver rolled onto his back and looked towards the gate where the smoking bulldozer still lay, half its blade blown off.

"I thought they'd think of something," Miller said, angrily. "But not *that* fast!"

"Come on!" Weaver shouted, springing to his feet and hurrying back to the hole they had occupied at the first attack. Behind them there was another explosion and then another.

He jumped into the hole, realized that he'd left his shotgun behind, and started to go back for it just as the smoking bulldozer shuddered and was shoved out of the way.

What came through the hole was impossible, a beast about the size of a rhinoceros, covered in scaly plates and strong enough, apparently, to move a D-9 by shoving with six stumpy legs. It let out a high-pitched bellow that shook the ground, then turned its head and launched a ball of green lightning from between two horns. The lightning seemed to float through the air but it must have been going fast because at almost the same instant it was fired it hit the trench line and exploded, blowing one of the machine gun posts into the air.

"Holy fucking shit," Sanson muttered, pumping rounds into the thing. Or at least at it; they were sparking on its plate and clearly not penetrating.

"Well, now we know what their tanks look like," the chief said. He still had the T. Rex and was aiming at the thing but not firing. "Come on, you bastard," he muttered.

The monster fired another ball of lightning and one of the houses behind them exploded in fire. Then it stopped and roared again.

As it did the chief fired one round.

Weaver had thought the world had exploded when the first round had been fired by the creature but he now had a new perspective. The air turned white and he found himself flung through the air by a tremendous force like a giant, ungentle, hand. He didn't even notice when he slammed into the back of the hole. He knew he passed out but it couldn't have been for long because the rumble from the explosion was still resounding when he shook his head and opened his eyes. For a moment he thought he was blind but realized that it was just an afterimage of the explosion; everything looked milky-white. He felt something liquid on his face and reached up. His nose and ears were both bleeding.

Sanson was lying in the bottom of the hole, unmoving. He was breathing but out cold. The local was in the bottom next to him, his head tilted at an odd and clearly unsurvivable angle. The chief was lying next to him up against the side of the hole, and sat up with what appeared to be a groan. That was when Weaver realized that all he could hear was a ringing in his ears.

He sat up and looked at the gate. There was a large crater in front of it. The bulldozer was over on its side. And there was nothing coming through.

The chief was looking at him and saying something. Weaver realized he could hear it, if barely. He was asking if he was okay.

"No," he said, shaking his head and pointing at his ears. "I can't hear!" He suddenly noticed that he had the world's worst headache.

The chief nodded and pointed at his own, mouthing "Neither can I." He opened the bolt of the T. Rex, wearily pulled some rounds out of his fatigues and thumbed them into the action. Then he shot the bolt forward, leaned back, closed his eyes and shook his head, clearly spent beyond human endurance, clutching the gun to his chest. After a moment he set his jaw, leaned forward and pointed the gun at the gate. He looked over his shoulder at Weaver and reached into his pocket. What he held out was a large goldish coin. He pointed to one side. It had a human figure on it and the motto: "The only easy day was yesterday."

Doctor Weaver looked at the SEAL, who was also bleeding from the nose and ears but clearly prepared to do battle, shook his own head and passed out.

# 5

"First report on Gate 417," Collective 15379 emitted.

"Go."

"Initial reports favorable. Group of ten level one ground combat units sent on survey. Encountered minor resistance."

"On immediate entry?"

"Yes. Or shortly thereafter. One GCU sustained terminal injuries, recovered and recycled. Two sophonts recovered, one terminal, one critical. Both terminated and examined." It sent a blip of biological information on the late Edderbrooks. "Initial invasion packet was started but before it completed gestation there was a magnitude 249 explosion at the gate and five farside combat units, estimated level one to three, entered the gate area. Sentries engaged and one reported full engagement. Slight variations from initial survey of sophonts." Another blip of data, this one defining Howse's protective suit as an extruded armor. "A response packet was sent through consisting of level one and two ground combat units. Level one units were repulsed by a heavy force of farside ground combat units designated one to four. Level two units pushed back first wave but were stopped and repulsed by a reinforcing wave of level two to four units; farside units manually blocked the gate. A group of level six units had arrived by then and reopened the gate. Initial entry appeared successful but first level six unit was destroyed, method unknown, which backblast severely damaged two more level six units, still recoverable. With only two level six units functional and all level one and two units terminated in the immediate gate area the attack was called off while more level six units are gestated. Colonization packet is gestated and only awaits successful opening of the gate."

"Heavy defense," Collective 47 noted. "Weapon type?"

"Chemical propellant and explosive. No plasma or quark weapons detected."

"I have sent a message to all nearby collectives and those with localized gate ability to forward all available level three though seven ground combat units and to begin a ten percent increase in gestation of all combat systems. When you have an overwhelming force available, strike. That will require at least seven cycles."

"I understand and comply."

"And send an emissary unit."

"An emissary?"

"Let us see how gullible they are."


"Dr. Weaver?" a voice said.

Bill opened his eyes a crack and then closed them against the light. It was moments like this that he dreaded. So far, it seemed okay. He felt sheets and the brief glimpse he had seen overhead indicated a hospital. So did the smell.

"Dr. Weaver?" the voice repeated. It was a woman. Nurse or doctor? Have to open the eyes again to check.

A large breasted redhead wearing one of those vaguely comical multicolored smocks that nurses seemed to be enamored of was standing by the bed with a cup of water.

"Before you ask, you're in Shands Hospital in Gainesville, Florida," the nurse said, holding a straw up to his mouth.

Bill took a sip, clearing what felt like a mound of plaster out of his mouth, and grunted.

"Bathroom?"

"How about a bedpan?" She smiled.

"No," he said, sitting up and wincing at the headache. "I can move." He checked his extremities to ensure that this was, in fact, the case. All working. All weak as hell but that would pass. He'd been in the body and fender shop before. "I can walk."

"You're not supposed to," the nurse said, firmly, pushing him back.

He slid his hand onto her thumb and exerted just enough pressure to prove that it *could* hurt. "I can walk. I'm going to walk. All I need is for you to help me with the IV cart."

She looked at him sternly, then shook her head and helped him to the bathroom. By the time he made it back to the bed he wondered if it had been a good idea; he was weaker than he'd thought.

"The gate?" he asked. He wasn't too sure exactly where Gainesville was from Eustis but if they'd lost the gate he didn't want to be close.

"Nothing else has come through," the nurse said, helping him into bed and settling the sheets to her satisfaction. "It's been all over the news. There's more National Guard and some Regular Army and Marines around it, now."

"There were some SEALs with me," Weaver said. He had a clear view of Sanson lying in the bottom of the hole.

"They're both here," the nurse said. "The younger one is still unconscious, not a coma, he'll be okay. The older one is already out of bed, against doctor's orders, and swearing at anyone who tries to get him back in. Now you just lie down and rest. A doctor will be here to see you soon."

After she had left Weaver elevated the bed—lying down hurt more than sitting up—and turned on the TV. He didn't have to flip through many channels; everything but the Discovery Channel and Disney were running all news all the time.

"We're reporting live from Eustis, Florida, where units of the Third Infantry Division, the same units that captured Baghdad, are just beginning to arrive. Bob Tolson is embedded with Bravo Company, First Battalion Ninety-Third Infantry, over to you, Bob." The voiceover was from New York or Washington but the video was from a news helicopter. There were green Army bulldozers and some yellow civilian ones digging big holes and a shot of a whole line of tractor trailer cars loaded with tanks and APCs.

Bill thought about the flaming debris falling from the sky and wondered at the balls it took to fly a helicopter in the area for no other reason than getting some nice stock footage.

"Peter, you should be able to see the activity around me," the local reporter said. "From the air it probably looks like chaos but I'm told it's a well orchestrated drill. I'm talking with Captain Shane Gries who is the commander of Bravo Company. Shane, thanks for taking a moment to talk to us."

"No problem, Bob." The video had cut back to the ground and now showed a youngish man with a square jaw, his helmet fastened and looking very neat.

"What do you think our chances are?" the reporter asked.

"Well, Bob, the enemy clearly has some very good firepower," the company commander responded. "But its action plan is going to have to be very simple, there is only one avenue of attack available. And if light infantry, which is what it faced before, could hold it and push it back, well, my boys will turn it into dog meat with their Bradleys and Abrams."

"By light infantry you're talking about the local militia?" the reporter asked. "What they're calling 'The Charge of the Redneck Brigade?'"

"Bob, I'm not about to dis those locals," the captain said, shaking his head. "They retook the gate and took plenty of casualties doing it. They're fine Americans and patriots and, truth be told, they probably shoot better than most of my boys. Some of them are still hanging around and as long as they want to, they can stay."

"I wasn't making fun of them," the reporter said with a tone of honesty.

"I know, but that redneck crack is getting under my boys' skin," the captain replied, sternly. "The day one of you reporters is willing to charge the gates of hell with nothing but some World War Two weaponry you can crack wise. Until then, treat them with the respect they deserve. They and the national guardsmen are going to stay here until, at least, the rest of the battalion arrives. I've been told that the short-term plan is to get the whole brigade down here, arrayed in layered defense. What they'll do after that I don't know. But I think that even the locals will admit that a battalion of mechanized infantry is probably enough."

"I notice that you've pulled further back from the gate," the reporter said, changing the subject hastily. "Is that wise?"

"Our Abrams and Bradleys are longer-range weapons," the captain explained carefully. "We're digging revetments for them and as soon as the engineers and civilian contractors are done with them they'll start on bunkers for the infantry that are forward of that line. But I don't want my command caught in another of those explosions; if the enemy had come through right after its rhino-tank exploded they'd have rolled over the defenders. Infantry positions are back two hundred yards and the Brads and Abrams are at two-fifty. That should give enough stand-off for secondaries. And, trust me, we can fill the probable avenue of approach with plenty of firepower even if we're that far back."

"Well, Captain, I'm sure everyone's glad you're on the job," the reporter said. "Back to you, Peter."

"That's good news from Eustis," the anchorman said. "Now turning to other news, the young lady who miraculously survived the explosion in Orlando has been reunited with her surviving family," the camera turned to what was clearly previously shot footage of Mimi, Tuffy tucked under her chin, hugging a heavy-set woman in her thirties. "Mimi Jones' closest surviving relative is Vera Wilson, who now has the responsibility of raising not only her niece but the strange alien playmate that adopted her. Our reporter, Shana Kim, talked with Mrs. Wilson earlier today."

The scene changed to what was clearly heavily edited footage as the heavyset woman, now wearing too much makeup of the wrong shade for television, was sitting on a plaid sofa and talking.

"Herman and I are glad to take Mimi in," the woman said, dabbing at her eyes. "I miss my Loretta, that's my sister, of course, but by the grace of God Mimi survived. Herman and I don't have any children of our own, not for want of trying and we both love Mimi very much and are glad to have her. She misses Loretta too, but she's taking it very well. She hasn't cried at all. I mean, she knows her momma is gone but we'll all be together in Heaven someday and that is a blessed relief to her."

"What about the alien?" the reporter asked. The camera gave a brief shot of the blonde woman in her twenties, looking serious and nodding her head. "Aren't you worried about it?"

"Tuffy?" the woman answered. "Well, he's pretty scary at first. I mean he looks like a big old terancheler. But he ain't done nothing wrong. I had to scold Mimi one time, nothing much just that she hadn't cleared her dishes, and I was sort of afraid to. But Mimi just nodded and did as she was bid and then told me that Tuffy said it was okay, I was right. That was pretty strange, I'll admit, but, like I said, he ain't done nothing wrong. I know they say he hurt that deputy, but I'm sure it was just a misunderstanding or something. I'm not afraid of Tuffy; he's sort of cute. Truth to tell, if he's that good a watch dog I'm glad to have him around what with all the child snatching and all. Couple of my neighbors asked if Mimi knew where they could get one for their own kids. Course she didn't. She doesn't remember where he come from."

"There's going to be a lot of interest in Mimi, you know," the reporter said. "How are you going to handle that?"

"Well, we're going to raise her as well as we can, as a God fearing young woman," Mrs. Wilson answered. "As to the reporters and such, I figure with all that's going on, Mimi and Tuffy won't be so interesting before long."

"And rarely have I heard the term 'nine day wonder' so well described," the anchor said, smiling. "A charity fund for the support of Mimi Jones has been established. Donations can be made to: The Mimi Jones Foundation, PO Box 4687, Orlando, Florida, 32798–4687. And in other news . . ."

"In other news that's going to be one very rich little alien," a voice said from the door.

Weaver looked up and grinned at Command Master Chief Miller, who was wearing a hospital gown tied in the back.

"You know your ass is hanging out in the breeze, right?" Weaver said, turning down the TV.

"Yep," the chief said, walking in the room.

"And you've got an IV insert stuck in your arm?"

"Yep," Miller replied, taking a chair. "And I told them they had thirty minutes to take it out or I was going to do it myself and bleed all over their nice, shiny floor. How you doing, Doc?"

"Tired, sore, hell of a headache."

"Pain is weakness leaving the body," the chief intoned. "You ready to get out of here?"

"I'd love to," Weaver admitted. "I don't think doctors know what the hell they're doing; there's a reason they call it a medical 'practice.' But we both appear to be a little short on clothes."

"Got some guardsmen on the way over with some chocolate chips," the SEAL said. "After which, by order of your friend the NSA, we're going to take a little drive up to a town called Archer."

"What's there?" Weaver asked, wincing.

"Guess."

Emma May Sands had turned seventy-nine the previous month. Two decades before when her late husband Arthur had retired they sold their house in Buffalo, New York, and moved to the small, rural town of Archer. It was not a "regular" retirement community and they had preferred it for that very reason. Archer was a small town consisting mostly of young couples who worked in and around Gainesville, generally in something connected to the university. There were also a few houses rented to students. It was a young town and despite the fact that Emma and Arthur knew they were old, they didn't want to feel old. So they moved where there were young people around for the life and vitality.

And they were close to Shands, which was one of the best hospitals in North Florida. Arthur had a heart condition and proximity to a good hospital was important.

Shands had not helped, though, when Arthur finally suffered a terminal stroke. It had come in his sleep, thank God, and he passed lightly. After his passing Emma's life hardly changed. She had to learn to cook for one but she continued to divide her time between the local Democratic Committee, which she had to admit was filled with hippy know-it-alls that didn't understand you could be a Democrat *and* a patriot, and activities associated with the Episcopal Church.

That was until a three-foot-tall cat scratched on her back door and calmly walked into the front room to watch Oprah.

She wasn't sure what to do. The cat walked on her back legs and, while she was clearly naked and just as clearly female, she didn't seem *bad*. The cat had gray fur tinged to black in a line along her spine. Her belly was a lighter gray, almost white, with another line passing up the middle between her . . . mammaries and more highlighting on the tips of her ears. She had slanted eyes and either some sort of makeup or another highlighting running back from her eyes in a line.

Emma had been watching the news—it was almost impossible to avoid unless you wanted to watch Discovery all day—and knew that aliens or something were landing in Orlando, but that all seemed very remote to her. Life in Archer had been much the same. Oh, there had been a rush on the grocery store like there was going to be a hurricane or something and a few of her friends had urged her to move back to Buffalo and stay with her children until everything passed over.

But that didn't mean she could pick up the phone and call the police and tell them there was a three-foot-tall cat sitting in the front room watching the news. Little old ladies that did that had to go to the nursing home. There would be a time for her to go to the nursing home but it wasn't that time yet.

So she went back into the room and watched Oprah. Oprah was cut off halfway through, though, with the news that more aliens, these ones bad guys, had landed in Eustis, which was closer to Archer than she really liked. There was a big fight going on between the aliens and the National Guard. She didn't like that, and when the cat saw the aliens she hissed and spat something that sounded like angry words, so, nodding in request to the big cat, she changed the channel to Lifetime and sat and watched an episode of *The Golden Girls*. When the show was over it was getting late and the cat stood up and nodded at her.

"I have to go," the cat said, very clearly. "I will see you tomorrow, Blanch."

Emma didn't bother to point out that her name wasn't Blanch. Tracy Cooper, the poor dear, whose mind was getting a little out there, sometimes made the same mistake.

Emma went to bed at her normal hour but couldn't get to sleep. After a while she got up and went downstairs and looked at Arthur's collection of books. She preferred to read mystery and horror novels but Arthur had been a big reader of all those trashy science fiction novels. She suspected that somewhere in those stacks and stacks of moldering paperbacks was what she needed to know to talk to an alien cat and let her know where the litterbox was, for example.

She finally picked one up that looked as if it had been read many times called *The Moon Is a Harsh Mistress*. It at least had a spaceship on the cover. She tried to read it but it made no sense. And the author couldn't write very well at all; he left out all the articles. Finally, after fifty pages, she gave up and turned off the light, falling almost immediately into the light sleep of old age.

In the morning, as she was making tea, there was another scratching on the door. It was that cat again, wearing something like a long trench coat and a brimmed hat like a fedora against the early morning rain.

"Good morning, Blanch," the cat enunciated precisely, taking off the coat and hat and shaking them.

"My name's Emma," Emma replied, taking the child-sized coat and setting it on the dryer with the hat perched on top.

"Mine is Nyarowlll," the cat said. "Good morning, Emma. May I watch television?"

"Please do," Emma replied. "I was just making tea and was going to have an English muffin. Or I think I have a can of cat food around?"

"No thank you, Emma," Nyarowlll said. "I am not hungry."

Emma rummaged in Arthur's boxes again and found a book called *Methuselah's Children*. It had the blurb "An Exciting New First Contact Novel" on the jacket so she thought it might help.

The book was not too long but it didn't have much in it about aliens until towards the end. She'd gotten up for lunch and fixed herself a tuna sandwich, offering some of the tuna to Nyarowlll on a plate. The cat was watching some sort of old science fiction show with a big clunky robot and a guy in a silver suit but she said that she did not want any tuna.

When Emma came back to the sitting room she noticed that this book was by the same author that had written that silly moon thing. Apparently he did know a definite article. Maybe the moon thing was his first book; first novels sometimes were pretty bad.

She finished the book—she was a fast reader—before dinnertime. When Nyarowlll came into the sitting room looking for her Emma narrowed her eyes.

"You're not going to change our babies, are you?" she asked. She had four children and two of them were still giving her grandchildren. Aliens had *better* not start changing babies. "We don't stand for that sort of thing, here."

"No, Emma," Nyarowlll said. Her diction had improved, smoothed out, and if she had an accent it was slightly Midwestern. "We do not change babies. Emma, I think the thing I need to say is: Take me to your leader." She stuck out one paw as if to shake hands.

Emma took the paw carefully, Nyarowlll looked as delicate as a big bird, and shook it, then put her other hand over it and said, gently. "Why don't I just call someone, okay?"

There was a big barrier of police tape around a small ranch house, with two officers sitting on the hood of their squad cars smoking cigarettes, when Weaver and Chief Miller pulled up at the address they had been given. They showed their ID to the officers, then walked to the front door of the house, which was being guarded by a SWAT team sergeant.

Weaver waved at the sergeant and showed his Pentagon ID again.

"I'm Dr. Weaver with the DOD," he said. "This is Command Master Chief Miller with SEAL Team Five. What do you have?"

"We received a call that a nonhostile alien was visiting this home. The home owner is Mrs. Emma Sand. When the first officers arrived they found a three-foot-tall . . . cat that walks on its hind legs. The homeowner alleges that the cat had been visiting for two days, watching television. When confronted by the officers the cat demanded to be 'taken to our leaders.'" The SWAT sergeant was visibly sweating. "Upon investigation we found another gate in the woods behind the caller's home. At that point we contacted the Department of Homeland Security, secured the area and awaited further information. The area is quarantined at this time but by the time we got here quarantine had already been breached."

"Felinoid," Weaver said, gently. "Three-foot-tall felinoid. Looks like a cat but it's from another world so it's not *really* a cat. And the other term you're searching for is 'bipedal.' That's walking on two legs. Gotta learn the jargon."

"Yes, sir," the sergeant said.

"We've got it," Miller said, tapping the sergeant on the shoulder. "You don't get this much in Archer, huh?"

"No . . ."

"Command Master Chief."

"No, Command Master Chief, we don't."

"Don't worry," Miller said, tapping him on the shoulder again. "We see it all the time."

They walked into the front room where a pleasant-faced older woman was sitting in front of a tea service talking in low tones with, yes, a three-foot-tall bipedal felinoid.

"Hello," Weaver said, nodding at the old lady. "I'm Dr. William Weaver with the Department of Defense and this is Command Master Chief Miller with the Navy. Are you Mrs. Sand?"

"Sands," Emma said, starting to get up and staying in her chair at a wave from Weaver. "Emma May Sands."

"And who is your visitor?" Weaver asked.

"This is Nyarowlll," Emma said, getting the vowels as close as she could to what was essentially a meow.

"Hello, Nyarowlll," Bill said.

"A doctor is someone who manages the physiology of your people?" Nyarowlll asked, carefully.

"It is also the term for an academic," Bill pointed out. "I am an academic who is studying the gates."

"I, too, am an academic," Nyarowlll said, somewhat excitedly. "I study the physical processes of our world."

"We're probably the same sort of academic," Bill replied with a closed-mouth smile.

"And your Navy, as I understand it, handles combat at sea," Nyarowlll asked, looking at the chief. "Does it not? But surely this is a situation for land security."

"I'm a SEAL, ma'am," Miller replied. "We handle ground combat as well."

"Oh, yes," Nyarowlll said, making a strange sidling motion with her head. "I saw a program on them on the Discovery Channel. Very good soldiers."

Miller decided to let that one pass.

"What can we do for you, Nyarowlll?" Bill asked.

"I am what you would call an ambassador from my world," Nyarowlll answered. "I have come to this world to establish friendly relations and trade. I would like to meet with your world leadership and, barring that, I would like someone who is capable of establishing communications to come to our world to meet with our leadership."

"Ah," Bill said, momentarily dumbfounded. "You have to understand that we are somewhat . . . uncertain about cross-gate contact. The first sentients we have . . . met from another intelligent society came through fighting."

"That would be the T!Ch!R!," Nyarowlll noted, letting out a stream of what was mostly clicks. "We, too, have had experience with them. They are a sort of pest that goes with the gates."

"Let me call someone and see what I can arrange," Bill replied, stepping out of the room. He pulled out his cell phone and called the NSA. He had an intermediate control at this point in the Pentagon but this seemed like something that needed a bit more direct approach.

He finally got through to her and explained what he had been told.

"Damn," the NSA said. "State is going to be all over this like stink and we *don't* actually know that she is friendly."

"Yes, ma'am," Bill said. "I'm wondering what they know about the gates. I've seen no sign of high technology about the visitor. But that doesn't tell us anything about the far side."

"Would you and Chief Miller be willing to travel to the far

side and investigate this society while I do battle with State back here?" she asked.

"Yes, ma'am," Weaver replied, sighing. "If Nyarowlll can survive on this side the converse is probably true."

"Tell her you've contacted your leaders in this government. Then, go through, make contact with their government but don't promise *anything*, understand?"

"Yes, ma'am," Bill replied.

"Good luck."

"Nyarowlll," Weaver said. "Or should I call you Dr. Nyarowlll?"

"Nyarowlll will do," the cat replied.

"I've contacted our leaders and told them what is happening. They asked me to go through and contact your leaders in turn. Would that be possible?"

"Certainly," Nyarowlll said, standing up. "Now?"

"Chief?" Bill said.

"Let me go get my bag," the SEAL replied, walking out of the room. When he came back in he was carrying an M-4 and wearing a combat harness. "Okay, I'm dressed."

"Will there be an issue with bringing weapons with us?" Bill asked.

"Not at all," Nyarowlll replied, walking towards the rear of the house. "It is a justifiable action. However, when you meet the emperor they will have to remain outside."

Bill mulled that over as they approached the gate. Two SWAT team members were watching it carefully, as if it would start dumping . . . whatever she'd called them at any time.

Nyarowlll stepped through with total aplomb and Bill followed her into the looking glass.

The far side was a large room, about fifteen meters high, with a concrete floor and walls. The ceiling, which looked to also be concrete, was held up with heavy metal beams that were riveted together. The construction looked vaguely familiar to him but he couldn't place it. Then he noticed the odor. There was a catlike musk but overlaying it was what he identified as wood and coal smoke. He hadn't smelled coal smoke in years but it was distinctive. There was also a smell like rotten fish or a salt marsh; the place must be near the ocean. The room was cold, cooler than the Central Florida evening they had left, and there were three small potbelly stoves heating it. One of them was glowing cherry red. The room was lit with a large number of lamps which Bill tentatively identified as oil lamps.

There were about twenty cats in the room, most of them colored like Nyarowlll and almost indistinguishable, but a few colored a light tan with brown markings. Some of them wore leather aprons and others bore harnesses made of leather and carried what looked like laser pistols that had been modified for wood stocks. One of the ones wearing an apron came over to Nyarowlll immediately and they carried on a conversation that sounded like a cat fight, meanwhile stroking each other's ears. After a bit of that Nyarowlll came back over to them and waved to one of the doors.

"We have a transfer device," she said, opening the low door and waving them through.

Bill had to duck nearly in two and when he reached the far side he saw another gate.

"This gate does not go to another planet but to a linked gate on this planet," the felinoid said, stepping forward. "It is quite safe."

Bill looked at the SEAL, then shrugged, following the cat through another looking glass.

In a moment he was standing in another room. It was much smaller with fine wood paneling, a terrazzo inlay floor, and lined with low—low even for the cats—benches that were covered in rich furs of an unusual shade of blue. There were two more of the soldier cats in the room, bigger and beefier than the ones in the gate room. Both carried the laser pistol/rifles and were eying the SEAL warily.

"I'll be just a moment," Nyarowlll said. "You'll have to leave your weapons here."

Nyarowlll spoke to the soldier cats and then passed through the door with a perfunctory ear wipe to each.

Bill got a more careful look at the weapons the cats bore and reached some conclusions. The body of the weapon was made of what appeared to be plastic or ceramic composite with a barrel that was metal, probably a heavy metal. The shoulder piece, on the other hand, was wood and was connected to the main weapon by metal bands that wrapped around a very strangely curved pistol grip. The ammunition pouches were formed and hardened leather secured by a brass clip. They looked about right for some sort of power pack.

"Doc," Miller said, glancing around the room. "These guys don't make those weapons."

"Yes," Weaver replied. He glanced over at the SEAL who was looking dyspeptic. "What's wrong?"

"Nothing," Miller said in a muffled voice. He was looking around at the floor with a pained expression and finally swallowed.

"Couldn't figure out what to do with your tobacco juice?" Bill said, smiling.

"Always something you can do with it," the chief growled. He unbuckled his combat harness and laid it on one of the couches, setting the M-4 down on top of it. Then he pulled out a clasp knife from his pocket, a pistol from the back of his trousers and a knife out of his boot. "That had better be here when I come back," he added, pointing at the pile.

One of the cats made a sinuous head motion then stepped over to the pile, lowering his weapon from high port. He gestured at the rifle in interest.

Miller picked up the M-4 and dropped the magazine, then jacked a round out of the chamber and handed the weapon to the cat who, after a moment's hesitation, touched a stud on his own rifle and removed a small, silver oblong and passed the rifle to the chief.

"There's no sights on this thing that I can see," the chief said as the cat hefted the M-4 and then looked at the sights. He said something to his companion who responded with a series of hacks. It might have been disgust, it might have been laughter. The cat lifted the M-4, figured out how to shorten the stock, which made it just about perfect for him, and looked through the sights, keeping his finger away from the trigger. The pistol grip was too large for him but so was the one on the ray gun.

"I bet one of those guys could handle the kick on an M-4,"

Weaver noted as the cat lowered the weapon and then examined the cartridges. He pointed out the bullets to his companion again who made a sinuous head motion and spat a couple of times. There was a discussion that sounded like two cats stuck in a barrel going on when the door opened and Nyarowlll, followed by a cat that just *looked* older, came through.

"The emperor will see you now," Nyarowlll said, gesturing through the door.

"Don't fiddle with that while I'm gone," Miller said, handing back the ray gun and then accepting his M-4 in return.

There was a short corridor outside the room and another door with two of the "heavy" cats guarding it. These bore not just the ray guns but short swords that looked oddly ceremonial. The older cat opened the door and they ducked through, it was very low for them although the corridor had been about normal height, into a small office. A cat that looked about Nyarowlll's age was sitting in front of a low desk that was just about covered in paper. On one side of the desk an odd, capped tube jutted up through the floor. Behind him was a large window that was open a crack at the bottom despite the chill. From it came the sounds of a street, if metal wheels on rock and a strange oinking could be called street sounds.

Five more cats were in the room, two heavies, one by the door and one by the window on the far wall and three that were all older than the cat behind the desk. One of them was wearing a combat harness that was missing ammunition pouches but did have some silver embroidery that might have been rank markings. He was an old tom, scarred in quite a few places, one ear nearly torn off, eyepatch over his left eye and missing his right arm from just below the elbow. That had been replaced with a steel metal skeleton that terminated in a hook. Despite all the damage he looked as if he could chew nails and spit them out as Rottweiler killers. Miller took one look at him and saluted.

"General," the SEAL said, holding the salute.

The cat looked at him for a moment, then crossed his arms in front of him, hissing something. Miller dropped the salute and turned back to the cat behind the desk.

"Dr. Weaver, Command Master Chief Miller, may I present His Majesty Mroool, Emperor of All the Mreee," Nyarowlll said.

"Your Majesty," Weaver replied, putting his hand over his heart and bowing slightly. The protocol was probably all fucked up. He probably just said that the U.S. was part of His Majesty's domain or something. But it seemed like the thing to do at the time.

"It here is good you visit," the emperor meowed. "Not many words yours. Nyarowlll tell who here."

"Also present," she said, gesturing at the three older cats standing by the wall, "are Secretary Owrrrllll who is something like our Minister of the Interior, General Thrathptttt, commander of our military, and Academic Sreeee, who is the senior minister for intragate affairs, something like your Secretary of State." Owrrrllll was a tabby as was Sreeee. About half the guards they had seen were female as well.

"Honored, gentlemen," Weaver said, doing a slight bow again. "Ladies."

"Our interest is to open up trade between our two peoples," Nyarowlll said as there was a yowl from the tube by the desk. The emperor uncapped it and spit a phrase into it, slamming it shut. "We have things we can trade with you. Our weapons are far superior to yours and we have the teleportation devices which you do not. I'm not sure what you have to trade with us." She made another of those head tossing gestures as if in dismissal.

"Well," Weaver said, dryly, recognizing a bluff when he saw one, "the first thing that comes to mind is a telephone system."

# 6

Miller and Weaver stood outside the palace watching the street scene. It was cold and misty and Weaver was shivering in the thin desert BDUs that he'd been given at the hospital. Miller didn't seem to notice.

The street was crowded with traffic, most of it carts pulled by long, low, beasts that looked something like six-legged, furry hippopotami. Pedestrians wore coats something like trench coats against the mist and many wore hats somewhat like fedoras. And it smelled, strongly, of chemicals, ammonia and others, that seemed to be coming from the manure of the draft-beasts. Weaver noticed for the first time that none of locals, the Mreee, except the guards, seemed to wear shoes. And few of them gave the two humans more than a glance. They didn't seem guarded, however. Just uncurious.

"We need to figure out where the high tech is coming from," Miller announced.

"Agreed," Weaver replied, shaking his head. "This looks to be about 1800s tech. Which doesn't square with them being able to open a gate. I don't even see signs of electricity."

"Something else," Miller noted. "That tom didn't get scarred like that from intracountry wars. Their 'empire' might be like the British empire but they all act as if there aren't other countries. So where'd he get so scarred up? Internal rebellion?"

"Maybe you attain rank by battle." Weaver shrugged. "I gotta get out of this weather, Chief."

"Yep," Miller said. He'd reclaimed his weapons after the meeting with the emperor and now he settled his M-4 on his shoulder. "Let's see how honest we can get Nyarowlll to be."

They found a guide who led them to a small room in the bowels of the palace. The building, really series of buildings, was large. The center of it was a massive castle on a hill but buildings had been attached that spread down the hill on every side. The emperor, strangely, had his main office right on the edge, by one of the side streets.

Nyarowlll's office, or the one she was occupying anyway, was closer to the castle, up the hill and partially dug into it; the back wall was gray stone of the hill's bedrock. The room was warmed by a small coal brazier that was attached to a tubular chimney.

"Nyarowlll," Weaver said, taking a seat on the floor instead of one of the spindly benches. "It's pretty obvious that our society has a much higher tech level than yours. And that you don't make those jaunt devices or the guns. Where do they come from?" There was probably some diplomatic way he was supposed to say that but he wasn't a diplomat.

"This is true," Nyarowlll admitted. "We get them from the N!T!Ch! who get them in turn from the @5!Y!."

"How do you *say* that?" Weaver asked. "Never mind."

"We have to pay very much for the weapons and the teleportation devices. Our mines are being bled dry of gems and currency metals. But we *must* have them to fight the T!Ch!R!." She stopped as if she hadn't meant to say that much.

"Oh, crap," Miller muttered.

The military had set up a secure communications room at the UCF gate so they were no longer broadcasting their secrets to the world. At the moment, Weaver was of two minds about that.

"The Titcher are a sentient race that has the ability to open gates and invades through them, colonizing the world beyond," Weaver said, looking at the screen that showed about half the Cabinet. "The Mreee have been fighting them for about fifty years. They have three gates, including the one that connects to us. One that the Titcher opened, one that was opened by the Nitch and the one that *they* opened, using technology that the Nitch sold them, to us. Nyarowlll is something like a natural scientist; they haven't really separated out physics, biology and chemistry yet. She's the closest thing they have to an expert on gate technology and alien technology. She wasn't really willing to discuss the military situation but it seems the Titcher are well established on the Mreee's world and they are trying everything they can to stop them. The weapons they get from the Nitch are apparently really powerful, but the Titcher forces, once they're established, produce immense fighting biologicals and millions of those dogs and thorn-throwers. I think we've only seen what they can fit through a gate."

"And if they overrun the Mreee?" the national security advisor asked. "Then they'll be attacking two gates?"

"That's right, ma'am, but that's not all," Weaver said. "I was asking Nyarowlll about gate tech and she was puzzled by our experience. They've only been able to open a couple of gates and it takes the tech they get from the Nitch who are getting it from . . . I can't even begin to pronounce it, ma'am. From the Fivverockpit. But the point is, she didn't know why ours were just opening and they'd only had contact with the Nitch and the Titcher before."

"We've had two more open," the President said. "One in south Georgia that is spouting out lava and another in Boca Raton that is just a disaster."

"Excuse me?" Weaver said.

"Everyone within fifty miles of Boca Raton is dead or hopelessly insane," the director of Homeland Security said, painfully. "Everyone. Millions of people. We have no idea why or what is causing it."

"And before you ask, no, you are not going to Boca Raton," the national security advisor said. "There's a line you just can't cross. A recon plane that was sent in crashed; anyone crossing the line goes insane. And it's a *line* from the reports we're getting. There should be a file there called Enigma Site; see if you can find it."

Weaver moved around the Top Secret files scattered, against regulation, all over the desk at the communications center and found the one marked Enigma. He opened it up and looked at the satellite photos.

"All there is is a gray blotch," he said.

"Indeed," the national security advisor replied. "A gray blotch that is some sixty meters wide, appears to be about one hundred meters high and does not cast a shadow."

"Nobody is coming out except those at the very edge," the Homeland Security director continued. "And all we can do with them is put them in straightjackets and sedate them. Psychiatrists hold out hope that with heavy medication they can get some of them back to a semblance of normal. But it's only a hope."

"Are they saying *anything*?" Weaver asked.

"Just ravings about formless shapes and huge shambling mounds," the national security advisor said. "And most of them aren't even saying that. Just screaming."

"Jesus," Weaver muttered. "Well, trading with Mreee is going to be hard. We might be able to get some weapons from them, thirdhand from the Fivverockpit, but I'm not sure they'll be worthwhile. I'm not sure, frankly, *what* they can give us. They don't have many of those teleportation belts and not nearly enough of the weapons. But we've got all sorts of knowledge that would help them and that they really need. And I submit that ensuring that we don't have one more gate spitting Titcher is probably worth whatever we give them."

"Any idea why the gates are opening, yet?" the President asked. "Or where they will open?"

"No, sir," Dr. Weaver admitted. "But I've been running around from one fire to the next and haven't really been able to give it much study. That's next on my list."

"When did you sleep, last, Doctor?" the national security advisor asked.

"Sleep?" he said. "A couple of days ago. But I'm okay, I can go for a while without it. I'll probably get some tonight."

"Okay, we'll talk tomorrow," the President said. "Let's hope that another gate doesn't open between now and then."

The lab was now in a trailer and Garcia was installed in front of a computer, looking at random scrabbles of white on black that Weaver recognized as particle tracks.

"Talk to me, Garcia," the doctor said, collapsing onto a computer chair.

"The gate seems to be generating one boson every forty-seven minutes," Garcia said. "If they're what is causing the gates we should have over a hundred of them by now. But the readings from Eustis show that while there's some muon emissions, there's no boson formation."

"Nyarowlll said that gates can only form at 'thin' spots," Weaver said. "Although they can open *to* them from anywhere. I wonder what 'thin' spots means? Is that where the bosons are stopping?"

"They've been increasing in mass as well," Garcia said. "And they seem to be generating in random directions except that some seem to be following the same path as previous bosons."

Weaver spent a little time figuring out how to pull up the course tracks on his own system, then studied them for a while. There was a pattern there but he wasn't sure if it was his imagination. He pulled up a pattern recognition program and fed a couple in and after a while it spat out some equations that he recognized as fractal generation. Taking the course tracks as shown and entering the equations gave him a complex fractal pattern for each of the bosons. Each was different but it spread out widely and in an apparently, but not truly, illogical fashion. Last he brought up a terrain mapping program and overlaid some of the fractals on it.

"Got it," he said.

"What?" Garcia asked, yawning. "You know it's two o'clock in the morning, right? And you've been working on that for four hours?"

"I guess," Weaver said. "The thing is we can determine where the bosons are going, now, and when they'll arrive at various points on their travels. And I think I can determine, based on what limited data we have, where they'll stop."

"You're kidding, right?" Garcia asked, sliding his chair over.

"No," Weaver said. "Look at this track, A-4, generated about an hour after you got the instruments up; thanks by the way."

"No problem," Garcia replied.

"Zig, zag, zag, seventeen degree skew turn, zag, increase in size of moment by a fraction and repeat. Run that through the equation, superimpose and, voila, passes perfectly through Eustis, Florida, after going in a vaguely circular direction past Sanford and Daytona Beach. Doesn't quite match up with Jules Court but damned close, close enough for these instruments and this map."

"What about the rest of them?" Garcia asked.

"I'm mostly backtracking at this point," Weaver said. "I think the Boca Raton boson was B-14. And am I imagining things or are they increasing in mass?"

"They're increasing in mass," Garcia said. "Or charge, not sure which at the moment."

"Charge," Weaver said. "Now it's starting to make sense." He brought up the computer again and started plugging in numbers, pulling them up from the data from the instruments. "I need to do a field experiment. Go find somebody with a Humvee."

"Now?"

"Now," Weaver said, not even looking up. "We're going to Disney World."

The staff duty officer had been reluctant to part with a Humvee and driver but when Weaver pointed out that he was going to be a making a report to the President in the morning, not to mention looking for where the Titcher might break through next, things got remarkably easier. The yawning driver took them down the almost deserted Greenway until it connected to Interstate 4 then turned south to County Road 535. More turns led to a guard-shack manned by a young guard in a blue uniform and a nylon jacket sporting an embroidered mouse that was world famous.

"Can I help you?" the guard said, looking at the driver of the Humvee. The only one available at that time of night was a recon Humvee that still had a 40mm grenade launcher mounted.

"Yes," Weaver said, leaning over the driver. "Could you direct me to Bear Island Road?"

"Sir, this is a restricted area," the guard said. "I understand that you think you need to enter here but we're considered a top target of terrorism. Nobody gets in without a pass that has to be preapproved by the security office. I don't see a pass. No pass, no entry."

"Too bad," Weaver said with a smile. "My orders from the national security advisor and the gun on the top of this thing, not to mention the very pissed off and sleepy SEAL in the back means I can go anywhere. Now, could you direct me to Bear Island Road?"

Chief Miller had just laid his head down for the first time in two days when he'd felt somebody kicking his boot.

"Come on, Miller, the game's afoot," Weaver had said, tossing him his M-4.

"What now?" Miller said, standing up. He was almost instantly awake but that didn't mean he was rested. He looked at his watch and groaned. "Jesus, I just got off the horn to SOCOM an hour ago!"

"You're a SEAL? You're complaining about a little sleep? Besides, how long were you out in Shands?"

"What?" Miller asked. "UNCONSCIOUSNESS does not COUNT."

"Whatever, come on. . . ."

So he was in no mood to be held up by some rent-a-cop. And he'd been waiting most of his adult life for a moment like this.

"Son," he said, popping his head up through the gunner's hatch and training the MK-19 until it was pointed vaguely at the guard. "We're in no mood for Mickey Mouse. Get out of the road."

"Where are we and why are we here?" Miller asked as the Hummer pulled to a stop on a stretch of deserted road. There was something that looked like a small factory just down the road and he could see lights and what looked like the top of Cinderella's castle off to the left. To the right was a drainage ditch half filled with water and then dense forest.

"I think I know where another boson settled," Weaver said, climbing out of the back of the Hummer and opening the hatch. "I need to get some readings. Help me with this."

"This" was a box about a meter square and a half meter high. There were also two car batteries to be lugged.

"We need more people," Miller said, lifting one end of the box. It wasn't all that heavy but it was bulky as hell. "Where are we going with it?"

"That way," Weaver answered, looking at a hand-held GPS and pointing into the woods. As he did a car made a screeching turn at the end of the road and came barreling down, yellow lights flashing. It slammed to a stop and two more security guards got out, one of them fingering his side arm.

"If you put your hand on that again, I'll feed it to you," Miller growled, flipping the M-4 up to a hip-shot position.

"What's going on here?" the driver said, coming around the car. When he saw the SEAL pointing an M-4 in his general direction he stopped and raised his hands. "Sir?"

"I think there's a boson over in those woods," Weaver answered. "Thanks for showing up. We needed some more help."

With the two security guards carrying the box and Weaver and the national guardsman carrying the batteries and Chief Miller following along, his rifle in no way pointed at the two guards, they managed to get the material across the drainage ditch and into the woods.

"About seventy-five yards that way and we'll take our first reading," Weaver said, pointing slightly to the right.

The woods were pine with palmetto undergrowth and hard going. The only light was the tac-light Miller had attached to his M-4 and it was great for illuminating about a one-meter patch but otherwise useless. The guards continually stumbled over the low, spiky, palmettos, occasionally letting out a yelp as one of the fronds pierced their pants.

"Can I ask a question?" the driver said, gasping. The box was a bitch to carry though a swamp and over palmettos.

"Sure," Weaver answered. He looked at his GPS again and stopped. "This'll do. Try to find a flat spot."

The palmettos were close growing but there were occasional open spots and the guards gratefully lowered the box onto one of them, wincing and grabbing at their hands that had been cut by the thin handles.

"What in the hell is a boson?" the driver said, sniffing. "Do you smell something?"

"It's what's causing the gates," Weaver replied. There were levelers on the bottom of the box and he was busy trying to get it level. "This is a muon detector. They should be emitting muons and we should be able to detect them within about a hundred meters."

"Doc," the SEAL said.

"There are two coated plastic plates inside. When the muons hit the plates they cause Cherenkov radiation, which emits a flash of light. Light sensors record the flash and with the two plates we can get a reading on which direction they're coming from. That way we can figure out which way the boson is and move it around until we find it. The particle itself will probably be invisible to the naked eye. . . ."

"Doc," Miller repeated, hoarsely.

"But we'll know where the boson settled. And from that we can extrapolate where more gates might open . . ."

"Doc!"

"What?" Weaver said, looking up as he realized nobody was listening.

No more than twenty feet away a large, round mirror was reflecting the lights from Cinderella's castle.

"The planet on the far side has a reducing atmosphere and what looks like an F class sun."

The military responded even faster now that there was an SOP for such things. In no more than two hours secure communications and a string of tents and trailers were set up along Bear Island Road and the national security advisor, rubbing sleep from her eyes, was shaking her head at the physicist's latest report.

"No signs of life at all; it might as well be the primordial Earth. Very low oxygen levels, high levels of ammonia, chlorine, methane and carbon dioxide. Rocky ground, very dry. Slight overpressure so we're getting a fair amount of their atmosphere leaking through."

"No signs of the Titcher?" the NSA asked.

"No," Weaver said. "From what Nyarowlll told me the planet would be of little interest to the Titcher. But what I don't understand is why a gate opened at *all*. I've come up with a list of GPS sites and the list is going out to local police for investigation. But if *this* gate is open, it means most, or at least many, of them are going to be open. This explains the magma pile in Georgia, at least."

"Do you think it's the same planet?" the Homeland Security director asked. "I've seen stuff about the early Earth, lots of lava . . ."

"Those shows are . . . slightly overdramatized," Weaver said, carefully. "At the point of advancement of the planet on the far side crustal formation seems to be complete and we'd expect similar tectonic activity to Earth or significantly reduced. This is going to be a good opportunity to find out which."

"But it's not a threat?" the NSA said.

"Other than atmospheric leakage, not so far," the physicist answered.

"How many of these things can we expect?" the Homeland Security director asked.

"Well, the UCF anomaly is producing about thirty bosons per day," Weaver said.

"Oh, my God . . ." the NSA muttered.

"If every one opens we're in for a world of hurt," Weaver said with a shrug.

"Even if they don't . . ." the NSA said. "How are these things . . . spreading?"

"They seem to be following, by and large, certain fractal course tracks," Weaver answered. "They zig zag around in an apparently random manner and when they reach a certain point, based upon their energy level, they stop. The energy level is increasing, though, so each one is going farther."

"And they're spreading across the world," the NSA said. "If they're up to Georgia then they're down to Cuba."

"Yes."

"Opening up in open ocean."

"Presumably."

The NSA put her head in her hands and shook it. "Sailboats cruising along and suddenly landing in other planets."

"Well, they'd have to be quite small sailboats," Weaver pointed out. "Otherwise they'd sort of . . . crash."

"Freighters," the Homeland Security director said. "Cruise ships! We need to get a hazard warning out for mariners!"

"That . . . would be advisable," the physicist said.

"We need to get that . . . anomaly turned off," the NSA said. "Soon. How many of these gates can the Titcher access?"

"Unknown," Weaver admitted. "We only have one emergence so far. If we have a couple more it will give me some data. In the meantime I'm as in the dark as you are."

"How do we turn the anomaly off?" she asked.

"Errr . . ." Weaver shook his head. "You remember how I mentioned the great big steel ball?"

"That will turn it off?" the NSA asked. "A billion dollars will be pocket change compared to this stuff."

"I also remember how he mentioned ten years," the Homeland Security director said, sourly.

"And it won't turn it off," the physicist pointed out. "What I *might* be able to do is steer the bosons somewhere controllable. Maybe. Nyarowlll admitted that *their* gate openings, the controlled openings, are on small islands with heavy guard facilities. Maybe steer them all to atolls or, I don't know, Area 51 seems appropriate."

"I'll pass that on to the President," the NSA said, dryly. "In the meantime, try to figure out how to turn off the anomaly and shut at least some of these gates."

"I'll put some of my people on the job of monitoring them once they're found and we're going to need a whole bunch of people suitable for surveying the far sides," the Homeland Security director said, sighing. "I'll put FEMA in charge of finding those people. They know every environmental specialty company in the U.S. This is going to start costing real money pretty soon."

"Look on the bright side," Weaver said.

"There's a bright side?" the Homeland Security director said with a grim laugh.

"Sure, besides the advances that this is going to make in science, we're looking at multiple *worlds* that are available for colonization. Sure, so far there haven't been many that have been worth much and the U.S. isn't really interested in getting rid of surplus population. But if we can figure out how to steer some of these things to India and China . . ."

"That's a point," the NSA said. "One bright point."

"So far we've encountered two civilizations," Weaver said. "One of them hostile and one friendly. That, I think, is pretty good odds."

"Three," the NSA pointed out. "If you add the Boca Raton anomaly. And I don't know if it's hostile or just so impossible to understand it will always be an anomaly."

"But the point is that we're encountering friendly ones," Weaver said. "It's not all doom and gloom. It's just very odd. But the U.S. is a master of handling oddities. We take cellular phones and the internet for granted. In time I bet that we absorb gates just as we've absorbed every other change. And, for that matter, make money off of them," he added with a chuckle.

"Okay," the NSA said, smiling. "I'll point that out to the President, too. Just as soon as he wakes up. I'm sure we'll be talking again, Doctor."

"Yes, ma'am," the physicist said as the transmission terminated.

He got up and stretched his back, then undogged the door to the communications center and stepped into the other room of the trailer. Miller was sitting at a short-range radio with his feet up on the ledge in front of it, his eyes closed.

"I thought that SEALs never needed to sleep?" Weaver said.

"I was just resting my eyes," Miller answered instantly and opened them. "I was talking to the director of security for the parks. I'm much more impressed with this outfit than I was just dealing with their rent-a-cops. They've got better environment suits than FEMA, a bigger environmental response team than most major cities and a 'county' SWAT team that is dedicated for the park and looks pretty damned sharp. The security director, who's an ex-Green Beanie, and I took a little stroll on the other side. Not exactly a garden spot, but you know Disney. He'd already talked to the director of parks and they're planning on turning it into an 'interplanetary adventure' at very high rates. Suit people up in environment suits and take them for a stroll on 'the primordial Earth.'"

"I just told the NSA that somebody would find a way to make money off of these things," Weaver said, sitting down. "You know, she wants me to either shut down the anomaly or figure out a way to move the gates. It occurs to me that the people to put on that would be Disney's Imagineers. They're some of the best engineers in the world, certainly the highest paid."

"We'll talk to them later," Miller said, standing up and taking the physicist by the arm. "We're headed back to base. Then you're going to bed. And you're going to sleep even if I have to hit you over the head with a blackjack. And I'm going to sleep, too. And I'm not getting up until tomorrow. By then there will be more news, more gates, more data and more emergencies. But *until* then, we're getting some sleep. Understood?"

"Understood," Weaver said, grinning. "If anything comes up, I'll tell them you're on another emergency somewhere."

"Yeah," Miller said. "In fact, I think I'm just going to check into a hotel. Maybe the powers that be won't find me there."

What they ended up doing was talking to the security director who, whether he was appreciative of them responding so fast to a potential threat on Disney property or happy that the SEAL hadn't killed his guard, arranged for rooms in the Grand Floridian. It was broad daylight when they made it up to their rooms but neither of the two cared. Weaver undressed, took out his cell phone, turned it off, plugged it into the charger he was carrying and hit the bed with his whole body. He never even pulled the covers down, he just fell asleep.

» » »

Shane Gries was sitting on the back of his M-2 Bradley Fighting Vehicle eating a hamburger from Burger King when he heard the distinctive WHAM-WHAM-WHAM of a 25mm chain gun. He dropped the hamburger just as the driver that was manning his own vehicle's gun opened fire and the first Abrams fired with an enormous slam of sound. He had his vehicle helmet on in seconds and plugged in to the intervehicular communications system before he popped his head out of the commander's hatch. What met his eyes was nightmare.

Something like a giant green worm was extruding through the gate, filling it from side to side. As he watched a ball of lightning jumped out from a horn on the side of one segment and impacted on an Abrams, which exploded in a ball of fire. He saw 25mm rounds bouncing off the armor on the thing and just as he wondered about Abrams rounds a "silver bullet" went downrange with a sound like ripping cloth, impacted on the armor of the thing and then, incredibly, bounced off, the depleted uranium arrow breaking into pieces and sparking fire.

"Holy shit," he muttered, keying the Forward Air Control frequency.

"Alpha Seven this is Romeo Two-Eight!"

"Romeo Two-Eight, this is Alpha Seven. Before you ask I've already called for JDAMs. Impact in forty-five seconds. Danger very God damned close!"

Shane switched frequency to the company net and shouted: "JDAM! JDAM! JDAM!"

A B-52 or B-1 bomber had been on continuous loiter since an hour after his company arrived, their Joint Directed Attack Munitions programmed to the location of the gate. Because of the danger of the gate the weapons they were carrying were M-82 two-thousand-pound bombs. In the event of their use the only thing the infantry could do was hunker down and hope like hell that the bomb hit the target and didn't hit them. If it came anywhere near the line it would probably kill half the company.

Artillery rounds were already starting to land but they had no more effect on the creature than the Abrams rounds. And, as he watched in horror, more bolts of lightning were jumping skywards. He looked up and winced at the first titanic explosion overhead. Then there was a tremendous roar in the sky and the contrail that had indicated the presence of the B-52 on station was abruptly terminated in a gigantic cloud of fire and smoke.

There were three segments through the gate, now, all of them belching chain lightning. The artillery started to dwindle as some of the lightning intercepted it overhead, the explosions raining shrapnel down on the beleaguered infantry company. But he noticed that the front segment had taken damage. It seemed to be crippled, being pushed ahead by the trailing segments, and was no longer firing. It could be hurt.

"All units," he called. "Try to aim for repeated hits on the same spot. Try to bust through this thing's armor."

The gunner had slid into his seat, replacing the driver who started the vehicle.

"Switch to TOW," Shane said to the driver, switching back to the company frequency. "All Brads, go TOW!" The Tank-killing, Optically-tracked, Wire-guided missile was the Bradley's premier antiarmor system. It was capable of taking out a main battle tank at four thousand meters. On the other hand, it was pretty inaccurate at less than a thousand meters, which was the current engagement range. Shane cursed, again, the directive that ordered him to "remain close to the gate." He was well inside his maximum engagement range, with no room to maneuver against this hell-spawned thing.

He looked to either side and saw that he had lost two of his precious Abrams, both of them billowing fire into the sky. They were mostly intact, ammunition magazine ports blown out but their turrets still in place, but from the looks of them the crews were gone. Whatever that thing was firing seemed to pierce the armor of the Abrams as if it was insubstantial as paper.

"Keep up fire," he commanded. "Keep hitting it on the same spots if possible. Do not retreat. Say again, stay in place, do not let this thing . . ."

It was his last transmission as a ball of plasma blew his Bradley sky-high.

» » »

Weaver rolled over and groaned at the pounding on the door. He sat up and stumbled over, cursing.

"Yeah, yeah, I'm up," he said, unlocking and unbolting it. Command Master Chief Miller was the one doing the knocking and at the look on his face Weaver woke up fully. "What happened?"

"The company in Eustis just got clobbered, again," Miller said, walking into the room. "It's all over the news."

"Let me take a shower at least," Weaver grumped. He turned on his cell phone, first, and shrugged at the multiple message icon. It could wait until he had a shower.

A science fiction writer he knew always carried a black backpack that he called his "alien abduction pack." "Everything I need to survive for twenty-four hours in eighty percent of terrestrial environments." It was really a "I crashed in somebody else's hotel room at a con" or "the airline lost my bags" pack. Weaver had started carrying one as well and he was glad for it now. He could shave with his own razor and brush his teeth with his own toothbrush. He'd used up the bottle of water the day before but that was easily remedied.

As soon as he was done with his shower, hair brushed, wearing new underwear thanks to the "alien abduction pack" again, he was ready to face the day.

Or, afternoon as it turned out.

As they walked out of the front of the hotel, Weaver hoping that the nice security director would make sure the bill or whatever was paid, he started listening to his messages. The national security advisor wanted him to call. A secretary at Columbia pointed out that he had missed a scheduled meeting with a client that morning. His girlfriend in Huntsville wanted to know when his plane was getting in and reminded him that they were supposed to go to a party that evening. It was still on, despite the news, but Buddy was retheming it an "Alien Invasion" party and what was he going to wear? His cell phone company reminded him that he was overdue on his bill and if the balance of three hundred dollars wasn't paid in two days his cell phone would be temporarily disconnected.

That reminded him that he didn't know how any of this was

being billed. He supposed he was working for Columbia but, come to think of it, nobody had signed a contract. He was basically working on the word of the secretary of defense. On the other hand, that ought to be good enough. But he hadn't talked to his boss at Columbia for that matter.

He keyed in the number and got a secretary, the same one that had called him about the missed meeting. He put her off and got ahold of Dan Heistand, vice-president for Advanced Development at Columbia.

"Hey, Dan," Weaver said as the chief pulled onto Highway 192.

"Weaver, where the hell have you been?" Heistand asked. He was normally a pretty mild fellow, so Bill was taken aback.

"I've been working on the UCF anomaly," Bill replied. "Didn't anybody tell you?"

"No," Heistand said, calming down. "Who brought you in?"

"The SECDEF. I had a meeting with the War Cabinet on Saturday morning."

"You're joking."

"No, he sent a couple of MPs to my hotel room. Speaking of which, I never checked out of that one, either."

"Where are you, now?"

"Disney World."

"Disney? What the hell is happening at Disney? Who's paying for this? How many hours have you billed? What's the contract number?"

"I don't *have* a contract number," Bill sighed. "Look, when the secretary of defense, the national security advisor and the *President* tell you to go to Orlando and send you down in an F-15 doing Mach Three, you don't say 'Oh, excuse me, Mr. President, would you mind signing this contract from Columbia Defense Systems so the billing will be straight?' Okay? As to how many hours I've been billing, except for four hours' sleep this afternoon and about three and a half unconscious yesterday . . . all the rest. Okay?"

"Unconscious?"

"I got blown up by one of those rhinoceros tanks," Bill said. "That was after the standoff in the house. Hey, did you know that an H&K USP .45 caliber pistol will kill one of those dog-demons if you hit it just right?"

"Bill," Dan said, then paused. "Forget everything I said."

"Already forgotten," Weaver replied. "Hey, if you want to be a help, find whoever has to sign the contracts, and I can imagine what howling they're going to make when they see my hourly rates, and get the whole team down to the anomaly site. I've got a national guardsman who used to be a physics student doing all my monitoring and half the analysis. He's been helpful and I'd like to keep him but I could use some help."

"Will do."

"And see if you can find a guy named Gonzales or Gonzalves or something in England, Reading, I think. Pure math guy. Ray Chen used to go to him for Higgs-Boson math he couldn't get. And send me some clothes. And get somebody to pay my cell phone bill."

"Okay," Heistand said, chuckling. "In retrospect, the meeting this morning wasn't all that important, despite the fact that there was about two million dollars in billing riding on it and you were the star of the show."

"Hell, Dan, I've probably billed a quarter of that just this weekend," Bill said. "Okay, we're pulling into a McDonald's to get some breakfast. As soon as I can slow down enough to do anything like a report I'll get it to you."

"Bye, Bill," Heistand said. "And, oh, *try* not to get blown up again, okay? You're my star biller."

"Will do," Weaver said, chuckling. Then he thought of something apropos of the order and frowned.

"Oh, one more thing, Dan," he added. "Send the Wyverns."

"That's a classified program, Bill," the vice-president said. "I can't just open up that compartment on your say-so."

"I've got the access I need to get it opened," Weaver replied. "But do you really want me to go that route? Call the DOD rep, explain the situation, get the compartment kicked open. But in the meantime, put them in their shipping containers and get them down to Orlando. I'm tired of nearly getting my butt blown off. Send the Wyverns. And their full suite of accessories."

"I had to call my boss, too," Chief Miller said. "What do you want?"

"Number one, Diet Coke," the physicist replied.

The SEAL gave the order and pulled around in the Humvee, the Mk-19 just clearing the overhead. The employees manning the windows were visibly bemused to be serving a Humvee with a grenade launcher being driven by a heavily armed SEAL.

"The Team didn't know where I was; they thought I'd bought it at Eustis," the chief said. "Even sent a damned counseling team over to my house: chaplain, a captain, the works. My wife couldn't decide if she was happy as hell that I was still alive or pissed that I hadn't called earlier when I called and told her they were wrong. They didn't even know that Sanson was in the hospital. Most of the casualties at Eustis were 'missing presumed dead' including the Old Man."

"I'm sorry about that," Weaver said. "Glasser was a good man." He looked over at the chief who was driving the Humvee with one hand and eating a Quarter Pounder with the other. "I didn't even know you were married."

"Three happy years," the chief replied around a mouthful of burger. "And twelve that weren't so bad either. Hell, every time I go out the door she figures I'm not coming home. The kids hardly know who I am. But she doesn't bitch about it. Well, not much. Somewhat more when I return from the grave."

"And kids," Weaver said, shaking his head. "It just doesn't fit the image of the world-traveler SEAL. How many?"

"Three," Miller replied. "Being a SEAL's just like any other job after a while. At first it's all 'oooh! I'm a SEAL!' and getting into fights in Bangkok. Then there's the 'okay, I'm a SEAL, that's my job and it's sooo coool' phase after you've been on the Teams for a while. Then there's the 'honey, I'm off to work' phase, which is basically me."

Weaver laughed at that.

"And one from my marriage to She Who Must Not Be Named," Miller added. "He's in the Army. Studying *computers* of all things. The rest are high-school and one in elementary school. Sixteen, fifteen and nine. Boy, boy, girl."

"And she's the apple of daddy's eye?" Weaver grinned.

"She's daddy's nightmare," the SEAL groused. "Daughters are nature's revenge on fathers. She's already got a string of boyfriends. She's going to be impossible when she's a teenager. I'm seriously thinking about putting her in a barrel when she turns twelve and not letting her out until she's eighteen and no longer my problem."

"Be a pretty messy barrel," the physicist pointed out. "Maybe with a mesh bottom? And rinse it out once a week?"

"Whatever."

When they got to the developing encampment around the Orlando anomaly they had some problems getting into the main camp. The guards there had never heard of a Dr. William Weaver, didn't care that they were in a National Guard vehicle and seemed only mildly interested in the fact that Command Master Chief Miller was a SEAL and had been one of the first people through the gate.

After a few calls and calling the Officer of the Guard they were let through but only on condition that they report to the camp headquarters and obtain proper passes.

Weaver had Miller drop him at the physics trailer, which had acquired a sign while he was gone. It was now designated "The Anomaly Physics Research Center" and had another sign that said: "Authorized Persons Only. All Others Keep Out. This Means You!" He figured he'd better get the proper papers later.

The guard on the trailer, however, had another opinion.

"I'm sorry, sir, I can't let anyone in who doesn't have the right pass," the guard, an 82nd Airborne private, said.

"Look, son," Weaver said, patiently. "This is *my* lab! This is *my* project. And unless the secretary of defense or the national security advisor have taken me off the job, that is *my* equipment in there."

"That may be the case, sir," the guard said, doggedly. "But unless you have the right pass, you're not going in."

Weaver had just opened his mouth when his cell phone rang. He fished it out of his pocket and held a hand up to the guard.

"William Weaver."

"This is the Secretary," the secretary of defense said. "There's supposed to be a FEMA representative down there to coordinate the tracking of the gates. You talked to him, yet?"

"If he's in my lab the answer is: no," Bill said, shaking his head. "I'm having a little trouble getting into it."

"Why? Lost your keys?" the SECDEF chuckled.

"No, the nice young man from the Army who is standing outside the door won't let me in."

There was a long pause as the secretary digested this fact.

"Let me talk to him."

Weaver handed over the phone.

"Private First Class Shawn Parrish, sir," the private said, politely.

"No, I don't recognize your voice, sir."

"Yes, sir."

"No, sir," this somewhat strained but determined. "But I'd be happy to call the sergeant of the guard, sir."

There was a long period while the private's face gradually got whiter.

"Yes, sir."

"Yes, sir."

"Yes, sir." This with a very white face.

"Thank you, sir."

"Dr. Weaver, I need to call the sergeant of the guard," the private said in a very small voice, handing back the phone. He pulled a civilian multiband radio off his LBE and spoke into it.

Weaver spent the next three minutes considering the nature of boson particles, muon detection and particle degradation. He'd been doing that a good bit while not being attacked by aliens or visiting alien planets in the last couple of days, which mostly meant while driving or eating, but every little bit helped.

The sergeant who came running up with two privates trailing him was panting.

"What do you got, Parrish?" the sergeant said, looking askance at Weaver's mussed desert camouflage BDUs, missing such items as nametags or rank insignia and worn over tennis shoes and a civilian T-shirt.

The guard pulled the sergeant aside and carried on a low voiced conversation of which Weaver caught only the exclamation: "Who? Are you sure?"

"Dr. Weaver?" the sergeant said. "Could I see some ID?"

Weaver pulled out his driver's license and Pentagon pass, then waited as the sergeant examined them and the list that the guard handed him.

"Sir, we'll get this straightened out," the sergeant said, handing back the IDs. "For the interim, I'll provisionally add you to the pass list on my authority. Please see that you get the proper paperwork as soon as possible."

"Will do," Weaver said. "Can I go in, now?"

"Yes, sir."

"Thanks."

"Sir, can I ask a question?"

"Yes."

"Was that *really* the secretary of defense?" the sergeant asked, clearly hoping that it was not.

"Yes," Weaver replied. "Want me to call him back so you can make sure?"

"No, sir!"

"Sergeant, I've been running around like a chicken with my head cut off since Saturday when the SECDEF, the national security advisor and the President had me flown down here in an F-15. I've been blown up, had to learn to use a pistol and a shotgun to keep aliens from eating me, learned more than I want to know about gate teleportation and had about four hours' sleep, and three hours recovering from a concussion, since. Could you do me a small favor?"

"Yes, sir," the sergeant said, smiling.

"Get somebody to find me the appropriate paperwork or something? If you need to talk to General Fullbright, do it. As the SEAL I was with said when we busted down the gates to Disney to find this latest gate, I don't have time for Mickey Mouse. Okay?"

"Got it, sir."

"Thanks," Weaver said, walking in the trailer.

There were three people crowded in the main room. Two of

them he vaguely recognized; the third was a total stranger, a blonde female. Not at all bad looking, little light on top but easy on the eyes. She was running some sort of track calculation on a new computer that had been installed while he was away.

"Dr. Weaver," one of them said, standing up and coming over to shake his hand. "I'm Bill Earp from FEMA, you might remember me . . ."

"From that remarkable safety lecture you gave Sanson," Bill said, shaking his hand. "Good to see you again."

"Good to see you," the FEMA rep replied. "First word we had from Eustis was that you were a goner."

"The report of my demise was exceedingly exaggerated," Weaver replied. "I'm sorry to say that Howse and, apparently, Lieutenant Glasser bought it. Sanson, Chief Miller and I were in Shands hospital. Where's Garcia?"

"Getting some rest, sir," the other male, a young soldier replied. "I'm Crichton. I was at the site . . ."

"You did the initial survey, sure," Bill said.

"I've got some radiological background," Crichton said. "I'm just trying to help out, keeping an eye on the boson count, mainly."

"FEMA sent me over to coordinate with finding the bosons," the safety specialist said. "I'm a chemist, not a physicist but I know the tune and can dance to it."

"Robin Noue," the young woman said, waving. "I'm a programmer . . . I *was* a programmer at UCF, in the AI Lab."

"Good, okay," Bill said. "What's the count on bosons and have they surveyed any more sites?"

"The count is up to over a hundred," the FEMA rep said. "We've managed to pick out thirty probable sites. Twenty have been surveyed. Five open gates, one into vacuum which displeased the guys that found it immensely; one of them nearly got sucked in. We sent out muon detectors to two of the ones that weren't open, all the detectors we had and we've got a call in for more. They found inactive, I guess you'd call them, bosons at both. Close enough to the course track."

"I've been trying to refine the course programming," Robin said. "I'm getting it fined down somewhat. What bugs me is that it seems to be following a uniform sphere, congruent to the gravitational field."

"It bugs me, too," Weaver admitted. "And five open gates from twenty bugs me more. Because I think that means the others are 'available' and that means that the Titcher can open them."

"That would be bad," the FEMA rep said.

"Understatement of the century," Bill replied. "Maybe of the millennium. How many base tracks are there?"

"Sixteen so far," Crichton said. "Every now and again a boson takes off on its own merry way. But most of them have been sitting in those sixteen base tracks and most of them have been following a 'top four.'"

"Which track is the Titcher track and is it the same as the Mreee track?"

"The Titcher track is designated track three," Crichton said. "And, yes, the Mreee gate is on the same track. Disney and one other open, near Miami out in the Everglades, are on track one. Boca and the Georgia eruption appear to be six and they're the only two bosons that have come out of six."

"Any dead bosons on track three?" Weaver asked.

"Oh, a shit-pot full," Crichton said. "Sorry ma'am."

"It's okay," Robin said.

"Okay, I'd say that those are a probable threat," Bill said. "Just a hunch. But I'd say it's a good area to point the military and local police towards. Open gates I don't think the Titcher can attack. But closed ones they can and the ones that they're most likely to be able to touch would be the ones on track three; those are the only ones that have been intentionally opened from the other side. Maybe the bosons on that one are really easy to detect or something; that would explain the Mreee as well. Oh, and maybe Boca, I've got no idea what Boca is."

"I do," Crichton said. "But it doesn't help."

"What?" Weaver asked, noticing the pained looks on the faces of Earp and Noue.

"They don't like the answer," Crichton said, seriously. "It's Cthulhu."

"What?" Weaver said, then shook his head. "Come on!"

In the 1920s a series of horror short stories had been written by a writer named Howard Phillips Lovecraft. The stories involved alien beings which had controlled Earth in the depths of time and then died out or been driven out by other aliens, leaving the way open for the development of man. The aliens were also reported to be sealed away in remote places, such as the depths of the ocean, and from time to time tried to "awaken." The best known of the stories was "The Call of Cthulhu" about just such an awakening.

"No, listen to me," the sergeant snapped, shaking his head. "I'm not saying it's *actually* Cthulhu but do you know the reason why H.P. Lovecraft started writing those stories?"

"No," Weaver admitted. "But that doesn't mean I'm going to buy your logic. On the other hand, say your piece."

"Lovecraft was a minor student of astrophysical science," Crichton pointed out, earnestly. "He came to the conclusion that if man ever actually *did* meet aliens they were going to be so different that there would be no way that man could interact with them. And if they could cross the stars they would be so powerful and so advanced that they would consider us as no more than ants. Total indifference. The 'evil' aliens in the Lovecraft stories aren't evil; they're indifferent. But their indifference and power, not to mention weirdness, kills us. Just like we kill ants. I'm saying that whatever is in Boca Raton meets the Lovecraftian definition of an alien; a powerful alien being that is indifferent to the secondary effects it is causing. And those secondary effects are not a defense but a function of what it is."

"That's it?" Bill asked.

"Yeah," Crichton said, sighing. "Stupid, huh?"

"Only in presentation," Bill replied. "Look, you don't say that 'it's Cthulhu.' You say: 'I think it's a Cthulhoid form entity.' 'It *is* Cthulhu' is both wrong—if you went up and asked it its name I sure hope it wouldn't answer 'Cthulhu'—and a good way to get dismissed as a crackpot."

"Yeah," Earp noted. "I had. But that explanation almost makes sense. Why's it driving people crazy, though?"

"Well, the answer to that is sort of out there," Crichton said. "But think for a second about a species that finds quantum mechanics logical. I remember my physics professor joking about that and Lovecraft. There's a game about those stories called *Call of Cthulhu* and any time you run into one of the monsters you have to roll a sanity check."

"Never played it," Weaver said. "But I get what you mean."

"Anyway, he was always joking that we had to roll SAN check when we got into discussions of quantum mechanics. Now, think about a species that actually finds it logical."

"Okay," the physicist said, wincing.

"Did you make your SAN roll?" Crichton said, grinning.

"Barely," Bill laughed. "I think I lost a couple of points, though."

"All right. Now think about such a species that is totally logical, like a Vulcan, maybe even higher form sentient, totally sentient that is, it doesn't have *any* subconscious. Just pure thought and logic."

"Okay," Bill replied.

"Now think about it if it's a broadcasting telepathic."

"Oh, hell," Bill whispered. "Now I see what you mean. Not evil, just totally indifferent and bloody dangerous."

"Bingo," Crichton said. "A Cthulhoid entity. Its purpose is probably unknowable at our level."

"It might not even be a real entity," Robin suggested. "It might be something along the lines of a probe. All the 'broadcast' might be secondary effects from whatever it's using for analysis of its surroundings."

"Robin," Bill said. "Write it up as a theory, post it to the Columbia research net with a suggestion that they try to get some sort of monitors in to see if we can pick up any specific traces of what it's generating. I refuse to believe that anything is impossible to understand."

"Even quantum mechanics?" Crichton said, smiling.

"Even quantum mechanics," Bill answered. "What's the word from Eustis?"

"The Titcher are in full control of both sides of the gate," Earp replied. "More units from the Third ID have responded but they can't regain control of the gate. They've managed to hold them to a perimeter but they're taking horrible losses doing it."

"Drop a nuke on it," Weaver said.

"From orbit?" Crichton asked. "Only way to be sure?"

"Pretty much," Weaver replied. "I don't know if National Command Authority has caught up with what a problem the Titcher are. If we don't push them back and close up that gate we're toast. As a species, I mean, not just the United States."

"They can only fit so much through the gate," Earp protested. "We can hold them back; we just need to get enough troops in place."

"And what if they open other ones?" Bill asked. "Besides, what we're seeing is what they can *fit* through the gate. We haven't seen what they're throwing at the Mreee. I think what we've seen is the tip of the iceberg. Once they start growing forces on *this* side of the gate it'll be all over but the shouting." He sighed and rubbed his face. "I think I need to tell Washington how to run the war. Again." He picked up his cell phone and punched in the number to the national security advisor.

"White House, National Security Advisor's Office."

"This is Dr. Weaver. I need to talk to the NSA."

"She's in a meeting at the moment, can I take a message?"

"Ask her to call me back as soon as possible," Bill said. "And she'll have to get me authorized a secure link. There's something she needs to know." He turned to the three in the room and frowned. "Not one word of this conversation leaves this trailer, understood?"

"Understood," Crichton said, looking at the other two. The two civilians looked shocked but they nodded their heads.

"You're serious?" the NSA asked.

Bill hadn't had any problems getting into the secure communications trailer. A light colonel had turned up, apparently briefed on the earlier SNAFU and abjectly apologetic. Passes had been tendered, a Humvee carried him over and he'd been ushered into the inner sanctum ahead of a line of officers including a very pissed-off-looking major general.

"Yes, ma'am," Weaver said. "I would strongly suggest nuking the site and setting up something like a nuclear land mine at all the others."

The NSA licked her lips and nodded. "Everyone is here right

now. I think I can get them all free. Stay there and I'll try to get them all into the Situation Room."

Weaver waited patiently until the view changed from the NSA's empty chair to the Situation Room. It was the same people he'd dealt with on Saturday. The President, the secretary of defense, the NSA and the Homeland Security director. They all looked worn; the director was actually looking haggard.

"Authorizations all straightened out, Doctor?" the SECDEF asked.

"Yes, sir, thank you."

"Okay, Weaver," the President said. "Explain why you think I should nuke one of my own cities."

"Mr. President, what I learned from the Mreee makes me think that it's the best possible option and we can't wait too long," Bill said. "The Titcher have a standard method of invasion. They take a bridgehead, establish a terraforming colony and then start replicating themselves from biological material on the far side. The terraforming process involves some sort of biological that eats and destroys all local life, spreading out from the bridgehead. As they get more material, you can think of it as fertilizer, they start building more and more Titcher and larger and larger combat organisms. The Mreee hold them off with those ray guns, which from the sounds of their effect are pretty powerful. We don't have any, yet, that I know of. Our tanks can just barely damage their worm tanks and from what the Mreee said, the worm tanks are the *little* weapons. If we don't stop them, soon, we'll be looking at Escape from Florida. And, sir, we've detected over thirty points that probably can be accessed by the Titcher and more are forming all the time. It might be necessary to nuke them not once, but repeatedly and in multiple different spots."

The President closed his eyes and leaned forward in his chair, holding his head in his hands.

"I'll take input from you one at a time," he said, sitting up and straightening his shoulders. "Homeland Security?"

"I'd like to kick it to the secretary, Mr. President," the Homeland Security director said. "We can evacuate the area. Most people have left of their own accord. Ten hours, maybe, to ensure evacuation. A clean weapon will minimize fallout. We can survive it. If Dr. Weaver is right, and we've gotten the same reports from the Defense and State personnel that have been meeting with the Mreee, then . . . I don't see any choice. If they break out in a more populated area . . . that will be harder. Eustis . . . is a small town. Break out in Atlanta or Cleveland or Los Angeles and . . . I'm not sure that bears thinking on."

"Mr. Secretary?" the President said.

"We have clean weapons," the secretary said. "Reasonably clean. The fallout isn't going to be that bad, especially if we can use an airburst, which will be hard because of their defenses. I'd wish we had neutron bombs but . . . we don't. We've lost nearly a brigade, more including the initial National Guard force, trying, and failing, to hold the perimeter. We don't *have* the forces to hold them, at present time, to a ground perimeter. I have been considering Dr. Weaver's suggestion for the last few hours myself and I have to concur. Delivery, especially airburst delivery, will be . . . difficult."

"National Security?" the President said.

"Concur," was all she said.

The President steepled his fingers and nodded. "Dr. Weaver, thank you for your help. I, obviously, want you to continue with your work. I cannot stress enough the importance of determinating how to control this phenomenon. For your information my decision is affirmative. Means and methods will be left to the Department of Defense in consultation with the Department of Homeland Security. Keep this under your hat until an announcement is made."

"Yes, Mr. President," Bill replied. "I will."

The President looked up in annoyance at someone off the camera and Bill saw an officer carry a message form to the secretary of defense. The SECDEF looked at it, nodded and turned back to the camera.

"There's been another Titcher breakout, this one in the hills of Tennessee," the SECDEF said. "A team found it looking for one of the inactive bosons. It appears that they are already colonizing. Several hills are covered in what is described as 'green fungus.' Doctor Weaver appears to have hit the problem on the head."

The President grabbed his head again and sighed, angrily.

"Doctor Weaver," he said, looking the camera right in the eye. "You *must* figure out how to close these GATES."

"I will, sir," Bill said. "I will."

# 7

"I have an authorized launch code, do you concur?" the captain of the USS *Nebraska* said.

"I concur," the executive officer said, swallowing hard. They'd already reprogrammed the targeting of the missile.

"I concur," the navigation officer said, pulling the red key out to hang on a necklace around his neck. The weapons officer was responsible for making sure the weapon launched and followed its track but if the sub didn't know where it was then it would hit the wrong spot. There's no such thing as a "near miss" with a nuke. Be off by a fraction and it was going to hit Orlando or Gainesville for sure. They'd checked the course track twice and even gone up to periscope depth for a GPS reading. It still didn't make him happy to be firing a nuke at Central Florida.

"Concur," the engineering officer said. He already had his key dangling from his hand.

"Concur," the weapons officer said. The youngest of the five officers required for launch authorization was silently crying.

"Insert keys," the captain said. When all five were inserted he continued. "On my count of three, one, two, three," and they all turned. They actually had a few fractions of seconds to play with but it was best to be sure. Green lights turned red and a klaxon started going off.

"Tube twelve is opened," the weapons officer said. "Tube twelve is armed and reports ready to fire." His hand shook over the covered switch.

"I'll take it," the captain said. He stepped up behind the weapons officer and lifted up the switch. "Are we targeted?"

"All clear," the weapons officer said, stepping back from a board he never wanted to see again in his life.

"Firing," the captain said, flipping the switch downward.

There was a dull rumble and then a shaking sensation as pressurized gas pushed the missile out into the water and then the missile ignited. The sub was moving and it ignited *behind* them but it still sounded like a depth charge going off close alongside.

"Send message to COMSUBLANT," the captain said to the communications officer. "1432 hours Zulu, this date, launched one missile from tube twelve. Target Eustis, Florida."

It had been necessary to do more than simply clear the area. The Russians were barely a nuclear power anymore but they still maintained a nuclear watch and informing them was a good way to avoid an accidental WWIII. Then there had been the press, and the United Nations. There had been acrimonious recriminations even before the launch on Tennessee, which, because it was an uninhabited area, had occurred first. Protests had broken out in Washington, New York and San Francisco, not to mention throughout Europe where major riots were reported. Then there was the Nuclear Test Ban Treaty, which prohibited nuclear testing, especially aboveground. A Presidential Finding had been written covering the fact that this was not a Test but an act of war. The Test Ban Treaty didn't cover those. Despite that fact, France, China and Pakistan had all immediately stated that they considered the treaty nullified and intended to restart nuclear testing immediately.

The Titcher had engaged the MIRV warheads on the way down. There had been some fear that the nukes might prematurely detonate—the Titcher weapons seemed to form some sort of fusion reaction when they impacted—but that was not the case. Four of the MIRV warheads from the first firing and three in Eustis made it through the Titcher fire and detonated.

"We've been asked to warn people, again, not to look in the direction of Eustis," the anchorman said. He looked haggard and worn from being on camera for most of the last three days. He was doing voice-over for low-light camera which currently showed an open field with a line of pines at the far end, the moon rising in the background. "Our cameras have been specially shielded but anyone looking at the impact from within about fifty miles is going to be flash-blinded. If you experience flash blindness, call your local 911 operator and remain calm. The blindness *will* pass. Everyone within seventy miles of the event is reminded to please open windows in your home and take pictures off the wall. Secure fragile objects. The military says that the impact will be at any time. All we can do, is wait."

There was a short, unusual, period of silence on the television and then the screen flashed white. The camera that had been being used for feed was *not* shielded but New York switched immediately to another which *was* and the video showed a series of domes of fire. The light must have been blinding; it was bright even through the heavy filters on the camera.

Dr. Weaver got up from the chair and went to the door, opening it and leaning out to look north. Sure enough, there mushroom clouds were twining amongst each other. Robin had squeezed into the door behind him and it was a sensation he thought he'd remember for the rest of his life, watching mushroom clouds reaching for the troposphere, roiling and pregnant with evil, while two small but firm breasts pressed into his shoulder blades. He noticed that he was enormously horny. And he remembered that he'd forgotten to call Sheila back and tell her that he wasn't in Washington and wouldn't be in Huntsville any time soon.

Just then the ground shock hit and he had to clutch the door frame to keep from being knocked out of the trailer. Robin grabbed him for the same reason and it just made things worse.

"We need to get inside before the blast front gets here," he said, leaning back into the room.

"Yes," she said in a small voice.

"We're right at the edge of where the military will let civilians stay," a reporter was saying in an excited voice. "We just got hit by the blast front . . ." For a moment he was drowned out as a wave of noise enveloped the trailer. It shook on its foundations and one of the computers gave a pop and the monitor showed "No signal" but other than that there was no damage. "And that was extremely frightening but we're in a bunker and we rode it out fine."

"Is there any danger of radiation in your area?" the anchor asked.

"Well, we've got radiation detectors and they haven't gone off," the reporter said. "The military says that the bombs are going to be as clean as they can make them, since they're bursting in the air. And the winds are from the west, so the explosion is downwind of our current location. Units of the Third Infantry Division are standing by and I can hear them revving up the motors in their big tanks and fighting vehicles. They're going to go right into the blast zone as soon as they get the okay and try to snatch back the gate from the Titcher. I understand it's going to be much harder in Tennessee where the terrain doesn't let them get their fighting vehicles up to the gate."

"Thanks for that report, Tom," the anchor said. "And you take care, you hear? We've got another report from Oak Ridge, Tennessee, which is close to the gate up there. Melissa Mays is standing by with a live report."

"I'm here in Oak Ridge where the best way I can describe it is a festival is going on," the reporter said in a bemused voice. "About a thousand people, lab workers, shopkeepers and others including schoolchildren were out to watch the nuclear attack on the Titcher stronghold. All of them were wearing the same dark glasses we had been issued by the military and when the bombs went off they broke out in spontaneous cheers. Since then it's just been an air of carnival. People have opened up beer kegs and started a barbeque in the town square. I'm talking with the mayor of Oak Ridge, Phillip Lampert. Thank you for speaking to us, Mr. Mayor."

"My pleasure, Melissa," the portly man said. He had a sandwich in one hand, a beer in the other and heavy, dark-tinted, goggles dangling around his neck.

"Can you explain these remarkable events?"

"Well, as I understand it, some sort of particle was generated at the University of Central Florida . . ."

"No," the reporter corrected. "I mean this . . . this . . . party. Most people would be crying at the sight of a nuclear weapon going off right next door."

"Well, little lady," the man said in a voice like he was speaking to a small child. "Since 1943, when the U.S. government decided that the best place to hide their new super bomb research was a sleepy little town in the Tennessee mountains, Oak Ridge has been the main site for nuclear research in the entire United States. Some towns have steel plants, some towns have the local car and truck plant, Oak Ridge has nuclear weapons. We don't make them here anymore, but we live with their existence every day of our lives and most of the people around here have never seen a shoot . . ."

"A what?"

"A nuclear explosion," the mayor continued. "Above ground nuclear testing was ended before you were born but they used to take our parents out to Los Alamos to see the shoots, sort of like taking the employees to another factory to see how their parts are used. Besides, from what I've seen of the Titcher, it was the smartest thing the President could do and it took a lot of b . . . courage. I'd rather watch fireworks than have them invade the town."

"But aren't you worried about fallout?" the reporter pressed. Surely some of these idiot rednecks were going to have to realize that setting off a nuclear weapon was much worse than any conceivable alternative.

"Little lady . . . I'm sorry, what was your name again?"

"Melissa Mays," the reporter said, tightly.

"Miss Mays, did you have a job when you were in high school?"

"Yes," she said. "But the question was about fallout."

"What was the job?" the mayor pressed.

The reporter took a moment and then said: "I worked in a McDonald's."

"And I'm sure you were a bright spot in that cheerless place," the mayor replied, giving her his very best "I know you think I'm a male chauvinist and I just don't care" smile. "Miss Mays, between my junior and senior year, and again between high school and going to UT, I worked in a lead-shielded room pouring batches of green, glowing goop from one beaker into another beaker. I met the woman who is still my wife in that lab. We have two beautiful children who are straight-A students and neither of them have two heads. Now, Miss Mays, do you *really* think I'm going to be troubled about a little cesium from an airburst?"

"No," the reporter admitted in a defeated tone. "Thank you, Mayor Lampert," she added then turned to the camera. "Well, that's the news from Oak Ridge, Tennessee, where the party looks to continue into the wee hours of the morning."

"Thank you, Melissa, for that . . . illuminating report," the anchor said, bemusedly.

"Gotta love high-tech rednecks," Weaver said, turning down the sound.

"I can't believe they're having a *party* for God's sake," Robin said.

"I can," Earp replied. "You've clearly never been to Oak Ridge. I think the mayor is wrong, the radiation has had an effect: they're all insane. No, they're crazy but not insane. They just know what they're talking about and it makes them seem a little crazy. The mayor was right. Nuking Eustis was a tragedy; people lost homes and possessions that they loved and cherished and they'll never get them back. There might have even been a few that were missed by the evacuation sweeps and were killed. The only thing that was lost in the hills of Tennessee were some deer and bear and undoubtedly some rare and endangered species of plants and salamanders. But they were going to be lost *anyway* if the Titcher weren't stopped. The Titcher consider it their job to make *everything* endangered, rare or extinct except Titcher. They're a pain in the ass. Wish we could be one to them."

Weaver was smiling at the rant but he stopped at the end. "Say that again."

"Well, the Titcher see it as their job . . ."

"No, the last bit," Bill said, closing his eyes.

"I wish we could be a pain in their ass," Earp replied.

"Got it," Weaver said, opening his eyes. "Thanks. I need to go find Chief Miller."


"I've talked with three or four other physicists today," Weaver said to the secretary of defense and the national security advisor. The President and the Homeland Security director were both out showing the flag and trying to explain why it had been necessary to nuke two spots in the continental United States. "And we're all pretty much in agreement that what the bosons are doing is establishing stable wormholes."

"And those are?" the secretary of defense asked.

"Basically what we're seeing," Weaver replied. "Instantaneous 'gateways' to another place. Meisner, Thorn, and Wheeler are the main guys to go to; hell that is why THE general relativity book is known as MTW rather than *Gravitation* as it is titled. I sent an email out to Kip Thorn and one of his colleagues Michael Morris but got "Out of Office" replies. I then tried Stephen Hawking but he didn't respond except to say that they were "interesting" which means he'll think about them for eight years or so and then point out several things I missed but conclude I was right despite not taking enough care in my assumptions. The one thing we're not getting is neutrino emissions, that I know of, but neutrino detection is very difficult. I've got a call out for a mobile neutrino detector but the only one is in Japan. The point is that one theory of wormholes is that if you dump enough energy into them, they destabilize."

"How much energy?" the NSA asked. "Electrical or what?"

"Well, bigajoules, actually," Weaver replied. "Like, a nuke."

"You want another one?" the SECDEF asked, angrily. "*At* the wormhole? A ground burst? Do you know what sort of fallout that will cause?"

"Yes, sir," Bill replied. "But I'm not planning on detonating it on *this* side."

"Oh."

"And I think we should send an assessment team in after the explosion, maybe before as well."

"You can't get an armored vehicle through the gate," the SECDEF pointed out. "And people outside of vehicles *will* be at risk from residual radiation."

"Not if they're in a Wyvern they won't."


"Oh. My. God." Chief Miller said in a voice of awe.

The suit was crouched on its knees, multijointed metal fingers splayed out on the recently laid gravel. Its "chest" was open and a seat and arm-holds were clearly displayed along with a complicated control panel. It was vaguely humanoid, like an artist's rendition of a robot, with an idealized human face on the "helmet."

"The original design came from a gaming company of all things," Bill said, walking around the suit. It gleamed silver in the overhead lights, a titanium shell laid on a Kevlar underlayer. "The first ones were unpowered and the best aerobic workout you'll ever have. But they were designed for a later powered version. We just tuned the design up, put in piezoelectric motivators, sealing, environmental systems and improved the electronic suite. Oh, and a little radioactive shielding."

"Why?" the SEAL asked.

"See the big box over the butt?" Bill asked. "Americium power generator."

"So I'm going to get irradiated when I use it?" the SEAL asked.

"I've got over a hundred hours in one." The physicist sighed. "You wear a radiation counter back by the reactor. So far I've picked up about as much radiation as you would at a day on the beach in Florida. Don't even get me started on flying; I took a radiation counter on a flight one time and it raised my hair."

"Really?" the SEAL asked. "I've flown in a lot of planes."

"Really," Bill replied. "Besides, it's the only power source we have that can run one of these things for more than a couple of hours. It's got some bugs, it tends to want to disco occasionally, but you get past it. This is just a prototype, you understand."

"How hard is it to learn to use?" the SEAL asked.

"Pretty easy," the physicist said. "The electronics suite takes some getting used to. Oh, it walks like Frankenstein and it feels as if you're on ice all the time, but you don't fall down."

"I don't like the idea of standing up all the time," the chief noted. "That just makes you a big damned target."

"Notice the wheels on the elbows, knees and, if you look, under the belly on there," Bill said. "It's actually easier to low crawl over a flat surface than to walk. You can't see unless you activate the camera on top of the helmet."

"I want," Miller said. "Oh, man, do I want. Screw the bugs."

"Good," the physicist replied. "This one's yours. As soon as we get you fitted."

"Why?" the SEAL said, suddenly suspicious.

"We're going to take a little stroll," Bill replied.

"Where?"

"Eustis."

"Oh, shit."


They rode on the front glacis of an M-1 Abrams, their armor-clad feet dangling over the front, one hand hooked over the barrel of the main-gun, the other clutching their weapon.

The "accessories" for the Wyvern had included a shipping container filled with appropriate weapons. These ranged from .50 caliber machine guns, the venerable M-2 or Ma Deuce that dated to WWII, through the more recently designed "Dover Devil" to a new Czech 12.7mm, then onwards and upwards culminating in a massive cannon that dominated one of the walls of the shipping container.

"What's that?" Chief Miller had asked. He was clearly a man who had never seen a bigger gun he didn't like.

"It's a South African one-hundred-thirty-millimeter recoilless rifle," the armorer said, proudly. He was a heavyset gentleman in his fifties, gray haired where there was any left, with a pocket protector containing five colors of pens and an HP calculator dangling from his belt. But he was clearly inordinately fond of his weapons. "It was one of the guns they were looking at for the Stryker Armored Gun System but they turned it down. It had been sitting around in a depot for a couple of years when we picked it up."

"Can you use it with a Wyvern?" the chief said, stroking the two-and-a-half-meter barrel. It had a big shoulder mount about a third of the way back from the end and an oversized grip and trigger.

"Oh, yes," the armorer said. "Reloading, of course, is slow."

"I'll take it," the chief said. "And one of those Gatling guns. And you got any pistols? How about swords?"

"Chief," Bill said, chuckling. "Even with the Wyverns there's only so much you can carry. Why don't you take the 30mm?"

"What 30mm?" the SEAL asked. "Besides, if I've got a choice of thirty or a *hundred* and thirty, I'll take a hundred and thirty any day. I'll just reload fast."

"This 30mm," the physicist replied, pointing to a weapon hanging on the left wall.

It looked . . . odd. It had clearly been modified for use by the mecha-suits but beyond that the barrel looked oddly . . . truncated. "What the hell is it?" Miller asked.

"Well, you know those guns the A-10s use . . ." Bill said, smiling.

"No shit!" the SEAL replied, clearly delighted. "Besides, there's no way you could fire one of those things off-hand in a Wyvern. The recoil would kill you."

"Oh, we had to modify the ammo a little bit," Bill admitted. "Just like the 25mm Bushmaster I'm going to haul. But it's still got depleted uranium penetrators and I think you'd be surprised at what you can do in a Wyvern. Just remember to lean into the shot."

So lying beside the chief was the 30mm chain gun and lying beside Bill was a modified 25mm Bushmaster, the same gun carried by the Bradley Fighting Vehicles. On their backs were integral ammunition packs but they'd been warned that the ammunition would not last long at full rate of fire. They had external radiation counters, which were running right up into the bottom of redline, internal radiation counters that were down in the bottom of yellow and riding behind them in pride of place a large sack.

The ordnance technician who had assembled the special satchel charge had explained it as carefully as he could.

"The material in the device is an expansion-form explosive," the tech said. "Instead of just exploding in one place the material continues to explode on the wavefront and expands through any open space. They tested it on an old mine back before the Afghanistan war and it blew out a steel door at the back side of three hundred meters of tunnel. The thing is, it will do a number on anything but, probably, those centipede tanks. But it's going to probably explode *out* of the gate as well. It's not as effective in an open area as enclosed, but it's going to be a hell of a blast in the local area. So you'd better run like hell."

"How long do we have?" the SEAL asked.

"How long do you want?"

"Seven seconds."

There was a short battalion of Abrams and Bradleys parked a thousand meters from the gate, all of their hatches shut and their environmental overpressure systems going full-bore. The ground radiation count was high and the vehicles were going to have to be decontaminated after they were withdrawn. More likely they'd be scrapped; after a few hours at ground zero they were metaphorically going to be glowing like a Christmas tree.

Airbursts of nuclear weapons were relatively clean and caused limited radioactive fallout. But the pulse from the fusion explosion irradiated everything in a large circle. The alpha and beta particles, as well as gamma rays, struck common materials, carbon, silica, iron, and transmuted them to radioactive isotopes. Sometimes they were split and formed highly radioactive isotopes of lower-weight elements.

So the ground zero of even the cleanest nuclear weapon was highly radioactive. The radiation would fade over time, most of the particles would degrade in no more than a year and while some lingering radiation would exist for thousands of years to come it would be not much beyond background. Hiroshima, which was hit by a relatively "dirty" bomb, had been resettled since the 1950s. The only sign that it had ever been destroyed by a nuclear weapon was the memorial at its city center.

In the meantime, though, Eustis was hot as hell.

As the Abrams drew to a stop in front of the gate it was the bad time. The firesupport from the vehicles in their defensive positions behind was blocked. If the Titcher came through the gate the Abrams would be blocking the defending units. So far, no Titcher had come through the gate since the explosion. But bad things tend to happen at the worst possible time.

So Weaver and the SEAL hurried. They had planned this carefully and practiced it once, all the time they felt they could afford. They set their weapons down, leaning on the front of the Abrams, and grabbed the big bomb off the glacis. It had been secured with duct tape but the tape tore loose easily at the yank from two Wyverns.

They set the bomb down a half meter from the gate, retrieved their weapons, set them down to either side of the bomb and then Weaver waved at the Abrams, whose driver put it immediately into reverse and stomped the gas.

Chief Miller, in the meantime, seemed to be doing a routine from *Saturday Night Fever*, his feet moving back and forth and to either side while his hands flailed wildly in the air.

"Excited, Chief?" Weaver said over the radio.

"Damned disco dance, you were right," Miller said, panting.

"Steady down, just quit trying so hard and it will damp out," Weaver replied. After a moment it did and the chief stooped and grabbed one of the handles on the bomb with both hands, hooking the release tab over his thumb. "Ready?"

"Ready," Weaver said, stooping and picking up the bomb.

"One," Miller said, starting the swing.

"Two," Weaver, replied.

"Three!" they both said, letting go just short of the apex of the arc.

Weaver turned and picked up his Bushmaster and then started into a clumsy run. The mecha-suits did tend to walk like Frankenstein, a problem of lack of mobility in the "ankle" of the suit and complete lack of feedback, but they could get up a fair turn of speed and he was going just about twenty kilometers per hour when a giant picked him up and tossed him in the direction he had been going anyway.

He hit hard and a yellow light popped up, indicating that his left arm power system was down. That was really going to suck.

He rolled onto his belly after a couple of kicks, centered his right arm under him and used it to lever himself to his feet. It would have been nearly impossible for a normal human but the Wyvern's design made it surprisingly easy. Which was good because he could tell from the feel that the left arm was under muscle power only. His internal rad counters were higher, also, and he figured he'd popped environmental somewhere. That was *really* going to suck.

The chief was up as well and running back to the gate so Weaver made the command decision that he'd ignore those minor little issues. He picked up his Bushmaster and clumsily trotted over to the gate, carrying the Bushmaster in his right hand.

"You okay?" the chief said.

"Couldn't be better," Weaver replied, hooking up his ammo feed slide. "You?"

"Peachy," the SEAL answered, manually cocking the 30mm. "Okay, let's rock."

With that the two of them bent over—the mecha-suits were fourteen feet tall and could barely fit together though the gate—and stepped, lurched really, through the looking glass.

"I think he's losing it," Crichton said, turning up the news broadcast.

"Who?" Earp replied, looking up from the latest bulletin from FEMA.

"The CBS anchor," the sergeant replied.

The anchor was beginning to show signs of the strain of trying to keep up with the news.

"Another Titcher gate has opened in Staunton, Virginia," he said, pronouncing it, correctly, as *Stanton*. "National Guard units have responded but the initial attempt by state police to stem the attack has failed with heavy casualties among the state police. In other news the State Department has announced that the Mreee have officially requested the loan of mobile nuclear weapons and that the Russians have agreed to sell the U.S. several SS-19 mobile missile launchers. . . ." The reporter, who had won his spurs in Vietnam reporting all the news that was detrimental to the United States and who had been a quiet, but major, advocate of the antinuclear/antimilitary brigade for decades, was reporting the latest news with a rictus smile. "The Mreee have relayed a request from the Nitch, a race of intelligent spiderlike creatures . . ." He stopped and giggled. "I can't say this. Yes, I know, I'm reading it on my TelePrompTer but this can't be happening! This JUST CAN'T BE HAPPENING!"

The screen changed to a female anchorwoman who was rubbing furiously at her nose with her index finger. She looked up in startlement and then recovered quickly.

"We seem to be having some technical difficulties in New York," she said with studied aplomb. "In other news . . ."

"Score one for reality overload," Crichton said as he turned the sound back down. "Failed his SAN roll."

"Just proud to be here," Earp replied.

"I gotta ask," the sergeant muttered. "Look, Earp's not a really common name . . ."

"My great-great-grandfather was a cousin," Earp replied. "A wanted felon up around Dodge City. They had a gentlemen's agreement; Wyatt didn't come up where Ryan was and Ryan didn't go near Tombstone."

"Thought it might be something like that . . ."

And in other news, Weaver tripped, almost immediately, on a dead dog on the other side of the gate.

The Titcher side of the gate was littered with dead and dying aliens, many of them torn limb from limb by the big explosion. As he lurched forward Weaver caught a glimpse of one of the rhino-tanks over on its side, one leg blown off and green lightning rippling over its surface.

There had been thousands of aliens in the gate room and most of them had suffered some effect from the expansion bomb. But many of them had simply been stunned or thrown off their feet and they were getting up and charging the humans who had been imprudent enough to invade their space.

Weaver felt glad he'd fallen as a line of needles passed through the space he would have occupied standing up. The armor of the suit *probably* would have stopped them but better to be out of the way. He toggled his top-side camera, brought the Bushmaster up to his shoulder one-handed, propped it up as best he could with his left hand and opened fire.

"I can't see!" Miller shouted. He was prone as well, with his chain gun up, but it was firing sporadically, many of the rounds flying over the heads of the aliens.

"Toggle your top camera!" Weaver yelled. "Setting Three! Setting Three!" He aimed at a rhino-tank that was just heaving itself to its feet and was pleased to see the 25mm rounds splash goo out of its side. The tank shuddered, did a couple of side steps and then lay down again, its legs twitching. Fortunately it didn't explode.

Other than that he wasn't getting very many impressions. The lighting in the room was badly damaged, probably from the explosion, but it was strong enough that it was interfering with the automated low-light circuitry of the cameras. They kept switching from normal to low-light setting. There was also a smell, harshly chemical with a slight undertone like rotten fish. He knew he'd smelled it somewhere before but he couldn't quite place it. On the other hand, he knew for sure that his quarantine integrity had been breached to hell and gone.

There were lots of thorn-throwers, lots of dogs and he was hammering out rounds, single shot, carefully aimed using the laser sight on the Bushmaster. Standard Bushmasters had neither laser sights nor a selectable switch but the armorer, who had a Ph.D. in engineering, was a foresighted man and had made some adjustments. Weaver noticed that the SEAL had started to get his fire under control and assumed he had switched cameras.

"What, exactly, are we doing here?" Miller asked as he took out another of the rhino-tanks. There were so many of the Titcher in the room the tanks couldn't seem to decide whether to fire or not. Or, maybe, they didn't want to damage the room. Good.

"Getting a look at what is on the other side before we nuke it," Weaver replied.

"Good, we've done that," the SEAL said. "Time to do the Mogadishu Mile."

"What?"

"Run away, run away!"

"Oh, okay," Weaver replied. He hooked his hand under him and pushed up to his knees then up to standing. Then he froze.

"What the fuck . . . ?" he heard Miller mutter.

The thing was probably just the right size to fit through the gate. It was, essentially, a mobile green cone that looked like nothing so much as a mound of manure. Tentacles that might have been purple extended from its base and it was glowing, faintly. It also was waddling towards them serenely through the chaos of the gate room.

"I don't know what the fuck that is," Weaver said, taking a step back and lifting his Bushmaster as well as he could with the functional right arm. "But I think we should shoot it."

"Damned straight," the SEAL said, flicking his selector switch from semi to full auto and letting out a stream of depleted uranium penetrator rounds.

What the SEAL had failed to consider was that he had previously been firing from the prone, where the mass of the suit was in contact with the ground. Also, he had been firing single shots, each of which shoved the heavy suit back a few inches. If things hadn't been so chaotic he might have considered the recoil of those shots. But he did not. So when he pulled the trigger, intending to send out a controlled burst of three rounds, the recoil staggered him backwards through the gate as his hand automatically clenched, a monkey reaction from falling, on the trigger.

The first round, however, hit the thing squarely on the front of the cone. The second was near the top, just to the left of a small, brightly glowing patch. Where the third was didn't really matter because by that time the thing had exploded.

Weaver had also been knocked back by the recoil of his weapon but he was actually in the process of gate transference when the explosion, categorized from later inference as right at sixty megatons, occurred.

Collective 15379 was nonresponsive. How interesting.

"*Collective 12465, report on physical conditions near Collective 15379,*" Collective 47 emitted.

"*Mushroom cloud and radiation emissions categorized as sixty megaton quarkium release,*" Collective 12465 reported. "*Outer collective processes 12465, 3456, 19783 damaged. All functions 15379 terminated.*"

15379 had reported attacks by fission/fusion weapons and had registered intent to respond with a quarkium unit. Collective 47 had automatically given assent. Once a bridgehead had been secured with sufficient standoff to prevent destabilization of the wormhole the quarkium unit would be detonated and then colonization could recommence with the local area seared of hostile forces.

Something had somehow predetonated the quarkium unit.

Collective 47 could not be said to feel anger or sadness at the demise of the subcollective called 15379. Collectives were, essentially, immortal and 15379 might have, in time, created as many subcollectives as Collective 47, thereby increasing the Race and ensuring its security. Not to mention that the subcollective was a major supplier of vanadium and a few other trace metals as well as a huge source of biological material via two slave races.

But the loss of Collective 15379 could be borne. It would decrease the status of Collective 47 to a degree and reduce its balance of essential trade. But those, too, could be borne. What was questionable was whether the Race could afford another species to damage it so severely. The Race had encountered many species in its expansion from gate to gate and some of them, the Alborge for example, were significant threats to the survival of the Race itself. If the Alborge ever exerted themselves they could erase the Collective in a span of time that had no meaning. But would be very, very short. The sophonts of world 47-15379-ZB might, in time, become such a race. *That* could not be borne.

"*All subcollectives,*" Collective 47 emitted. "*Reestablish contact with gates to world 47-15379-ZB. Initiate twenty-five percent increase in all combat unit systems, ground, air, space and liquid, emphasis on systems level four through seven. Order all slave races to initiate assault plans; deception plan is terminated.*"

Collective 47 was going to war.

Susan McBain was puzzled.

The portal in Mississippi that had so startled the survey team by its vacuum opened onto a planet. It wasn't quite a vacuum, simply very thin atmosphere. About what you'd expect on Mars. The planet looked a bit like Mars, as well, except for the lambent purple sun that was setting in the east. It was dry and desolate, the ground scarred for miles and miles, somewhat like the outskirts of Newark.

None of that had Susan puzzled.

What was bothering her was the biology of the planet, such as it was.

She had received samples from the initial survey team and decided that they just couldn't be right. The survey team was an environmental company that normally responded to hazardous waste spills. It had gone to the far side, collected samples of soil and air, and returned. Then a large metal plate had been put over the gate to prevent more loss of atmosphere.

Despite the fact that the survey team was supposed to avoid contaminating the samples, they had to have done so. Otherwise the biology of the far world made no sense.

Oh, it was alien, to be sure. She had tentatively identified a type of archeobacteria in the soil and it was unlike anything from earth. But what was bothering her was dichotomies. The soil was almost entirely depleted of any form of nutrient; there was no phosphate, nitrate or any trace material useable by plants in it. It was almost, but not quite, pure silica and iron with some traces of elemental carbon.

However, "almost" wasn't "pure." Besides the archeobacteria, there were traces of proteins all over it. More proteins than you'd get, say, in clean sand in the desert. And the proteins were not the same as those found in the archeobacteria. Not even vaguely the same. They used completely different amino acids for one thing. Amino acids different from Earth's and different from the Mreee. In fact, the only place she'd seen amino acids like those were from Titcher remains. Which was why she suspected contamination. The same company had done some clean-up work with the Titcher and the only thing she could think was that they had contaminated the samples.

So she had leaned on her connection to the Anomaly study and gotten a plane from the Army to carry her up to the site. An airlock had been installed vice the former plate and she had first gotten into an environment suit then had herself decontaminated. Then she went through to the other side.

The Army had wanted to send a security team through with her, but she had cited the possibility of contamination. Actually, she just was tired of dealing with soldiers.

The far side had been as described but Susan had noted something that had passed right by the survey team. Yes, it looked like an abandoned primordial planet from one perspective. But Susan had grown up in the phosphate mining zone of Florida where the highest hill in the region was mine tailings. And if you let your mind wander you could imagine you were in the middle of a giant strip mine. Maybe one that was as big as the world.

She put that aside and walked well away from the gate until she got to the edge of a hill that she was pretty sure the survey team hadn't tested. She got down on her knees and started collecting samples. Technically she should throw a ring and make sure that it was random sampling but at the moment she was only trying to satisfy her own curiosity.

As she was tipping a sample into a canister it fell over and she noticed that the ground was shaking. She considered the possibility of earthquake but the shaking was rhythmic and rapid, BOOM-BOOM-BOOM, more like artillery fire or something. She looked up and around and that was when she saw it.

There were mountains to the east, how far away was hard to tell in the thin atmosphere, and without anything for a comparison she had assumed they were far away, maybe twenty or thirty miles, and quite large. But they must have been closer

and smaller because walking around the edge of the nearest
was a giant green daddy longlegs. It was half the height of the
mountain, at least. Her mind buckled as it tried, and failed, to
put the beast into anything like normal reference. Then she
noticed that, following it and running among its six legs, were
smaller creatures. Even at the distance she could recognize the
rhinoceros and centipede tanks of the Titcher. There were other
things, as well, like smaller spiders, about twice the height of
the rhino-tanks. But the thing about all of them were that they
were tiny, like grains of sand, next to the giant daddy longlegs.
The thing was as big as a mountain, maybe as much as a
*thousand* meters high.

And it was headed this way.


"What happened?" Miller said as his eyes opened. He was in
a hospital again. This was getting annoying. And he had another
blinding headache. He pushed that aside, willing himself to
ignore it; pain was weakness leaving the body.

"You're in Shands Hospital," a female voice answered. "There
was an explosion at the gate."

"Not again," he muttered. "Look, call my wife and tell her I'm
alive this time; she was furious the last time I disappeared."

"I'll make sure she knows," the nurse said, giggling.

"How's Dr. Weaver?" Miller said, sitting up. He felt incredibly weak, like he had the flu or something. He put that aside
as well. There were things to do.

"I don't know," the nurse replied. She was a mousey female
with short brown hair. "There was no Dr. Weaver admitted with
you." She put her hand out as he started to get out of bed. "You're
really not in any condition to go anywhere, Mr. Miller."

"The hell you say," the SEAL replied, sliding his legs out of
the sheets and sitting up. There was an IV in his arm and he
noticed that this time it was a yellowish liquid that he recognized as plasma or platelets. "Where'd I get hit?"

"You didn't," the nurse replied. "But you did sustain some
severe radiation damage. It appears that a nuclear weapon was
detonated on the other side of the gate. It apparently sent out
a lot of radiation."

"Oh, hell."

"The gates in Eustis, Tennessee and Staunton are all closed, with a big burst of radiation at each. And there's an admiral that's been calling for you every couple of hours."

"Shit, shit, shit, shit . . ."

Bill tried to open his eyes and realized that he didn't have any eyes to open. There was no sensation of heat, of cold, of having a body at all. There was no sound, no light, no sensory input at all. The universe was formless and void.

"*Sensory deprivation,*" Weaver thought. Okay, what happened? He remembered stepping back to the gate. And a flash, he thought. "*Am I alive?*"

Well, sure, otherwise who is asking the question.

"*What am I?*" he asked. Where am I? could wait. Get down to base principles. "*I am a thinking being.*" Good, so he at least existed in some form. But sensory deprivation was tricky. The brain anticipated continuous feedback, little signals sent down the nerves and received back like a computer network that is constantly sending out packets. If it didn't get feedback it sent out more and more packets until it overloaded. Which was why sensory deprivation was such a great tool for torture.

"*On the other hand, that assumes I have a brain,*" he thought. And nerves.

"*This really sucks,*" he thought, bitterly. So, what had happened? He and Miller had shot the cone thing as they were retreating out the gate. Something had happened after that. There had been quite a few attack units in the gate room, like they were staging for another assault. So the cone thing was probably supposed to follow up the assault. Maybe some sort of weapon. A nuke? Possibly. So had they predetonated it? If so, as close as it was to the gate, the wormhole, it could have destabilized it. If so, what did that mean to him? Maybe he *was* dead and this was the afterlife. If so, where were the angels? Then he thought about a few of his life experiences and considered the alternatives. Okay, where were the demons with pitchforks?

"*Neither a particle nor a wave,*" he thought. Caught in Schrödinger's box. I'm a cat that might be alive and might be dead. Now if I just had some equivalent of opposable thumbs, or, by preference, a crowbar. *"Excuse me? Would you let me out of here?"*

He suddenly found himself in a car, going down a winding mountain road. There was a huge semitrailer in his rearview, riding right on his tail. He instinctively knew that if he slowed down the semi was going to run him right over and he really would cease to exist. But he couldn't go too fast because around every turn there were low-slung police cars with beady-eyed officers clutching radar guns. If he went too fast the police would catch him and then he would cease to exist as well. He didn't know how he knew that but it was an absolute certainty as strong as the fact that he had to breathe.

He looked down at his speedometer and slowed down, slightly, but nearly ran off the road, actually bouncing off a guard rail and barely regaining control of the car. He got back on the road but by that time he had lost track of how fast he was going and tried to look at the speedometer again. It was impossible; he couldn't know how fast he was going and *where* he was at the same time.

"Oh, shit," he muttered, careening around the twisty road, trying to watch the road and instruments at the same time and failing miserably at both. "I'm an electron."

The crazy road race continued for some time, sometimes uphill and then, crazily, he would find himself going downhill without having reached a crest, the semi always on his tail, crashing into him any time he slowed down too much. When they were going uphill it would fall behind a little bit but it would come barrel-assing up behind him on the downhills. And always there were the police.

He got to a trance-state where he had a vague notion of where he was in the road and also how fast he was going. Not a perfect control of either, but a good approximation. He was all over the road though. And then, suddenly, the road ended in a guard rail right around a steep corner. He slammed on the brakes but the semi hit him from behind and he found himself flying through open space. Then the car, nose down, hit a wall on the far side and exploded.

He came to, lying on the ground at the bottom of the mountain, pieces of the car all around him. He could barely see them, out of the corner of one eye. He tried to move his head but it was immobile, his vision skewed up and to the left. He rolled his eyes and saw his torso, only slightly bleeding, lying on the ground next to him with a leg on top of it. Then the leg jerked into motion and slid over to the shoulder socket and attached.

"That's not right," Bill muttered, wondering how he could speak without lungs to provide the air.

There was more thumping and bumping around him and then he could turn his head. He got to his feet, clumsily, leaning slightly to one side, and looked down.

He had one leg and one arm attached as "legs." He had a leg as his right arm and his left arm was attached, backwards, on his right. One buttock was just below him on his chest and he noticed that it wasn't his chest but his back; his head was on backwards. And there was something tickling his hand.

He pulled the hand around, holding it upwards behind his back where he could see it. What was tickling his hand was Tuffy.

"You're real," he said. He noticed then that there still was no sensation. He hadn't felt the turns on the road or land under his feet. He could see, but there was no sound of wind, no smell, no feel. Except for the tickling sensation from Tuffy's fur.

"What is reality?" The words formed in his head. They weren't even words, just the knowledge that such words had formed.

"I'm a physicist, not a philosopher," Bill replied. "You're real."

"At your level, what is the difference?" The words were like lead weights in his mind.

"We're better at sums," Bill said. "And you're real."

"I thought that physicists hated it when people said 'sums'?" the creature replied, honestly sounding puzzled.

"I'm supposed to have legs where legs go and arms where arms go and you're arguing semantics?"

"Nonetheless, when all was uncertain you clutched for the certainty of philosophy," the creature said.

"Descartes was one of the greatest mathematicians of all time," Bill replied. "I didn't read about him in a philosophy course, I read about him in a tensoral calculus course. His 'I think because I am' thing was just blind panic."

"Yet you continue to use your mind, to apply logic, even when your butt is sticking out of your chest. Many would have gone insane."

"I made my SAN check," Bill answered. "I was an electron, all that 'I can't know my velocity and location at the same time' bullshit in the car. Now I'm a busted-up electron that has been badly reassembled. I suppose it's a metaphor for something. I'm still trying to figure out the cops. They looked just like Virginia State Patrol, except that Virginia State Patrol doesn't usually have fangs that are dripping venom and yellow eyes."

"Who do you think keeps an eye on the particles in your universe to ensure they don't exceed the speed of light? And who destroys them when they do?"

"Cops with yellow eyes and fangs?" Bill said. "Makes as much sense as anything Einstein ever said." Bill thought about something else and found himself laughing out loud. "And blue lights!"

He found himself back in the car, in the race down the hill. Tuffy was hanging from the rearview like a brown, fuzzy dice, swinging back and forth, attached by a silver thread that looked infinitely thin.

"Uncertainty principle," Bill muttered. "I got it the first time." His body was whole again, two hands on the wheel, bitterly trying to stay on the black stuff.

"All of reality is based upon uncertainty," Tuffy said. "Certainty is impossible."

Bill was certain that the police would kill him if he sped up. So he sped up. Before long he had a chain of police cars following him, blue lights flashing. One pulled alongside of him. He looked over and the cop reminded him of a Virginia State Patrol officer that had pulled him over on I-81 the one time he had been stupid enough to drive to Washington instead of fly. Same fat face, same expression of casual disinterest in his existence.

The dripping fangs and yellow eyes like a snake's were at variance, though. So was the cop's action, which was to ram into the side of the car—Bill suddenly realized it was a Pinto—and shove it off the road into space. He'd somehow expected a ticket and a lecture on safe driving on twisty roads.

The cop car followed and the whole line behind it came along, the line of cars flying off into the canyon and impacting on the wall on the far side.

Bill woke up back on the ground. This time both his arms were in the place his legs should be, his torso had been switched for his abdomen and his head was on sideways. Tuffy was perched on his butt, which was about where his shoulder should be. That was when Bill realized he had his head up his . . .

"You're real," Bill said. "I don't know about any of the rest of this Heisenberg stuff and I refuse to believe that I'm an electron, especially one with free will. But you're real. And I think you're trying to tell me something. Couldn't you just send an e-mail?"

"Yes, Bill, I'm real," Tuffy replied. "I'm the realest thing you'll ever meet. Realer than a mountain falling on your head. Realer than a planet, realer than stars. More real, by far, than death. I'm as real as it gets."

"This isn't real, I know that," Bill replied. "I can't be talking without lungs."

"Who says that you're talking?" Tuffy noted.

That was when Bill realized that he couldn't actually hear himself talk.

"So what is reality?" Bill asked. "Really."

"Do you want to see?" Tuffy asked.

"I've always wanted to see," the physicist admitted. "Since the first time I asked myself that question."

"I thought you said you weren't a philosopher," Tuffy said, dryly.

"Well, you were right, at this level the *only* difference is that we're better at sums."

"Okay, I'll show you reality."

Bill suddenly found himself squeezed in on every side. There were Tuffys all around him, pressing him in, making it hard to breathe. They were on his back, in his hair, pressing against his mouth.

"SAN check time," he said, noticing that he did not, in fact, have to breathe and that he hadn't actually spoken. Just that certainty that he had.

"You're doing well," Tuffy said. It was all of them and one of them at the same time. "This is the ultimate reality."

"What? Fuzzy stuffed animals?" He noticed that while there was a moment of panic it was actually quite comfortable. He also noticed that what he was standing on was Tuffys; they were squirming under his feet.

"Your scientists describe universes as soap bubbles," Tuffy replied.

"For the masses, yeah," Bill said. "I can do the sums, though."

"Equations, Bill."

"Not if you're a high-tech redneck," Bill replied. "Then it's sums."

"As you will. But what they do not ask is: in what medium do the soap bubbles float?"

"Well, they do," Bill pointed out. "But it's like asking what's the whichness of where or what is East of the Sun and West of the Moon."

"This is the reality beyond the universes, the whichness of where."

"Plush children's toys?" Bill asked. He'd had a girlfriend once who had collected Beanie Babies obsessively. It pained him that she might have had a better handle on reality than he did.

"Sometimes, bubbles are created within the bubbles," Tuffy replied. "When they reach the wall of the outer bubble, if there is a bubble on the other side of the wall, they open a hole between the bubbles. Just for a brief moment, or eternity in another way of speaking. This form that you see is obviously not our real form. We are what is *outside* the soap bubbles. The child was carried through in the instant of the bubble being formed, caught in the interstices between the walls, where *we* live. She, in a way, made this form, a form that she could understand and love. So, to you humans, yes, reality is plush children's toys."

"And now I'm caught in it, too," Bill said. "That thing exploded and shoved me into the interstice, right?"

"That is as close to the reality as you're going to get, yes," Tuffy answered.

"How do I get back?" Bill asked. "Click my heels together and say: 'There's no place like home'?"

"This is the reality that is everywhere and nowhere. You've always been home."

There was a brief moment of disorientation and Bill was lying on his back. He was in the Wyvern. The cameras were all inoperative but he could see through a small armored plate in the chest. There was blue sky above him with high cirronimbus clouds drifting across it. All of the electronics on the Wyvern were out but he could still move his arms and legs, and fingers seemed to be where fingers were supposed to be and toes were down where toes were supposed to go.

He got the arms of the Wyvern moving and rolled himself over on his belly, then levered himself onto his side.

He was at the edge of a town. The walls of the strip-mall in view were pockmarked with bullet holes and one end had burned. He could see buildings in the distance that were somewhat higher. The place had a familiar feel and after a moment he figured out why.

"Staunton," he muttered. "Why the hell did I have to end up in Staunton?"

# 8

Major Thomas "Bomber" Slade was the S-3 (Operations) officer of the 229th Combat Engineering Battalion (Light, Sappers Lead), based in Fredericksburg, Virginia. The short, stocky, erect officer had arrived three hours before with the main body of the engineering battalion that was tasked with designing and beginning construction upon interlocking defenses to attempt to stem further Titcher incursions through the Staunton wormhole. He was currently observing the wormhole from the front glacis of an M-88 engineering vehicle, that being the only place in relatively short range that wasn't radioactive as hell.

Major Slade was an "active reserve" officer. That is, he no longer held a regular Army commission, despite being a product of the United States Military Academy (West Point, NY). He had resigned his regular commission as a captain to embark on a career as a civilian civil engineer. He had his bachelors in civil engineering from West Point and had attained a masters from Rensselaer Polytechnic in New York while in the United States Army. After serving with the Army in several positions, notably as a company commander of the 82nd Airborne Division's light engineering company, he felt that he had limited chance of eventual advancement to high rank in the regular Army. This was as a result of the incident that had given him the moniker "Bomber" Slade.

As a young lieutenant he had been tasked with clearing a live fire range of unexploded ammunition. His platoon had spent two weeks carefully policing the combined arms' range for unexploded ordnance ranging from small mortar "sabot" rounds, which were about as dangerous as firecrackers, up to five-hundred-pound bombs. They would comb one-hundred-meter by one-hundred-meter segments and put white flags on any ordnance that was detected. Then, when the area was fully surveyed, they would carefully lay small charges of Composition Four on any of the unexploded ordnance, "daisy-chain" the explosives together for simultaneous detonation and then, having removed to a distance considered safe, detonate the charges thereby blowing up the dangerous munitions that had been lying around.

They had done this for two weeks and at approximately three P.M. on a Friday the range had been declared, by Lieutenant Slade, clear.

Unfortunately, Lieutenant Slade was a meticulous officer and he had ensured that only sufficient C-4 had been used on each munition to ensure its destruction. Furthermore there had not been as many exploded munitions as were anticipated. Therefore, there was a large quantity of C-4 left over, approximately thirteen hundred pounds. Once drawn from the ordnance corps, munitions are extremely hard to return, even if it is, as most of this was, in unopened ammunition boxes. It entails vast amounts of paperwork and annoyingly intense questions from various ordnance officers and NCOs who are, understandably, unhappy to have "irregular" munitions in their storage bunkers.

Therefore it was Lieutenant Slade's decision to detonate the C-4 on site.

The careful and cautious manner to do so was to detonate the C-4 in small lots, carefully moved from the site of the central group of material. But it was late on Friday, the platoon had been out on the fricking range for two weeks and everyone was ready to head back to quarters, grab a shower and then hit the bars on Bragg Boulevard. Including Lieutenant Slade. It was, therefore, his decision to detonate the pile of explosives as one lot, a sort of going away present for the exhaustive work of clearing the range.

Being a combined arms' range there were more than sufficient bunkers and trenches at a reasonable distance to ensure the safety of the working detail and the C-4 was placed well away from anything that might suffer undue harm, such as a passing tank. Therefore after rigging the pile to blow, the platoon retreated to the bunkers and Lieutenant Slade clacked the claymore firing device that was connected to the blasting cap by a very long wire.

The explosion was more than thrilling. Everyone had inserted earplugs but several of the platoon complained of ringing in their ears and Private Burrell developed a small nosebleed. Despite that fact the platoon, speaking loudly as was necessary because everyone was at that point a bit hard of hearing, packed up and headed back to barracks feeling that they completed a job well done.

What Lieutenant Slade and his platoon sergeant, a staff sergeant who would later leave the U.S. Army at about the same time as Captain Slade, failed to consider was the method in which wave fronts from explosions propagate. They are, essentially, sound waves. Secondary effects can be mitigated, therefore, by the presence of obstacles, such as the pine trees that just about cover the ranges of Fort Bragg. However, if there is no intervening obstacle they are mitigated only by distance. And it had been a very *loud* explosion.

The 82nd Airborne Division's quarters are laid out between Ardennes Street and Gruber Road. On the far side of Gruber Road are the motorpools of the division and on the far side of the motorpools are training areas detailed to the various battalions. They begin the vast stretches of training areas that make up the bulk of the Fort Bragg reservation. There are very few buildings other than motorpools on the far side of Gruber. The exception is the division headquarters, which is placed on the top of a hill just about centered on the division. The front of the headquarters, which faces the division, is given over to reception and security areas as well as offices of the lowly in the headquarters. The back of the headquarters is reserved for higher ranking officers. And right at the rear of the headquarters is the office of the commanding general. Behind his desk is a large plate-glass window so that by no more than turning his chair around the general can look out over the vast stretches of land where his troops are busily training.

Thus it was that the commanding general of the 82nd Airborne Division, who was finishing up paperwork for the week and looking forward to a cold martini and maybe a smile from his wife, suddenly found his back covered with glass as a resounding explosion occurred somewhere on the ranges.

Lieutenant Slade was required to reply by endorsement as to his reasoning that led to the commanding general's window being broken. Furthermore, the incident was reflected in his next officer's evaluation. Officers' evaluations are carefully considered reports that bring the term "hyperbole" to a new level. Lieutenants that managed to avoid pissing in potted palms or screwing the commanding general's underage daughter still had phrases in their reports that indicated that they were the next Napoleon, but with higher moral standards. Anything other than such phrases led to officers that *were* so described being promoted ahead of those who *were not*. It was assumed that if you were not the next Napoleon, you simply were not Army material.

Lieutenant Slade's next efficiency report had the phrase "sometimes given to acts of less than calculated logic." In a civilian environment that might have been overlooked. But even for a second lieutenant, this was the kiss of death to an army career.

Thus "Bomber" Slade, after an otherwise exemplary career, chose to hang up the uniform, go back to his hometown of Fredericksburg, Virginia, and go to work building apartments and retaining walls in suburban developments.

However, he did not leave the Army entirely. He joined the Virginia National Guard which had its engineer battalion headquarters located in Fredericksburg (one of the reasons he had joined the Army in the first place) and after another company command and staff time was eventually promoted (despite the efficiency report and probably with a helping hand from the West Point Protective Association) to major. He acted for a while as the assistant division engineer then became the S-3 (Operations) officer of the battalion. Life, really, wasn't all that bad. He would have preferred, of course, to have deployed with The Division (former members of the 82nd always refer to it as *The* Division as if there were only one) to Iraq. But life goes on. And he'd built quite a few nice retaining walls instead.

Then came the gates.

Now he was, unquestionably, doing the work that he had looked forward to all his adult, and much of his preadult, life: defending the United States from attack by armed enemies. They were aliens, of course, but that just made it better. He *was* a reader of science fiction and aliens were a nice, morally clean enemy. You couldn't get worked up over mounds of alien carcasses. The only post traumatic stress syndrome that was going to come from fighting the Titcher was related to possibly losing.

At the moment, however, the enemy seemed to be unavailable.

There had been reports that a team had entered the Eustis gate and that something had happened there. At the same time radiation counters in the units that had been fighting in Staunton had gone wild. The aliens, who had been pouring through in an apparently unstoppable tide, had suddenly stopped coming through the gate. The remnant, mostly dog-demons and thorn-throwers with a few rhinoceros tanks, had been mopped up by the survivors of the first National Guard company to be thrown in and locals who, like those in Florida, had turned out with everything from hunting rifles to one squad in an old M-113 Armored Personnel Carrier complete with M-2 .50 caliber machine gun.

None of them had gotten close to the gate, however, because the ground was still reading very hot. There had been no explosion, just a sudden jump in the radiation count. And now the gate was acting . . . odd. Instead of a flat mirror it was rippling, reflecting the light in a pattern of every color of the rainbow.

That, however, was not Major Slade's concern. He was tasked with designing the defenses to be emplaced to cover the gate. There were tanks and fighting vehicles dug in on the hill but the division commander wanted a complete and thorough prepared defense with interlocking fire, bunkers, communications trenches and all the rest.

So Major Slade sat down on the front glacis of the engineering vehicle, laid his map across his lap and pulled out a camouflage colored portfolio, unzipping it and opening it to reveal the 8½x11 lined pad therein. Then he pulled a Cross pen out of his left chest pocket and began to sketch, occasionally picking up the binoculars or referring to the map on his lap.

It was while he was examining dead-zones around the gate, spots where direct fire could not be placed on the enemy, that the mecha-suit appeared. It seemed to hang in air, almost insubstantial for a moment but that might have been an optical illusion, then dropped to the ground. It was human shaped, about four meters tall, or would be if it were standing up. He looked at it again and made a moue of uncertainty. He had three children, all boys, and they were great players of computer games when they weren't watching Japanese anime. Major Slade, for that matter, had spent a couple of years religiously reading the Battletech series until it turned to utter dreck. And he damned well knew mecha when he saw it. And as far as he knew, the United States Army did not have any mecha units. If they did he'd turn in his commission and reenlist as a private if that was what it took to join.

The mecha rolled over on its side and seemed to be looking towards the town; there was a small rectangle of what looked like glass on the chest of the suit. Then it lay back down on its back, as if exhausted.

Major Slade pounded on the driver's hatch with the handle of his locking blade knife until the vehicle commander, wearing a gas mask, popped out of the hatch.

"We need to go down and pick up that soldier," Major Slade said.

"What the fuck is that?" the vehicle commander, a sergeant, asked in surprise. It was clear that none of the crew had been watching the gate which, given that the Titcher might appear at any moment, was just criminally stupid. What they'd probably been doing was sitting as high up as they could, fearfully watching the radiation detectors.

"It's a mecha-suit," the major replied, picking up his materials and climbing up the armored engineering vehicle. "One of ours."

The major was not aware that the Army had mecha, but that did not mean that he thought the suit was alien. Oh, he could get his head around some race, as yet uncontacted, having mecha. There were numerous arguments against mecha as a combat system. Joints were much more prone to mechanical breakdown than the simple track and drive wheel system of an armored fighting vehicle. They also had a higher profile than tanks and more surface area to hit. But the major had known that the Army was eventually going to go to something like mecha for infantry. The weight that infantry soldiers were expected to carry was growing every day as more and more "vital" systems were discovered. Properly designed mecha would simply amplify the abilities of the infantry.

Thus another race could be using them for combat, say against the Titcher; one such might have been "sucked in" by whatever destabilized that gate. And he could allow the logic of them being humanoid; covergent evolution and all that. He could even allow the logic of them being vaguely human facially; he had seen the mask sculpted on the "face" of the suit. Although that was pushing the bonds of credulity.

But lying on the ground next to the suit was what appeared to be a cut-down 25mm Bushmaster from a Bradley Fighting Vehicle. He couldn't imagine precise covergent evolution of the Bushmaster. Among other things, it had some real design drawbacks.

Ergo, it had to be a human. Furthermore, it had to be a human from a time sometime near the present. It was probably *from* the present.

And it was right in the middle of one of the hottest patches of radiation in the world.

The vehicle lurched into motion and he, carefully, climbed up onto the turret and held onto the commander's machine-gun mount as it slowly negotiated the rubble on the hillside.

The mecha had gotten to its feet and was now lurching in the general direction of town. It didn't walk very well; every step seemed to be dragged out of some recesses of energy. And the steps were not graceful at all, foot by foot lurches, arms held at the sides. It had left the Bushmaster on the ground and now plodded its weary way up the hill, one slow step at a time.

It didn't seem to notice the engineering vehicle until they were about fifty meters away. Then it stopped and raised its right arm, waving it back and forth slowly, very much like the droid in Star Wars but slower and with much less enthusiasm. But Slade waved back and motioned for the mecha to stay where it was.

When the engineering vehicle stopped it was within a meter of the mecha. Slade called for a Geiger counter and went forward, waving the wand over the suit. Sure enough, it was hot enough to fry eggs.

"Stay in that," he yelled. He could see a human face peering at him through the armored glass.

He climbed back up onto the turret and ordered them to pick the mecha up with the manipulator arm.

The manipulator arm was a relatively recent addition to the engineering vehicle. It was designed to pick up mines and "Improvised Explosive Devices." It should, however, be able to lift the mecha. If it was even working; the arm was complicated and broke down on a regular basis.

The one on this vehicle was working, though, and it lurched out of its protective cover and jerked creakily towards the suit. The operator, probably the vehicle commander, clearly didn't have much experience using it. But it managed to clamp onto the chest of the suit, lifting it up by hooking under the shoulder.

"Let's get out of the rad zone," Slade yelled down into the vehicle.

He watched carefully to ensure that the suit was not damaged by the movement. But the driver or the vehicle commander had already thought of that and the vehicle backed up the hill, the suit held well off the ground to avoid obstacles, and slowly bumped to the top and over the other side.

The burst of radiation that had come from the gate had, fortunately, been blocked by the hill. Otherwise the vast majority of the defenders would have died of radiation poisoning. But the back side of the hill was clean and there was a decontamination station set up at the base of it. The driver pivoted the vehicle and carried the mecha down to it, where the suit was lowered to the ground in the middle of the road where the decontamination station had been set up.

"What the fuck is that?" one of the decontamination team yelled through his mask. He was wearing a rubber environmental suit that was half covered in suds and had a scrub brush in his hand. The Humvee that he had been working on was sitting in the road.

"Mecha-suit," the major said from his place of approximate safety on the top of the vehicle. "One of ours. There's somebody inside. How do you want to handle it?"

As he asked that the suit rolled to the side then got up on its knees, slowly. The decontamination team backed up and one of the MPs from the contaminated Humvee drew his sidearm.

"Put it away," Slade said. "I told you, he's one of ours."

"We don't have anything like that, sir," the MP yelled.

"That you know of," Slade replied.

The front of the suit opened outwards and a man wearing a black, skintight, coverall stepped out and walked quickly away from the suit, rubbing one shoulder and stretching.

He turned around and waved at Slade as soon as he was well away from the suit. "Thanks for the ride. This is Staunton, right?"

"Right," Slade said.

"I need a secure line to the Pentagon," the man said. "Right after I get whatever they give you for radiation poisoning. Oh, and I could really use a beer."

"We have a report from Chief Miller on the events at the Eustis gate," the secretary of defense said. "We had assumed that you were killed in the explosion."

"No, I was caught in the gate failure," Bill replied. "At that point I experienced some rather unusual communications. I'll make up a report on it as soon as I can with the strong caveat that I'm not sure whether it was real or a sensory-deprivation-induced hallucination. But I think I know what's going on and I've got a pretty good idea how we can get some control over the gates."

"Good," the national security advisor said. "How?"

"The anomaly in Orlando is a boson generator," Bill said, taking a sip of Miller Light. "I mean, that's pretty obvious but I know, now, how it's working. Bosons require high levels of energy to occur. The anomaly is an opening to a realm outside the normal concept of 'universe.' That is, it's not opening to another universe, it's completely open to utter unreality. The reason that we're opening gates to other planets is that linked bosons create stable wormholes through that intermediate unreality. The reason that they're on other planetary surfaces is that they are inactive bosons left over from previous generation. I think that if we looked hard at all the sites we'd find evidence of previous civilizations. Furthermore, the bosons are resonating on a specific frequency. They only link to bosons on that same frequency. I think that's why the Titcher can only get through certain bosons."

"Can I ask you a question off the subject?" the President said. "More of a point of order. It's not normally the case that one of my subordinates sits in a secure communications facility sipping on a beer during a report."

"Doctor's orders," Bill said, taking another sip. "Honest to God, Mr. President. I know that you don't care for it, and why, but I'm balancing health and need. The only thing you can do for radiation sickness is get as much of the radiation out of your body as you can as fast as you can. The most efficient way to move it out is water transfer, drink a lot and go to the bathroom a lot. Beer is even better than water at both. As soon as I'm off the horn with you guys and get a few things moving, I'm going to sit down with a couple of cases and drink them as fast as I can. In the meantime, I'm staying on the sober side. Just."

"Oh," the President said. "In that case, I hope I never get exposed to radiation."

"Your theory that sufficient energy will destabilize the wormholes seems to be correct, by the way," the secretary of defense said, changing the subject. "The Titcher gates, as well as the Mreee gate, have all shut down and generated a blast of hard radiation. I'm not sure why in the case of the Mreee gate."

"Oh," Bill said, taking another sip. "That's because the Mreee are bad guys."

"What?" the national security advisor snapped.

"The Mreee are working with the Titcher," Weaver replied. "They use the same resonance bosons as the Titcher and when I went into the Titcher gate room my environmental system had been breached. I smelled the same smell there that I did at the Mreee gate. I'm pretty sure that just about everything the Mreee told us was a lie, at least about their trying to hold off the Titcher. The gate room, all that concrete, was probably *inside* a Titcher organism. Not on an island. The island lie was to explain the smell. They're not trying to hold off the Titcher; they already lost."

"Oh . . . damn," the secretary of defense said. "Are you sure? The Mreee took a couple of our officers up to watch the fighting. They were using those blasters to really sock it to the Titcher."

"Disinformation," Bill said. "The Titcher don't care how much is destroyed as long as we left a gate open and undefended. We were even getting ready to send through support that we wouldn't have been using against them at other gates. But, really, how much did we *see* of the Mreee? Just where they took us with those jaunt belts. Total area a couple of square miles, most of it in buildings or cities. The evidence against the Mreee is pretty strong. I'm sorry I supported them in my initial evaluation. That was my mistake. Fortunately, we found out in time."

"We've got teams over there," the national security advisor said. "From State and Defense."

"They might be just fine when, if, the gate opens again," Bill said. "In which case I strongly suggest that they be 'called home for consultation.' Then again, I'd suspect that they'll disappear in the interim. And even if they didn't, the gate room must have taken one hell of a whack. It was on the same boson track as the rest. That probably transmitted the wave front of particles."

"They've attacked, in some strength but not as much as normal, on another track," the national security advisor said. "The open boson in Mississippi. We're holding them and they've apparently retreated for the time being."

"I'd guess that that was a leftover from a previous civilization on that planet," Bill said, thoughtfully. "There wasn't an organism at the gate so they're having to move them over from wherever they have forces. Which makes the point that we really have to hold them here."

"Why?" the secretary of defense asked.

"We're opening multiple bosons along multiple tracks," Bill pointed out. "The Titcher seem limited to just one resonance, one track; they don't appear to have our version of a boson generator. If they break out on Earth, we're going to let them out across the entire circuit; thousands of worlds they've never been able to touch. And the generator is not going to shut off for thousands of years."

"Oh . . . shit."

The boson in Horse Cave, Kentucky, was quite invisible to the naked eye. The survey team from Louisville that found it, an environmental company again, which normally responded to spills generated by CSX railroad, had had one team member, in fact, walk right through it. It gave off no radiation that was detectable with a Geiger counter. It had no apparent physical presence. But it was giving off a continuous stream of muons.

As Weaver had been assembling the materials he needed for his experiment he had kept one eye on the news and came away with an even greater cynicism than was his wont. The fact that the bosons were generating muons had become common knowledge and it had created a real hysteria, exceeding, if possible, the hysterias about the use of nuclear weapons. Which was far greater than the hysteria generated by invading aliens, although of the three they were far and away the greatest threat. Muons were subnucleic particles. They didn't generate "radiation," they didn't cause cancer, they didn't make two-headed babies. Hell, there are about 10,000 muons per square meter at sea level continuously coming from active galactic nuclei and quasars and other cosmic stuff and that hasn't caused us any problems in five billion years. But try to tell that to reporters.

They had found a slew of so-called "scientists" who had trotted out elaborate . . . lies about the danger from muons and bosons. Did they bother to tell people that light particles were bosons? Hell no! They were based on no scientific evidence, but the falsehoods were much more interesting to the news media than the occasional countering truth from physicists who actually knew what they were talking about. People who had never heard the term "muon" until they saw it on the evening newscast were now running around hysterically trying to find muon detectors and calling up environmental companies to have them come in and check their homes for muons and bosons.

Bill had been at a scientific conference where a psychologist had laid out the theory of hysteria. In chimpanzee society when faced with an overwhelming or previously unknown threat, such as the first time they heard a rifle shot, the tribe would act in a hysterical manner. Some would try to fight, some would run, some would bluff, others would hide or simply collapse. With no way to logically evaluate the threat, the very randomness ensured that some would survive and, presumably, reproduce. It was an evolutionary method to ensure survival.

It was a pain in the ass in humans, though.

And the protests. Oh my God. Rioters had trashed the physics department of the University of California, destroying hundreds of man-hours of work, some of it directly linked to boson research which might have helped fix the anomaly in Florida. Antiscience hysteria was sweeping the nation, hell, the world. The anomaly site was an armed camp now that protesters had decided it was safe to picket there.

In Horse Cave, Kentucky, however, things were placid. The area that the boson had generated on was an open field just up the road from Park, a natural depression, a shallow forty-acre sinkhole, with a stream running through it. The county road had a sign about a quarter mile north that had a horse and buggy on it, indicating that Amish used the area. The county had sent over a couple of sheriff's cars and a few reporters had come down from Louisville, asked him some questions, most of which he'd either lied about or avoided answering by invoking national security, and left. Fortunately they left before the units from Fort Knox showed up.

The boson had been chosen for the experiment for several reasons. The area was rural, well away from major roads, so if the worst happened minimal damage would occur to humans and their possessions. Even if they got a Cthulhoid entity through the gate, the worst that it would mean was having to change the route of I-65 by a few miles. The depression meant that the boson was easily defended. And it was only two hours from Fort Knox which was the Armor Home of the U.S. Army and which had a vast stock of armored vehicles for the Kentucky Army National Guard. A goodly few of them were being arrayed on the slopes around the depression.

"This is a track one site," Bill said to the National Guard battalion commander. "The Titcher attacking in Mississippi are coming through a track one, but that seems to be a world that was held by another civilization; there wasn't a Titcher organism on the far side. So far all the gates *they've* opened have come from track three. So we're pretty sure that there aren't Titcher on the other side of this gate. On the other hand, it doesn't mean there's not *something* hostile. On the gripping hand, most of the gates have been neutral. We may not be able to open it. We may find that there's nothing on the other side. We just don't know."

"Okay," the lieutenant colonel said. "When do you open it?"

"As soon as you're in position," Bill answered.

"We're as ready as we're gonna get," the colonel replied. "Blast away, Doctor."

Particle accelerators were delicate things that were normally only found in laboratories. And the rest of the mechanisms involved were even worse, not to mention being hastily thrown together by the team from Columbia. There was, therefore, an inflatable shelter, courtesy of the United States Army, thrown up over the boson.

Bill walked down the hill, which was knee high in grass and covered in lovely white flowers, to where the team was making final adjustments. The equipment also required enormous quantities of energy, which was another reason for using this boson; there was a high-tension power line trailing across the back side of the property. Army electrical power specialists along with some bemused electricians from the local power cooperative had tapped into the line, run it through an Army field substation and trailed arm-thick power cables down to the devices in the tent. They were now all connected and would soon be drawing enough power to brown out the surrounding area.

"All set?" he asked.

Mark Rosenberg was a member of his team at Columbia. The heavyset, just below medium height, brown-haired man was an electrical engineer with a background in the nuclear industry. After getting laid off in a round of cuts he had submitted his resume to Columbia, expecting to end up working in one of their few remaining defense factories. Instead, he had ended up working with Bill doing whatever they were doing that week. The team's purpose, up until the opening of the gates, was finding problems that the U.S. military had and then solutions. It had all been highly classified work which sometimes resulted in major successes but often resulted in minor failures. However, the military had a host of problems it wanted fixed and much preferred to dump them on what were generally called "Beltway Bandits" than detail officers who had real day-to-day jobs to trying to find solutions. Good, problem solving, officers were always in short supply. It made more sense to have them fix those problems that only the military could solve, like figuring out exactly how much firepower to use against Iraqi guerilla forces by trial and error, than sitting in offices trying to figure out how to determine the whichness of where. Occasionally the team's problem-solving skills had a great effect and thus the military felt their money had been well spent. One soldier's life saved was equated to just about a million dollars. The team's output had probably saved, here and there, over a hundred lives if not more.

But since getting the call to go to Orlando, Mark had been on what the military called "the sharp end." He'd suited up more times than he ever did working at Savannah River, he'd watched two nuclear detonations and he'd scrounged more weird materials, from more sources, than he'd ever imagined. The linear accelerator, for example, had had to be hand built on site from parts scrounged from research laboratories and factories ranging from Missouri (at a steel plant) to England (Reading University). And the circular magnetic whatchamacallit, its temporary official name, had started off life as a device to wrap tubes with in plastic. He'd found it on eBay being sold by a company in Seattle that was tired of it jamming all the time. The express overnight shipping had cost more than the machine.

"Probably," he said, checking a connection. "This is the most jury-rigged piece of crap I've ever seen in all my born days."

"It only has to run for a few seconds," Bill replied. "It either will work or it won't."

The boson generated muons in every direction. But by careful study they had found that in one direction, more or less pointed west and down towards the earth, it was generating over one hundred times the output of any other direction. The devices had been aligned carefully. The circular magnetic whatchamacallit was aligned perpendicular to the stream while the accelerator was aligned opposite of it. In a few seconds they were going to find out if it was possible to open a gate intentionally. If they could open one, they might be able to close one as well.

"Let's get out of here," Bill said, gesturing to the door of the shelter.

"I'm sure not going to stick around," Mark replied, closing the door to the connection and wiping his hands on a scrap of rag. The one thing he'd enjoyed about the recent jobs was getting his hands dirty. Both working for Savannah River and Columbia had involved far more time sitting in offices than building things. And he dearly loved to tinker with electrical contraptions.

They walked up the hill and through a stand of old trees where a farmhouse had apparently once stood, then across the road and down the slope on the far side. In the tobacco field on the far side the army had kindly constructed a bunker. It was a hole in the ground, covered with scrounged heavy timbers, I-beams and corrugated steel, which had been piled six layers deep with sandbags. Bill had been surprised and amused to find that the Army had an automatic sandbag filler. Construction of the bunker, using civilian backhoes, the sandbag filler and a small army of soldiers, had taken less than six hours. It was large enough for the team and all their gear. Another bunker a short distance away, connected by a reinforced and covered trench, held the military command post.

Bill picked up a field phone and cranked it.

"Bravo Company," a voice answered on the other end.

"All your people ready?" Bill asked.

"Hold one," the soldier answered. In a moment he was back. "All clear."

"Initiating," Bill said, nodding at Mark.

Mark nodded back and pressed a button on a hastily rigged control panel.

There should have been an explosion or a blast of light. Some sort of decent special effect. But there wasn't. The cameras in the inflatable shelter showed the whatchamacallit starting to spin. It got up to full speed and then, suddenly, as the lights in the bunker dimmed slightly, there was a round mirror hanging just off the ground.

"Kill it," Bill said. "Send in the evaluation team."

Bill walked out of the shelter and up the hill where the trees were and watched as a Humvee bounced down the hill. Five men in environmental suits, carrying a selection of heavy weapons, jumped out of the Humvee and entered the inflatable shelter. Bill waited impatiently and then one came out of the shelter and waved a hand.

Bill caught a ride with the battalion commander as he drove by on the way down the hill. When he got to the bottom he waved a hand at Command Master Chief Miller who was stripping out of his environment suit. Miller had lost quite a bit of what remaining hair he had left but otherwise was recovering nicely from his exposure to a blast of neutrons and fairly hard gammas.

"Desert environment," Miller said. "Some mountains nearby. What look like ruins at the base of the mountains. No animals seen or plants. And no Titcher for sure. Air monitors say it's got enough oxygen, slightly elevated carbon dioxide. Pressure is about earth normal. Cold as hell, though; temperature on the far side reads five degrees Fahrenheit."

"Did you say ruins?" Bill asked.

"We can't say that the entire world is desert," Bill noted over the secure link. "We can only see the tiny slice on the other side of the gate. The archeologist we conscripted from the University of Kentucky estimates that the ruins are at least ten thousand years old. We've found some biologicals at this point, but they're all lower order, our equivalent of insects and lichen."

"Did the Titcher wipe them out?" the President asked.

"No, there's no sign of Titcher biology," Bill said with a shrug. "Everything has a lifespan, Mr. President. Species rise and fall, at least if you look at the evolutionary record," he noted, carefully. "Civilizations rise and fall, too, as do planets. Eventually, our sun will go cold and the earth will pass into history. It won't happen for millions of years but it appears that it already has happened on that planet. I'd be surprised if the ruins don't turn out to be older than they appear. I suspect that the race that made them died out or left, to somewhere warmer at a guess. The boson that we connected to was a remnant from when they had lived on that planet, raised their children, built their civilization."

"It feels sad," the national security advisor said. "But it doesn't do much for us at present."

"It tells us we can open gates," Bill pointed out. "I don't think that the Titcher can come through a gate that is opened to a world that they don't control. On the other hand, quiescent bosons are a threat."

"So are gates," the secretary of defense said, dryly. "We don't know that the Titcher are the only threat. Look at the Mreee. Not to mention the Boca Raton anomaly. We need to figure out a way to *close* them and keep them closed."

"I'm not sure that's possible with any near future technology, Mr. Secretary," Bill said. "I've spoken to several other specialists and it's a general agreement that it would take orders of magnitude more power, precisely applied, to close a wormhole, permanently. The quiescent bosons that we've connected to indicate that it *is* possible, but the how remains a mystery. What we have been able to do, based on these experiments, is figure out how to *channel* the boson output from the Orlando generator. The bosons seem to choose their channels based upon maximum probability in the local environment. By applying an induction field, a very high order induction field, we've managed to get the bosons to avoid track three. So there are no more bosons generating on the track the Titcher use. But there are over a hundred quiescent bosons currently scattered around on that track, from Florida to France. It continues, apparently, to be closed, but it might open at any time."

"Any suggestions what we can do about *that*?" the President asked.

"Remember that great big Van de Graaff generator I was talking about?" Bill said. "We think that the bosons are moveable if they have a charge applied, same with the gates. But we need some huge Van de Graaff generators to apply that charge. After that I'd suggest moving them somewhere remote, Frenchman Flats comes to mind, and leaving them. Maybe even bury them in an old mine or something, with a nuke set to detonate. We won't be able to do that in weeks, maybe not in years, we may be talking about decades, but it's doable. Assuming that the reality matches with theory."

"And you can't turn off the Orlando generator?" the national security advisor asked.

"No, ma'am," Bill said. "Same problem. I've looked at some of Ray Chen's surviving notes; he had some on his home computer. And I've talked it over with Dr. Hawking and Dr. Gonzalvez. But it comes to the same conclusion. We'd need about one GAEE, that's pronounced gee, or a Global Annual Energy Expenditure—that is about $1 \times 10^{18}$ Joules . . . a hell of a lot in other words, and something that could actually channel it, which doesn't exist even in theory, to pump enough power into one of those gates to close it. There are some very out there theoretical materials that might be used, but I think even then all we'd get is destabilization and the materials vaporizing in a microsecond or two. And the vaporization would be a high energy event, think explosion. We could drop a nuke on the other side of some of the gates that are on other tracks and try to destabilize those tracks. But we already know about the secondary effects. How many areas do you want to irradiate? There's a gate in the suburbs of Los Angeles, now, and another in Cleveland. Both of them open onto abandoned worlds. But drop a nuke in one on that track and we might end up with neutron pulses on all the others."

"Not good," the President said.

"No, Mr. President," the national security advisor replied. "Especially since some have opened in Europe as well. I can imagine the reaction of the French."

"Did you know that one of the planets has been tentatively identified?" the President said.

"No, I didn't," Bill answered, excitedly.

"I don't know the jargon," the President added. "But it's supposed to be relatively close."

"BT-315-9," the national security advisor said, consulting a note. "It's a star something like ours. . . ."

"G class?" Bill asked.

"Yes, that's what it says here. About sixty light-years away. It's on track one. The gate is in Missouri. One of the survey team knew something about stars and thought she recognized some of them. So a team of astronomers went through and took a look. They're pretty sure that it's that star. They took readings on some others and they all tracked back to that location. Now they're sending in excited reports, something about triangulation, and they want to somehow establish a major astronomy base on the other side."

"I can understand why they're excited," Bill said. "And I agree. But it has some impact on the other problem. I'd like to get some research done at the other open gates. It might turn out that they're all relatively local. By the same token, it might tell us how much power is required to open a gate that's not relatively local. And it tells us that we're at least in the same universe. He . . . heck, that's practically right next door. As far as we knew before that, we might have been opening into other universes, much less in the same galactic quadrant."

"And this is important, why?" the defense secretary asked.

"Well, I'd personally like to know where the Titcher are in 'real' space, Mr. Secretary," Bill pointed out. "Just in case they have space travel technology as well."

"Oh, how truly good," the secretary said.

"They might and they might not," Bill said, excitedly. "But it clears up the major point that the gates can open in *this* universe. And that, Mr. President, is a very, very good thing indeed."

"We're opening another one?" Chief Miller groused.

"Yep," Bill said. The current boson was located in Indiana, well out in a cornfield. A forty-acre section had been hastily mowed down and revetments constructed for units of the Indiana National Guard. A presidential order had been signed calling all units of the National Guard to federal service. There had been barely a squeak from Congress over the supplemental appropriation bill; at this point just about every state in the Union had one or more gates open in it and multiple identified bosons, many of them what the news media referred to as "Titcher bosons."

"Are you sure this is a good idea?" Miller asked as Bill and Mark checked the alignment of the linear accelerator. The accelerator had been modified so that it could be pivoted over a narrow arc, both horizontally and vertically.

"Yep," Bill answered. "You wanna go get suited up?"

"How do I get out of this chickenshit outfit?" Chief Miller muttered, but he went to get suited up.

"You gonna tell him?" Mark asked as soon as the SEAL was out of the building.

"Nope," Bill answered. "I might be wrong. I don't want him letting his guard down."

They were looking at the screens on the same hastily cobbled together control panel. Mark had taken a few hours that were otherwise unoccupied to run up a CAD diagram of a properly designed gate opening system. Columbia had dithered for a few days about whether to patent it or classify it and decided on the former. Now a construction firm in Taiwan was working on a new and improved version. Given that Columbia had the patent on the process, if the next experiment worked his option shares were going to go through the roof.

"Initiating," he said, flipping the switch. The Circular Inductance Generator, formerly known as the circular magnetic whatchamacallit, began to spin. The lights briefly dimmed. Nothing.

"No formation," Mark said.

"Track it around a little," Bill answered. "Our aim might have been off."

The device, still operative, was tracked back and forth.

"We're using a hell of a lot of juice," Mark pointed out.

"The government's paying," Bill replied.

Then a looking glass appeared in the air.

"Formation," Bill said over the radio as Mark started shutting down the systems. "Survey team in."

They watched external monitors as a Humvee bounced down the hill. Then a group of five heavily armed men in environment suits, their body posture making them appear as if they were being hard done by, walked into the shed and then into the looking glass.

It was sort of like doing a tactical entry. Sort of. You never knew what was on the other side of the door. Miller knew that he should be getting blasé about it, but instead each successive entry was getting more and more on his nerves. And something about Weaver's attitude, they'd been around each other enough at this point to tell when the Doc was planning something devious, had him worried.

So he took point. If it was going to be really bad, better that he be the one figuring out what to do about it than the newbie they'd just gotten in from Coronado.

He hefted the MG-240 that he had started carrying as a personal weapon and looked over his shoulder at the team, most of whom were similarly armed.

"Anybody head sweeps me and I'll kill you even if we survive," he growled, then stepped into the looking glass.

He automatically stepped forward to let the team out into the area around the gate then dropped to one knee. Sweep left, impressions, very earthlike, sweep right, green grass, blue sky, look outward, hill, guns, tanks!

He raised the MG-240, his finger going to the trigger, and then stopped.

"Everybody freeze," Miller snapped over the radio. Then he looked around and swore as he lowered the machine gun. "I'm gonna kill that motherfucker."

"Kansas!" Miller snapped over the cell phone. "I thought I was going to another fucking planet and you sent me to *Kansas*?"

"You'd have preferred another planet?" Bill asked.

"No, not really," Miller admitted. "'What did you do, today, Daddy?' 'Oh, went to another planet. This one had a gravity that was high enough I got squashed flat which is why I look like a pancake.' It's gonna happen sooner or later."

"Agreed," Bill said. "Which is why we're going to start shifting the bosons to internal gates. Instantaneous transportation! What man has been dreaming about for decades!"

"One or two persons at a time," the SEAL noted. "From gates in some really odd places. It's not going to take the place of planes any time soon."

"Yeah, but we're having more bosons produced all the time," Bill pointed out. "Spreading out all over the world. We've already got the ability to open one in, say, Virginia, and one in, say, France. And people can just walk in one and out the other. But movement can also be controlled. Set up customs, that sort of thing. And now there's a direct link between Kansas and Indiana. Don't know what use *that* will be, admittedly, but I could see a shipping company setting up a conveyor belt that shifts stuff across the gate. FedEx, maybe."

"Yeah, open one up in New York and another in California and they won't even have to *look* at 'flyover country' anymore," Miller said, grumpily.

"I even know which two gates," Bill replied. "They're next on the list. The only problem will be crowd control."

"Rental car agencies are going to love you." The SEAL grinned.

"So does my boss," Bill replied. "The contract with the DOD had a normal disclaimer about 'civilian use' of anything learned from my research. The accountants at Columbia are already having spasms. They're looking at it as a license to print money. A fee for opening the gates and a percentage of any profits."

"People from other countries opening up clandestine gates to the U.S.," Miller noted. "The new illegal Zimbabwean problem."

"You're such a grump." Bill laughed.

"Open up the Titcher gates, first," Miller said.

"Oh, definitely," Bill replied. "Just a question of from where to where. Once opened, we still don't know how to close them. And moving them will be . . . difficult."

Bill had called Sheila, finally, and told her that he was a little busy with some stuff he couldn't talk about and that he wasn't going to be in Huntsville any time soon. She'd taken the hint and dropped him an e-mail detailing all the reasons she was glad he was out of her life, including that his best friend in Huntsville was much better than he was in bed.

Columbia had a division that was supposed to handle civilian uses of any of their developments. They had taken over the gate opening system as soon as the first one was opened between a farmer's field in the Hudson Valley and a suburban backyard in East Orange County, California. They were, in Bill's opinion, handling it badly and the news services were paying more attention to that than the still quiescent Titcher gates. But Bill had figured out the theory; it was up to other people to mishandle the marketing and public relations.

He'd gotten sorely out of shape lately so he'd picked up a mountain bike in a sporting goods store in South Orlando and brought it up to the anomaly site. After reading the e-mail from Sheila he took the bike down off its rack, clipped his cell phone to his waist and went out biking.

Most of the remaining roads around the anomaly site had been closed but the majority of the TD area was still off-limits to unauthorized personnel. Which meant it was perfect, except for the terrain, for biking. He headed down a track towards the river to the west and rode along what had once been suburban streets. Nature had already started to prevail in the area. Grasses that had not been uprooted were starting to sprout green and along the river, which had been partially shielded, saplings were starting to grow. A few trees that had merely been pushed over were sprouting new growth upwards. Life goes on.

But not if the Titcher came back. The Titcher would turn this all into their green fungus, if not their vast strip mines. The records from the Mississippi gate had been studied and the conclusion was that it was a world the Titcher had destroyed and abandoned.

He stopped down by the stream and looked at the water, thinking. The water had run brown with silt for the first few weeks after the explosion but now, with the majority of runoff that would occur having happened and the plants coming back, it was clear as gin. Clearer, he suspected, than before the explosion. There were fish in it, as well, big guppy-looking things, some of them with bright blue tails.

They had been unable to close the remnant Titcher bosons. The destabilization seemed to spread along the "track." Which meant that besides the gates in Tennessee, Eustis, Staunton and Archer, presumably, they had to worry about thirty inactive bosons scattered from Northwest Florida to Saskatchewan. And he had no idea how soon the destabilization would go away. Just a pretty strong gut feeling, based on very limited theory, that it wouldn't be long.

He got back on the bike and pedaled up the shallow hill towards where UCF used to stand. And the anomaly was still pumping out bosons, although they had limited it to three tracks at least: one, two and four. They were all over the western hemisphere at this point, except Tierra Del Fuego, and had spread as far as the Philippines and Tibet. They were coming out a shade more slowly, now, having lost nearly four seconds in the past month. Which meant the rate wasn't going to change appreciably any time soon. In the meantime, since they weren't closing them as fast as they were being produced, the bosons were a menace that might produce more things like the Titcher, or the Boca Raton anomaly, at any time.

The answer to that was to link the gates as fast as possible, which was one of the reasons that he was getting ticked with Columbia's civilian applications side. The news media was getting huffy because they saw it as a money grab by Columbia, which was not only a big corporation but a, horrors, Defense Contractor. They hadn't even touched on the fact that as long as the gates were open, they were available to any species that had the capability to open them, friendly or hostile. And despite his initial pronouncement, all the species they had encountered seemed to be hostile.

That was bothering the SETI folks no end, but they were blaming it on the way that the government had handled first contact. They seemed to be ignoring the fact that First Contact from the Titcher was the snatching of two innocent retirees.

Columbia's civilian side, meanwhile, had gotten wrapped up by their lawyers. Gates gave instantaneous and unhazardous communication from Point A to Point B. But that wasn't enough for the lawyers. They were trotting out all of the potential horrors that might be involved, litigation-wise. If someone tripped on the exit from the gate, who would get sued? Columbia, that's who. If someone got hit by a truck, said truck delivering materials to a gate, who would get sued? That's right, Columbia. If a gate was opened to one Point B and another Point B was considered to be more economically viable, who would get blamed? You guessed it.

So the gates remained closed while the news media howled about monopolies, the Congress held fact-finding commissions, the lobbyists ran around asking for bills and unknown potential aliens rubbed their hands in glee at all the available bosons.

And, oh, yes, transportation remained via car, truck and airplane.

Humans could not be the only sentient race in range to detect them that would sooner or later notice the available bosons. Someone was going to open one up. And, like the Titcher gates, Bill anticipated that it would be sooner rather than later.

"Boson fourteen is linking to a remote active boson; direction galactic hubward."

Tchar looked at the viewscreen and frowned at the face of his littermate, Tsho'an.

"Dreen?"

"Probably not; this is a Class Nine boson, not a Class Six."

"It could be a remnant," Tchar said.

"It just started linking," Tsho'an argued. "That seems to suggest that the remote was recently formed. We are not alone. Well, alone with only the Dreen for company."

"Yes," Tchar replied, grunting in black humor. "We need Unitary approval to open a remote gate. Especially after the disaster with gate seven. I'll submit a request."

"Do you think we'll get it?" Tsho'an asked.

"I really don't know. I think that they would like to see all the bosons turned off. The transportation guilds have been complaining, again, about incursions on their authority. Move it as quickly as possible to Sector Nine, just in case it is a hostile entity. If it is, we'll have to set up quarantine measures. I'll send a message to the Unitary Council. We will see about opening it."

"They could be friendly," Tsho'an pointed out. "Any support against the Dreen would be useful."

"I was going to bring that up," Tchar noted, closing the connection.

"It had been quiescent for two weeks," the physicist from the French Academy of Sciences said. Bill knew him, slightly, from scientific conferences they both had attended prior to the opening of the Chen Anomaly. He and Bill disagreed on just about every major scientific topic that existed, especially if it had a political flavor. They cordially detested one another, in fact. But they were buddies compared to most of the aliens humans had encountered. "Then a gate formed. The farmer who owns the vineyard contacted authorities immediately, of course. Then *they* came through. Before our reaction team could arrive, I might add."

*They* were five beings in armor that was marked with a muted, vaguely sand-colored camouflage. The beings were bipedal, nearly three meters tall, with three fingers and a thumb. Other than that it was impossible to determine what they looked like in their all-covering suits. They might not be that tall, if the suits were made like Wyverns.

One of the beings was talking in pantomime with a human wearing an environment suit. The aliens' weapons, presumably weapons, that they had been carrying on entry were stacked up by the gate. They were large guns that looked similar to rifles but instead of a conventional barrel they had large bores that looked vaguely like a blunderbuss. Bill suspected that they fired something other than nails. The ground was torn with tracks from armored vehicles and the French Leclerc Mk2 tanks that surrounded the gate had effectively destroyed the vineyard.

Bill walked towards the group as the academic sputtered behind him. He touched the person in the environment suit on the arm and smiled as the woman turned towards him and widened her eyes in surprise that he was not similarly dressed.

"You washed them down, right?" Bill asked. "So far we haven't found anything on any of the worlds which is infectious." He reached into his backpack and pulled out a picture, holding it up so that it could be seen by the nearest of the aliens.

The alien let out a hissing howl that sounded remarkably like one of the dog-demons and could best be written as "Dreeen." The picture had been of a dead dog alien.

"Yeah," Bill said, nodding. "We call them Titcher." Then he extracted his laptop and opened it up. He was no wiz at three-D modeling but there were various cartoon programs available in two-D that worked. He brought up a program and ran a short video he'd composed on the way over.

First there was video of the Titcher, taken at the attack in Eustis by a TV cameraman who would probably win some sort of posthumous award. Then there was video of Nyarowlll shaking hands with Bill, clearly in a friendly manner. Then there was some video of the nuclear attacks in Eustis and Tennessee and more video from the aftermath, centering on all the dead Titcher. Then there was a cartoon, poorly done, of Nyarowlll smiling at Bill and then, when he turned his back, sticking a knife in it. Then there was another cartoon of Nyarowlll with her arm around a Titcher dog-demon.

The alien he had been talking to waved at the other four and they crowded around while Bill showed the video again.

They nodded at each other, waving their necks back and forth, but didn't seem to be talking although there was some sound coming out of the suits. It took Bill a minute to realize that they were probably speaking via radio or some equivalent.

The first alien, he seemed to be a boss, waved at the screen on the third run-through and Bill froze it on a picture of Nyarowlll.

"Dreeen," the alien said.

"Mreee," Bill replied. "That one's Nyarowlll."

The alien cocked his head to the side. "Nyarowlll, Mreee."

Bill touched his chest. "Bill." Then he pointed at the screen. "Nyarowlll." He pointed at himself and the other humans around. "Human."

"Oooman," the alien replied. "Adar," he added, pointing at his chest.

"Humans," Bill said, then pointed at Nyarowlll. "Mreee. Bill. Nyarowlll."

Bill backed up to the point that had Nyarowlll being friendly then to the rough cartoon of her putting a knife in his back then to the picture of her being friendly with a Titcher. Then he brought up another, a video of the suited aliens, the Adar, side by side with the Titcher, one armored arm over the back of a thorn-thrower.

There was a hiss at that from the boss alien and he waved it away, spitting, clicking and gabbling in apparent anger.

Bill showed the scenes with Nyarowlll again and then waved at the pictures. Then he held up a hand and shrugged. It was anything but a universal gesture, but the alien, the Adar, seemed to get the point. Humans had been bitten once, that was going to make them shy.

The aliens waved their arms at each other for a bit, then the boss reached out carefully and touched one of the controls on the laptop, starting the footage. He ran it forward to the nuclear blasts and stopped at the mushroom clouds.

"Dreeen."

"Human," Bill said. "We did that."

"Adoool," the alien said. "Adoool." He pointed around at the tanks. "Adoool."

"Soldiers?" the French woman in the environment suit said. "War?"

"Actually," Bill replied. "I think it's more like 'smart' or 'good damned job.'"

The alien reached up and manipulated some latches on his neck at which one of the others waved a hand. He waved back and then took off his helmet, snuffling at the air.

He wasn't pretty. There were three eyes, one on either side of its head and one placed more or less where a human forehead would be. Just below it was an opening and below that was a wide beak, flat and round. Its skin was a pale bluish color.

"Tchar," the alien said through the snout; his mouth remained closed. "Tchar," he added, tapping his chest. Then he pointed at Bill. "Bill. Tchar."

"Hello, Tchar," Bill said. "Pleased to meet you. I hope."

# 9

"The Adar appear to be about fifty, maybe a hundred, years advanced upon us. They use neural implants, their primary air method of transport is suborbital rockets that work off of laser launch technology, they have very advanced computing devices and the guns that they were carrying seem to be some sort of plasma-toroid generator. They're not super guns, but they'd probably take out a Bradley Fighting Vehicle from the pictures Tchar showed me. They do not *appear* to be friends with the Titcher or Dreen as they call them. They've showed us pictures of their planet, had one team over on a suborbital rocket from which a large area was visible, and appear to get the point that we're not going to just fall for the friendly alien thing. Once bitten twice shy and all that but *this* time the aliens appear to be friendly."

"That's good," the President said. "If true."

"Yes, Mr. President," Bill replied. "If true."

"Most of the time the Adar team on Earth have been using their communicators," the national security advisor said. "They appear to be radios, they're giving off RF emissions, but we haven't figured out exactly how they're broadcasting or what is being said. So we haven't been able to get much of their language. Dr. Avery from the State Department, however, has been communicating with some of their people on the other side, we don't know if they're leadership or not, and he's making headway. He thinks he's gotten about a five-hundred-word vocabulary so far."

"Avery's amazing," the secretary of defense said to the President. "He can pick up an Earth language just listening to it for a couple of hours. If anyone can decipher their language he can."

"They're being helpful in that as well," the national security advisor said, biting her lip. "I'm inclined, this time, to side with them being friendly. As friendly as could be expected. They appear to have a couple of internal gates open as well and the means to move them; they apparently had the theory of wormhole formation and *then* started making bosons. And Dr. Weaver will be gratified to learn that the way they move them is by using very large Van de Graaff generators."

"Yes," Bill said. "Maybe we can buy a couple off of them."

"I still want a full analysis this time," the President replied. "As much as we can determine of their economy and order of battle. I don't want to be fooled again. It's not good for politics and it's not good for America. Dr. Weaver, any idea when the Titcher gates might open?"

"No, Mr. President," Bill replied. "Tchar took me to what they call their Dreen gate. It's in the same area as the one that connects to us, a big open desert area with some mountains in the distance. Except for some of the colors it looks a lot like Groom Lake. They have the Dreen gate surrounded by their tanks inside a large hole in the ground that they can fire downwards into. And there's a big device right opposite it. Again, this was all pantomime, but I get the impression that it's got something like a nuke in it that they can trigger if their gate stabilizes. It wasn't stable, though; it was rippling just like ours. I tried to get some idea if they knew how long they stayed down but that was just too complicated. If Tchar knew what I was talking about, he couldn't answer me. Among other things, sir, they don't have our clock, obviously. Their planet seems to have about a thirty-hour day and I have no idea what their year might be. I started to try to get him to count it out in Planck seconds since every physicist in this universe would know what that is . . . but for the life of me I couldn't think of how to pantomime 'what is the time delay if you count that in the smallest possible time increment allowed in this universe?' I'm open for suggestions on that one."

"Ask Dr. Avery to concentrate on that question," the President said to the national security advisor.

"I will, sir," the NSA said, then temporized. "The thing is, they might take it as a request to find out about their nuclear capability. We'll have to know things like the yield of their weapons and delivery methods. If they started asking *us* those questions, I'd be uncomfortable."

"Tell him to explain why we're asking, first," the President said. "I'm sure they'll understand in that case." He frowned and then shook his head. "They seem to have a point, though. Don't we have some artillery-fired nukes? Is there any reason we can't fix up something like that at all the sites?"

"I don't think we have any left in inventory . . ." the secretary of defense said.

"We don't," the national security advisor said, definitely. "But there ought to be some way to set up a launcher on a standard Mark 81 MIRV warhead, and we have a bunch of those in inventory." She smiled for a moment and shook her head. "We're supposed to come up with things like that, Mr. President. What do you want to do, work us out of a job?"

"No, but I do want to make sure the Titcher stay on their side of the gate," the President answered. "Get that set up as soon as possible. Not just at the open gates but at the inactive particles as well. I don't want to be caught with our pants down again. Then there's the inactive particles. Dr. Weaver, Columbia is taking far too much time in opening them."

"I have to take the Fifth on that one, Mr. President," Bill replied, formally. "It's not my department and the one time I brought it up I was reminded of that fact."

"Well, I'm not afraid to bring it up," the President said, somewhat angrily.

"I'll call Kevin Borne over at Columbia," the secretary of defense said. "I know they've got some issues but I'll point out that they really don't want to get us upset with them. I'll be pointed about that fact, rest assured, Mr. President."

"Just get it done," the President said.

"There's the point that there is still only one gate generator," Bill pointed out. "It takes a skilled team about ten hours to set up, then there's transportation time. Even if they had gotten on the ball right away, and ignored arguments about which gates should open where, there wouldn't be many linked, yet. There is a firm that was scheduled to build some more, but I don't know the status of that project."

"I'll talk to Kevin and light a fire under him," the secretary of defense said. "If there's something holding it up besides lawyers, money I guess would be the answer, I'll talk about that as well."

"I think that's all we have," the President said. "Let's hope the Titcher gates don't open soon."

"Robin," Bill said, from his office. "Could I see you for a second?"

"Sure," the programmer replied, walking to the open door.

"Come on in and close the door," Bill said, opening the refrigerator by his desk. "You drink Pepsi, right?"

"He said as he slipped in the strychnine?" Robin asked.

"No," Bill said, chuckling. "I got a call from the Columbia rep in Paris. The Adar are asking about the boson generator. Communication is still spotty so they've asked me to go over there and try to figure out how to communicate what's going on and what we think happened. You're better at 3-D modeling than I am. I'd like to just make up a little cartoon to show what we think happened and what is happening now. Could you do that?"

"Sure," Robin said, smiling. "It doesn't require modeling at all. I'll just do a rip on an Unreal Tournament engine; that will give enough detail for what you're asking about."

"Great," Bill said. "Can you do it on a plane?"

The biggest problem had been passports; Robin didn't have one. By the time they were in D.C., though, one had been prepared and they took a trans-Atlantic flight, First Class, on British Airways.

It was a hell of a lot better than his first flight to Paris when they'd loaded him in another F-15 and flown nonstop with one aerial refueling. The service was much better, from some very pretty young English stewardesses, and Robin was good company.

They'd laid out the script for what they wanted to impart on the way to D.C., then Robin had started modeling it on her laptop. By the time they got to Paris the video, which had had some glitches, was working fine. They spent the night at the embassy, then took a French Alouette helicopter to the Adar gate site.

The French military was, apparently, not taking the Adar at their word. The vineyard was now ringed by entrenchments and a large concrete bastion was under construction. But the Adar representative, wearing a respirator, was apparently willing to ignore the formalities. Perhaps that was because when they stepped through the gate, also wearing respirators since the Adar atmosphere was high in carbon dioxide compared to Earth, there was a similar military buildup on the Adar side. There was also a large device that looked vaguely like a tank without the treads. The weapon it mounted had a large bore but no larger than that on an Abrams. Bill suspected, though, that it was something much more powerful than a 120mm tank cannon. If the humans turned out to be less friendly than it appeared, the Adar were clearly willing to close the gate with all due force.

Rather than flying casual diplomats all over their globe, the Adar had set up a meeting center near the Terran gate. Bill saw quite a few humans, most of them apparently international diplomats uncomfortable in their respirators, moving around the grounds. The Adar that had greeted them on the Terran side accompanied them by ground vehicle to the meeting center, which was a large building that had the vague feel of a hangar, sectioned up by hasty plastic panels, and turned them over to another guide. He, in turn, led them to the back of the center where a more substantial office was located.

In it were Dr. Avery, wearing an oxygen nosepiece and toting an oxygen bottle, and three Adar. There was also an Adar-sized conference table surrounded by chairs for the Adar and a few human swivel chairs that had been brought through the gate. All the Adar looked the same to Bill and he suspected that it was the same with them. But one of them stepped forward and crossed his chest, bowing slightly.

"This is Tchar, Dr. Weaver," Avery said. He was a slim man with an erect carriage, a former Navy officer who had attained the rank of rear admiral before retiring. He weighed 173 pounds, which was the same weight he had been upon entering the United States Naval Academy in Annapolis. "You met him before."

"A pleasure to see you again, Tchar," Bill said, pulling aside his respirator then clamping it back down. "I see you've found a better solution, Admiral Avery."

"A necessity of the mission, Doctor," Avery replied. Before he did he took a breath through his nose which slowed his speech, but it was better than shouting through a respirator or pulling it aside. "Do you think we can explain the gate phenomenon to the Adar?"

"We can't even explain it to ourselves, Admiral," Bill admitted. "Miss Noue?"

Robin set her laptop on the table as Avery and the Adar sat down. The laptop was nearly at Avery's eye-level due to the height of the Adar table. She keyed the video and then sat down herself.

The scene was a daytime, apparently viewed from the air. The notional camera swooped in over some suburban tracts and roads and then showed a stylized college campus. A few students were walking around the campus, carrying books or laptops. The camera zoomed in on a building and then through the wall into a laboratory. A few people were grouped around a device. The only portion that was clear was a linear accelerator. A man that didn't look like Ray Chen but did have vaguely Asian features said: "Let's see what happens," and pressed a button.

The camera cut back to outside the building and there was

a flash. It cut to farther away and watched the shockwave roll out from the building and the mushroom cloud form.

The next sequence was video from the news choppers on the day of the event. They showed the police helicopter closing in on the base of the dust cloud and then the shot of the Chen Anomaly. And the bug that first fell out.

The next sequence was computer animation again. The anomaly was shown and then particles zipping out. The "camera" showed one of the particles zipping away down between and through buildings, then zoomed out to show that it was covering a portion of the globe. It came to rest at a random spot and then, a few moments later, a gate opened.

Another was shown zipping not far from the anomaly on the map and then a gate opening in a dark wood. Dog-demons, and they had been the hardest to create of all the images, came out of the gate sniffing the ground. They went into a house and came out dragging two people, taking them into the gate. Last there was a shot of the fighting in Eustis.

"And the rest you know," Bill said as the video stopped.

One of the Adar said something to Tchar and he made a gesture like a horse tossing its head. He said something to Admiral Avery, crossing his arms in front of him.

"Tchar says that he grieves for the pain inflicted to us," Avery translated. "But he is also puzzled." The translator nodded for the Adar to continue.

"He says that he is puzzled by the scene in the laboratory. Unless we have something to use great power, I think he means something like superconductors, that he is unaware of, there did not seem to be enough power available to create a single boson, much less many of them. He also asks how many bosons we have generated. I'm not sure that we can answer that. Also, be aware that the other gentleman is called Tsho'futt. He appears to be picking up English rather quickly."

"It's common knowledge in general on our world," Bill pointed out. "They'll find out sooner or later and I don't even have an exact number. Tell him over thirty for each one of their days. And, no, Ray Chen's accelerator should not have been able to make a single boson, much less many."

This was translated and Tchar made another head gesture, waving one hand and speaking.

"Only one boson that they have generated seems to be accessible to the T!Ch!R!," Avery said, doing the closest approximation of the word Bill had ever heard. "He wants to know if you know if the T!Ch!R! can access only certain bosons and if you've identified them."

"Yes," Bill said. "Twenty-one of them were generated on that fractal before we learned how to prevent it. They are scattered across our country but not in other countries, not in France near your gate."

Tsho'futt made a noise that sounded like pain and so did Tchar as the words were translated.

"What have you done about that?" Tchar asked through Avery.

"An explosion happened on the Dreen side that destabilized the entire fractal. But we don't know for how long. Do you have any idea?"

"Was it your device?" Tchar asked.

"No, one of theirs," Bill said, pulling out a sketch of the thing in the gate-room. It was the best they could do from his and Miller's recollection; both of their camera systems, which had been recording the events, had been erased. Miller's was straightforward EMP damage; the scorching was noticeable. Bill wasn't so sure about his; the systems weren't functioning when he got back to earth but after replacing a few parts they worked fine. The recording chip, however, had been erased. It was fully functional, there just wasn't anything on it.

The Adar examined the picture, then set it on the table.

"We have seen nothing like that," Avery translated. "As to the question of time, Dr. Weaver, we're working on that. We've shown them the time pieces we have and vice versa but we're still working out what it means." He listened as Tchar spoke, nodding.

"Tchar said that they have had the gate restabilize three times since they have opened it. They were hit by the T!Ch!R! when they first formed the boson, a heavy attack which they repulsed on the ground. Then they brought up the . . . it's not a device to throw a nuclear warhead, we're not sure what it is exactly, but it *is* a weapon. They triggered it at the gate and shut it. But it opened again . . ." He listened and pulled out a piece of paper. "I think it's seventeen of their days later."

"Holy . . ." Bill said. The Adar day was approximately thirty hours long. That meant less than three weeks. There had been more time than that already. "Do they know what . . . we need to know what kilotonnage they use!"

"That is more difficult," Avery said when he translated. "Time we're getting better on. And I'm aware that science is supposed to be a universal language, but only in certain details and not in the notations." He smiled thinly at his little joke.

Bill was well aware that many scientific baseline measurements were taken from nonuniversal constants. The meter was a fraction of the Earth's diameter, as best it could be measured in the seventeenth century, and only later defined as a certain number of light waves of a particular wavelength. Joules, the internationally recognized standard for energy, were similarly arbitrary. But one was not.

"Singlet transition," Bill said, pulling out a sheet of paper. He made a dot on the paper then drew a circle around it and placed a smaller dot on that circle. Then he drew a squiggly line hitting that circle. Then he would drew a larger circle around the thing showing the dot jumping from the inner circle to the outer circle. "I should have set this up as a cartoon, but most physicists would understand it if I showed it to them," he added, sliding the picture across the table to Tchar. Tchar tilted his head and considered the picture for a moment, then tilted it the other way. Then he picked up the pen and began to draw.

The picture that he slid back to Bill was . . . incomprehensible. There was a complicated group of figures at the center with another figure in an oval off to the side. There were three more symbols spaced around the central symbol. Overall, it looked like a Chinese charm or a mystic spell and Bill wasn't sure what they represented.

"What is this?" he asked, looking at Admiral Avery.

"He says it's a drawing of an atom," Avery replied. "Look, Bill, some things are intuitively obvious to *humans* because our societies evolved in connection with each other. I have no idea what that's saying, exactly; we haven't gotten that far. For all I know, it could be saying the same thing as yours. What is a . . . singlet transition?"

"The energy necessary for an excited electron to jump from one orbital level to another. It's a base energy equation."

"Try something else?" Robin asked. "Calories? That's just the energy necessary for one gra . . . damn, we'd have to get measurements for a gram, right?"

"Right," Bill said, leaning back and steepling his hands. Then he leaned forward and tapped the symbols. "Does this represent an atom? Are we sure of that?"

"Yes," Admiral Avery said. "They consider it a transitional state, which is interesting. But it's definitely an atom." He spoke to Tchar for a moment and then shrugged. "Tchar said it's the smallest possible atom."

"Hydrogen, good," Bill said. "What amount of energy is released when one of these atoms fuses into the next largest atom?"

Avery translated that and the Adar got a distant look. Admiral Avery explained that he was accessing their datanet.

"I wonder if it's like ours," Robin said. "One-third data, two-thirds pornography and singles sites?"

Tsho'futt made a hacking noise and translated the question. Tchar continued to look distant but the third Adar, who had not been named, said something.

"Announcements of tcheer," Tsho'futt said in not bad English. "And much announcements of herbal remedies to prevent loss of youngness."

"Tcheer is the reaching of bonding age of a sexual transfer intermediate," Avery said, tightly. "Nonsentient. I suspect we just discovered what their pornography is."

"The wonders of science," Weaver replied.

Tchar spoke and Avery paid rapt attention.

"Tchar says that he can see where we are going and he thinks we can come to some conclusion on energy level translations," Avery said. "When we have those, we might have a measurement of their weapon's yield. And he's willing to let us know what theirs are if we tell them what ours are."

"Ouch," Bill said. "We'll get the materials but the rest we'll have to kick upstairs."

Three hectic hours later they had a measurement.

"Ten megatons, give or take," Bill said, looking up from the calculator on his laptop. "I wonder if it's straight geometric progression or nonlinear or what?"

He and Tchar had spent most of the time, with Avery as an interpreter, discussing the formation of bosons and boson gates and their characteristics. They had come to a mutual understanding of muons, neutrons, neutrinos and quarks. Because they weren't generated by inactive bosons or nuclear weapons, quarks had been a little harder, but Bill was pretty sure they were talking about the same particles. They'd also discussed, badly, quantum mechanics. Bill got the impression it was as insanity causing for Adar as for humans.

The French physicist, Dr. Bernese, had turned up and had joined in the discussion for a while and then politely excused himself as it turned to weaponry. He was a firm member of the nuclear disarmament committee and while he appreciated the current necessity he deplored actually discussing them.

Bill, on the other hand, had, without getting into anything that would violate security, discussed them with wholehearted abandon. The Adar, it turned out, did not use fission-fusion devices but something else. Tchar was somewhat reluctant to specify what it was but he noted that the results that Bill described from the gate room might, in fact, have been the same thing. Bill was pretty sure that the thing in the gate room had been an antimatter containment system, but when he brought up the subject of antimatter, after having a tough time explaining it, Tchar had been more than happy to discuss the material. Ergo, it was not their weapon system.

Antimatter was the reverse of normal matter; at its most basic a positron was an electron that had a positive, instead of a negative, charge. Antimatter that was placed in contact with regular matter would explode, violently. Both it and the regular matter it encountered immediately transmuted into energy. It had been produced, in minuscule quantities, in the big matter-accelerator at CERN in Switzerland. Minuscule being individual antiprotons and antihydrogen. Producing it wasn't actually all that difficult, but storing it for any amount of time used up so much energy that the final output was a negative.

Bill had postulated that the thing in the gateway had been a carrier for antimatter. Positrons could be kept from contact with regular matter by inducing a magnetic field around them, generally called a containment bottle. The thing had *looked* like some sort of containment bottle, if such was made by a species that used biology instead of mechanical devices.

But Tchar had hinted that there was something else, something more powerful as an explosive than antimatter. And the Adar had it. In sufficient quantity to use it as a weapon.

"Something like that would be a tremendous fuel source," Bill said, dangling for information.

"It was what I was working on before we opened the first gate," Tchar said, then changed the subject.

The Adar had formed the bosons with the purpose of creating gates for transportation on their own world. They had just about exhausted their easily worked areas of fossil fuels and relied heavily on nuclear fission power to provide motive transport. Even the suborbital rockets that they used instead of most aircraft were powered by nuclear fission. But it had the same byproducts that it did anywhere; spent fuel rods that even when recycled left behind unusable radioactive byproducts that had to be stored for centuries. The Adar did not seem to have the, often irrational, human fear of nuclear power and its byproducts, however. Or, at least, Tchar wasn't letting on if they did. The one thing Bill had decided in the three hours was that, besides being a crackerjack physicist, Tchar would have made one hell of a poker player.

But finally the measurements were completed as were the calculations.

"They used the same weapon, every time?" Bill asked.

Avery did not seem to have minded three hours of translation, sometimes very esoteric translation. The old admiral was as fresh as when they had started. If anything, he looked more enlivened by the conversation.

"They did," he said to Tchar's reply. "The suggestion was made after the first to vary the power to determine if the portals stayed down for more or less time but the Unitary Council, their Cabinet if you will, did not want to take the chance."

"And we don't know what the output was on the Dreen side," Bill mused. "Okay, Tchar, Tsho'futt, Mr. Unintroduced, I thank you for your information. Can I tell you anything we've missed?"

Avery translated this and then shrugged. "I don't think we have anything they want in the way of information. Except data about boson formation beyond what we can translate."

"I've got one more thing to cover," Bill said. "But, with the permission of the Adar, I'd like to only discuss it with Tchar and for him to be willing and able to keep it to himself for the time being. It does not relate directly to security of either of our worlds but to . . . the philosophy of physics."

Avery frowned but translated the request. There was a discussion among the Adar and then Tchar spoke.

"The one who has not been introduced," Avery said, "requires that he stay. Are you familiar with the Japanese method of negotiation?"

"No," Bill said. "I've dealt with Russians before . . ."

"With the Japanese, the more senior of the negotiators will often spend the entire exchange with his mouth shut. The junior does all the talking. In this case, it appears to be protocol to completely ignore the third party, who I would guess is a senior scientist or politician."

"Scientist," the unintroduced Adar said, suddenly. "And linguist."

"I want to express that the following information is known to very few people," Bill said. "Our President, his national security advisor and the secretary of defense. Besides those persons, I have told no one else. And despite the fact that it appears that it has security implications because of the personages involved, I'm certain it does not. It does, however, I believe, relate to the physics of boson formation and gates. And I would be willing to discuss it with you. If you understand the importance of securing the information carefully."

The Adar discussed this again and then Tsho'futt got up and left the room.

"Your artass will leave or stay?" Tchar asked, pointing at Robin.

Avery looked confused for a moment then chuckled, dryly. "It had been assumed that since Bill was doing all the talking, Robin was his . . . control."

"I hope not," Bill said, looking over at Robin. "Got anything you want to tell me?"

"Only that I hope I get to find out what you're talking about," Robin said.

"Robin, you're a great person, but . . ."

"The answer is no," she said, shrugging. "I'll figure out a way to drag it out of you. One day." She picked up her materials and left.

"Does your artass wish to do the translation?" Avery asked, carefully phrasing the question to Tchar.

Tchar responded with a head motion that indicated negative.

"Admiral Avery," Bill said. "I have to ask one technical question. What's your clearance?"

"Sonny boy," the admiral answered, tartly, "I was doing nuclear negotiations with the Russians when you were a gleam in your daddy's eye. My clearance is higher than yours. You can judge for yourself the need-to-know but I don't even talk in my sleep."

"Sorry," Bill said, chuckling. "Okay, here goes. The first thing to understand is that humans are subject to hallucinations."

"I don't have an Adar word for that," Avery said then spoke to Tchar for a moment. "Okay, they have something similar. I think I can work with it, anyway, but it has religious connotations."

"Well, so does this," Bill said and then launched into a repetition of his experiences in Eustis during the gate malfunction. He didn't leave out the fact that he had been tired at the time, up too long and wired to the max, perfect conditions for hallucination. He pulled out notes and referred to them, notes he had made shortly after his experience against letting anything get in the way of the memories. They were as close to verbatim of the exchange he had experienced as he could manage. Stuffed children's toys were a bit of a problem but he had a picture of Tuffy and Mimi on his laptop.

When he was done the as yet unintroduced artass sat forward, turning his head from side to side and examining him critically with his third eye, which was high on the head as if to check for overhead threats.

"Wonder if you dream," the artass said. The words were dragged out and hollow.

"Yes," Bill replied, looking into the weird alien face and wondering what was going on in his mind.

The artass started to say something then spoke a word at Tchar who spoke at length to Avery.

"Human scientists try to separate science and what we would call philosophy or religion," Avery said. "The Adar do not. They said that the one thing in your ramblings that made true sense was that, at our level, science and philosophy are brothers. To them, science, philosophy and religion are intertwined."

Tchar looked over at the artass, who made a head motion. Tchar continued.

"Our greatest saints," Avery translated, "experienced visions just such as yours, visions that asked them to open up their mind and explore what is reality. What is the universe? If bosons can contain a universe, who is to say that we are not experiments in some cosmic laboratory? Are we the result of one of the stuffed Tuffy dolls saying: 'Let's see what happens.'? Is God one? Is God omniscient and omnipotent? Or is God many researchers, searching to understand Their own reality? Are we made in God's image as lab rats? Or are we, too, researchers, furthering Its quest for understanding? At our level of physics, these are viable questions, not to be dismissed. As you apparently dismiss them." Tchar made another head movement as Avery completed the translation and then said something quietly.

"He grieves that you do not open your mind to the wonder of the universe."

Bill, who felt that he had spent the better part of his life doing just that, was taken aback.

"Actually," Bill said, shrugging, "what you're saying sounds about right. But it's less a question of the scientists than the religious persons. Most scientists at my level, who work with advanced physics, are just fine with God as researcher and us as assistants. Perhaps it is the way that God is portrayed among my people. Very few of the religious are scientific and vice versa. In early science, many of our discoveries were made by religious persons. But as time went by the belief structure of religion seemed to interfere. To most of our religious persons, if they think about it at all, things either are or are not. God made gravity pull to keep people from flying into space. That's good enough. That attitude creates a good bit of friction, but the friction for physicists is simply that they won't bow their heads to the unthinking and say 'yes, you're right about God and I'll stop researching since it's pointless.'"

Tchar looked over his shoulder but the artass was simply watching Bill.

"Then, perhaps," Tchar said, carefully, "we should be talking to your religious leaders."

"Good luck," Bill laughed, hollowly. "Hope you don't get lynched."

Avery winced but translated the statement.

"This would happen?" Tchar asked.

"Probably not in the United States," Bill admitted. "But if you went to Mecca and preached your word of God, you'd have your head taken off. And I don't think the Reform Baptists would be really open-minded, either."

This required a good bit of back and forth between Avery and Tchar, each explanation requiring more explanation. Finally the artass spoke to Avery and Avery nodded.

"They, too, have religious sects," Avery explained. "But very few are antiscience although some are militant to a degree. One sect provides the bulk of their fighting forces. In fact, as they seemed to indicate, science and religion among the Adar seem to go hand in hand. I think, once they get the language down, they could have a very instructive time talking to some religious leaders I know."

"I will consider your words carefully," Bill said, wondering if he could get his mind around God as a researcher. It certainly made more sense than "in six days he created the earth and then kicked Adam out of the garden for simple curiosity."

Maybe that was it. From the very beginning, curiosity among the religious had been degraded. "Don't eat of the fruit of the tree of knowledge, or you, too, will be thrown from the Garden."

He knew that early science had been heavily supported by religion. Even some of the urban legends surrounding "religious bigotry" about science were false. Galileo, for example, rather than being a victim of religious bigotry had been a victim of simple failure to rigorously base his conclusions. The theory of planets going around the Sun and the Moon going around the Earth required a theory of gravity and calculus to explain it. Since Galileo could not show conclusive proof of *why* his theory worked, the best scientific minds of his day, admittedly supported by false theories that had built up starting with Aristotle, dismissed his work as fraudulent. But it had been his inability to show a method, rather than pure religious bigotry, that had doomed him. That and the fact that he was a revolting son of a bitch. The pope of the day had protected him from his detractors, but that was all that he could do. Galileo, himself, made it impossible to do any more.

For that matter, it was not those who believed that the world was flat who argued most vehemently against supporting Columbus' mission that had found the "New World." It was, instead, the best scientific minds of Isabella's court, who pointed out that going west, instead of around Cape Horn, was an impossible distance, with the technology of that day, to India. They had determined the size of the globe and the distances involved and realized that Columbus would be out of food and fresh water before he was halfway there.

Fortunately, before he was a third of the way there he landed in the Caribbean. But they didn't know that was there. And Isabella, the poor dear, was too stupid to understand their math.

Nevertheless, religious bigotry against science did exist. The

Scopes Monkey Trial and continuing bills to try to enact "Cre-ationism Science" as being on the same order as evolution. The hysteria about the current boson formation which was being supported and exacerbated by religious leaders.

He wondered if one of the first people to convert to the Church of Adar or whatever might not be William Weaver.

"I'll think about it," Bill repeated.

"Do," the artass said. "Open your mind. Or we all may fail."

Admiral Avery accompanied him out of the meeting room where they picked up a visibly curious Robin and headed back to the gate. When they were on the other side, and out of hear-ing, Avery touched Bill's arm.

"I just figured something out," Avery said.

"What?" Bill asked, wondering if Tuffy was really God. The Church of Tuffy. Somehow, it just didn't have that ring. Tuffy's Redeemed Church? Nope. He remembered the interview with Mimi's aunt and thought about what that good woman would have to say if he tried to tell her Tuffy was holding God.

"Those defenses the Adar have on their side," Avery said, looking around to ensure nobody would overhear.

"Yes?"

"They're not for us. They're for if . . . when the Titcher over-whelm us."


"The largest nuclear weapon we have in the inventory is the Mk-81," the national security advisor said, nervously. "That's right at two megatons. You're saying that that will only close the gate for, what? A couple of weeks?"

"Maybe three," Bill said. "Right now it's been closed for more than a month. And I somehow suspect that something that size wouldn't shut down all the gates simultaneously."

"We've converted Mk-81s and mounted them at the three gates," the secretary of defense said. "But at that rate . . ."

"A potential of a nuke every three weeks on a potential twenty-two gates," Bill replied. "And that assumes that every one works; the failure rate for nuclear weapons we're not even considering."

"True," the national security advisor said, biting her lip. "To be sure, we should have two or three at each gate. And you don't have any idea what this weapon system they use is?"

"No, ma'am," Bill said. "That is, I've got a couple of theories but nothing I can test."

"Between twenty-two and sixty-six nuclear weapons every three weeks," the secretary of defense said, shaking his head. "We're going to have to begin scrapping our nuclear arsenal and converting them for gate closure. We're going to have to go back into the nuke building business. In ten years we're going to have to have a flock of breeder reactors just to keep up with the plutonium usage. And if any of the devices fail . . ."

"Then we're going to have to retake the gate," Bill answered. "Wherever it is, from Eustis to Saskatchewan. And the only way we've been able to do that is by nukes."

"And we're only set up at the active gates, anyway," the national security advisor pointed out. "Dr. Weaver, are you *sure* they won't destabilize all the gates with one nuke?"

"No, ma'am," Bill said. "But I wouldn't have expected them to destabilize the way they did at all. It may destabilize some, it may destabilize all of them. It may only destabilize the local gate. It's something that we just don't know and haven't experimented with."

"Could you?" the President asked.

"Certainly," Bill replied. "Test it on one of the gates that is in an out-of-the-way area. Drop a nuke in it and see if it destabilizes the whole track." He thought about it for a moment and then nodded. "I think Track Four would be best. There's a gate in Northern Ohio, out in the country. The planet on the other side is a low atmospheric pressure planet with virtually no life. Certainly nothing sentient that we've encountered. Understand, sir, it *will* irradiate the immediate area on our side, just as the blast at Eustis irradiated Staunton. But we can do the test."

"Nothing more remote?" the President asked.

"There are a couple of bosons out in the desert areas," Bill said. "We could probably test open them and see what's on the other side. Or, maybe, do a link between two bosons in deserted areas, but that would leave one nuke on the Earth. I think that would definitely violate the test ban treaty."

"Not to mention ruin any chance of reelection," the President said, dryly. "Dr. Weaver, on my authority prepare to send a nuke through the Mississippi gate; get the Titcher over there off our backs for the time being at least. Cleanup can be arranged." He reached into the interior pocket of his jacket, pulled out a card that looked somewhat like an American Express Gold Card and shook his head. "When I came into office, we were, more or less, at peace. Since then we've had 9/11, the Iraq War and now this. No President had authorized the use of a nuclear weapon since 1945. Now I'm getting to the point I'm wearing out the plastic on this thing. Dr. Weaver, find a better way. We must all pray to God that you find a better way."

"Yes, Mr. President," Bill said. "And you should really talk to my counterpart among the Adar sometime, Mr. President."

"Why?" the President asked, coldly.

"He said almost the same thing to me yesterday. That I should pray to God."

"Mrs. Wilson, I really need to talk to Mimi alone," Bill said.

As Mrs. Wilson had predicted, with the exception of very occasional "local interest" programming when the news was slow, and it had rarely been slow lately, the media seemed to have forgotten Mimi and Tuffy.

The Wilsons lived in a ranch house in west Orlando, an older neighborhood but pleasant and not run down, probably built during the first rush of construction after Disney World was completed. It had a pleasant "Old Florida" feel with oaks in the yard that had grown well in the succeeding thirty years.

The interior was neat as a pin and done in a country manner. Mimi had been carefully dressed for the interview in a flowery dress, Tuffy perched on her shoulder. She was seated on the same plaid couch that had been in the news broadcast, which turned out to be in a "Florida Room," a room filled with windows to bring the light indoors. Bill sat to one side in an overstuffed, matching armchair. Mrs. Wilson was seated beside Mimi, on the far side from Tuffy he noticed, eyeing him warily.

"I don't think that's good," Mrs. Wilson said. "I don't think it's proper."

"Ma'am," Bill said, as politely as he could. "I'm here at the direction of the President of the United States to ask Mimi some questions. If you want to stay, what you have to understand is that the questions, and any answers that I might get, are matters of National Security. You can't ever talk about them."

"You're going to ask Mimi the questions, aren't you?" Mrs. Wilson said, puzzled. "What about her talking about them?"

"I've got a feeling that she won't," Bill replied. "It has to do with Tuffy. I've met other aliens like him, I think. I need to ask *him* the questions, frankly. I'm just hoping that he'll answer."

"People have asked him things before," Mrs. Wilson said.

"They're not me," Bill replied. "If you're staying, you have to understand that this is like knowing the names of spies or knowing how to build nuclear weapons. You can't ever let *anyone* know that you even know those things."

"Do you?" Mimi asked, suddenly.

Bill looked at her and shrugged. "If I did, I couldn't tell you."

"Auntie," Mimi said. "Tuffy asks you, nicely, if you could let us talk. Alone. He doesn't think that you would like some of the things they have to talk about."

"What about you, honey?" Mrs. Wilson asked.

"I'll be okay, Auntie," Mimi replied in very close to a monotone. "The Lord is my shepherd."

Mrs. Wilson considered this carefully and then stood up. "You going to be long?"

"I doubt it," Bill replied. "If we are, it's going to have to be a very strange conversation."

Mrs. Wilson, with occasional backward glances, left the room.

"What are you?" Mimi asked. "You're a doctor you said."

"I'm a physicist," Bill answered. "I'm called a doctor because I went to college a lot."

"What's a physicist?" Mimi asked.

"A person who studies how the world works," Bill answered. "Why gravity pulls things down."

"Because it likes us," Mimi answered then giggled. "Tuffy says that gravity is the world giving us a hug. I'm going to be a physicist, too, when I grow up. I need to know the words. For Tuffy. He's smart, so smart I feel dumb all the time. But he helps me with my work. He doesn't do it for me, but he explains how I can do it. School is getting pretty boring."

"Have you told anyone else that?" Bill asked.

"No, Tuffy said I shouldn't," Mimi replied. "My teachers just think I'm really smart. They don't know Tuffy's smarter than them. He's smarter than you, too. And he says he's met you before. Not at the place where everything blew up. Someplace else. I don't understand what he's saying. Something about between the small bits."

"In the space between the atoms," Bill said, wonderingly.

"He says something like that. Even smaller."

"Can you tell Tuffy I need to close the gates?" Bill said. "There are bad monsters coming through. They'll destroy everything. I don't think you would be killed, I think Tuffy would probably protect you. But everything else will be gone. There won't be any colleges for you to go to."

Mimi considered this carefully and then looked at the giant spider on her shoulder.

"Tuffy says I don't know the words," Mimi replied, softly. "I don't know the mathematics. He's been showing me some of it, but we're not far beyond something called algebra. He says that's not even close, yet. He can't say the words." She looked at the spider again and nodded.

"Tuffy says, when you take a grain of sand and cut it, then cut it again and again, getting smaller and smaller, when you get to the smallest bits that you can possibly cut. When you get to the bits that are smaller than those, bits that won't cut because they flow away like air, like water, like trying to cut sunshine, that is the secret of closing the gates. But you need a lot of them. More than he thinks you can make. Enough that they get in the space between the gates, in the space between the smallest bits and smaller, and push the gates apart. The gates are the lock and the key to the lock as well." Mimi grabbed her head and shook it, a faint trickle of tears coming out of her eyes.

"Tuffy says that's as much as I can take," she said, in a very small voice, suddenly just a six-year-old girl who was old beyond her years. "He says I shouldn't talk about it right now. That if the bad monsters come he'll take me in his arms, as Jesus took up the small children, and take me to a place where there aren't any monsters."

"Mimi," Bill said, softly. "I'm going to do everything I can to make sure the monsters don't come here and you don't have to go away. And thank you for your help. You're a good girl, the best girl in the world, and Tuffy's a great friend to all of us."

"Can you really keep the monsters from coming?" Mimi asked.

"If I can find a small enough knife," Bill replied, looking at the shifting dust motes in the light through the window.

It was three A.M. and Bill still couldn't sleep. He'd ridden back to the encampment around the anomaly at two, sure that he was exhausted enough from riding all over North Orlando to turn his mind off. But it hadn't happened. It wasn't functioning right, either, twisted in the mire of images. Tuffy, the shattered man, patrol cars with evil police, the grains of dust in the light, bosons that had happy faces on them. Ray Chen smiling as he pressed a button that changed the world. He picked and pried at particle theory, but it was no use. He'd had a drink and that hadn't helped; it just seemed to make him think faster and more chaotically. Finally he'd gotten up from the couch where he'd been sitting and made his way from shadow to shadow until he reached his exercise bike and started furiously pumping.

He'd been at it for an hour, trying to use up all the energy in his body so that maybe his mind would rest, when the door to his trailer opened and Robin walked in.

"I heard the squeaking of that damned thing from over in my trailer," Robin said.

"Sorry," Bill replied, letting it coast to a stop. "I just can't get my mind to work. It's spinning around like an out-of-control boson. Occupational hazard."

"Tried having a drink?" she asked, stepping into the trailer and flipping on the light over the stove. She was wearing a robe and bunny slippers.

"Yeah," Bill said, leaning on the bike and frowning.

"A glass of warm milk . . . perhaps?" she intoned with a faint accent.

"Maybe an Ovaltine?" Bill replied, smiling. "I wish there was a book in some musty room. But all there is are these strange dream images and hints that I think I'm supposed to be smart enough to figure out."

"You've lost some hair," Robin said, frowning. She walked over and touched where some had fallen out.

"Radiation damage," Bill replied, shrugging. "It'll grow back. Most of it."

"Anything else wrong?" she asked.

"My white blood cell count dropped for a while," Bill admitted, frowning. "Other than that, no damage."

"None?" Robin asked, rolling the word off of her tongue.

"Nope," Bill said, finally getting the hint.

"QUARKS!" Bill shouted.

"What?" Robin panted, clearly exasperated. "Is that a normal thing to shout at a moment like this? Usually it's 'Oh, My, God!'"

"It's what they're talking about!" Bill said, taking her face in his hands. "Quarks!"

"I have *no* idea what you are talking about," Robin said, coldly. "But if you do not return to the business at hand you're going to be unable to explain it to anyone. Except, maybe, if I'm kind, as a soprano."

"Oh, right. Sorry."

"The key to the gate is quarks," Bill said. He had more to go on at this point than just raw speculation. With that link in hand he had seen the theory of gate formation clearly and had even worked out most of the physics. He hadn't waited for much in the way

of peer evaluation; among other things he was as anxious as the
government to classify the data. Because it worked as a weapon
as well as a gate. "When the Chen Anomaly formed we didn't
have a universe inversion; we had a high rate of unlinked quark
emissions. That was what caused the explosion."

"How high a rate?" the national security advisor asked.

"Oh, the total emission was probably right at two or three
hundred thousand particles," Bill said.

"That's all?" the President asked. "I mean, these are smaller
than atoms, right? It takes a lot more uranium than that to get
a nuclear blast . . ."

"Yes, sir," Bill replied. "But their destructive power is orders
of magnitude higher than any substance except strange matter.
And we don't have any theory on how to form either one in
any quantity. Even the biggest supercollider only forms one or
two at a time and those almost immediately link. But the point
is that we *may* be able to adjust one of the inactive bosons to
form a stream of unique quarks, one particular type, strange,
charmed, whatever. That way, they don't link at all; it's like
pushing the same poles of a magnet together. If we can, we
can capture them and move them to one of the gates. When
it opens, we pop them in and get either a big explosion, low
in neutron emission, on the far side or, possibly, we collapse
the gate. I'm virtually certain that a large enough quantity *will*
collapse the gate. Permanently. It will not only close the gate
it will eliminate the bosons on either side."

"Hold on," the national security advisor said. "I know just
enough about quarks to know that they *always* link. A muon is
two quarks, right?"

"Yes," Bill said, frowning. "But they have to have the right
color to link . . ."

"Color?" the President said, puzzled.

"Ai-yai-yai," Bill said, frowning again. "Okay, quarks are
described as coming in flavors and colors. Why? Because they
were discovered by physicists who didn't have much else to do
but come up with strange terms. The point is that you have to
have a quark and an antiquark of two different colors to create
a muon. In this case, we'll create a stream of a single type of

quark, probably strange since that seems to be the easiest to create for some reason."

"You've already been experimenting with it?" the NSA asked.

"Oh, yes," Bill replied. "Otherwise we'd be spinning our wheels. The problem isn't tuning the boson to produce them, it's capturing them. . . ."

"And you're going to do that, how?" the NSA asked, fascinated.

"We're looking at two different possibilities," Bill admitted. "We might put two bosons in close proximity. Have one produce a stream of similar color muons, ones that can't bind to strange quarks, and set up a magnetic field to create a capture bottle. The muons will pass through the field and create a sort of stream field that will surround the quarks. I'm not sure that one will work but it's less energy intensive than the other way."

"What's the other way?" the President asked.

"Well," Bill said, his face working, "the other way is to create a miniature white dwarf. But that's going to take a whole lot of power."

"A white dwarf?" the defense secretary said, grinning. "You're serious?"

"Yes, sir, Mr. Secretary," Bill replied. "All a white dwarf is is a collection of electrons. What we'll do is create an electron field and then use a magnetic field to sort of cup it. Then we'll shoot a whole bunch of quarks into the cup and wrap the electrons around the quarks, compressing them at the same time, sort of like catching water in your hand. Some of the quarks will escape but, hopefully, not enough to destroy the containment vessel. The only problem is, maintaining it will require a whole lot of electricity. But it will work for sure."

"And then you slip this . . . device into the gate?" the secretary asked. "And that destroys the bosons."

"Yes, sir," Bill said.

"Destroying whole universes?" the President asked.

"Errr . . . possibly," Bill replied. "But current theory is changing as to the nature of bosons; at this point theory is pointing to them being gates to other universes, or links, rather than the universes themselves."

"How much?" the secretary of defense asked. "How many particles?"

"Probably on the order of a million, Mr. Secretary," Bill said. "We'll have to see what the rate of emission is of the boson."

"How long to do the experiment?" the national security advisor asked.

"There's a boson conveniently settled in Death Valley," Bill replied. "We'll have to assemble the materials and set up a base camp. A week, maybe less. Getting enough power to it will be the key."

"I want Dr. Weaver to have whatever he needs to get this experiment running," the President said to the secretary of defense.

"I'll see that he gets it," the secretary replied. "You're saying that these things are the equivalent of nuclear weapons?"

"Yes, Mr. Secretary," Bill said, frowning. "More like nuclear explosive material. That's why I've been pretty careful about spreading the theory around. If the theory is right, making unlinked quarks and then capturing them is going to be relative child's play. Any decent physicist with access to a boson could make them."

"Giving every two-bit country on Earth nuclear weapons." The national security advisor winced.

"Close one Pandora's Box and we open another," the President said.

"That's science for you, Mr. President."

"Remember Ray Chen," Bill said as his hand hovered over the initiator.

The base camp had been set up ten miles from the inactive boson. A bunker, constructed of concrete filled sandbags and steel beams, had been built a mere five miles away. Comfortably cooled by an air-conditioning unit, similarly protected, it had independent power and materials to dig out if it were covered by an explosion. It was there that the team had assembled to study the anticipated quark formation.

In the end the muon field plan had been a bust. A brief, and mildly traumatic, experiment had proven that they'd be unable to hold the field closed well enough to capture sufficient quarks. Bill was almost sure that tinkering would fix the problem, but they didn't have time to play around with the idea so they'd set up the white dwarf bottle instead.

The problem, of course, would be moving it; they were going to be using several megawatts of power just to create the field and about a half megawatt per hour, if they could spin the electrons in a toroid, to maintain it. The Army was trying to find a portable half-megawatt per hour generator, thus far with little success.

Mark was there, having assembled another whatchamacal-lit device on less than a week's notice. Bill Earp from FEMA, who pointed out that for once the agency might as well get there *before* the disaster. Sergeants Garcia and Crichton who had been useful military liaisons. Robin had been writing code, with Garcia's fumble fingered help, eighteen hours a day for the last four. The only person missing was Command Master Chief Miller, who Bill, after a certain amount of argument, had sent off on a different project. But everything was finally in place and it was time to find out if it worked.

"Let's see what happens," Bill Earp said, inserting earplugs. "Everyone got their plugs in? Safety first."

Bill already had earplugs in and he hoped he wouldn't need them. If everything went as planned nothing would happen, outside of some changes in very sensitive instruments.

He looked around one more time

"Everybody ready?" Bill asked.

"Ready, sir," Garcia and Crichton said.

"Let's get it over with," Robin said, yawning.

"Gotta test it sometime," Mark said.

"Just proud to be here," Earp intoned.

Bill pressed the button.

Nothing blew up. The lights dimmed rather deeply, though.

He looked over at Garcia who was frowning.

"Something's happening," the sergeant said. "We've got fluctuations in the magnetic containment bottle."

"Power's going somewhere," Mark added. "Quite a bit. We keep this up and we're going to start affecting California's power requirements in a bit."

"More fluctuations," Garcia added a few minutes later as everyone was congratulating themselves. He had stayed glued to his monitor, however, his brow furrowed in a frown. "The electrons are starting to slip. I think we're . . ."

There was a very slight ground shudder and everyone looked at the external monitors. In the distance was dust rising from a small explosion where their expensive and difficult to build quark generator now appeared to be so much metal and plastic scrap.

" . . . losing it," Garcia finished. "Negative signal."

"Back to the drawing board," Bill said.

"It looks like it's working this time," Garcia said, watching his monitors carefully. "The Quark Hotel is in operation."

Analysis of the data that they had gotten before the explosion indicated that some of the quarks, rather than being fully trapped in the bottle, had gotten caught in a magnetic eddy. When their local charge overcame the eddy they reacted, violently, with the surrounding matter and released the rest of the quarks to do so even more energetically.

The containment bottle had been upgraded and redesigned so that, as Garcia put it: "Quarks go in, but none get out."

It had been instantly dubbed the Quark Hotel.

"Negative radiation emissions," Crichton said. "But the rate of entry is really low. It looks like only a quark per second."

"Not fast enough," Bill said. "We need to increase the rate by a couple of orders of magnitude."

"Up the power input?" Mark asked. "We need to increase the size of the bottle anyway."

"Maybe," Bill replied. "We're probably only catching a fraction of the potential stream. But we don't have the generators for that. We're already pushing a hundred kilowatts through at the moment. To up it we'll need big power. I don't think we can do it here unless we can get some really monstrous generators and then we'll be hauling in diesel so fast the experiment is going to be pretty damned obvious."

"So what do we do?" Robin asked.

"Shut it down," Weaver replied. "We can do it, we just need another boson that has access to a lot of power. Set the quarks on battery backup. We need to see if we can *move* the containment bottle, anyway. I'll have to kick this upstairs."

"So that's where we're at," Bill said. "We can make the material, we can even contain it and move it, with relative safety. But we need orders of magnitude more power. I don't think the rate of capture will be linear, more like asymptotic . . ."

"What?" the President said. "You're usually pretty good about avoiding extreme jargon, Dr. Weaver, but . . ."

"That means for a little more power we'll get a lot more result, Mr. President," Bill said. "But we're still looking at needing to have something on the order of a megawatt or more of power. We're going to need to move someplace that has that sort of power available."

"Savannah River?" the secretary of defense said, looking over at the national security advisor.

"Oak Ridge, Savannah River, Hanford," the NSA said with a shrug. "All have secure facilities, all have access to enormous power. Take your pick."

"Savannah River," Bill replied. "Mark worked there. He'll know where to set up and who to see when we need something. And besides, there ain't much left of Oak Ridge."

"Get moving, Doctor," the President said. "We may not have much time." He looked up as someone entered the Situation Room. The agitated messenger walked up to the secretary of defense and whispered in his ear at which message the secretary's face suddenly looked every day of his seventy-odd years.

"We're out."

# 10

Despite the logistics involved it had taken far less time to set up than the period the gates were destabilized. Collective 47 had a total of nine subcollectives to draw upon, less the late Collective 15379. Bosons were energy intensive to generate but six of the collectives had created at least one, in some cases two. Collective 47 was able to generate three.

In addition each of the collectives had disregarded trade and internal improvements to increase combat unit production. Each of the potential gates, and the three that had previously been opened, now had an overwhelming force stationed by it ranging from class one to class seven ground combat units along with twenty percent more air defense units than standard. The biologicals of the new world would not be permitted to throw their fission weapons onto the bridgeheads this time.

Last, and certainly least, all three of Collective 47's subraces had been levied for support. In some cases this included combat units. Primarily it had been contribution of biological materials to be converted to Collective combat units. One gate had been entirely ceded to the subraces and would be assaulted by a combination of Mreee and N!T!Ch, using weaponry the

N!T!Ch had obtained from the Slen. They, too, however, would be supported by Collective air defense units.

A new subcollective, designated 16743, had been established at the locus of the former 15379. It was in its infancy, a colony organization rather than a truly functioning collective, but it served to support the forces sent to those open gates by the other collectives. In addition, Mreee biologicals were being added to the subcollective to accelerate its formation; as the holder of two of the open gates it was an important strategic locus and needed the boost.

All was in readiness when the gate fractal stabilized.

"*All Collectives,*" Collective 47 emitted. "*Initiate gate formation.*"

Even for the collective this took a few moments. In the interim, Collective 16743 sent a weak emission.

"*Fission detonation, Gate 763, Gate 765, Gate 769. Assault formations destroyed. Gates closed. Twenty percent damage to collective. Initiating repairs.*"

Best to get this over with as quickly as possible. Collective 47 had considered using the race on the far side as a subrace, but it was simply too dangerous. All would have to be destroyed.

"*All Collectives,*" Collective 47 emitted as the gates popped open. "*Initiate assault.*"

Dave Pearce threw his queen of diamonds on the pile and watched as Jim Horn covered it with a king. That was okay, it was his sole diamond. When somebody brought out that ace they were hoarding they were in for a surprise.

Dave was whistling in his teeth, a sure sign that he was out of one suit, Sergeant Horn thought to himself. He knew the song, vaguely, something about Hallack or Harlack or something. Pearce was always whistling it, to the point that it got on his nerves. Especially when it meant the specialist was out of a suit and waiting to hop on his ace. You'd think that with an ace, king combination, you'd get at least two tricks. But in the last two weeks he swore that he'd seen every possible combination of tricks and rubbers possible in the game of spades. There wasn't much else to do but play.

The duty was incredibly, unmitigatingly, boring. Hell of a lot more comfortable than Iraq, though. The track three boson had formed in the living room of a suburban home in Woodmere, Ohio, a suburb of Cleveland. After the danger of the boson became evident, the house, then the surrounding houses, then a good part of the town, had been evacuated. The house, a pleasant single-story ranch, had been cleared by moving crews and then leveled, as had several of the surrounding houses and most of their landscaping, creating open fields of fire. Last, defensive positions had been scattered around the boson and units of the Ohio National Guard were established in the positions. Well, were supposed to be established in the positions. There was always one member of the unit on the tracks at all times, but most of the rest of the brigade had settled in the abandoned houses; they were far more comfortable. The local electric company, as a gesture of patriotism, had left the electricity running. So the troops had hot and cold running water, a place to sleep out of the weather and flush toilets. Cots, and then beds, had appeared. Except for the boredom, which was relieved by television and endless games of spades, not to mention Nintendo, Sega and Gameboys and for a fortunate few internet connections, it wasn't bad duty. Definitely better than the six months the unit had spent in the Sunni Triangle.

They all knew that the balloon could go up at any time and they'd been told it could occur without warning. But they also figured that the big brains would give them a little warning.

So Sergeant Horn was more than a little surprised when he threw his ace down, fully prepared for Pearce to trump the damned thing, and was rewarded, instead, by the explosion of a claymore mine.

Claymores were directional mines, a small box on legs that could be pointed at the direction an enemy was likely to approach from, in this case directly at the inactive boson. Normally they were command detonated, that is a soldier would close a "clacker" which sent an electrical signal to the mine telling it that it was time to perform its function, namely spilling out 700 ball bearings at approximately the speed of rifle bullets.

When the combat engineers set up the defenses for the boson, however, they laid in a rather extensive minefield around the concrete slab that had once been a ranch house. The first line of defense was a series of claymore mines on trip-wires, so that anything coming through the gate, should it form, would be met by a hail of ball bearings.

It also served as an efficient signal that the shit had just hit the fan.

The four card players tossed down their hands and picked up their weapons, rushing to their bunkers as fast as they could. But there were nine people currently in the house and by the time Sergeant Horn squeezed through the press at the door, more mines were exploding. And then the first incoming hit the house.

The plasma weapon hit on the roof and tossed burning debris down into the living room, setting fire to the table where they had been playing and tossing burning cards through the air.

The overpressure from the blast threw Sergeant Horn and Specialist Pearce out of the door in a tangle of limbs. The sergeant was the first to recover, sitting up and shaking his head, then grabbing his M-16 and continuing on to his bunker. Or where his bunker had been. Which was now a hole in the ground.

There was a protective berm that had been thrown up around the boson and Horn crawled to the top of it, looking over the edge. What met his eyes was a nightmare.

The collectives had not bothered with assaulting the gates with low-class ground combat units. Coming through the gate was a segmental class seven combat unit. It was tossing plasma charges off its horns at everything that looked like a threat. Four Abrams were smoking wrecks as were all the Bradleys and most of the bunkers that were supposed to shelter the infantry. And the thing just kept coming out of the gate, like a giant nightmare centipede, pouring fire in all directions.

As he watched, though, the thing hit one of the antitank mines the engineers had installed. The massive explosion punched up through the thing, sending a self-forging round upward through the first segment. The secondary explosion, even at five hundred meters, tossed the sergeant off the berm and down into the grass yard of the burning house.

He shook some life back into himself, again, and climbed back up the berm, wishing that his LBE hadn't been in the bunker. All he had to fight with was a single magazine for the M-16.

It wasn't going to matter, much, though. The front segment of the monster was a smoking wreck but it had already been detached and the thing continued to extrude. Now fire was leaping into the sky, intercepting incoming rounds of artillery. There were more antitank mines, but Horn was pretty sure there wouldn't be enough.

"Anybody got a radio!" Horn yelled. "Call somebody and tell 'em this thing ain't going to stop any time soon!"

"This is Bruce Gelinas in Woodmere, Ohio, where units of the Ohio National Guard have again been repulsed from an attempt to retake the Cleveland Gate. Fighting is reportedly heavy and from the looks of the casualties I'd have to agree. Besides the segmented tank there are now rhino tanks and something like large spider tanks, along with large numbers of dog aliens and thorn-throwers. The unit has had to retreat, twice, and now is simply trying to slow the monsters down as well as it can. More units are being brought up but the situation looks very bad."

"Bruce have you been able to talk to anyone from the National Guard, there?" the anchorwoman in New York asked.

"No, the spokespeople don't seem to be available," Bruce said. "From what I heard they were issued weapons and have been sent in to replace losses in the infantry units, which are taking a real beating. I spoke, briefly, with a sergeant who had been injured in the initial assault. . . ."

The scene cut to a recording of a soldier on a stretcher, his left arm in a thick bandage and scorch marks on his uniform. His face was partially bandaged and he could only see out of one eye.

"Sergeant Horn, you were part of the gate defense force?" the reporter asked.

"We couldn't stop it," the soldier said, almost incoherently. "It took out the Abrams before we even knew it was there, it was blowing up everything in sight! It took three mines and it didn't stop it, it just kept coming!"

"We have further reports that an attempt to deliver strategic nuclear weapons was unsuccessful," the reporter said, again live. "Orders to prepare for a strike were issued and we were warned, then nothing. Heavy fire could be seen from the direction of the gate and it apparently intercepted and destroyed the incoming nuclear rounds. As I said, at this point it looks as if nothing can stop the Titcher. This is Bruce Gelinas, in Woodmere, Ohio."

"Thank you for that . . . disturbing report, Bruce," the anchorwoman said. "Breakouts are reported at all of the formerly inactive bosons, ranging from Georgia to Canada. In addition to Titcher attacks, the gate in Oakdale, Kentucky, appears to be sending out Mreee soldiers and some sort of giant, silver spiders. We go now to Erik Kittlelsen who is reporting, live, from near the front lines. Erik?"

"We're live in Oakdale, Kentucky," the reporter shouted at the microphone just as an explosion occurred, very close, in the background. "I'm with Alpha Company, 1st Battalion, 149th Infantry Battalion of the Kentucky National Guard!" He looked over his shoulder at the wall of earth behind him and then back at the camera. "The attackers here seem to be Mreee and what the military now believes to be Nitch, the giant spider species we had previously only heard about from the Mreee. It's clear, now, that the Mreee were allies of the Titcher all along!"

"Erik, we're getting some very disturbing reports from other defenders," the anchorwoman said. "How are things, there?"

"Not good, Roberta," the reporter shouted, then hit the ground as an enormous explosion occurred close enough that the flash could be seen even with the camera pointed at the wall of the trench. In a moment he was back up again, though, and the camera was back on him. "The Mreee and the Nitch are using some sort of homing explosive round. Even if they appear to be missing, the round tracks in on our combat vehicles and bunkers! Infantry are doing better but not much. And they have antiair and antiartillery support from some sort of Titcher weaponry. They're holding them to a perimeter for the time being, but more of the Mreee and Nitch are pouring through the gate and the gate is on a hilltop, they can drop fire on our lines and it's hard to even get a head up with all the . . ."

The screen went blank then showed the anchorwoman again.

"We appear to be having some technical difficulties," the woman said. "We'll try to get Erik back as soon as possible."

"Not this side of the grave." Miller grunted, setting down his beer.

"No," Bill said, through steepled fingers.

They were alone in the physics trailer at the anomaly site. The SEAL was wearing a skin-tight jumpsuit, and Weaver fatigues. Bill looked up at the SEAL and shook his head.

"You smell like a goat," Bill commented.

"It's your fault," Miller replied, noncommittally. "What are you going to do?"

"Why does everyone want to know what *I'm* going to do?" Weaver replied, angrily.

"Because you're always the man with the plan," Miller explained, shrugging, and taking another sip of his beer. "So . . . what are you going to do?"

"By the time we create enough quarks to matter, we won't be able to get to any of the gates," Bill said, thoughtfully. "Even if we were set up in Savannah already. Which we're not. And we can't knock back any of the assaults with nukes, because we've exhausted half our subs firing into them to no effect. Something the news guys apparently haven't found out. But there is one bright spot."

"What?"

"We know that with the right technology, SDI works," Bill said, still in a thoughtful tone.

"Very funny."

"I think there's only one thing to do," Bill said, sitting back.

"And that is?"

"Beg."

"Beg the Titcher to not kill us?" Miller asked. "I don't think that's gonna work."

"No, beg for help," Weaver replied, pulling out his cell phone. The charge was low; he'd forgotten to charge it up last night. He hoped it would last long enough. "First I'm gonna beg for an airplane. A few. One for me, one or more for you."

"Why?"

"I'm going to France. You're going to Kentucky."

"I think I'm getting the better deal," Miller said, watching the world end, live.

"We need Tchar," Bill said, striding through the Adar gate with Admiral Avery. "Even more important, we need that artass guy."

"You don't speak directly to him," Avery pointed out. "That's important. If he's not available we can't even ask where he is."

"We need somebody like him," Bill replied. "Somebody who can make policy decisions."

"We get what we get," Avery said.

Avery spoke to one of the Adar guards on the gate and was directed to the meeting hall where they were directed to sit in one of the cubicles.

"Our world's dying while we sit here," Bill pointed out.

"I know that as well as you do, Doctor," the admiral replied, tartly, and Bill remembered that he had started off life as a "nuke," working the ballistic submarine fleet. His remarkable ability at languages had been put to use later. The admiral, in his own way, was a warrior, a man who had carried a key that could lead to the extermination of millions of lives and who had run the risk on every deployment of having to use it.

"But," the admiral added, more thoughtfully, "the longer we sit here, I suspect, the better."

"Why?" Bill asked.

"If we'd been received immediately, we would have gotten, at most, Tchar," the admiral said. "If we're being kept waiting it's because someone who *can* discuss policy is being summoned and briefed."

Bill shrugged, then pulled out a calculator and started tapping keys.

It had been a four-hour ride from McCoy to France in another F-15. Bill was logging up some serious hours in that jet at this point. Then a brief ride by helicopter; one had been waiting with the rotors already turning when he landed. By the time he got to the gate, the news had worsened. Huge areas around the gates had been opened by the Titcher and, in those where the areas were in view from a safe distance, the Titcher "fungus" was already spreading. Even if he closed the gates, it might be too late to save the world.

Finally, after an interminable wait that turned out to be all of twenty minutes, another Adar came to the cubicle and waved for them to follow. They were taken to the same meeting room that had been used during their previous, less hurried, visit. Tchar was waiting for them and so, to Bill's relief, was the unnamed artass.

"Tchar," Bill said, inclining his head.

Tchar spoke hurriedly to the admiral, who shook his head.

"They've already been informed of the breakout," Avery translated. "They ask if you think it's possible to stop the Titcher."

"I'm not the Army Chief of Staff," Bill replied. "But the frank answer is: no."

"Why then are you here?" Avery translated. "Do you seek shelter for your people? Our foods cannot be mutually consumed. There is no way that we can support many of you on this side. If you, yourself, and a few others wish to flee, that can be granted."

"No," Bill said, "I've come for help. I have spoken to God, as you told me to, and he has told me that there is a way to break the gates. But it requires a large amount of quarks, free quarks. We have figured out a way to produce them, but not enough and not in time. I am hoping that you have such a way, such a weapon. I think you do."

"And if you get such a weapon, even supposing we have it, what would you do with it?" Tchar asked.

"There is one gate I believe possible to retake," Bill answered. "I would use it on that gate. It should shatter the entire fractal, if the math is right. At the very least it will shut all the gates, giving us time to retake them and set up more effective defenses at each. But, again, my understanding is that it will turn them off, perhaps more."

The artass suddenly leaned forward, examining Bill with the single eye in his forehead. He peered at him for a moment, then spoke.

"You say you have spoken to God," Avery translated. "What did he say."

"To cut matter to the smallest form it becomes, when it will no longer cut because it is light, it is water. That is the secret of the gates," Bill answered, staring back.

"And if I told you we had tried this method and failed?" the artass asked.

"I'd say you didn't use enough," Bill replied. He turned back to Tchar and nodded. "I think I should add something. When the Titcher take our planet, they will gain access to the bosons already generated and the boson generator. That means *any* bosons you make will be potential gates. You could find yourself in the same predicament we are."

Tchar didn't answer, just sat looking at Avery. Nor did he turn his head to the artass.

"Please," Bill said, looking at the artass, now. "In the name of all that is holy, in the name of God, please. Help us."

The artass looked at him out of both side eyes then said a word.

"I don't recognize that one," Avery said. "*Artune a das?* There are some similarities to other words. Destroyer of Small Things?"

"There is a device," Tchar said, abruptly standing up. "Come with me."

He led them out of the building to a rank of small cars, somewhat like golf carts. All four piled in one and then he put it in gear.

Bill had previously seen the Adar drive but had never been in any of their vehicles. The thing looked like a golf cart and was open on all sides but it drove like a Ferrari. He held on for dear life as Tchar, who apparently considered this no more than normal, rocketed across the compound and around a series of buildings. Pedestrians, clearly, did not have the right of way and he nearly smashed some poor human that had never heard of Adar driving techniques.

They stopped at the base of the mountains that half ringed the site where there was an open corridor leading into the mountain.

Tchar and the artass led the way; the guards at the entrance, which had the sort of blast doors Bill had only seen at a very few military installations, stood aside at their approach, saluting cross armed in the Adar way.

"I would be delighted to figure out who the artass is," Avery whispered as they strode down the tile-lined corridor. It was sloped downward, with several doglegs, heading deep into the bowels of the mountain.

"I am K'Tar'Daoon," the artass said in very clear English. "The Unitary Council is composed of nine members, each with their own separate area of responsibility. We do not break it out the same way that you humans do. I would be something like your secretary of high technology defense. I am currently the rotating head of the Unitary Council."

"Holy crap," Bill whispered, then realized that the question had not been translated. "Sorry."

"You said that you spoke to God," the artass replied. "And I sensed no lie in you. You are a fortunate man to have been able to speak to God, twice. Such a person does not deserve to die at the hands of the Titcher." He paused in front of a blast door and made a complicated hand gesture. "On the other hand, the philosopher/scientist Edroon pointed out that alliances are based upon mutual need as well as friendship. Your point about the Titcher taking your planet was well timed." There were guards in front of this door, as well, and Bill considered them to be nervous. It was hard to read body language among an alien species, but they didn't look very happy.

The artass placed a hand on a pad and then leaned his forehead on a curved plate. This placed his center eye against the plate and Bill suspected something like a retina scan was being conducted. As the artass leaned back the door swung ponderously open.

It was not, by any stretch of the imagination, the last door to be accessed. There were a total of four, the last requiring that two more Adar, who were awaiting them, give their identity and approval.

When the last door was opened it revealed a small room

with shelves along one wall. There were several devices on the shelves, including one long line of what looked like small artillery shells. On the opposite wall was a vault which the artass opened by a combination. It was the first nonelectronic security device Bill had seen.

The artass pulled a box from the vault and then closed it. But Bill got a glimpse in the vault and saw that there were two more. The vault was, otherwise, empty.

The two stranger Adar were standing to one side as the artass came out with the box. They, too, looked strangely nervous, turning their head from side to side to watch the box that the artass carried, with apparent indifference, by one of two handles placed at either end.

The box was about a half a meter long, a quarter meter deep and wide, and colored a rather pleasant shade of violet. It appeared to be made from plastic or carbon fiber. On the top were a series of symbols and some readouts.

"I will brief you carefully upon the use of this device," the artass said. "Then I will carry it to the far side of our mutual gate. After that what you do with it will be up to you."

"Yes, sir," Bill said, eying the box warily.

"This is an ardune," the artass said. "The ardune requires a period of time to become useable." He pressed a key and a bar on the top of it outlined in blue and began slowly flashing. "It will require half a cycle, some fifteen of your hours, for it to become fully useable."

"Fifteen hours," Bill said, looking at his watch. "Got it."

"Each ardune uses a different initiator key," the artass said, pointing to the symbols. Bill noted that there were fifteen, three rows of five. "In this case, you press these five," the artass continued, not actually touching the keys. "When you do, this indicator begins to blink," he said, pointing to a readout that was, at the moment, quite dead. "You press this key and it increments up in time. It is in our sadeen which is about two thirds of your seconds."

"Okay," Bill said.

"It only increments to thirty sadeen," the artass continued. "Twenty of your seconds."

"Okay," Bill said, his stomach clenching.

"You then have to input the code again. You have thirty sadeen to reinput the code, after which the counter resets and you have to start all over again. When you complete the second input, the countdown starts."

"Okay," Bill said, breathing out. "Can I input all but the last key as long as I don't go over the thirty sadeen?"

"Yes."

"Can I turn it off?" Bill asked. "I mean, after the countdown?"

"Key the sequence again," the artass said. "If you have time."

"Key the sequence again," Bill nodded, realizing why the guards and the two other Adar, probably nearly as high rank as the artass, were eying it they way they did. This was a nuclear suicide device. "Just like a security alarm. Got it."

"A few warnings about the ardune," the artass said. "Obviously, it must be used immediately. If you get it to the other side of the gate, and it stays there, all is well. The effect around the gate area, however, may be hazardous."

*I bet*, Bill thought.

"Last warning about the ardune," the artass said. "It is heavily armored. That is because, as you surmise, the material it contains is explosive. If the armor is penetrated or the containment fails, it will predetonate. The development of material is nonlinear, however. It will be at least one of your hours before it is significantly hazardous. However, by the time it reaches full power, if the case is cracked, say by a Titcher plasma weapon, the results will be . . . unpleasant."

"What's the output?" Bill asked.

"You would define it as six hundred megatons," the artass answered. "If it does not destroy the gates, it will assuredly destroy your world, probably cracking it open and fragmenting it into space. In which case, our world will be secure."

*"Unpleasant." Understatement of the . . . of all time!*

"How do I know it won't blow up the first time I input the code?" Bill asked, sweating.

"You don't."

》     》     》

When they reached the Terran side of the gate, the artass handed Bill the bomb and then went back to his side without a backward glance. Tchar looked at Bill, unreadably, for a moment, and then stepped back through as well.

Bill looked at the admiral and shrugged.

"You going back over?" Bill asked. "I understand they've set up a greenhouse over there. If this thing goes off, on the wrong side, you'll make it."

"What's the point?" Avery replied. "All my children and grandchildren are over here. Nope, I think I'm going to pack up my tent and see if I can still get a flight back to the States. If we're going to all die, I'd rather die on my own soil."

"Well, I've got a plane to catch," Bill said, looking at the bar on the ardune. It was still barely showing any increase.

"That you do," the admiral said. "Good luck."

"Thanks."

The F-15 had state-of-the-art communications and it was in the middle of the Atlantic. It was an even better place to hold a secure conversation than most secure rooms.

"I have obtained a device from the Adar," Bill told what he'd come to think of as the Troika. "It will destabilize, probably destroy, the gates and the boson fractal. All I have to do is get it to the other side."

"That's going to be hard," the secretary of defense said. "Actually, that's a bit of an understatement. That's going to be damned near impossible."

"We're holding the Mreee, right?" Bill asked. "Can you pull forces off elsewhere and throw them at that gate? I just have to get this thing over for a few seconds and then the Titcher threat goes away, permanently. Or, at least as permanently as we're going to get. We're losing everywhere else, right? Let the Titcher have the territory, we can get it back. We just need to close the gates."

"He has a point," the national security advisor said. "You're sure this will close the gates?"

"Yes," Bill replied, definitely. But a faint quaver in his voice must have given him away.

"What are the secondary effects?" the national security advisor asked, guardedly.

"Oh, if I get it to the other side, minimal on this side," Bill answered. "I'm not even sure there will be a neutron pulse, this time. Don't see why there would be. The gates should just disappear as if they never existed."

"And if you don't get it to the other side?" the President asked. "And it goes off on this side?"

"That gates will still get shut down," Bill replied. "As long as I can get it close to one of them."

"And the secondary effects?" the national security advisor asked.

"Oh, pretty bad," Bill said, his head light. "Just about as bad as can be imagined. Some of the guys in nuke boats might be okay, if they're, say, well out in the middle of the Pacific and really deep. There's women on some of them now, right? So the human race won't be entirely eliminated. If the world doesn't crack and turn into a new asteroid belt," he added, honestly, in a voice out of nightmare.

There was a very long pause that was ended by the secretary of defense clearing his throat.

"Dr. Weaver, what sort of magnitude are we discussing here?"

"Six hundred megatons," Bill said, looking at the device in his lap.

There was another long pause.

"Dr. Weaver," the national security advisor said, in a voice that was high and strange, "I'm reminded of an expression from the Vietnam War. Something about destroying a world to save it."

"We're doomed anyway, ma'am," Bill replied, his voice firm now. "The Adar have had this capability for some time, how long I don't know, but long enough to use it on their own gate. They haven't. The question is: why?"

"Why?" the President asked in a firm tone.

"Because they're not desperate, Mr. President," Bill answered. "I guess the question is, how desperate are we?"

There was another pause.

"Mr. Secretary?" the President said.

"Sir?"

"Transfer all available forces to open the Oakdale gate," the president said. "Dr. Weaver."

"Yes, Mr. President?"

"Try very hard to set it off on the other side of the gate. And may God grant us victory on this day."

The F-15 never even returned to Orlando. Instead, taking a snaking course that followed relatively safe lanes around the area the Titcher interdicted, it flared out and landed at Louisville International, the closest airport with runways long enough. A Blackhawk—a special operations variant, he noticed—was waiting just outside the gates to the airport and as soon as Bill was in and strapped down, in one of the crew-chief seats that had a great view out the Plexiglas window, it took off. The flight started low and got lower the closer they got to the alien incursion.

Bill had thought that riding in an F-15 was wild, and it was, but even though the Blackhawk was going a fraction of the speed of the fighter, the fact that it was doing so, towards the end, actually *below* the treetops added a certain degree of frisson to the experience. So did jerking up to avoid power lines and then back down, quickly, to avoid fire from the hills to the east.

It was right at 130 miles, straight-line, from Louisville International to the Oakdale gate. Even in a Blackhawk it took over an hour to make the flight, twisting and turning at the very edge of the experienced chief warrant officer five's capability. Towards the end the chopper cut south and, keeping a ridgeline between itself and the gate, actually passed the gate to the Army assembly point in Jackson.

Naturally, Bill thought, the most assaultable gate would be just about the least accessible. The road network in the area was, to say the least, primitive. To get the bulk of the combat forces to the region required going down Highway 402 out of Lexington and through Winchester, to Highway 15. Highway 402 was a multilane highway, limited access for most of its length, and it had been taken out of civilian service to move the vast fleet of tanks and fighting vehicles that were headed for the gate. Highway 15, on the other hand, was a two lane, twisting, road that snaked through the hills in the area, hills which were just starting to leave the rolling bluegrass and edge up into the Appalachians. Highway 402 was a logjam of low-boy trailers trying to turn onto 15, which was worse.

Many of the soldiers being sent to try to retake the gate were Ohio national guardsmen who were, for reasons unexplained, being removed from defending their own homes and driven to the wilds of Kentucky. They were, to say the least, less than thrilled. Others were coming up from Tennessee, again National Guard with a leavening of air assault troops from the 101st at Fort Campbell. They took the Daniel Boone Highway, a limited access toll road that, again, had been placed in military service, and then turned north on the same Highway 15.

What the more astute soldiers noticed was the distinct lack of support vehicles. Missing from the logjam were the fuel, food and ammunition trucks they were used to seeing accompanying their formations. They had been given a basic load of ammunition and food at an assembly point in Louisville and their tanks were full. But there were no apparent plans for resupply. What that told those astute soldiers was far more grim than the fact that they were being taken away from their homes and families.

Furthermore, the assembly area in Jackson was a nightmare. The small town of a bare 2500 souls was more of an elaborate crossroads on two minor highways. It was the county seat of Breathitt County and, notably, its largest town. In an area with barely a square acre of flat land; it occupied a section of large, relatively flat, and therefore flood-prone, shoreline along the North Kentucky River.

"As a spot to assemble a battalion of tanks, much less a short division," Brigadier General Rand McKeen said, dryly, "it leaves a lot to be desired."

Low-boy trailers could be heard in the background, snorting around turns and backing and filling, trying to find places to drop all the tanks and fighting vehicles they carried. The town, even before the heavy reinforcements had arrived, had been largely abandoned and tanks now parked in yards, alleyways and streets, trying to ensure that they knew where their higher control was and, more importantly, which way the enemy might come from.

Even defining "higher" was difficult. The units were drawn from four different divisions, two brigades from Kentucky National Guard, one brigade from Ohio, one from Tennessee and a battalion of light infantry from the 101st. General McKeen, assistant division commander of the 101st, had been placed in overall command.

"And you're not an armor officer," Command Master Chief Miller noted. "Sir."

"Nope," McKeen said, smiling faintly. He was a tall, rawboned man with a lantern jaw, wearing his helmet very straight with the chinstrap neatly fastened. He also was weighted down with an infantryman's combat harness, loaded with magazines, and carried an M-4 rifle. "I'm not. But I suddenly got dumped with four brigades of National Guard armor and a direction of the President to take and hold one hilltop with them. So I guess that's what I'm going to have to do."

"Certainly you have enough forces," Bill said.

"Well . . . yes and no," McKeen replied. "The Mreee and Nitch, if that's who those spiders are, don't seem to be fighting all that hard. The local National Guard commander had positions along all the ridgelines around the boson. Some of them got pushed out and the Mreee took the town of Oakdale, pushed down the valley and took Athol and pushed over the nearest ridge towards Warcreek. But the local National Guard forces held them up in every direction, despite the Mreee having more forces and those damned rayguns of theirs. The rayguns don't appear to track in on infantry. And that's what I meant by 'yes and no.' If I go barrel-assing down 52 with all these Abrams and Bradleys, we're going to get blown to hell, Doctor. Frankly, it would have been much better to just send the whole 101st. But we're spread in penny packets on other missions. So here I sit, a light infantry specialist with a classic light infantry mission and a whole passel of mechanized infantry on my hands."

"So what are you going to do?" Bill asked.

"Take the gate," the general replied, smiling faintly again. "As to how I'm going to take it, Dr. Weaver, that's for me to know. As I understand it, my mission is to get you and your SEAL team up to the gate. And the very least, *you* have to be alive.

That is what I intend to do. *How* is up to me. The *when* is, according to my orders, up to you."

Bill looked at his watch and shook his head.

"The . . . device we need to insert will not be ready for nine more hours," the physicist said. "Can we hold on that long?"

"As long as the Titcher don't reinforce their 'allies,'" the general replied. "In fact, I'd appreciate at *least* that long to get this amazing cluster . . . stuff fixed. Normally this sort of movement would take days, for exactly the reason that you see on the roads. As it is, we're doing the best we can with the time we've got. Ten hours would be preferable."

"The device won't be ready for nine hours," Bill repeated. "Thereafter . . . well, would you like to be sitting on a nuclear hand grenade that already had the pin pulled and was just being kept from blowing up by holding down the little lever thingy?"

"Spoon," the general said, his face going blank. "Is that what this thing is?"

"Worse," Miller said, his face grim. "Much, much, *much* worse."

"The best scenario is that we get it up to the gate, through the gate and blow it on the other side," Dr. Weaver said, blowing out as he said it. "Then the gates all shut down and we all go have a beer."

"Miller time," the SEAL said, one cheek jerking up in a rictus of a smile. Weaver had explained exactly what Sanson and the rest of the platoon were guarding.

"Next best scenario, and it's a real serious drop, is that we get it *close* to the gate, this is not close enough, and it blows up," Bill said.

"How serious a drop?" the general asked.

"You don't want to know," Bill replied.

"Really," Miller said. "I wish he hadn't told me."

"That bad?" the general said, lightly. "I wish he hadn't told me, too. If you get it close to the gate and can't get it through, then what?"

"I'll blow it," Bill replied. "It will destabilize this fractal track. It might even blowback along the fractal. I'm not sure what that will do to the Adar, or to us, if it happens, but it's going to do worse to the Titcher. This is about more than America, more than any personal needs, wants and desires, more than the needs of the human race, this is about the future of multiple races. If the Titcher get out on this planet, with that runaway boson generator Ray Chen created, there's no stopping them. If we're lucky, there will be survivors in nuke boats at sea and places like Cheyenne Mountain."

"And the worst case is you never get near the gate," the general said, licking his lips. He hadn't realized it would be that bad. After twenty-five years of service in uniform he was used to taking risks with his life and the lives of the soldiers he commanded. But this was risking the fate of all humanity.

"Yes, sir," Miller replied. "That would really and truly suck."

"Well, for the first time today, I understand my orders," the general said. He gave the physicist a half salute and walked back to the lawyer's office that he had taken over as a command center.

"You think it's gonna work?" Miller asked.

"It'd take a miracle."

"The gate is at the head of this narrow ravine that branches off of the main Clover Branch valley," the S-3 of what was being called Joint Task Force Oakdale said, pointing at the map. The major was normally the S-3 of the 37th Armored Brigade Ohio National Guard. As a full-time reservist he was decently capable of arranging the operations of his brigade, whether it be summer training, training schedules for the battalions scattered throughout Ohio or peacekeeping in Bosnia, Iraq or Afghanistan.

Planning a desperate assault on a mountaintop in Kentucky for four brigades and a battalion of regular soldiers was a different ballgame.

"The Mreee hold most of the Twin Creek Valley as well as Keen Fork and Bear Fork, but are being held up on ridges on three sides by units of the Kentucky National Guard."

There was an "ooowah!" from the back of the crowded tent and the S-3 smiled thinly.

"Part of this is probably because the Mreee seem willing to

stand on their gains. But a continual trickle of reinforcements has been coming through the gate, both Mreee and Nitch. It is believed when they have sufficient force they intend to assault, probably in the direction of Jackson. Most of the reinforcements have been moving up the Twin Creek Valley to assemble opposite the defenses near Elkatawa."

He turned back to the map and frowned.

"The assault on the bridge will be along four axes. The majority of the 35th Brigade will move into positions opposite the Chenowee build-up and prepare for a direct frontal assault up Highway 52. In the meantime, 1st Battalion 149th Infantry with supporting units from 2nd Battalion 123rd Armor will move up to the vicinity of Lawson where they will prepare for an assault over the ridges along the axis of Warcreek-Filmore Road. Once established on the ridges they will advance along the axis of Keen Fork. There is an unnamed road running along the creek that junctions with Warcreek-Filmore at the ridgeline. It is anticipated that the majority of this advance will be dismounted as the named roads are the only ones that will be functional for mechanized systems. Thirty-fifth Brigade, less one battalion, will move as soon as possible to the vicinity of Copebranch. When they are in position, they will move down to strike the enemy positions near Athol. This has to be the first assault made. The intention is to force the enemy to redeploy troops to repel it before the other two brigades engage.

"Second Battalion, Third Brigade of the One-Oh-One will be moved up to the vicinity of Elkatawa. They will then dismount and move up onto the ridgelines currently held by 2nd Battalion, 149th Infantry of the Kentucky National Guard. Their objective will be to move, hopefully undetected, along the ridgelines to the vicinity of Highway 541, then stage a dismounted assault upon the gate under cover of the mounted and dismounted assaults from the other directions. Your northern border will be the general axis of Warcreek to the Warcreek-Filmore Road with southern border the ridges overlooking Highway 52. But movement is to be along the ridges. Kentucky National Guard patrols have found what may be a clear lane, nearly to the gate opening. The Second Battalion will be accompanied by units of SEAL Team Five and Dr. Weaver, who will be carrying the gate closure device."

"So, what you're saying," the brigade commander of the 1st Brigade said, "is that we're on the nature of a great big diversion."

"Yes," General McKeen said, looking over his shoulder. "Is that a problem?"

"No, sir," the colonel replied, grinning. "We'll just be as diverting as hell."

"If you can take the gate, any of you, do it," the general said. "Push for it like hell. But the 101st battalion is, hopefully, the key. They've got more experience moving dismounted and they can move through the hills better than your troops probably can. The Mreee seem to be just tacking down the ridgelines, concentrating on forming their forces in the valley. We're going to use that to butt-fuck them. Once Dr. Weaver and the SEALs insert the device, the gates close. At that point, it's all over but the mopping up. Not just here, everywhere. Ohio, Tennessee, Georgia, Alabama, from Florida to Saskatchewan. It's all up to us. And we're going to do the job. Any questions?"

There were none. The S-3 turned over the briefing to the Assistant S-3 who ran through the movement lanes, phaselines and other nitpicky details of the attack. He studiously ignored the portion on artillery support; there was none for the simple reason that it didn't work. He also ignored resupply and post-assault consolidation. This was an all or nothing attack. There would be no resupply and if it failed there would be no need for reconsolidation.

Bill tuned that out as he tried to quiet his own fears. He had written down the instructions on how to set the bomb, but if the artass had made a mistake it was going to be a lousy time to find out right in front of the gate. So far it had only been Mreee and Nitch on this gate, but that didn't mean that the Titcher might not show up at any time. They were racing against a series of deadlines, some of them unknown and unknowable. He glanced at his watch again. Five hours.

Finally the briefing was over and the various officers filed out of the large tent, some of them joking halfheartedly. They all

knew that they were going into a gauntlet from which most of
their forces, their soldiers, their children, would not return.

"Dr. Weaver?" a lieutenant colonel said as they were leaving.
"Lieutenant Colonel John Forsythe, I'm the battalion commander from the One-Oh-One. You're with me." He was a tall
officer with a clean-cut look and a square jaw. He looked like
Hollywood's idea of an airborne battalion commander.

"We'll meet you at the assembly area, sir," Miller interjected.
"We've got some special materials we need to assemble and we have
our own transportation. It was in the movement supplement."

"All right," the colonel said, nonplussed. "Be there on time."

"We're the timing, Colonel," Bill said. "The whole thing starts
when we're ready." He glanced at his watch. "Five hours."

"Understood," the colonel said, clearly *not* understanding.
"Just be there."

"We will, sir," Miller replied. "With bells on."

As it turned out it took just over four hours until all the
units were in position and Colonel Forsythe found out what
the "special materials" were.

"What the fuck, pardon my French, is that?" the colonel
asked, looking up at the kneeling mecha-suit.

After the first Wyverns had worked out so successfully, Bill had
convinced Columbia to fast-track construction of the Mark II. The
Mark II had a bit more fluidity, less of a tendency to disco at just
the wrong moment and the stylish face had been removed. The
whole upper half had, in fact, been significantly lowered and the
armor had been modified into reflective glacis ridges. The suits
were also camouflage covered and, in the case of the nine that
the SEALs were now suiting up in, covered further in a special
camouflage netting that would break up their outlines.

"It's a Mark Two Wyvern armored combat mecha," Bill
responded. He was now wearing the skin-tight black coveralls
that were necessary to properly "fit" the Wyvern and he ran his
hands over the suit proprietarily. "The Mark Twos are armored
about like a Bradley and can carry some serious firepower. They
also are going to be better armor for the ardune."

"The what?" the colonel asked.

"The gate closing device," Bill replied, glancing at the light violet box. It had been carefully placed on the back of the truck that had carried the Wyvern to their assembly area and his eyes, and those of most of the SEALs, were never far from it. The blue charging bar on the top now within a smidgeon of reading full. Bill's Wyvern had been hastily modified with a metal box to carry it and he had carefully ensured that the Wyvern finger systems were dexterous enough to key the arming system. He hadn't had the guts to actually key the full sequence, though. "The SEALs and I will let you carry the assault up to the gate but if you get bogged, we're going to go through on rock and roll. The ardune *will* be placed on the other side of the gate, and it *will* be triggered, one way or another."

"I want your people to understand something," the colonel said. "I know they're SEALs. I know they're the best of the best. I know that the mission is important. But you don't go until *I* say you go, understood?"

"Yes," Bill replied. "The flip side being that when it is time to go, you let slip the hounds."

"I will," the colonel said. "But I let them slip. My assault, I'm in command. You're just supernumeraries until we get up to the gate. You're in line between Bravo and Charlie company, right ahead of my section. Get suited up, Doctor."

Bill nodded and stepped into the suit. Once fitted, the Wyverns were relatively easy to take on and off. He simply put his hands in the controls, settled his feet into their holders and pressed a button. The front closed and he was ready to fight. With one small exception.

Miller came over carrying both his own and the doctor's weapons. Miller had insisted on another 30mm but the doctor had opted for a .50 caliber Gatling gun. The Mreee and the Nitch were not as hard targets as the Titcher units and Bill felt that the gun, which was the first Gatling gun accessorized with a semiauto selector switch, was more in keeping with the threat. Miller's philosophy, on the other hand, had not changed. More firepower is better firepower.

Bill picked up the big gun in one hand and waited until the command master chief had hooked up the feed tube and checked the connections. Then he keyed the external speaker and raised one hand in a half salute.

"Ready when you are, Colonel," Bill said.

"Maybe I should think about putting you on point," the colonel replied, then hefted his own M-4. "Okay!" he said, raising his voice. "Let's roll out!"

"This is Juliet Five-Four," the commander of the 35th Brigade said over the command net. He was half whispering despite the rumble from the command Bradley he was in. "Our advance scouts have the Nitch lines in sight. Ready to initiate."

"Juliet Five-Four, this is Sierra One-one," Task Force Command said. "Stand by. We're awaiting word from the Lima Eight-Six units that they're in place."

"Fucking One-Oh-One," the colonel bitched. "They think they're so hot shit and here we sit waiting on them."

"I dunno, sir," his S-3 opined. "Them ridges are a bastard. I hunt in country like this and making that movement, stealthily, in three hours? I would have been awfully surprised."

It had been a total bastard of a march.

The distance wasn't far, no more than three miles in a direct line, but they hadn't taken a direct line. The guide from the Kentucky unit was a short, broad young sergeant, dark hair covered by a floppy "boonie" cap and a dark growth of beard apparent in a five o'clock shadow. He had led them up and down hills, across streams and along knife-edge ridgelines, never in one direction for very long.

Bill was glad that the Mark II had more maneuverability, otherwise the march would have been impossible. It was necessary at times for the mechas to walk one foot in front of the other, something impossible with the Mark I. And while they were not holding up the advance, they definitely didn't feel slowed by the soldiers in front of them; it was all the clumsy mechas could do to keep up with the pace.

But the unit had stopped, all of the soldiers dropping to a squat and facing outward for threats as the colonel held the radio and talked to someone.

Bill kicked in his external directional mike and shamelessly eavesdropped as the Kentucky scout came back down the line and squatted by the battalion commander.

"Honest to God, sir," the scout said. "They wasn't there five hours ago."

"Picket," Miller said over the radio. The SEALs had been training with the essentially effortless suits for two weeks and he'd learned some of the ins and outs, too. Like the directional mike. "The Mreee have a picket up on our line of march."

"What do we do?" Bill asked as the colonel shook his head and looked at his map.

"Take it out," Miller replied, stepping forward in a crouch. "Excuse me, Colonel."

"Yes, Master Chief," the colonel said, clearly annoyed.

"Sir, taking out sentries is our specialty," Miller pointed out, ignoring the fact that the colonel had missed the "command" part.

"I don't think that, despite your wonderful camouflage job, you can exactly sneak up on these Mreee," the colonel said, sarcastically. The suits were well camouflaged, visually, but even with the enhancements they were as noisy as a platoon of regular infantry.

"I wasn't planning on using the suit, sir," the SEAL said, politely. He turned and made a series of hand gestures towards the other SEALs, who were down on their knees and elbows to reduce their visibility. One of the suits sat up and kneeled, opening along the front. The SEAL within stepped out and around the suit, opening up a side-panel on the ammunition storage box. From it he extracted a silenced M-4, a black balaclava, a combat harness and a camouflage "ghillie" suit made, like those over the suits, of netting strung with soft colored cloth. In a moment he was suited up and soft footed over to Miller's position. Bill noticed that he was wearing what appeared to be dyed black moccasins.

"Russell is our team sniper, sir," the command master chief said. "The wind is towards us. He can take down the picket and no one the wiser."

The colonel looked at the two SEALs and shook his head.

"Sorry, Chief," the colonel said. "I should have known you weren't an idiot. Go."

Russell looked at the scout and then gestured with his chin towards the front of the battalion.

Bill dialed up the directional mike and followed them out of sight. He could hear the scout moving quietly through the underbrush along the ridgeline, but not a sound from the sniper despite the encumbering camouflage. He waited what seemed an interminable period and then heard two muted cracks, something like firecrackers that had been placed under a jar.

"They're down," the colonel said. "They didn't appear to have a radio or any other communications devices."

Bill wondered about that, thinking about the Adar and their implants. But the Mreee really did seem to be a relatively low-tech race that had somehow acquired a set of high tech implements. The battalion started moving again but the suits had to wait while Russell made his way back. The SEAL quickly trotted into view, though, and stowed his dismount gear, suited up and they were on their way.

As they passed the two Mreee bodies, Weaver wondered what they had thought, sent to an alien land by their allies? Their masters? Set up on a hilltop that was unlike anything from their home world. What were they thinking? Were they hoping to go home, alive, to their mates? To their littermates? Or were they looking forward to killing the humans?

He also wondered what the soldiers thought at a time like this. He had never even considered joining the military; he had nothing against it but science had been his passion since an early age. What was Russell feeling? Did he have any feelings about killing the child-sized felinoids at all?

He remembered the expression on the SEAL's face as the balaclava had been taken off and he stowed his gear. Cold, clear, professionally interested in getting his gear away and back on track as swiftly and efficiently as possible. What drove these human killing machines?

Bosons made more sense.

The sun had set and away from city lights there was limited visibility. All the troopers of the 101st, though, had flip-down monoculars on their helmets and the reduced lighting seemed to affect them not at all. The suits, of course, had night vision systems and they could see, if not as clearly as day then clearly enough. They even had thermal imaging systems and Bill flipped them on to get a look at how it felt in a real mission. The soldiers ahead of him were white ghosts and the overall impression was, if anything, worse than with the night vision systems. He quickly switched back.

The battalion reached its first phaseline, Highway 541, and spread out to either side, probing for Mreee sentries. They found none. The lone picket on the hilltop seemed to be the only force the Mreee had out on this wing. As soon as everyone was in position, the colonel sent the code word and the whole battalion, plus the mecha, swiftly crossed the road and settled into the woods on the far side. They were within a mile or so of the gate and still seemed to have been undetected.

The colonel spoke into his radio and then waved the battalion down; now was the time to wait. Bill turned up his external audio to listen to the night. There was the sound of an owl, unaware that the planet had been invaded by aliens, calling forlornly for a mate. A cough. A slight rattle of equipment from down the line. Then, in the distance, a sound of firing that rose to a crescendo, quickly. A shattering explosion. Then, more firing, closer.

The colonel still waited, monitoring his radio. Bill looked at his suit clock and noted that the bomb should have fully cooked by now; it had taken that long to get into position. But there was only one ridge between them and the gate. The firing to the south and the west was joined by more to the north and there was a brief flash of actinic fire to the south that lit the crouched infantry for a moment like day. Finally the colonel stood up, saying something on his radio. There was a rustle from either side as the battalion began to move up the steep slope.

Still, as they moved, nothing. Then, from the north, there came the sound of a fusillade of shots and a ball of plasma lit the air.

Contact.

Bill switched over to thermal imagery and could see ghostlike images at the top of the ridge. There were several of them in view and even as he drew a bead on one with the laser mount on the Gatling gun, a ball of plasma flew through the air and impacted near the line of infantrymen, throwing two them to the ground to roll in agony at instant third-degree burns.

Bill closed his finger on the firing mechanism, rolling the fire through the figures on the ridgeline. One of them seemed to separate into two and another flew backwards. He could hear firing on either side of him, now, loud, but the audio sensors quickly dialed down. The figures on the ridgeline had disappeared. He could hear shouting and realized that it was he who was doing it, bellowing in rage as he tried to force the mecha up the steep slope. The ridge got steeper towards the top; a short bluff was apparent. Bill realized he could never get the suit up and over it and looked around for somewhere he could climb up. Suddenly, he felt himself lifted up and half thrown onto the top. He stumbled onto his face and then lay prone, moving forward on knee and elbow wheels to clear the spot he had been lifted up on. Another suit landed next to him and his systems automatically designated it as Seaman First Class Sanson.

Bill was right in the area that he had fired at and he saw, for the first time clearly, the effects of the Gatling gun. Two forms, their images fading with their internal heat, were on the ground. Three, really, because one of them had been cut in half by the fire from the gun. He started to heave but suppressed it with a mighty effort; it wouldn't kill him in the suit or damage the electronics, but it would have been damned messy.

He slid forward, looking to either side and seeing human forms running across the top of the ridge. He pulled up a location map and they were within a few hundred yards, no more, of the gate. He pulled himself upwards then ducked as a ball of plasma flew through the air. More firing was apparent from the area of the gate and Bill popped his head up for just a moment to get a look. He didn't know how many Mreee and Nitch had been passed through the gate, or how many had been moved up close to their intended assault point, or how many had been drawn off by the earlier attacks. But based on the images in the valley, most of them were still down there. His thermal imagery system couldn't separate them out.

Plasma rounds were impacting all along the ridgeline, now, as the forces around the gate realized they were being flanked. Bill heard screams to either side and realized that there was no way to get in view of the fire and survive. On the other hand, there were so many targets down in the valley it would be hard to miss. So he raised the Gatling gun up over the lip of the ridge and fired it without looking.

The other mecha had joined him and were doing the same thing. Most of them had Gatling guns with two 25mms and the chief's 30mm. Miller was one of the few not firing. He was lying on his side, apparently peacefully watching the scene and occasionally reaching behind him and lobbing something overhand into the valley.

"Having fun, Chief?" Bill asked, watching his ammunition counter. The Gatling was going through rounds at an alarming rate. He decided that when he was down to one quarter of his ammo load, he would stop firing.

"Loads," Miller replied. "Made up some improvised explosive devices while we were waiting. Bouncing Betties on a timer. Thought it was an appropriate time to expend them."

"We could use some fire support," Bill said through gritted teeth. Holding the gun overhead and firing it, even with the mecha's powered support, was not easy. One of the SEALs screamed and flopped backwards, his arms blown off by a plasma round. The scream was surprise rather than pain since the area that had been hit didn't vent into the suit and his "real" arms were down in the body.

"Saving it for something worthwhile," the chief replied.

Bill dropped his weapon and snaked forward, taking a quick look over the edge.

Where there had been bodies too numerous to count there were now . . . bodies too numerous to count. But most of them weren't moving. Some were, however, and plasma fire was still dropping on the lines, some of it damned close to the position the mecha had taken. But now fire from the infantry on either side, with the plasma somewhat suppressed, was beginning to get the upper hand. Bill saw a line of tracers lazily float down the hillside, missing their intended target high, then correct into the moving form of one of the giant spiders. It collapsed. The infantry medium machine guns had been set up along the lip of the hollow and now were steadily eliminating the resistance.

He brought the big Gatling gun up and started searching for targets as the rest of the mecha pushed forward on either side and did the same. Even Miller leaned over the lip and started sending individual rounds downrange. Seeing that he couldn't detect if they hit or not he switched to full auto and stroked the trigger, sending burst after burst, almost every one including a tracer, into the carnage in the hollow. The lines of explosions were easily detected by the thermal imaging scope, brief, bright, dots of white heat that gradually faded in the cool night air. Sometimes they left behind cooling bodies as well.

"I think it's time to go," Bill said.

"Roger," Miller replied, tersely. "Switch to the battalion command freq."

It took Bill a moment to fumble for the sheet of paper that had the information, read it by the dim redlight in the suit and switch his frequency. By the time he did, the argument was in full swing.

" . . . don't care, Uniform Two-Four," a voice Bill didn't recognize said. "We're still encountering resistance. Until it's suppressed stay in position."

"They *are* suppressed, Major," the SEAL said, tightly. "We need to get this box in position, *now*, before they can regroup or reinforce!"

"Where's the colonel?" Bill asked.

"Lima Eight-Six Bravo is unavailable," the new voice said. "This is Lima Four-Five; I'm in command."

"Colonel Forsythe bought it," Miller said. "Major White was the battalion XO, he's in command, now."

"Have you ever heard the term communications security, Uniform Two-Four?" the officer said, clearly furious.

"This is an encrypted link, Major." Miller sighed. "And our opponents have shown no sign of having intercept capability.

And we don't have time to diddle around with codes. We need to move, sir, right the fuck now."

"I am in charge of this operation, Uni . . . Mi . . ." the major spluttered. "You will move when I tell you to move and not one moment before."

"Major, for God's sake," Miller said, nearly shouted. "Take not counsel of your fears. We need to *move!*"

"That's what you SEALs thought in Panama, right?" the major snarled back. "Well this is a hell of a lot more important than making sure Noriega missed his plane. And we will *not* move until we have full control of the situation! This is Lima Four-Five, out!"

"Switch back to SEAL net," Miller said. "This is whoever the fuck I am leaving the net."

Bill punched the numbers in for the other frequency, which he remembered, and keyed the mike.

"What do we do, Miller?" he asked. He was down to one quarter ammo and had stopped firing. Miller was still sending the occasional burst into the hollow. Only an occasional burst of plasma, poorly aimed, was returned.

"Miller?" Bill asked as the silence lengthened. "Hey, am I on the right freq?"

"Yes," a voice answered. It was one of the SEALs, but he didn't recognize the voice. "Keep the chatter down."

"Miller!" Bill said, half afraid, half furious.

"SEAL Team Five," Miller said, stonily. "Sound off."

"Six." "Four." "Seven." "Five." "Eight." "Nine." "Three. Here, weapons inop."

"Two?" Miller said. "Two?"

"Two's gone." Bill recognized the voice this time as Sanson. He sounded . . . cold.

"SEAL Team Five," Miller said. "Prepare to assault gateway on my signal. Three, go ground tactical."

Bill manipulated the security settings on his radio as he prepared to stand up. The settings could be reset so that the commanders could speak to subordinates without being overheard. It was on the same frequency but anyone without the proper setting would only get a hissing in their ears. His suit and Miller's were dialed in on the security setting.

"Miller?" Bill said. "Is this a good idea?"

"Tactically?" the SEAL answered. "Yes."

"I mean, doesn't the military sort of frown on chiefs, even command master chiefs, not listening to majors?"

"Yes," Bill said, tersely. "It's called disobedience of a direct order from a lawful superior under combat conditions. It means I won't be getting a pension. On the other hand, I *will* be boarded by the United States Government, at no expense to myself, at a pleasant place called Leavenworth. Get the fucking box in the gate, Doctor. Leave the rest for me to worry about."

"SEAL Team Five," Miller said, his voice cold and professional as he reset to general communications settings. "Let's roll."

Bill started to stand up, then rolled over instead and lowered his feet over the slight bluff at the top of the ridge. The slope of the ridge down to the hollow was covered in light scrub—had apparently been cleared off a few years before—which broke under the weight of the mecha. But going downhill was, if anything, harder than going uphill in the suits. He more or less slid on his butt, half out of control, down the slope to where it flattened out. He felt rather than saw some plasma detonations, but they weren't close to him so he ignored them. There was no way, as out of control as he was, that he could return fire, anyway. He was having enough trouble just hanging on to his weapon.

Finally the out-of-control slide stopped and he hefted his weapon, levering himself to his feet and getting ready to run to the gate. Then he paused. Face it, it was the job of the SEALs to clear the way. He was just there to set the ardune. Let them go first.

He looked around and found it surprisingly hard to spot them; the suits had a radiator on their back, just below the americium battery pack, but other than that spot they didn't radiate heat. It was another benefit of the suits and if he survived he planned on adding it to his after-action field-test report.

There was no more plasma fire coming at them and as the SEALs slid forward, swinging their weapons from side to side, and scanning for threats, he followed, concentrating on the gate.

It was visible even in infrared, emitting a slightly higher temperature than the background. The planet on the far side must have been warmer and with a slight overpressure because wisps of what looked like fog in the thermal imagery were drifting up and out of the gateway. He quickly ran the fifty meters to the gate and set his Gatling gun on the ground, turning and fumbling to open up the container that held the ardune, just as one of the suits exploded in plasma fire.

# 11

"General Thrathptttt!" The runner was panting but he straightened and bowed to the commander of the combined Mreee N!T!Ch! assault force. "A group of human infantry has infiltrated to the gate area. They pushed off the forces on the ridge to the east. They are attempting to seize the gate."

General Thrathptttt spat a curse and looked at his map. The detail was poor, it had been found in one of the human stores in the small town they had taken, but it was clear what was happening. The humans had used their heavy forces as diversions and then sent in an infiltration force to seize the gate, cutting off his reinforcements. He'd left light forces on the ridge, banking on pickets to tell him if there was an attack from that direction. If there was, the forces near the gate should have been able to reinforce the ridge, easily. But the humans were tricky, worthy opponents. He was pleased.

"We can let the reinforcements handle it," one of his aides said. He had been updating the map and now put a marker on it for an unknown force at the gate.

"No," Thrathptttt said. He fingered his eyepatch in thought. It was a long time since the Mreee had faced worthy opponents and he remembered what had happened, then. But the humans were not as much to be feared as the Masters.

"Have runners sent to Mraown company and S!L!K! company. Have Mraown come over this ridge on them. Take the ridge and provide covering fire. Let the N!T!Ch! go up the road and recapture the gate."

"That will weaken our defenses along the road to Waaaar-crick," the aide protested.

"And the humans will drive through them, eventually," the general said, looking at the map and fingering his patch again. "Which will leave Mraown in position to catch them in the flank as they pass. We can push reinforcements from Flefffpt up the hill as well when they come through. Have Mraown and S!L!K! retake the gate area. The rest will be easy."

"Son of a bitch," Miller snarled. He didn't know if this was forces retreating from the mech attacks or units sent back to reinforce the gate. But he did know that they were bloody well screwed. The ridgeline to the west had just spotted itself with what were apparently Mreee and he could see a whole passel, company, maybe battalion, strength, of Nitch running up the road into the hollow.

"SEALs, form perimeter around the doc," Miller snapped. "Engage targets of opportunity. Keep fire off the doc."

That was pretty difficult, however. The Nitch had eight legs and two "arms" which they used to carry slightly larger versions of the "raygun" the Mreee had been armed with. They apparently had trouble moving among the trees—their feet spanned nearly three meters across—but they could skitter along the road, fast. And they were stable enough to fire at the same time. Which these were doing. They were still a couple of hundred yards away and most of the fire was going overhead, but it was still brutal.

And the Mreee on the ridgeline could pour fire into them, just as they and the 101st had poured it into the scattered bodies of Mreee and Nitch in the hollow. Admittedly, they seemed to have some trouble spotting the SEALs and their fire was pretty inaccurate. But as each SEAL fired, tracers from their weapons revealed their location. The fire had already taken out one of the suits and would soon start pounding the rest.

"Major, we need heavy fire-support here," Miller said on the battalion frequency. He had assumed the prone position and was now sending carefully aimed bursts into the Nitch charging up the road; he considered them the worst of the two threats.

"We're on it," the battalion commander replied. "This is why I said hold up."

Miller didn't bother to point out that if the major had started the assault earlier, the bomb would already be in the gate.

"Yes, sir," was all he said. "All the fire support you can provide would be appreciated."

"Alpha, Bravo, concentrate on the spiders," the major said on the battalion frequency, disdaining callsigns. "Charlie, engage the cats on the ridge. Maximum firepower; keep 'em off the SEALs."

"This must have been how Shughart felt," Russell muttered on the SEAL freq as Miller switched back.

"Target-rich environment," Ryan replied. "Nice to know somebody loves . . ."

"Seven down," Russell said.

"Loves us," Sanson finished.

For Sanson it was something on the order of a dream come true. Sure, he hadn't risen out of the waves to take out a sentry on the beach, but this was the next best thing. He'd never been some anime geek but the suits, he had to admit, were damned cool and the firepower they supported was just awesome. He was toting a .50 caliber Gatling like the doctor and the thing would just saw one of the spiders, much less the little cats, in two. On the other hand, it ate rounds like there was no tomorrow and he was down to just stroking the trigger, watching his waterfall counter get closer and closer to the bottom. And there just seemed to be more and more of the damned things. Which was cool, too, in its own way. Target-rich environment. *Better than Mog.* Much better than what the old guys talked about in Iraq and Ashkanistan.

He triggered another burst, just barely stroked the trigger, and ten more rounds poured out of the Gatling, tearing one spider in half, you could see the parts separate on the thermal imagery, and getting a piece of the one next to it. Probably got the one behind, too. But that was it. He hit the firing circuit again and was rewarded by having the barrels spin around and around making a cute ratcheting noise and a whine. Fuck.

"I'm out!" he shouted, pushing the weapon to the side and looking around. He had an M-4 in his pack but no way to access it without bailing out, which he was loathe to do. On the other hand, he was lying on top of a dead Nitch, he'd been using its thorax for cover, and there was a Nitch plasma gun sitting on the ground not too far away. He shinnied forward and picked it up, trying to examine it. But there was nothing to see under thermal imagery. He switched to night vision and saw that there were some levers and buttons on it. Nothing that looked like a pistol grip or a stock, though. He set it against his shoulder, awkwardly, he was really just holding it up with his left suit-hand, and pushed one of the buttons. Nothing. He pressed another. Nothing. Then he pressed the first one again.

There was a burst of light from the front of the weapon and a sapling about twenty feet away blew up, showering them in bits of stem and dirt.

"Hey!" he yelled. "The plasma guns work!" He took more careful aim this time and pressed the button again, the bolt of lightning tracking over the heads of the closing Nitch. He felt like a damned fool missing *that* big of a target from *this* close. He lowered the barrel, slightly, and fired again. This time two Nitch were turned into spider-goo and a couple behind them dropped to the ground, their legs writhing frantically on the ground.

"Awesome . . ." the SEAL whispered. He never even felt the bolt of plasma that dropped on him from the ridge above.

Miller looked over at where Sanson had been turned into a blazing pile of carbon and titanium and then back at the oncoming Nitch. Not so oncoming anymore, though. The fire of the SEALs, not to mention support from above, was having an effect. He had switched the 30mm to single shot and had been hammering out round after round. Each of the rounds blew a spider apart, okay, he admitted it was overkill, and between his fire and the fire of the other SEALs the phalanx that had been attacking them wasn't gaining any ground.

But they were still being slaughtered by the Mreee up on the ridge, that was what had gotten Sanson and Ryan, and if they didn't get taken out pretty soon they were done for.

Of course, if the doctor could ever get the box in the gate, they could do the Mogadishu mile and leave the clean-up to the National Guard. If.

"How's it coming, Doctor?" he said, calmly. Didn't want to spook the guy, not with that thing in his hands.

Weaver was lying behind the bulk of the dead Petty Officer Ryan's suit, using it for cover from the fire from above and the road. It was not so much that he was a coward, although anyone would be a bit anxious in this situation, but if one of the plasma rounds hit the ardune, it was going to detonate on Earth. Which would be bad.

He'd initially ended up on the side with the box down. After rolling over he'd fumbled the metal container open and pulled out the ardune. He fumbled it around to where he could see it through the armored glass in the chest of the suit and cursed under his breath. It was night; he couldn't see it. He shoved it up to where it was visible from his low-light circuit and cut to light enhancement. The symbols on the front still weren't visible; the vision just wasn't detailed enough.

"Miller," he said, as calmly as he could. "Does anyone have a flashlight?" He'd argued for some sort of a light on the suits, but the military didn't want them. Not white light, which was what he needed. The symbols were purple on violet; red light wouldn't help one damned bit.

"Shit," Miller muttered. He stopped firing for a moment and fumbled in a container, finally extracting something and arming it. He threw it to the side of the gate where it flashed into white heat.

"What the hell is that?" Bill asked. The late Ryan's suit left the box in shadow so he tilted it up to where there was light enough to see. It was damned near as bright as day.

"Thermite grenade," the SEAL said. "And I just lit our position so get a fucking move on."

"You're carrying thermite grenades?" Bill asked, starting to key the symbols. One, two, three . . .

"You never know when they're going to come in handy," the SEAL said. Plasma was falling all around their position now that the Mreee on the ridgeline could see them clearly. There was another cut-off scream as a SEAL suit was hit.

Four . . . Bill was struck in the side, the box knocked out of his hands, as a Nitch coming out of the gate caught him with one of its front legs. He grabbed the leg and with half hysterical strength, aided by the suit, ripped it off. As the Nitch, pouring some sort of goop out of the hole, stumbled downward, he struck upwards and punched it in the thorax. The blow was unthinking, a Wah-Lum ground fighting move backed by all the power of the suit. His arm sunk into the thing's thorax up to his elbow.

"They're coming through the gate!" Bill yelled, rolling to where the box had fallen. "Shit, shit, shit, shit!" He picked it up in one hand and pointed the .50 caliber at the gate, hosing rounds in the hope that he could hold off the forces on the other side.

"What?" Miller yelled.

"Besides the fact that we're surrounded and about to get overrun?" Bill laughed, hysterically. "I had the damned thing half keyed! I don't know if I can start over or what!" He fumbled the box around to where he could see it, again, but the light from the thermite grenade had been extinguished. "Aaaaagh! No light!"

"Stay cool!" Miller yelled. He turned around and started throwing things through the gate. One of them blew up before it went through and threw shrapnel all over Bill's suit.

"Don't hit the ardune!" Bill yelled, desperately. "I need *light*!"

One of the SEALs stood up with a plasma gun in his hand and started firing upwards. On the second shot he managed to nail the crown of a large oak that overhung the gate area. It had, miraculously, escaped fire to this point. But at the impact of the plasma round the crown burst into immediate flame.

The SEAL was hit before he could even drop the weapon. The smoking legs of the mecha were thrown in two directions but they were all that was left of the suit.

"You got light," Miller rasped.

Bill thought, frantically, about his instructions. He hadn't asked what happened if the code entry was interrupted. Better to try finishing it. He hit the last symbol and was rewarded by a blinking light. He started pressing the counter.

"How long?" he yelled.

"Not very," Miller replied, looking around. There were only two SEALs still firing besides himself.

Bill pressed five increments on the counter, about seven seconds, thought about having to key the second code, and pressed five more. Then he keyed the code, took the box in both hands and threw it through the gate as hard as he could.

It entered the gate and he started to get up but it bounced back and landed behind him. Immediately following it was a centipede tank.

"Fuck!" Bill shouted. "IT'S LIVE, ARDUNE IS LIVE, CENTIPEDE!"

Miller turned around and pulled out his last thermite grenade. He had noticed that the centipedes seemed to have some sort of mouth or breathing organ on their front. It was heavily armored and turned down, impossible to hit with a round, but he wasn't planning on shooting it. He pulled the pin on the grenade, took two steps and shoved it up the opening as hard as he could, leaning the mecha into the face of the tank and pushing back, trying to keep it from extruding all the way out of the gate. His feet started sliding back as he counted.

"Three, two, one," he muttered, wondering what hell was like. Probably pretty similar to Leavenworth, but longer.

Bill got one hand on the box and turned around. The centipede more than half filled the gate opening but he took two steps and leapt onto it, directly between two of the hornlike plasma generators. Taking the box in both hands he threw it towards the gate again, as hard as he could.

» » »

Bill never was sure what he saw in that moment. For just a second he thought that stars appeared in the gate as it turned black and lights flashed in it. But they seemed to be moving lights, moving in some complex pattern that defied explanation. The image was there for only a moment but it seared itself on his soul. He knew, in his heart, that they were not just stars, not burning bits of gas, but souls, entities. Perhaps even fuzzy children's toys, waving a farewell salute. He felt, in that brief instant, that he truly knew what it meant to touch the face of God.

Then the world went white.

Miller saw the gate go black for a moment, then disappear, leaving the rest of the centipede, and Dr. Weaver's suit arms, either on the other side or in some nowhere place. And then he felt the thermite grenade pop.

The explosion was not a plasma explosion. More like a very large transformer blowing up. Very large. Miller felt himself picked up and thrown through the air. It was a vaguely peaceful feeling, much better than the desperate combat he had been involved in a moment earlier. Right up until he hit the burning oak tree.

"Dr. Weaver?"

Pain. All-enveloping pain. Lots of it.

Weaver got one eye opened and groaned, or tried to; it came out as a croak. He swore that if God made the pain go away he'd live a good life and never, ever, do anything even slightly risky again. Wah-Lum? Hah, no chance. Mountain biking? And risk road rash? He'd buy a house on one level, never climb stairs again, never run, just walk. Nothing that could cause so much as a scrape. Blunt knives in the house. Put rubber on all the corners. His nerves felt jangled. Please, God, just let the pain go away.

He got a look at the ceiling and it wasn't good. It looked like the inside of a tent. There was a groaning from nearby and then a hoarse shriek. He tried to move his fingers and was rewarded with a lance of pain again, bad enough that he nearly passed out.

"Dr. Weaver?" the voice said, again.

"Ow," was all he could get out.

"Are you in pain?"

"Owwwww!"

"I'll get a doctor."

He swiveled his one good eye around and saw that there was a line of beds, filled with casualties. It was a tent, a big one.

"Dr. Weaver?" a female voice said. "I'm going to give you some liquid Valium. We're running low on morphine; we've got more casualties than we're supposed to have for a field hospital this size. You're in no danger. You have some serious burns from an electrical fire and a broken arm. Other than that, you're in good shape compared to most of the rest of the injured. We're going to be moving you, soon, to another hospital. Just rest as well as you can."

"Uhhh," Bill said and then God answered his prayers and made the pain go away.

"Hey, Doc, you're not out of bed, yet?"

Weaver looked up from the mess of gruel that the hospital considered a nourishing meal to where Miller was being wheeled in the door by a candy striper. The chief had a big bandage over one eye, an arm and a leg in casts and a very nonpermissible cigar in his teeth. He'd managed to find a set of BDUs somewhere, though, and he had a new set of rank pinned on his collar, a yellow bar with a black check in it that Bill recognized, now, as the insignia of a warrant officer.

"Like a bad penny, you keep showing up," Bill said, grinning. He grinned a lot these days; the world hadn't come to an end.

Things were still bad. The gates, and the track three bosons that generated them, were well and truly gone. But the Titcher/Dreen had established large bridgeheads before that happened. They were using their surviving forces and the bridgeheads to begin colonization, continuing to create monsters that were a tough battle to destroy. But, slowly, they were being pushed back. Where the bridgeheads were observable from the distance, it was apparent that the Dreen, as they were being called now, built special-purpose structures to produce their fighting forces, some for dog-demons, some for thorn-throwers, others for the mosquito-missiles. As that became obvious, artillery was brought to bear from long range, saturating the air defenses until the structures that provided the missiles and centipede tanks, which were the only things that stopped air assaults, were destroyed. After that it was a matter of killing the monsters and their structures faster than they could be produced. It was working, slowly.

In the meantime, the "real" world had continued though. Units had had to be redeployed from Iraq and the nascent democracy in that country was having a hard time with ongoing guerilla activity. Terrorists had exploded a truck bomb in New York, killing nearly fifty people. But that was probably going to be some post-9/11 high-water mark; the Middle East had other problems.

Dreen pockets had broken out in several different, decidedly odd, places. They were all out of the way and most had not been noticed until they were well established and started spreading.

One was in the Bekaa Valley, in Lebanon, near a center for Hamas and Hezbollah recruitment and training. Hamas, Hezbollah and the Syrians who actually owned the territory, immediately blamed it upon the United States and sent out proclamations that *they* would reduce the incursion in short order. The proclamations had been going out, steadily, for a week. There was no indication that they had had any real success. Indeed, news reports filtered from the U.S. government said that satellite imagery indicated at least a twenty-five percent spread.

Another was just north of the holy city of Qom in Iran. It had apparently started at the head of a valley which housed an experimental farm run by the Iranian Ruling Council, the fundamentalist religious council that ruled upon shariah law in Iran and was the actual government behind the scenes. An "unnamed U.S. spokesperson" had pointed out that the farm was one of several sites in Iran suspected of running a clandestine biological weapons program. The Iranians hotly denied the accusation and stated that it was a plot of the Great Satan and the forces of the Revolutionary Guard would quickly contain and destroy the infestation. Like the infestation in the Bekaa Valley, it was still spreading.

So was the one just south of Mecca, this one conveniently near the coast at another "experimental farm." The area was a Saudi military reservation and the Saudi National Guard had assaulted the infestation with Abrams tanks and Bradley fighting vehicles. Survivors from the group stated that upon entering the fungus area it had attacked the tanks, choking their systems.

The Saudi government had not charged the U.S. with planting the Dreen infestation on holy ground, but the mullahs throughout the world were more than happy to blame it on the Great Satan.

Qom was the holiest city in the Shia version of Islam and Mecca was the holiest city in Islam, period. Both the Iranian Ruling Council and the Mullah of Mecca had pronounced jihad against the alien invaders and mujaheddin from the Philippines to Algeria, not to mention various western countries, were being flown in by the Saudis and the Iranians to try to fight the infestations. The bulk of their fighters would have probably come from the Bekaa Valley, but they were all extremely busy. Or being converted to more monsters.

The fungus and growth structure of the Dreen had been, at this point, carefully studied by the U.S. government. It was determined that the fungus spread via a small wormlike creature that had been specially modified to convert terrestrial biology to Dreen. As it did so, terraforming the soil, eating plant and animal material, the "fungus" spread behind it. The fungus was anything but, an entity that not only gathered energy from a chlorophyll analogue but had an extensive vascular network for moving materials from one place to another. In addition, it could sprout structures that reproduced the megafauna that did the work of the Dreen. The fungus, left alone with some functional materials it could "eat," pure fertilizer would work, and sunlight, could spread and grow unchecked. It also was damned hard to keep contained if it had materials available, sprouting subgrowths that would attack any container it was placed in. It was considered a level four biological hazard. It was, however, responsive to burning, acid and certain powerful herbicides and did not grow well on soil that had not been preprepared for it by the worms.

One scientist had done an analysis and concluded that one human body could be converted into a dog-demon in two days. Or two humans in three days for a thorn-thrower, given the structures to make same.

Reports from the Bekaa Valley indicated that, the majority of their Katyusha rockets and a goodly part of their artillery rounds having been expended trying to break into the main areas, the Syrian, Hamas and Hezbollah forces were now attacking with rifles and flamethrowers and sustaining heavy casualties. The response by American military spokespeople was notably unsympathetic.

"You look good," Miller said. "Hey, honey, can I talk with my friend alone for a minute?" the chief added to the candy striper.

"Of course, Mr. Miller," the girl said, smiling. "I'll come back in about fifteen minutes, okay?"

"Works," Miller replied. He gestured at the turned-down TV where the latest news from Mecca, via Al Jazeera, was showing. "Bit of a bastard, ey?"

"Well, I know *you* didn't do it," Bill said with a chuckle. "And I know *I* didn't do it."

"And I happen to know that *we* didn't do it," Miller said, shaking his head. "Give us some credit, okay? Besides, I checked with the Teams and they'd know if anyone did. They did it to themselves. Okay, maybe with some help from the Israelis."

"Give," Bill said.

"All the outbreaks are at places where terrorists or terrorist sponsors have been working on bioweapons," the SEAL said, taking a puff on the cigar. "We don't know how they got the Dreen material there, but that's where all the outbreaks occurred."

"Any word on what we're going to do?" Bill asked.

"Well, the Teams are sitting back, watching the tube and laughing in their beer," Miller answered. "The Ayrabs can't fight for shit. There's a lot of cultural reasons for it, some of them pretty complex, but it's true. In a situation like this, they're the worst *possible* group to try to stop the Dreen. But they're pouring fighters in like water, just the sort of bastards that run around sniping at our troops, blowing up innocent Israeli civilians and flying jetliners into our skyscrapers. They've got lots and lots of mujaheddin, but no matter how many they throw at the Dreen, they're not going to push them back. The Dreen are the purest flypaper for those boys. Wait a year and there won't be enough mujaheddin left on earth to bury their dead. If they can find the bodies."

"Wait a year and the Dreen will be making those mountain-sized tanks that Dr. McBain saw on Ashholm's World."

"Oh, they won't wait a year," Miller admitted. "I figure, in a few months they'll all get back-channel messages that the U.S. is willing to help them out. The help will be a nuke. Several nukes, actually, the only way to be sure. They can take it or leave it. By then, they'll take it. The muj will be dialed down to a fraction of their former strength and maybe there will still be a few of the worms sitting around. The ragheads will also see, clearly, what the U.S. *can* do if it cares enough to send the very best. Nuclear weapons rising where the mullahs cannot ignore them. I suspect that they're going to have a slightly different view of the 'Great Satan' after we carefully drop nukes so they *miss* Mecca and Medina."

"Nukes can't get through," Bill said then shook his head. "Send in artillery, first, saturate the defenses, run them out of mosquito-missiles and then . . . boom."

"Yeah." Miller chuckled around the cigar. "Boom. I think they ought to drop one on Tikrit and Fallujah while they're about it, but nobody ever asks me. Hell, drop a ripple across the Bekaa Valley and I'd be happy. Let the Dreen have the whole thing, *then* pop it."

"Works for me," Bill said.

"But we have other things to do, Dr. Weaver," Miller said in a very formal tone. "I need influence."

"How much?" Bill asked. "I notice you're not in Leavenworth right now and you seem to have been promoted."

"Well, yeah," the SEAL said in a slightly embarrassed voice. "Submitted an honest report as to the actions in taking the gate. I'll admit there was a slightly awkward moment or two, but they would have looked silly court-martialing a wounded hero. It's pretty much been noted that I've got over twenty in and I can take a hint. As soon as I'm fit for duty they'll suggest that maybe I should retire and I'll take 'em up on it. What the hell, I've already saved the world, once; leave it to the young kids for the next time. But we've still got one thing we need to take care of."

"What?"

"Thrathptttt."

"Mr. President, what Warrant Officer Miller said makes sense," Bill said, carefully. "We need the information."

"I agree with that," the President replied. "But I'm not sure of the rest."

"General Thrathptttt, after the gate was closed, mousetrapped one of the National Guard Brigades," Bill pointed out. "I'm sure the secretary will agree on that?"

"Yes," the secretary of defense admitted, tightly. "He did."

"He then told it that he would surrender, on terms, or he could go down fighting," Bill noted. "He had the *choice* of killing a large number of our troops. He knew he was doomed, anyway. But he *chose* to let our soldiers live. I think we owe him for that. And we need the information; the Dreen are still out there, somewhere."

The President looked at Weaver over the video link for a long ten seconds and then nodded his head.

"Approved."

Miller and Weaver were standing when the guards brought General Thrathptttt into the interrogation room. Weaver was in civilian clothes and Miller in desert BDUs with a web belt and a holster holding an H&K USP .45 caliber pistol.

The sergeant with the two guards frowned and shook his head.

"You can't have a weapon in the same room with a prisoner," the sergeant said. "It's against regulations."

"Sergeant," Weaver answered before Miller could open his mouth. "Did you happen to see my orders?"

"Yes, sir," the sergeant said, carefully.

"My orders say that your regulations are superceded, understand?"

"Yes, sir," the sergeant replied.

"You can go."

"Sir," the sergeant said, again, with a pained look on his face. "This isn't about regulation. You're both injured and . . ."

"Sergeant," Miller said, chuckling. "The day I can't handle one three-foot-tall cat, even with one arm and one leg broken, I'll just have to turn in my trident. Clear?"

"Yes, sir," the sergeant sighed.

Thrathptttt had been seated in the chair in front of the table by the two guards and all three of them left. The chair was an adjustable swivel chair so the Mreee could sit at the table at something like normal height.

Bill and the SEAL had slightly less comfortable folding metal chairs into which they lowered themselves.

"General," Miller said, inclining his head.

"Chief Miller," the general replied. "Dr. Weaver. I am pleased to see that you both survived."

"Pleased enough to talk with us?" Weaver asked.

"No," the general replied. "I am not required to answer your questions."

"No, you're not," the SEAL answered. "Although, God knows, we've got a lot of them. We *need* to know about the Dreen. Where they are. If they have interstellar capacity. If they do, when they might show up. Anything at all that we can find out. And ain't none of you cats talking. We didn't capture but a handful of Nitch, what with nobody really wanting a ten-foot spider near them, and the ones that we did we can't communicate with. So we'd really like to ask you about the Dreen and we'd like you to answer those questions. But, you know what, General, I'm not going to ask you about any of that stuff."

"Good," the general said, straightening. "Can I leave, now?"

"No, because I am going ask you one thing, General," the SEAL said, leaning forward. "Why? When I saw you the first time I thought to myself: 'That is one hardcore motherfucker of a cat.' I don't respect many people, much less aliens, on first meeting. But I respected you. And I'm pretty good at first impressions. Pretty good. And I still say you're an honorable guy. The way you let those National Guard soldiers off *proves* it. Not only to me, but to the President. So I gotta ask, General, soldier to soldier: Why?"

The general looked at him for a long moment, as if he was going to spit or cough up a hairball and then he looked away. Silent. Bill was smart enough to hold his tongue. So was Miller for a while.

"You might be wondering, if I'm talking soldier to soldier, why I brought this pasty-faced academic with me. I brought him because he deserves an answer, too. He's a lousy shot and hasn't got the situational awareness of an ant, but we both stood our ground at the gate and he got his share of a bodyguard in Valhalla. He took the job and he closed the gates. I think he probably killed a great many of your people. If your world was on the other side of that gate, likely it's gone. At his hands. But he's here because he deserves the answer, too. For honor and for standing his ground."

"If my world is gone, so much the better," the general said, softly. There was a long silence and then he made a faint mew. "The reason we don't talk to you, Miller, is because we know the depths of dishonor. And we find it hard, impossible, to share them."

"Well, I'm black ops," Miller said, leaning back. "It ain't all fields of glory. One of our mottoes is: We do a lot of things we wish we didn't have to. So: Why?"

The general made another mew and looked away, silent for a moment, then he looked back.

"I was a young officer, what you would call a lieutenant, when the Masters came to our world.

"The banners of Tchraow flew from sea to sea, upon them the sun never set. We had bested the Raaown, we had conquered the Troool, an ancient and powerful land. The White Empress held sway over a vast empire. And then we were given word that in the unsettled lands a new power was arising. I was a young officer in charge of a small unit in the expedition that went out to pacify this new threat.

"We came upon Master forces far from their bases. The ones

you call dog-demons and the thorn-throwers. Our sraaah riders fell upon them in a terrible charge and it was a complete defeat. The infantry stood their ground against the Masters for as long as they could but we had only cannon and poor rifles to try to hold them. They broke us. A regiment that had never been broken and they broke us like a twig.

"I was carried back on a stretcher, hundreds of your miles. It was upon the Plains of Shraaaan that I took this," he said, gesturing at his eye. "And other hurts. But I survived. All the resources of the Troool empire were gathered, host upon host. General Mreooorw, who had defeated the Raaoown, was sent from Tchraow though he was old, old. You call me a general?" the cat said, looking at Miller. "That, *that* was a general. He had never lost a battle, but he lost one then. We met them on the Plains of Mraaa, a vast host, shining in the sun. Cannons ranked league upon league, in perfect positions, our infantry filled the valley and the hosts of sraaah riders were like the ocean's waves." He paused a moment, savoring the image.

"And they destroyed us. Of that vast host no more than one in ten survived. I was one of those unlucky enough to stumble away from that black field.

"Again and again we met them but we could never defeat the Masters. In time, we lost Troool to them and some of us, a fragment of the Tchraow who had been masters there, fled back to our homelands.

"Tchraow was far from Troool and we thought we might be safe. We sent out more forces, aiding other lands, I did my time in that duty, but always the Masters were undefeatable. They spread, land to land, sometimes slowly, sometimes in jumps. They created vast weapons of war, air-beings that blotted out the sun, giant Nitch-like creatures that burned the land as they came, every footstep a disaster, spitting fire from their mouths. Water did not stop them for they could fly through the air. Nor did distance.

"Finally, they sent the N!T!Ch! to us. The N!T!Ch! had been slaves long before our world was conquered and they managed to communicate with us. The Dreen held hundreds, possibly thousands, of worlds. They spread by the gates but also by biological systems that drift from solar system to solar system, looking for fecund planets. One such had found our planet and it would be fully colonized unless we submitted to the Masters. The Masters would let some of us live if we submitted tribute to them. Metals, many that we had never heard of before, certain types of gems and . . ." He paused and did spit, "'biological' materials for their expansion."

"Biological?" Bill asked. "Herd animals?"

"Those and the bodies of our people," the general said with a snarling yowl. "We were defeated. We knew we were. There was no choice. So we made that devil's bargain. We sent our best to slave in the Master's mines. We sent our litters to the Masters to be 'reprocessed.' Our herds, our bodies, whatever it took to keep us alive. And when they called for us to trick you? You think we paused? Do you think we cared? After giving of our own bodies? My litters . . ." The general paused and his face worked in anguish. "My children . . ."

"General," Miller said, after a pause. "We need one more service of you. You must ask your people to give us information. We need to know about the Dreen."

"The Dreen," the cat spat. "Better to call them that. We called them the T!Ch!R! because that was the name the N!T!Ch! used. We learned, soon, that it simply meant 'the Masters.' They had come to regard them, simply, as gods. I suppose we would in time as well. This," he said, holding up his arm, "this I lost to the Dreen. My eye, my arm, bits of my flesh, my children. My honor."

He hung his head again and rowled, a cry of anguish and anger that seemed to hang in the air even after he had finished, then set his features.

"I will give orders that my people will communicate with yours," he said, looking directly at Miller. "We have little time. There is no food upon this planet we can eat. The food your scientists gives us still lacks something. In short, we, probably the last of our species, are dying and there is no escape. We will aid you, but I want something of you, as well. I think you know what it is."

"I do," Miller replied. "I understand. If it had not been for

Dr. Weaver, here, and about a hundred years of technological advancement, I'd have been in your position. I hope that I could have survived it and done what I had to as well as you. For my world and for my children."

"Tell Sraaan, he is my aide, that the code is 'Mraaa.' It was the last, the best, time of our people. He will know what to do." The general hung his head and then looked up at Miller. "May I have my choice, now?"

"Yes," Miller said, nodding. He drew the pistol and racked a round into the chamber. Then he dropped out the magazine and pocketed it. "I am glad that my first impression was not wrong. I wish that the universe was not so cruel. I would have liked to have stood side by side with you in battle. May we meet upon the shining fields, battle evil all day, feast all night and rise anew to do battle once more."

"That is not your local faith," the general said, interested.

"I am not a Christian," Miller said, laying the pistol on the table. Then he stood up and saluted the general. "See you in Valhalla, General Thrathptttt."

Weaver stood up as well and inclined his head, then the two of them went out the door. The guard on the door looked at them quizzically, then his eyes dropped to Miller's empty holster and he started to reach for his radio.

Miller lifted one hand and looked him in the eye.

"I'm here on Presidential orders, son," the SEAL said. "Don't force me to make you eat that radio." There was the sound of a pistol shot and he closed his eyes, his lips moving. All that Bill could catch was something about shining fields.

# EPILOGUE

"Our Dreen boson has closed as well," Tchar said, nodding to Bill as he stepped through the Adar gate.

"So I heard," Bill said, looking around at the Adari facility. There were even more humans than had been there before the Kentucky battle. "Which doesn't explain why I'm here. There are plenty of diplomats around."

"The artass wishes to speak with you," Tchar said, waving him into one of the Adar scooters.

"About what?" Bill pressed, knowing it was probably useless.

"The artass will explain," Tchar said as he engaged the gears and screamed out of the gate area.

Bill held on for dear life as Tchar jetted out of the facility and towards a range of mountains across the vast salt plain. Like Groom Lake the Adar gate facility was placed as far away from civilization as possible, probably for the security of their world. Bill wished they could do the same on Earth. But the Chen Generator was still spitting out bosons. They'd started moving and linking them finally and he could see a time when there'd be a market for them. Instantaneous transportation was finally here.

All they had to do was keep it from linking off-world. Sooner or later the Dreen would find a secondary route of attack.

They drove up to the mountains and as they approached, doing at least two hundred on the flats, Bill saw that there was a large building set into the ridgeline. It was low and apparently made of concrete. More like a bunker than a home but he suspected that was exactly what it was.

Tchar slowed as they approached and then hit the long drive up the ridge still doing around a hundred. Bill managed to hang on through the bump and lift as they entered the drive and then Tchar hit the brakes, throwing him forward.

"Next time, I drive," Bill said.

"The controls are ill-suited for humans," Tchar replied, gesturing for him to enter a doorway in the side of the bunker.

They descended three levels to a heavy security door guarded by two of the Adar soldiers. Then through a series of corridors to a small room that Bill was pretty sure was on the back side of the facility.

"Please sit," Tchar said, gesturing to a human desk chair at the Adar-sized table. "Would you care for refreshment? We have water and your human Coca-Cola. It seems that your caffeine is similar in chemical composition to our gadam and has the same effect. Indeed, caffeine seems stronger. Further, your Coca-Cola is processable by we Adar. It has become something of a hit on our world."

"Leave it to Coke," Bill muttered. "Just wait until McDonald's figures out your food. But, no, I'll just wait."

"It should not be long," Tchar said, stepping out of the room and irising the door closed.

Bill pulled out his PDA and brought up a set of news articles he'd downloaded before coming to France. Unsurprisingly, the incidence of terrorism, in Israel and internationally, had dropped to nearly zero. Most of the mujaheddin types that were serious about the "cause" had been turned into Dreen fodder over the last few months. Now, there was a real dearth of mujaheddin willing to fight the Dreen these days, no matter how much money got thrown at them. Heck, there appeared to be a real dearth of mujaheddin left, period.

Saudi had been the first country to ask the U.S. to help and, as Miller predicted, they ended up using nukes. Iran was still trying to convince themselves they could handle the infestation but there was no effective control left in Lebanon. The "refugees," multigenerational residents in any sane world, that lived in the area of the Dreen infestation had become real refugees as the Bekaa Valley slowly got covered in the Dreen fungus. The so-called government of Lebanon, which had been controlled entirely by the Syrians, had more or less packed up and left. The country was a total mess. Nobody knew who was in charge and the civil war had broken out again in earnest, but this time with people fighting to get away from the Dreen. The spread was heading in the general direction of Israel and Weaver was pretty sure when it got to be a threat to that country they'd nuke it and let bygones be bygones.

The big question in everyone's mind was if the Dreen could come at the Earth from space. And that had led to a new space race, but an international one. It wasn't going very well in Bill's opinion; NASA was still in charge in the U.S. and NASA couldn't get its butt out of gear to save the Earth. But enough money was getting thrown around sooner or later some of it would stick to good ideas. But they were still playing with chemical-powered rockets and that wasn't going to do it if the Dreen were interstellar capable.

There were a bunch of theories about FTL out there, some of which might work. Bill had pretty much planned to use his influence and knowledge of boson physics to form a start-up. There had to be a way to use the bosons to power a ship, maybe even an FTL ship. Something better than chemical rockets.

He flipped over to another screen and was doodling equations when the door opened and Tchar and the artass entered.

Bill stood up and half bowed to the artass, who he now realized was something like the World President. The artass apparently didn't notice, simply taking a seat on one side of the table as Tchar settled at the end.

"We have a device," Tchar said, whistling tonelessly for a moment. Bill suspected it was a throat clearing. "We found it on an abandoned world. It appears to be of an ancient technology.

We have, thus far, performed a few experiments with it and been unable to determine its purpose. We know it releases energy, in excess of input, but we are unsure why. Simple energy release does not appear . . . rational."

"Energy in excess of input sounds great," Bill said, frowning. "I can think of any number of reasons you'd want that."

"Not the way this releases energy," Tchar said, pulling papers out of a pouch. "These are our experimental findings. We have had them translated into English. It has been recommended that you, personally, be given the device to continue the experiments."

"Well . . . thanks," Bill said, glancing at the artass and then away. "But if you guys . . ."

"You have touched the face of God," the artass said, quietly. "You are worthy. May your travels be honorable and increasing in knowledge." He nodded at Bill, then stood up and walked out.

"I would suggest you read the briefing papers carefully," Tchar said, standing up also.

"How big is this thing?" Bill asked. "Can we get it through the gate? What's it look like?"

"All of that is covered in the papers," Tchar said, waving at them. "But you can get it through the gate, easily. You have an expression in your engineering, a 'little black box,' yes?"

"Yeah," Bill said, puzzled.

Tchar reached into another pouch and removed . . . well it looked like a black deck of cards. Or a card-sized "monolith" from *2001*. He set it carefully on the table and then slid it across to Bill.

"Do not let it be in contact with significant voltage," Tchar said, whistling again. "That would be . . . bad."

Bill picked up the black box and looked at it. As an anomaly it was classic.

"This is it?" he asked, incredulously.

"May your journey of knowledge be more fruitful than mine," Tchar said, gesturing at the door. "A guard will conduct you back to the gate."

» » »

After reading the briefing papers, carefully, they had chosen to conduct their first test on a deserted world connected to one of the gates. Bill still couldn't believe his eyes as he looked across the ten-mile-wide crater.

"Yep," Warrant Officer Miller said, leaning sideways on his four wheeler to spit. "Putting a charge on it sure causes one hell of a bang."

"A double A," Bill said, shaking his head. "A friggin' double A. I hope like hell nobody ever really figures out this technology or kids will be making hundred-megaton nukes for sixth-grade science class."

They rode down the side of the newly formed, and quite warm, crater with Bill keeping a careful eye on the mounted Geiger counter. But there was, effectively, no radiation over background. The explosion had blasted material into space, but with no evidence of a nuclear explosion. The ground wasn't even glassed.

They finally reached a spot near the center of the crater and started hunting around. It took them nearly an hour but, sure enough, there was the little black box, sitting in the dirt as if it had fallen there, entirely unharmed.

"This is just bizarre," Bill said, shaking his head and picking up the box. "It's not even warm."

"I am," Miller said. "Let's get out of here."

"We're going to need to find another world to blow up," Bill replied, starting his four-wheeler.

"Damn," Miller said as they cleared the gate. They'd waited a few hours for the area to cool off but there was still a tornadic wind blowing dust around. "What did you do this time, Doc?"

"Look at the sky," Bill said, wonderingly. Clouds were running in every direction as if the entire atmosphere of the planet had been disturbed. As it should have been given the incredible mass of dirt in view. The explosion had apparently dug an even bigger crater and the side of it looked like a small mountain range. "I hope like hell we didn't dig to the mantle!"

"We're going to need more people to help hunt for it this

time," Miller said. "Next time, we're not going to use as much juice."

"It was a *car* battery!" Bill snapped. "How was I supposed to believe twelve friggin' *volts* would cause this sort of explosion? There is no rational explanation for this!"

"Holy Toledo," Miller said, wonderingly. He hit the gas jets on his EVA pack and turned around. Sure enough, the gate was floating in space. "Didn't we just put this thing down on a planet yesterday?"

"That's not the scary part," Bill said, spinning around. "Didn't there used to be a sun?"

"Uh . . ." Miller said, spinning himself. Sure enough, the nearest star was far, far away. "Did it move?"

"No, I think it went away," Bill said, turning and looking out towards what he thought was the plane of the ecliptic. There might have been a faint line of light out in every direction. "The term we're looking for here is nova. Maybe supernova."

"That explains the explosion through the gate," Miller said. "Good thing we fed it through two planets, first. If it had blown back in Arkansas things would have been bad. By the way, how are we going to find a black box in the middle of interstellar space?"

"We know the direction of the box," Bill said, sighing. "If it runs to form, it's going to be floating right where we left it, relative to the gate."

They jetted outward and found the device in less than fifteen minutes. It appeared to have remained stationary when everything else . . . went away.

"Right," Bill said, grasping the enigmatic device and pocketing it. "Three phase current is definitely *out*."

"Okay, I think I know what it's doing and why," Bill said, addressing the Troika with the addition of the national science advisor. "It's forming a micro black hole."

"Now, those I know something about," the President said. "Wouldn't stuff be sucked into them?"

"With a stable black hole, yes, Mr. President," Bill replied.

"But a micro black hole is unstable. Theoretically, they were only formed during the big bang. And they don't hold their matter inside, but let it out. What happens, I think, is that the device grabs all the matter in a certain area, based upon input, and uses it to form a black hole. But part of that matter is its power input system. When that goes away, the hole destabilizes and releases all the trapped matter as energy."

"Causing a very big bang," the national security advisor said.

"A very big bang," Bill said, nodding.

"So it's a bomb," the secretary of defense said. "A reuseable nuclear hand grenade?"

"Maybe," Bill said. "Maybe not. I've got another idea."

"Well, don't leave us guessing, Dr. Weaver," the national science advisor said, acerbically.

"Well, I got to thinking, sir," Bill said, musingly. "There was this *Star Trek* episode where the Romulans were trying to use micro black holes for an improved warp drive . . ."

"You think it's a drive system?" the national security advisor said. "Really?"

"Really," Bill said, grinning. "And I think I can figure out how to apply power to form the black hole off to the side. Using that we can generate a warp field. Theoretically. It makes more sense than a reuseable bomb."

"Now that's a very big thought," the President said, sitting back. "We can go looking for the Dreen. But . . ."

"There's a billion 'buts,' Mr. President," Bill said, nodding. "But the major truth is that, yes, we can try to find the Dreen before they find us. And we've got a technology we might be able to bootstrap for more ships. I don't think we can replicate that device but we can start working on something similar."

"I'm thinking of the international implications," the President said, frowning. "Everyone is going to want in on this. And, frankly, I don't know that I *want* everyone in on it."

"And a real space ship is not going to be easy," the secretary of defense said. "I took a look at some of the space stuff for space defense. And I remember there are a lot of problems with space ships."

"Nothing we can't overcome," Bill said. "I've got the basics in my head. We can get into space, find the Dreen before they find us, fight back. And . . . heck, explore. We can get into *space* Mr. President! Not go to the Moon and never go back. Go to other *stars!*"

"To go where no man has gone before?" the national security advisor asked, smiling.

"If you want to put it that way, ma'am," Bill replied. "But for science, for safety, we need to *try.*"

"How much?" the President asked.

"A lot," Bill admitted. "And if you want to keep it secret, more. But . . . the basic ship can be built around a submarine design. I think we could even let Groton or BAE build it. They don't talk. It will have to be *big*, though, and a big new sub class . . ."

"Twenty, thirty billion," the secretary of defense said, wincing. "Getting that through Congress will be hell."

Bill turned to the President with a look of pleading on his face. "Mr. President?"

The President looked at him for a moment, then looked away in thought. Everyone was silent as he considered the question. Finally he looked at the physicist again.

"Nobody is going to say I sat on my ass when there was a chance to find the Dreen," the President said, nodding. "Approved. We'll find the money somehow. It looks like the U.S. is going to get a new class of nuclear submarine. And Dr. Weaver gets to go see his stars."